The Curse

The Curse

BIG-TIME GAMBLING'S

SEDUCTION OF A SMALL

NEW ENGLAND TOWN

~

A Novel

Robert H. Steele

Levellers Press
AMHERST, MASSACHUSETTS

Published by Levellers Press, Amherst, Massachusetts.

The Curse is also available at special quantity discounts to organizations,
corporations, and other special markets. For information, contact
Levellers Press, 71 South Pleasant Street, Amherst, MA 01002
www.levellerspress.com

The Curse is a work of fiction set against a background of
true historical and contemporary events. The town of Sheffield,
Connecticut does not exist, and the casino, Indian tribe, and characters
associated with the town are products of the author's imagination and
are not to be construed as real. Any resemblance of the characters associated with the town to persons living or dead is entirely coincidental.

Book design by Kim Llewellyn
Maps by Beehive Mapping

Printed in the United States of America
ISBN 978-1-937146-17-7
10 9 8 7 6 5 4 3 2 1

~

Contents

Contents · VI

Author's Note

The Curse is a novel about the arrival of big-time gambling in New England and its impact on a small, quintessential Connecticut town. The town, which I have chosen to call Sheffield, is fictitious, as are the characters, Indian tribe, and casino associated with it. The historical and contemporary contexts, however, are real, and I have done my best to render them as factually as possible.

Connecticut is home to two of the world's largest and most spectacularly successful resort casinos: Foxwoods, opened by the Mashantucket Pequot Tribal Nation in 1992, and Mohegan Sun, opened by the Mohegan Tribe of Connecticut in 1996. In 2008 the Mashantuckets added a new $700 million hotel and casino to their reservation under a licensing agreement with Las Vegas's MGM Grand. Known as MGM Grand at Foxwoods, it effectively gave Connecticut its third casino. Collectively, the three casinos ended 2008 with approximately $2.2 billion in gaming revenue and 20,000 employees.

Prior to 1988, casino gambling was prohibited everywhere in the United States except Nevada and New Jersey. Passage of the Indian Gaming Regulatory Act of 1988 dramatically changed that. Native American casinos quickly spread across the country and in the process spurred the legalization and opening of non-Indian casinos in a growing number of states. The resulting wave of new casino construction has increased the number of U.S. casinos to more than one thousand, including some 460 Indian casinos in 28 states and 560 non-Indian "commercial" casinos in 22 states. It is an explosion that has literally turned casino gambling into America's new national pastime, with higher attendance than professional baseball, football, and basketball combined.

Now, starved for cash and loath to raise taxes, more and more states are looking to casinos and other forms of gambling—from scratch-off tickets to the new frontier of internet waging—as "painless" ways to increase revenue, setting the stage for a new wave of gambling expansion.

July 2012

MASSACHUSETTS BAY COLONY

Boston

PLYMOUTH
COLONY

Windsor

Connecticut R.

Hartford

CONNECTICUT COLONY

Wethersfield

Providence
Plantations

N
A
R
R
A
G
A
N
S
E
T
T
S

Pequot R.

MOHEGANS

PEQUOTS

SAYBROOK
COLONY
Fort Saybrook

Weinshauks

Mystic

Narragansett
Bay

Pawcatuck R.

Long Island Sound

Atlantic Ocean

N

Southern New England, 1637
with present-day state boundaries

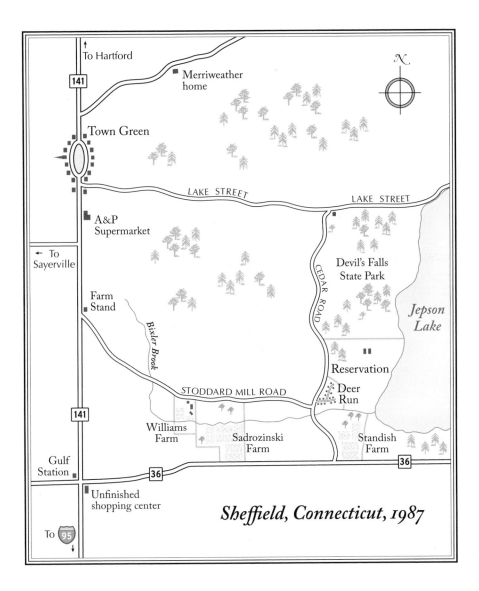

To Hartford

141

Merriweather
home

N

Town Green

LAKE STREET   LAKE STREET

A&P
Supermarket

← To
Sayerville

Devil's Falls
State Park

CEDAR ROAD

Jepson
Lake

Farm
Stand

Bixler Brook

Reservation

STODDARD MILL ROAD

Deer
Run

141

Williams
Farm

Sadrozinski
Farm

Standish
Farm

36

Gulf
Station

36

Unfinished
shopping center

Sheffield, Connecticut, 1987

To 95

I

~

Mystic

May 25–26, 1637

The combined English and Indian army trudged steadily through the southern New England woods, heading west toward Pequot country. There were seventy-seven English soldiers in all, led by Captain John Mason and accompanied by seventy Mohegans and more than four hundred Narragansetts. Their target was the newly fortified Pequot village at Weinshauks, near present-day New London, where the Pequots' grand sachem, Sassacus, was believed to be along with some six hundred warriors.

It was Thursday, May 25, and the afternoon had turned unexpectedly hot and humid, slowing the army's pace, but Mason remained determined to attack the Pequots that night. His plan was to catch the Pequots by surprise, kill Sassacus, and destroy the tribe's ability to threaten the new English settlements in Connecticut.

A tall, burly, battle-hardened soldier, Mason had fought with England's expeditionary army in Europe, but he had never faced a challenge like the current one. The Pequots were the most warlike of the New England tribes and a wily and elusive enemy who were terrorizing the English up and down the Connecticut River. Mason did not know the territory, was almost totally dependent on his Indian guides, and was gambling on being able to reach Weinshauks without being detected.

He also had two other concerns.

One was the reliability of his Indian allies, who were strung out for half a mile ahead of the English troops. Both the Mohegans and Narragansetts considered the Pequots their enemies, but all three tribes were believed to have intermarried over the years, and Mason could not be certain how loyal the Mohegans and Narragansetts would prove in an all-out war against their foe. In fact, it appeared from the number of stragglers the English were encountering on the path that some of the Narragansetts were already deserting.

His second concern was what he could expect from his own men. Twenty of them were trained soldiers who had been dispatched from the Massachusetts Bay Colony, based in Boston, but the rest were Connecticut settlers from Hartford, Windsor, and Wethersfield who, except for the officers, had little or no military experience. To make matters worse, the heavily armed men were sweltering in their thick buff corselets, and several had passed out along the trail. Unless it cooled down soon, there was no telling what condition they would be in by the time they had to fight.

The army finally came to a halt at a ford on the Pawcatuck River, which was a good eighty yards wide at that point and bounded on the near side by a strip of stony beach. According to the Narragansetts, the Pawcatuck marked the beginning of Pequot country, but the Narragansett and Mohegan scouts had already probed well beyond the river and reported no signs of the enemy.

Mason signaled his men to fall out, and the soldiers rushed down to the river, dousing their heads and faces in the cold, clear water, then retreated back to the tree line, where they collapsed in the shade to rest.

⌒

Ethan Williams stripped off his bandolier and corselet, and sat alone under a river birch sipping water from a canteen and letting the heat drain out of him. Twenty-two years old, just over five eleven, and with flaming red hair, he was younger, taller, and in better condition than most of the other Englishmen, but he had stumbled and hurt his knee crossing a stream earlier in the day and had thrown up twice from the heat. When he finally began to feel a little better, he nibbled on a biscuit and some hard cheese, and was about to stretch out when Lieutenant Robert Seeley came up and dropped down beside him.

Seeley was the second in command of the Connecticut troops and, like Ethan, from Wethersfield. He'd taken Ethan under his wing ten days earlier, when the Connecticut men and their Mohegan allies had boarded three small ships in Hartford and begun the trip down the Connecticut River to Saybrook Colony at the entrance to Long Island Sound. The small colony had started in 1635 as an English fort designed to control the river, and its garrison maintained close contact with the upriver towns.

The Connecticut troops were joined at Saybrook by the Massachusetts men, who had recently arrived to help defend the fort against mounting

Pequot pressure. The mixed Connecticut, Massachusetts, and Mohegan force then sailed from Saybrook past Weinshauks to Narragansett Bay, where they disembarked, recruited their first Narragansetts, and began to double back toward Connecticut to surprise the Pequots. Mason's plan was to rendezvous with his ships following the attack and return to Saybrook.

Seeley regarded Ethan carefully. "Yer leg still hurtin', lad?" he asked in his nasal East Anglican twang. He'd seen Ethan fall and was concerned he was developing a limp.

"'Tis nothin'," Ethan insisted, not wanting to admit how much the knee hurt. He slapped at a deer fly on the back of his neck and rubbed the bite. "How much furtha?" he asked.

"Six, seven hours ... maybe a little more," Seeley replied. "Depends how offen we hevta stop."

"Looks like we've lost some a' the Narr'gansetts," Ethan said, gesturing to the area where most of the Narragansetts seemed to have congregated.

"Aye," Seeley acknowledged. "Now that they can begin t' smell the inimy, seems a lot of 'em are hevin' second thoughts. Cap'n thinks at least a hundred hev turned back."

"After all their blabbin'?" Ethan scoffed. "Weren't they the ones who said we dursn't look upon a Pequit but that they'd slay 'em for us?"

"That wuz this mornin'," Seeley replied. "They obviously fer the Pequits more 'n we thought."

"What about that uppish one who boasted he'd kill twenty Pequits? You s'pose he's among the missin'?"

"I dunno," Seeley deadpanned, "but I s'pect he wuz the fust t' scoot."

"Yer probably right," Ethan said, chuckling at Seeley's dry wit. He liked the man immensely. He was straightforward and unpretentious, an able officer who took a personal interest in his men. He'd spent hours with Ethan discussing the background of the war and the Indian tribes involved.

As Seeley explained it, the Pequots, based along the northeastern shore of Long Island Sound, and the Narragansetts, based farther to the east, were the two largest tribes in southern New England and longtime rivals, while the Mohegan tribe was little more than a small tributary of the Pequots. Yet the Mohegans' chief, Uncas, was an extraordinarily ambitious and shrewd warrior who was said to be related by blood to previous Pequot grand sachems and to have recently lost a bitter political struggle with the Pequots' current leader, Sassacus, to head the Pequot nation. Spurned by the Pequots, Uncas had apparently seen the colonists' arrival in Connecticut as an opportunity to forge an alliance with them against the Pequots, and he'd quickly offered to join the English in their assault on the Pequots' stronghold.

Still, with the Narragansetts beginning to desert in large numbers, Ethan couldn't help but worry about Uncas as well. The colonists had made an enormous bet on his remaining loyal, and if he chose to abandon them now, the expedition would be in peril.

"And Uncas?" Ethan asked Seeley. "You think he'll stay with us?"

"He swows he will," Seeley said.

"You believe 'im?"

"He's stayed so fur," Seeley replied, "and I see little profit for him t' leave now. But I hev t' admit I don't like what I'm seein' from the Narr'gansetts. If they can change their minds that quick, then presumably so can Uncas. Remember, the man's playin' his own game, and he's already changed sides once. I jest don't want us bein' caught off guard if he does it agin."

With that, Seeley stood and checked the time with the width of his hand against the horizon. From the angle of the sun, it looked to be about four o'-clock. "Come on," he said. "Time t' go."

Ethan nodded, and eased himself off the ground, favoring his right leg as he got up.

"Stand still," Seeley said. He removed a strip of cloth from his pack and knelt down to tie it just below Ethan's kneecap, pulling it tight and closing it with a simple knot. "Should'a done it earlier, but that may help," he added, springing back up.

"Thanks," Ethan said, "but don't be worryin' about me, Lieutenant. I'll be fine."

"Good," Seeley said, placing his hand on the younger man's arm, "because yer the last man I want t' lose in this fight. None of us that know what happened t' Susan will ferget it, Ethan, and I figure you got more right t' git back at these bastards than any man here."

Ethan nodded almost imperceptibly and began to collect his gear.

⌣

Once across the river, the army resumed its march, continuing west along the narrow forest trail. Mason estimated that no more than two hundred of the Narragansetts had crossed the river with him, and most of them had fallen back to walk behind the English column rather than in front. Uncas warned that all the Narragansetts would desert before they reached Weinshauks, and Mason was beginning to fear he might be right. The key now was to keep Uncas and the Mohegans with him, and to ensure that his own troops were physically up to using their superior weapons to best effect. A dozen of his men carried eight-foot-long half-pikes, but most of the soldiers were equipped with matchlock muskets or, in a few cases, newer and more efficient snaphance muskets. The matchlock used a slow-burning wick secured by a movable arm to ignite the gunpowder when the trigger was pulled, while the snaphance ignited the powder by striking flint against steel and didn't require the constant adjustment of a wick. Both, however, fired lead balls that tore holes and smashed bone in their victims.

An hour later, the English troops, with Mason and Seeley in the lead, finally emerged from the forest into a cornfield newly planted by the Pequots. They had cleared the field by girdling the trees and burning the trunks and branches, and planted the corn in little hills among the stumps. They had set up a small hut in the middle of the field for watching the crops, although no one was manning it now.

Uncas and a sachem named Wequash were waiting at the edge of the field when Mason arrived, and the English commander stopped and called his officers together to review how far it was to the Pequot fort.

Uncas, who spoke in broken but understandable English, initially did most of the talking, and Ethan, who had been walking just behind Seeley, edged forward to try to hear. Though he'd seen Uncas from a distance many times, Ethan was now within just a few feet of him, and he was struck by the man's commanding presence.

Wearing only a breechcloth and moccasins, the Mohegan chief was tall and powerfully built, with broad shoulders, a coal-black scalp lock, and a stern, heavily tattooed face made fiercer-looking by piercing black eyes and streaks of red war paint. He spoke forcefully, gesturing frequently with his large hands, and knelt at one point to draw a map in the dirt. His dark skin glistened from the foul-smelling bear fat the Indians used to grease their bodies and repel insects, and Ethan winced as he caught the scent.

Uncas said the Mohegan and Narragansett scouts were now reporting they had come upon a second Pequot fort that was closer than the one at Weinshauks. According to Uncas, the newly discovered fort was at Mystic, only about half as far as Weinshauks from the army's current position.

The existence of two forts created a quandary for Mason and his officers.

Captain Underhill, the commander of the Massachusetts men, urged that they march directly to Weinshauks and attack the fort there that night, which would give them the best chance to kill Sassacus.

Seeley, however, argued that going directly to Weinshauks would be fraught with risk.

"The men 're spent," he said, "and even ef we march hard, there's no way t' make Weinshauks till after midnight. 'Twould be fur wiser t' rest t' night and attack Mystic at daybreak when we're fresh and the Pequits 're still asleep."

Furthermore, he continued, the deeper they moved into Pequot country, the greater the danger of being discovered. "Should we bypass Mystic and be spied on 'r way t' Weinshauks," he warned, "we could be caught 'twixt both Pequit forces and slartered."

"What say you, Mr. Bull?" Mason asked, turning to another of his lieutenants.

"'Tis true Sassacus is the main prize," Bull responded, "but Robert's right. The men simply ain't in any condition t' attack Weinshauks t'night."

Uncas waited his turn, then strongly backed Underhill, urging that they go directly to Weinshauks to maximize their chances of killing Sassacus. He knew the Pequot sachems, he declared, and it was Sassacus who was leading the drive to expel the English from Connecticut. They could kill a hundred Pequots, he insisted, but it would do no good unless they "cut off the head of the snake."

Mason hesitated, reluctant to go against his fellow captain and concerned about alienating Uncas, but in the end he sided with Seeley and Bull.

"I shall be much grieved if Sassacus escapes," Mason finally said, "but as Mystic is nearest, it seems the best choice. Dependin' on how we fare at Mystic, we can decide whether t' attack Weinshauks on the way t' our ships in the mornin'."

The decision made, the army set out again.

The path wound through mile after mile of forest, threading its way past oaks, birches, and chestnuts, skirting swamps laden with cedar and red maples, and passing through great stands of white pines that soared nearly two hundred feet into the air. The woods provided welcome cover for the small army, but Ethan feared that at any moment they might be spotted. The Indians regularly burned the underbrush in large sections of the forest, and there were areas where one could easily walk between the trees and see several hundred feet ahead. Even if someone in the vicinity wasn't close enough to see the invaders, he'd presumably be able to hear the tramp of boots and the occasional clatter of weapons. Ethan could only pray that there wasn't a Pequot hunting party nearby or that none of the Mohegans or Narragansetts decided to run ahead and betray the colonists in favor of their own blood.

Shortly after nightfall, the column came to a low-lying stretch of ground between two hills near the head of a narrow river. According to the Indian scouts, the Mystic fort lay just two miles to the south.

Mason ordered his men to pitch camp and get as much sleep as they could; he wanted to be on the move before first light. Ethan slumped down against a small boulder and massaged the ache in his knee. The air had cooled; it was a pleasant, moonlit night, with a soft breeze coming up from the Sound. Ethan ate his next-to-last biscuit, downing it with a few ounces of beer left in a second canteen, then tried to sleep. Whether it was the ache in his knee or the hardness of the ground, sleep didn't come, and he lay awake listening to the sounds of the forest and the occasional strains of singing and chanting that drifted up from the Pequot fort.

His mind drifted back to England and the long journey that had brought him to this moment—lying in the wilderness, thousands of miles from his birthplace, waiting to attack the fearsome Pequots in the morning.

〜

Ethan Williams was one of a steadily growing number of Puritans who had settled in New England since the founding of the Massachusetts Bay Colony in 1629. The Pilgrims had founded their own colony at Plymouth in 1620, but it remained small, and it was left to the Puritans to expand into the rest of New England.

Still technically members of the Church of England, the Puritans were reformers who sought to cleanse the church of its Roman Catholic trappings and, in general, restore it to the simplicity of the early church established by Christ. Their theologians rejected all rituals not rooted in the Bible, sought to do away with hierarchical structure, and opposed any other practices they believed interfered with man's ability to forge a direct relationship with God. The only acceptable form of church governance, they insisted, was one in which each individual congregation functioned independently, based on its own covenant with the Lord.

Unsuccessful in their reform efforts and under growing persecution by the mother church, the Puritans came to America seeking a refuge where they could freely practice their religion and build a Bible-based commonwealth they hoped would be a shining example to the world.

The only child of devout Puritan parents, Ethan had grown up in a small hamlet twenty miles northeast of London, faithfully learning the Scriptures, attending services with his mother and father, and accompanying them to the Sunday afternoon and market-day lectures where visiting Puritan preachers delivered fiery sermons.

Man, the preachers thundered, was sinful by nature and could be redeemed only through the grace of Christ. That redemption, the Puritans held, involved an intense spiritual conversion from sinfulness to righteousness that might be triggered by a particularly fervent sermon or other religious experience. God had predetermined who would be saved, yet no devout Puritan could be certain he had been chosen and hence strove mightily to assure himself he was one of the "elect" by living the kind of righteous life he assumed the saved would live. This entailed developing his moral conscience, which was regarded as the voice of God, taking responsibility for his actions, continually striving to improve himself, and constantly measuring himself against others.

Ethan proved a dutiful son, learning the carpentry trade from his father, and then, after his mother died in 1635, leaving England with his father for the new Puritan colony at Massachusetts Bay. His father never quite reached the New World, however, dying from dysentery the final week of the grueling two-month Atlantic voyage. When Ethan stepped ashore, a young man of twenty, he had never felt so alone.

Ethan was initially assigned to stay with a family in Watertown, one of the settlements that had grown up around Boston. But good land was already becoming scarce in the Bay Colony, and he became intrigued with stories about the fertility and beauty of the Connecticut River Valley, and about the new towns of Hartford, Windsor, and Wethersfield that settlers from the Bay Colony had established on the Connecticut, a hundred miles southwest of Boston. According to the stories, the area along the river was blessed with broad natural meadows that offered an abundance of rich, loamy soil, in contrast to the stone-infested ground that seemed to make up so much of New England. Moreover, it was said that, as in many other parts of New England, disease had killed more than half the Indians in Connecticut in recent years, increasing the willingness of the Indians to sell land and greatly reducing the likelihood of any serious resistance to Puritan settlement there.

Ethan watched a growing number of families leave Watertown for Wethersfield, and he heard of whole church groups leaving the Boston area for Windsor and Hartford in the spring of 1636. People said there were already more than twenty Watertown families in Wethersfield by midyear, and in July he joined the next group leaving for the new settlement.

Ethan's party of five men, three women, and four children traveled overland for nine days, hauling their possessions in four oxen-drawn carts and driving ten head of cattle, a dozen goats, and seventeen sheep before them. On the afternoon of the eighth day, they reached the eastern hills overlooking the Connecticut and stood awestruck; the lush green valley and seemingly endless ribbon of river stretched from north to south as far as the eye could see. God, Ethan was certain, had led the Puritans here just as He had led the Israelites through the wilderness to the land of Canaan three thousand years before. And God, Ethan was equally sure, had visited a plague on the Indians just as He had on the Egyptians, intervening once again to guide his chosen people to the Promised Land.

⮌

After Ethan arrived at Wethersfield, he was initially seized by doubts over the wisdom of leaving the relative comfort of the Bay Colony. The previous winter had been brutally cold and slowed the town's development, so that Ethan and his traveling companions had no choice but to lodge in the now-crumbling mud huts the first arrivals had built on the riverbank two years before. The streets of the town were mere paths where cattle and chickens wandered, there were severe shortages of everything, from seed to cloth, and wolves and bears prowled the area, threatening livestock and anyone foolish enough to venture out at night.

Nevertheless, Ethan could feel the enormous energy the settlers were putting into the new town, building their houses and barns, clearing the commons for pasture, and planting their crops. The settlers had purchased the surrounding land from the local Indians, the Wongunks, and had put up twenty-two thatched-roof cottages around or near the commons. They didn't yet have a meetinghouse, but they had formed a church whose members held services in one another's homes. In addition, a natural landing at a bend in the river was making the town a convenient port of call for ships sailing up-river from Saybrook and Long Island Sound.

A skilled carpenter, Ethan immediately found work helping to build houses and barns and repair visiting ships, and he used the small amount of money his father had left him to begin building a small cottage of his own.

Happily, he also found a bride, Susan Willis, the eldest daughter of John and Hannah Willis. The two young people were delighted to discover each other in the sparsely populated frontier town, and Susan's parents were equally pleased with the tall, earnest, red-headed suitor.

Ethan had first seen Susan at services following his arrival in Wethersfield, and then had seen her working in the fields a few days later as he was on his way to the river. Though he had continued to see her occasionally when he passed that way, he had never gotten close enough to speak to her until he was hired to help repair her father's barn, which had been damaged in a September windstorm. Susan had come out to the barn with water for him and her father, and her father had introduced him as a "smart lad" who knew more of his trade than anyone else in town. Susan had smiled politely as she handed Ethan the ladle. She couldn't have been more plain in her simple wool cloak and linen cap, but Ethan immediately felt a spark that carried him for days.

The courtship lasted through the winter, with Ethan and Susan given just enough privacy to determine if they were truly attracted to each other. Ethan recalled the first awkward supper at her family's home, he and Susan stealing glances across the table, and the feeling he had when she accidentally brushed his arm as she cleared the plates. He'd never forget the night they were finally put to bed together with the wooden bundling board between them, Susan's legs securely wrapped in a bundling apron that left her upper body uncovered.

Two weeks later, the town's minister conducted a formal betrothal ceremony for the couple, in which he delivered a lengthy sermon on marriage, and Ethan and Susan posted their banns, publicly announcing their intention to wed. On April 15 the couple was married in a brief civil ceremony, as was the Puritans' practice, at the Willis home, with the family and a dozen friends looking on. There were no religious vows or wedding rings, just a single question Ethan answered so enthusiastically it brought giggles and blushes from more than a few members of the otherwise solemn gathering.

After a modest dinner, the guests toasted the newlyweds with cups of steaming sack posset and escorted them to Ethan's house, where they put the bride to bed in her wedding-night gown and then stood outside, giving the couple a rousing shivaree of banging and bell-ringing that carried for miles through the frosty night.

⌒

Ethan had been told in Massachusetts that the remaining Indians in the Connecticut River Valley were friendly, but in Wethersfield he immediately began to hear stories about growing tension with the Pequots, who held the land to the southeast.

Dutch traders, it was said, had killed the Pequots' previous leader, Tatobem, and the Pequots had responded by killing a European sea captain and eight of his crewmen. Unfortunately, the Pequots retaliated against the wrong Europeans: the seamen they killed turned out to be English rather than Dutch, and the English demanded justice for the murders of their innocent countrymen. The Pequots dragged their heels, refusing to turn over the killers, and the incident precipitated a series of moves and countermoves that had set the English and Pequots at each other's throats. Boston sent out a sea-based expeditionary force in August 1636 that killed several Pequots and burned a number of their wigwams, and the Pequots retaliated by attacking the small English garrison at Fort Saybrook. The Indians maintained an almost continuous siege of the fort through the fall and winter, lying in wait for anyone who ventured out, and killing, wounding, or capturing and torturing more than a dozen men.

By early March, the threat to the fort had become so grave that the upriver towns sent seven men, including Captain Mason and Lieutenant Seeley, to help with its defense, and shortly thereafter Captain Underhill and his nineteen soldiers arrived from Boston to reinforce them.

⌒

There was little further news from Saybrook for the next month, and Indians were the last thing on Ethan's mind as he and Susan began their new life together. The Willises presented the couple with a team of two oxen, and John Willis saw to it that they were allotted a prime strip of land in the great meadows that stretched between the river and the town.

With the days getting warmer, Ethan and Susan rose early on April 23, hitched their wagon to their new team of oxen, and set out to begin the spring plowing. Ethan touched the brim of his hat and Susan smiled as they passed other settlers preparing their wagons and encountered others already out in the fields.

The sky had turned a deep blue by the time they arrived at their tract in the upper meadows, and they stood for a moment in the wagon admiring the view that swept down to the river and beyond. The warm sun and the smell of the rich, dark earth were exhilarating after the long, hard winter, and as Ethan grasped Susan's hand to help her down, he felt a greater sense of happiness and well-being than he'd ever known.

Ethan had some difficulty getting used to the two oxen, but he managed to plow two long furrows before stopping back at the wagon to adjust the heavy yoke fastened about their necks.

"They've a mind o' their own, don't they now?" Susan called brightly, putting down her hoe and coming over to help.

"They surely do," Ethan replied, intending to add that he suspected her father had given him these particular animals to test him. But before he could say it, Susan let out a scream, and when he turned he saw seven or eight settlers running furiously toward them in the distance. To his astonishment, the settlers were being pursued by a large band of Indians who appeared to be coming from the village.

Ethan's first thought was that it was impossible for Indians to be attacking this far north. The local river Indians were friendly, and the nearest Pequots were thirty-five miles downriver at Saybrook. Yet it had to be the Pequots.

Ethan doubted anyone in the fields that morning had a musket and saw immediately that the attack could turn into a massacre. Without further thought, he grabbed his axe and seized Susan by the arm, propelling her in the other direction.

"Run t' the landing!" he commanded. "The ship I worked on yistidy should still be thare."

"I'll ne'r make it," Susan protested, hiking her skirt over her knees and beginning to run.

"You must," Ethan shouted. "'Tis our only chance!"

Susan looked back and saw the Indians spread across the open meadow, coming hard.

"Don't look, jest *run!*" Ethan ordered.

They ran side by side, Ethan looking back every few seconds. The Indians were gaining fast, hatchets now clearly visible in their hands. Ethan saw one colonist and then another go down to the sound of wild war whoops as the Indians began to overtake their prey.

The next time Ethan glanced back, the main body of Indians had broken off toward the southeast, but two were no more than forty feet behind him. There was no way they were going to make it to the landing. He yelled for Susan to keep running while he tried to fight off their pursuers, but as he turned to face them, Susan stumbled, and within seconds the two Indians were on them. Ethan swung his axe viciously, chopping into the first man's upper arm and knocking him to the ground. The second Indian flew at Susan, caving in the left side of her head with a single blow of his hatchet.

Gasping for breath, Ethan locked eyes with Susan's attacker in a moment of pure hatred, but before either could act, gunfire erupted in the distance. The Indian glanced at his wounded comrade, who was struggling to his feet, and then both Indians turned and fled.

When Ethan went to Susan, she lay lifeless, the side of her skull a mash of blood, brains, and bone. Carefully, he picked her up in his arms and carried her to a clump of bushes, where he placed her in the shade and slumped down beside her. He had no idea how long he sat there, cradling her head and stroking her blood-smeared hair, the magnificent morning suddenly turned to death and ruin.

The sun was high in the sky by the time Susan's father finally found them, Ethan still sitting next to Susan, but now with his blood-soaked shirt draped over her head. Her father and two neighbors had been searching the meadow for them after finding their abandoned wagon and two dead oxen at their plot. The three men helped Ethan up and gently laid Susan's body in her father's wagon. Mr. Willis and Ethan mechanically climbed aboard, and they slowly set off, Ethan holding Susan's small, cold hand and the two neighbors walking behind. It was the most doleful procession, a woman later said, that she had ever seen.

⏝

As the pieces began to come together, the townspeople learned that a lone horseman riding south of town that morning had seen a large Indian war party coming up from the river and had galloped as fast as he could to the village, where he encountered a group of women at the south end of the Commons. The women had refused to believe that hostile Indians could be in the area, and the man had ridden on in a frantic effort to find someone who would heed him.

The women fled toward a nearby house when they saw the Pequots, but the Indians managed to seize three daughters of William Swayne, killing one and carrying off the other two as captives. Seeing the Commons deserted, the rest of the Indians turned east toward the river, where they came upon Ethan and the others working in the fields. In all, the Pequot war party had killed six men and three women, abducted the two younger Swayne girls, the eldest of whom was sixteen, and slaughtered more than a dozen cattle.

⌒

The attack on Wethersfield was the final straw for the three Connecticut River towns. Isolated and vulnerable, they called a special session of the General Court in Hartford, where representatives from the three settlements met to discuss the crisis.

On May 1, 1637, in a small, windowless building that served as Hartford's meetinghouse, the court officially declared war on the Pequots, and within hours each of the towns held emergency meetings to deliver the news. Ethan and his neighbors listened somberly in Wethersfield as the town's constable read the pronouncement:

> It is ordered that there shall be an offensive war against
> the Pequot and that there shall be 90 men levied out of the
> 3 Plantations, Hartford, Wethersfield, and Windsor.

The levy called for Hartford to contribute forty-two men, Windsor thirty, and Wethersfield eighteen, and the order named John Mason, a professional soldier from Windsor, as the army's commander. The call-up affected virtually every able-bodied man in the three river towns, underscoring the all-out nature of the war the Connecticut colonists were about to wage.

Ethan was among the first to report for duty, and Mason and Seeley came home from Saybrook to take charge of the new army. A mix of excitement and dread gripped the three towns as they prepared for war, outfitting their soldiers and gathering provisions to send with them.

There was little time to train the men, but when the troops assembled in Hartford on May 15, the town's renowned preacher, the Reverend Thomas Hooker, exhorted them to take the "Lord's revenge" upon their enemies. The Connecticut colony was in a fight for its survival, Hooker declared. "Do not do the work of the Lord's revenge slackly."

More than a hundred fifty officials, family members, and friends crowded the landing at Hartford later that morning as the army's three small ships, including a pink, a pinnace, and a shallop, started downriver, their white sails billowing in a stiff northerly breeze. Ethan stood on the narrow stern of the two-masted, square-rigged pink, taking in the spectacle and watching the landing slowly recede. He was filled with apprehension but determined to press on. For him, it was a mission of divine retribution.

∽

The fleet put in at Saybrook for two days, during which dozens of unnerving stories swirled through the fort. There was wild speculation about the size of the Pequot force at Weinshauks and gruesome accounts of the torture the Pequots had inflicted on the men they'd captured; in one case they peeled back their captive's skin and inserted red-hot embers against his raw flesh. The men were cheered upon learning that the two Swayne girls had been rescued unharmed by the Dutch, but then deeply troubled by the girls' report that the Pequots had acquired an arsenal of sixteen muskets, along with powder and shot.

Increasingly worried about the enemy's strength, Mason and his officers decided that rather than sail directly to Weinshauks to attack the Pequots, they would sail to Narragansett Bay, try to persuade the Narragansetts to join them, and march back to Weinshauks from the east in an effort take the Pequots by surprise. Meanwhile, Captain Underhill volunteered to join the expedition with his Massachusetts soldiers, allowing Mason to send twenty of his Connecticut men home to defend their towns against any new Pequot assaults.

Finally, loaded to capacity with ninety Englishmen and seventy Mohegans, the three ships left for Narragansett Bay on Friday morning, May 19, passing Weinshauks that afternoon. The Pequots were alarmed when they caught sight of the fleet, fearing a possible attack, but they relaxed their guard as the ships passed in the distance, concluding that at least for now, the English had no stomach for a fight.

Arriving at their destination Saturday evening, the colonists and the Mohegans spent the Sabbath onboard their ships, then were kept from landing for the next two days by howling winds from the southeast. They finally went ashore on Tuesday evening, leaving thirteen men to sail the ships back to the rendezvous point. Perhaps offended that the English had put the attack against the Pequots in motion without consulting him, the Narragansetts' grand sachem, Minatonomi, was initially cool toward Mason, warning that the Pequots were "very great captains and skillful in war" and expressing doubt that Mason and his small army could defeat them on their own. He agreed to provide Mason with guides, however, and then surprised the English by providing the more than four hundred warriors who started out with Mason on Thursday morning, May 25.

The long, hot march on Thursday brought the allied army to its current camp at the head of the Mystic River, where Ethan now lay staring at the stars. Drained and exhausted, he finally fell asleep.

The next morning Ethan felt someone shake him.

He sat bolt upright, momentarily confused.

"What time is it?"

"Fust light," Seeley answered hurriedly, already moving on to the next man. "We're late. We hevta move quick or we'll lose the advantage."

Ethan tried to focus. Men were waking up around him, strapping on equipment and picking up their muskets and pikes. His mind cleared and he scrambled to his feet.

As the soldiers assembled, the guards who had been posted throughout the night were spreading a mix of good news and bad. The good news was that their Indian scouts had heard the Pequots singing and rejoicing until well past midnight in celebration of what they believed to be the colonists' fear of them. The bad was that the scouts believed the Pequot fort was impregnable and that most of the remaining Narragansetts had deserted, leaving only fifty or sixty at most.

Mason quickly huddled with his men, stressing the importance of catching the Pequots while they were asleep and hopefully exhausted from their reveling.

"The village kivers about two acres," he said, "and is surrounded by a twelve-foot-high palisade of logs as thick as a man's leg and sharpened at the top. There're loopholes in the palisade they can shoot through unless we git there fust."

"How do we git in?" one of the soldiers asked.

"There're two entrances," Mason answered, "both with narrow passages they block with boughs and bushes at night. We'll need two men t' pull 'em out."

Mason said it appeared the fort contained four or five hundred Indians, including men, women, and children, and as many as seventy dwellings, which he described as typical ten-by-fifteen-foot oval wigwams covered with mats of iris leaves and rushes. The goal was to get inside the fort, kill as many of the enemy and seize as much plunder as possible, and then head toward their ships. They'd leave the question of what to do about the second fort until they'd finished with the first.

After a brief prayer, the army set out, with Mason and Seeley again at the head of the English troops and Underhill and his Massachusetts men at the rear.

The English moved briskly, trying to make up for lost time. But after a mile and a half, there was still no sign of the fort.

Ethan could see Mason was becoming uneasy.

"You think the guides've misled us?" Ethan heard Seeley ask in a low voice.

"Dunno," Mason replied, his eyes trained on the Mohegan guide ahead of them, "but tell the men t' be on guard."

Seeley turned to Ethan to pass the order down the line.

"On guard . . . be alert!" each man in the column whispered to the next. Ethan fingered the hilt of his sword, peered into the surrounding forest, and strained to catch any suspicious sound. If the English were ambushed now, they would be annihilated.

Moments later, the path unexpectedly opened onto another cornfield, where Mason stopped and angrily summoned Uncas and Wequash.

"Wer's the fort?" Mason demanded, eyeing his allies warily.

"At the top of the hill," Uncas replied, pointing upward.

Looking up, Ethan could make out the dark outlines of the palisade, which sat at the top of a long, gradual hill littered with charred tree stumps. To reach it, they'd have to cover a good hundred fifty yards in the early-morning light.

"Wer're your warriors?" Mason asked.

"In the woods," the chiefs replied nervously, pointing to the southern edge of the clearing.

"Go tell 'em they shouldn't be afraid, but should stay with us," Mason said. "Tell 'em they can stand at what distance they please, but they should stay and see now whether Englishmen will fight."

The chiefs nodded and hurried off to talk to their men.

Underhill came up from the rear slightly out of breath; after a brief conference he and Mason agreed to split their forces, with Mason attacking the main entrance from the northeast and Underhill attacking the second from the southwest. The two groups moved as swiftly and silently as possible up the hill, the soldiers running low to the ground and using the stumps as cover. Ethan was right behind Mason and Seeley, praying his bad knee wouldn't buckle and there were no Pequot guards to sound the alarm.

Another fifteen feet and they'd be there. Suddenly a dog barked from inside the fort and someone began shouting "Owanux! Owanux!"—the Indian word for "Englishmen." Mason immediately ordered some of his soldiers to fire into the fort through the openings in the palisade and others to guard the perimeter, while he rushed to the main entrance with the rest.

The entrance was blocked by bushes as high as a man's chest, but Mason clambered over them. Once Seeley and Ethan cleared the passageway, the soldiers flooded inside with their swords in their right hands and their muskets in their left. Underhill's men broke through the second entrance in a similar manner, trapping the Pequots between the two English forces.

In the bedlam that followed, Indians ran through the lanes and alleyways; some hid in their wigwams, and others struck back both singly and in groups. Underhill's troops encountered fierce resistance from the outset, arrows bouncing off their helmets, slamming against their leather armor, and sometimes ripping into unprotected flesh. Two men were struck in the face, others in the legs and shoulders, and Underhill himself was hit at close range by an arrow that tore through his corselet into his hip.

Inside, the English quickly became separated in the turmoil, and shortly after entering the fort, Ethan saw Mason storm into a wigwam by himself. Ethan called to Seeley that they should go after him, but before they could get there a soldier named Hydon rushed in ahead of them. Bursting into the hut, Ethan saw two bodies on the floor and Hydon rushing at an Indian about to loose an arrow at Mason's head. Hydon sliced the bowstring with his sword a split second before the shooter could let fly, then hacked the man to death.

When Mason and his companions returned to the lane, several Indians fired arrows at them from behind another wigwam. Three arrows struck Mason's helmet, and one hit Seeley just above his right eye, somehow lodging in his eyebrow. Mason pulled it out, while Ethan fired at the fleeing Indians and Hydon rushed to the aid of another soldier grappling with two Pequots nearby.

Mason and Seeley paused while Ethan poured a new charge of powder down the barrel of his musket and rammed a lead ball and wadding on top of the charge. The three then started up the lane in a small phalanx, forcing a dozen Indians into the path of soldiers coming from the opposite direction. The approaching soldiers shot at the fleeing Indians, dropping three of them in their tracks, and pursued two more into a wigwam, where they dispatched them with their broadswords.

The English had been in the fort for less than fifteen minutes, but Ethan could see that Mason was becoming frustrated with the hopelessly disorganized nature of the fighting, and Ethan himself was beginning to fear the soldiers were in danger of being picked off or overwhelmed in the confusion.

Their muskets gave the colonists far more firepower than the Indians had, and the thunderous noise and clouds of smoke they produced wrought terror inside the fort. But the muskets were heavy, clumsy, and unreliable, often requiring the shooter to rest the weapon on a forked stick when he fired, and an Indian could get off as many as five arrows before a solider could reload and fire again. The English increasingly went to their broadswords, but as they did, their advantage began to ebb, more Indians fought back, and the Connecticut troops' inexperience became more evident.

Passing two soldiers who appeared dazed and confused, Mason turned to Seeley and Ethan in anger.

"Rot these bloody Indians!" he cursed. "We'll ne'er kill 'em this way. We must burn 'em!"

With that, Mason headed back into the wigwam where he'd nearly been killed and brought out a firebrand that he put to the roof mats, igniting them instantly. Carried by swirling embers, the fire spread quickly, leaping from one wigwam to the next.

Seeing the flames, Underhill lit his own fire on the other side of the fort with a train of powder, and as the two fires raced toward one another, Pequot men, women, and children fled their burning huts, screaming above the musket fire. Confusion turned to panic as whole groups of Indians fled one way only to run directly into a line of soldiers, from whom they wheeled in terror and headed back the other way, in some cases running directly into the flames they were trying to escape. Ethan watched one young Pequot turn and attempt to loose an arrow at his pursuers, but the fire burned his bowstring before he could get off his shot. Within minutes, the stench of burning flesh was everywhere.

As the flames grew higher, the soldiers fought their way out of the fort and, together with the troops outside, surrounded the entire palisade in order to intercept and kill anyone who tried to flee the inferno. Ethan took up a position near the main entrance and waited with his musket at the ready. Seeley stood off to Ethan's right, and the Mohegans and Narragansetts formed a second and third cordon around the doomed fortress.

Some Pequots climbed to the top of the palisade and tried to jump, but the colonists shot them the moment they appeared or ran them though with their swords or pikes as they hit the ground. One man was shot while being handed a child. Another, on fire when he jumped, was shot and left to burn at the base of the stockade. Suddenly a group of thirty or forty Pequots burst out of the main entrance in a mass bid to escape, sprinting in various directions. Ethan and the soldiers around him opened fire, but most of the Pequots got through the first line and headed toward the outer circles of Mohegans and Narragansetts, who awaited them with their arrows and hatchets. Even then, some of the Pequots managed to break clear, and Ethan and several other soldiers joined in trying to chase them down.

Ethan caught up with one of the Pequots, a lean, hard-muscled man about twice his age, and knocked him to the ground from behind with the butt of his musket. The Indian went down, rolled once, and came back up on one knee, grasping his hatchet in his right hand. Ethan drew his sword and approached the man, who stared back defiantly. Ethan could see that the man's left arm was badly burned and that he was bleeding from his right temple, but he felt nothing for him as he began to raise the sword.

"You slay too many," the Indian cried, startling Ethan with his English. "*Matchit.* 'Tis evil. May the gods drive you from our land!"

"Damn your gods, you heathen savage!" Ethan screamed, and raised the sword over his head. Just as he did, the Indian sprang forward and swung his hatchet at Ethan, slicing into the outer layer of his corselet just above his heart. Ethan instinctively stepped back, then came down with a blow that severed the man's head.

⤳

The English and their Indian allies killed more than five hundred Pequots at Mystic on that Friday, May 26, 1637, including some hundred fifty Pequot warriors who had fatefully arrived from Weinshauks the evening before. Two English soldiers were killed and twenty wounded, while several Narragansetts were killed or wounded by friendly fire in the Pequot breakout. Seven Pequots were taken captive, and seven escaped, spreading the alarm to Weinshauks.

With their ammunition depleted and some of their men so severely wounded they had to be carried, the English gave up any thought of attacking Weinshauks and instead, accompanied by the Mohegans and the remaining Narragansetts, retreated toward their waiting ships. Sassacus sent some three hundred warriors from Weinshauks to intercept them along the way, but the army, with critical help from Uncas and the Mohegans, repeatedly repulsed the Pequot attacks.

Shocked and dispirited by the disaster at Mystic and convinced they could no longer stand up against English power, the remaining Pequots abandoned their villages and dispersed into the countryside, the largest group fleeing west along the Connecticut coast. Later that summer a combined force of English and Mohegans caught up with the main body of Pequots in a swamp near current-day Bridgeport and captured or killed most of them. Sassacus himself managed to escape briefly to the Hudson Valley in New York, but was slain there by Mohawks apparently seeking to ingratiate themselves with the victorious English.

Most of the surviving Pequots were divided among the Mohegans and the Narragansetts, pressed into servitude to the colonists, or shipped as slaves to Bermuda and the West Indies. Back in Hartford, the colonial government declared the Pequot nation dissolved forever.

2

~

A Man Who
Believes in Himself

March 6–9, 1987

Josh Williams sat at the elegant rosewood conference table with twenty of his fellow executives listening to United Insurance's new CEO, Tug Caldwell, outline his vision for the company.

At age thirty-eight, Josh was a trim six-foot-one, with a crew cut and chiseled profile that suggested military officer or college coach rather than one of the company's fastest-rising corporate stars. He had almost single-handedly turned around the Chicago insurer's commercial lines business and was being prominently mentioned as someone who might run the division now that its longtime head, Jack Snow, was being pushed out the door by the new management. Caldwell's secretary had, in fact, called to ask Josh to stay after the morning meeting, and Josh's own secretary had whispered excitedly that she'd bet anything he was going to be offered the job. If so, it was going to be the biggest day of his professional life.

On the surface, Caldwell seemed an odd choice to head the nation's fifth-largest insurer, having come from a media company that owned a string of radio and TV stations. But there was no denying he had tripled that company's stock price in less than three years, and there were high hopes he could do something similar for United. Furthermore, Josh had to agree that Caldwell looked and acted the part. In his late fifties and perhaps an inch taller than Josh, he was an imposing figure, with silver hair, steel-blue eyes, and a bluff, engaging personality that had won him a growing legion of followers on Wall Street. The latest issue of *Business Week* had named Caldwell one of the nation's top ten CEOs, and *Forbes* was predicting he'd shake up the insurance industry just as he had broadcasting.

Once the last of the other executives had left the room, Caldwell sat down next to Josh.

"Thanks for staying," Caldwell said, giving Josh a friendly smile. "I'm sorry we haven't had time to have a real one-on-one yet, but I've been reviewing your record and am very impressed with the way you've turned the division around. You keep up that kind of work, and you'll have my job before you know it!"

"Thank you, Mr. Caldwell, but I'm not the only one who deserves recognition," Josh demurred. "A lot of people contributed."

"Sure, I know," Caldwell acknowledged, "but you made it happen. And by the way, Josh, call me Tug; all my friends do.

"In any case," Caldwell continued, "now that Jack Snow's leaving, you're the guy I'd like to see replace him. Means moving up to senior vice president. Think you're up to it?"

"Yes, sir, I do," Josh replied confidently.

"Good," Caldwell said. "That's what I like, a man who believes in himself. We'll announce your promotion next week. And although you didn't ask, let me assure you it'll mean a nice bump in your comp. Double your current salary, to be exact, plus a bonus plan and an options package that can really mean something once the stock takes off."

Caldwell paused for a moment to let his largess sink in. "I'll have Sullivan from H.R. go over it with you," he continued, "but as you see, I like my top people to be well-paid."

"That's very generous," Josh replied with an appreciative nod. "I just hope I can meet your expectations."

"I have no doubt you will," Caldwell said reassuringly, and he turned to collect his papers as though the meeting were over.

"And, oh, Josh, just one more thing," Caldwell added, turning back to his newly anointed SVP. "K&L's CEO, Fred Knapp, approached me the other day and said he hoped we'd be able to start doing business with them again."

Josh's antennae went up immediately. K&L was one of the largest insurance brokers in the country, and Jack Snow had dropped them because one of their top people had suggested United participate in a plan in which K&L would steer large excess casualty policies to a select group of insurers. These highly lucrative policies were attached to a company's primary insurance to provide added protection against catastrophic events like an oil spill or fatal plant explosion, and they gave insurers and brokers opportunities to make hundreds of thousands, even millions of dollars in premiums and commissions. K&L, however, had proposed an arrangement in which it could earn even higher fees in the form of hidden contingent commissions paid by the insurers to whom K&L steered the business. The basic idea was that several participating insurers would submit bogus high bids to help push a contract to another insurer in the group with the understanding they could expect to have the same done for them on future deals.

"I'm afraid Jack Snow stopped doing business with K&L for a reason," Josh said cautiously.

"You mean because of their approach to the excess casualty market?" Caldwell asked.

"Well, I don't know how much you know about what they were proposing, Tug, but basically they were offering to bring us business if we'd coordinate bids with some of our competitors. Either we'd be expected to submit an inflated bid to help a competitor win or keep the business, or our competitors would be expected to inflate their bids to help us. To me, it was nothing but a bid-rigging scheme designed to jack up K&L's commissions and screw its clients."

Caldwell winced slightly at Josh's description of the proposal.

"You know, Josh," he said, "I've looked at this, and I think you're being a little hard on K&L. They're one of the top insurance brokerages in the country, and Fred Knapp is one of the smartest guys in the business. I think he'd argue that they bend over backward to help their clients put together exactly the right risk packages and then place those packages with the best insurers available. Granted, their brokers may be a little aggressive, but you've got to be aggressive to compete."

"Mr. Caldwell," Josh replied, "I'm as aggressive as anybody, but what K&L was proposing was wrong and, in my opinion, illegal."

"Have they ever had any trouble with the regulators, or been accused of any kind of impropriety?" Caldwell asked.

"Not that I know of," Josh replied, suddenly feeling defensive.

"Well, I think you've got to be a little more flexible, Josh," Caldwell said. "My understanding is that K&L is the hottest broker in the industry right now, and without taking anything away from what you've done, it's clear we've got to find additional ways to build the business. We don't have forever to get this company airborne, and I'm counting on big things from commercial lines."

Josh asked, "So what are you saying? You want me to go back to K&L and talk to them?"

"Yeah, I do," Caldwell replied. He wasn't smiling now, and Josh could feel his cold blue eyes boring into him. "Better yet, why don't I bring Fred Knapp and a couple of his people in here to talk to both of us? Is that agreeable?"

Josh knew the right answer politically: *Sure, why not; maybe they've backed away from their original idea, and it certainly won't hurt to talk.* But there was something in his character that simply wouldn't let him say it. He could picture the K&L executive who'd outlined the proposal, and while he had no proof, he had no doubt K&L was already implementing it with other firms.

Josh couldn't believe his new boss was pressing him this way. Was it some kind of test, or was this Knapp a buddy Caldwell was trying to do a favor for? Or was it simply that Caldwell was so intent on results, he didn't care how he got them? Suddenly Josh's exhilaration over the promotion was gone, and he began to feel he was facing the kind of moment of truth he'd read about but never expected to confront himself.

"I don't know," Josh finally said, raising his eyebrows and shaking his head uncertainly. "I have to tell you, Mr. Caldwell, I really feel uncomfortable about talking to them further on this. Can you give me a day or two to think about it?"

"Sure," Caldwell said coolly, "It's Friday. Why not take the weekend to think it over and let me know Monday? That way, assuming we're on the same page, we can announce the promotion on Tuesday."

So the business with K&L is a deal breaker, Josh thought as he and Caldwell rose and stood facing each other.

"Remember what I said about being flexible," Caldwell added, extending his hand and giving Josh his legendary iron grip. "I expect flexibility in my executives. And I'm looking for team players."

❧

Josh returned to his office and stood at his window, staring down fifty-five stories at Michigan Avenue and replaying the conversation over and over in his mind. His first thought when he left the conference room was that he had just made the biggest mistake of his life, jeopardizing the chance to head a key division of a major insurance company at age thirty-eight. But as the day progressed, he became increasingly angry with Caldwell for putting him in a corner.

How, Josh repeatedly asked himself, could he work for someone who didn't respect his opinion on a critical matter like this, let alone who seemed so little troubled by the ethical issues involved? And it wasn't just a matter of ethics. If they got tangled up with the kind of scheme he was sure K&L was running, he and Caldwell could conceivably go to jail. The publicity alone could damage United for years. Furthermore, he was furious at the way Caldwell had tried to bully him into submission.

Yet he wanted the job, and his family deserved the security and lifestyle it promised. Hell, the stock options alone could be worth millions. Maybe he could hang on for a couple of years, find a way to delay working with K&L, even come up with enough ammunition to persuade Caldwell to back away from them. After all, he'd been working toward a position like this his entire career; even if he were lucky, it could take years to find another one like it. If he didn't swallow his pride and self-righteousness he was not just going to miss out on the promotion; he was going to have to leave United altogether, because there'd be no place for him under Caldwell.

Unable to concentrate on his work that afternoon, Josh decided to pack up early and catch the 4:30 train home. He rarely left before 6:00, but there was no sense sitting around without being able to get anything done. Once on the train, he tried to read a magazine, but that proved impossible. His mind was stuck on the day's disaster and how it was likely to affect the rest of his life.

⌒

Josh had grown up on the family farm in Sheffield, Connecticut, a small town in the southeastern part of the state, and he had essentially been away now for twenty years. Called "Red" by his friends because of his reddish-brown hair, he'd graduated second in his class from Southeast Regional High and captained its tennis team. Eager to see other parts of the country, he'd accepted a scholarship to Stanford , where he studied economics and played tennis, and had spent his college summers hitchhiking around the United States or working at resorts up and down the New England coast. After graduating from Stanford, he joined the Army, winding up running espionage agents in Vietnam for Army Intelligence and almost coming home in a body bag in 1972 when he stumbled into a firefight. He'd then spent a year assigned to the Pentagon, getting to know Washington firsthand and watching the President and the war unravel.

By age twenty-five, he decided it was time to get serious about a career and entered the MBA program at Wharton in Philadelphia, where he was eventually recruited by United. Shortly after arriving in Chicago, he met Sharon Holmes, a pretty, vivacious midwestern girl with emerald-green eyes and an irresistible smile who was an up-and-coming copywriter in the company's marketing department.

He recalled vividly the day he'd first seen Sharon. She'd stepped into a crowded elevator and smiled as she squeezed into a space in front of him. She was wearing a simple white blouse that set off a deep summer tan and was standing so close he could smell her fragrance and at one point feel a wisp of her short, honey-brown hair against his chin. The effect was like being hit by the thunderbolt the Italians joked about. He remembered looking down at the nape of her neck and the swell of her breasts, and thinking she was the most captivating woman he'd ever seen. When she got off the elevator two floors before his, he took a chance, following her out, then catching up and introducing himself as they walked along the corridor toward her office. They later laughed a thousand times at his audacity, but he always insisted it had worked out "exactly" as he'd planned. Within a week they'd had their first date and begun a whirlwind romance that ended with them getting married in her hometown of Des Plaines four months later.

For the next eleven and a half years Josh moved steadily up the corporate ladder, and Sharon gradually gave up her career to become a full-time mother. The couple now had three children—Matthew, ten, Sarah, eight, and Jacob, three—and the family had settled into a comfortable suburban life fifty minutes from Josh's downtown office. Now, he felt, he was about to let them all down whichever way he went.

It was obvious to Sharon the moment Josh walked in that something had gone wrong, but it wasn't until they got the kids to bed that they were able to sit down at the kitchen table and talk about it. Josh poured himself a drink, which he never did that late at night, and proceeded to recount the day—his excitement at the call from Caldwell's secretary, Caldwell's praise for his work, the job offer, the money and stock options, and finally the way the whole thing had fallen apart. He was certain Sharon's first reaction would be to step back, take a deep breath, and suggest they use the weekend to come up with a way to work things out. But she surprised him.

When he'd finished, she sat quietly, then simply shook her head and smiled at him.

"I wish I could help, Josh," she said earnestly, "but I know you too well. You're never going to be happy working for Caldwell, and you'll be miserable trying. It might be a little tough while you look for something else, but you'll find it. You're simply too good a man to be held back, Josh." She leaned over and kissed him.

It was the greatest relief Josh Williams had ever felt.

$$\smile$$

Josh called Caldwell's office first thing Monday morning and made an appointment to see him.

Caldwell was working at his desk when Josh entered his office at 10:00, and he motioned for Josh to have a seat while he finished signing some papers.

"So," Caldwell said, finally looking up, "did you have a chance to think things over this weekend?"

"Yes, I did," Josh said.

"And?" Caldwell asked, glancing casually toward his in-box as though the meeting were merely a formality and there could be only one answer.

"I haven't changed my mind," Josh said firmly. "In my opinion, K&L's simply not the kind of firm we should be dealing with."

Caldwell started to respond but apparently thought better of it and instead simply sat appraising the younger man.

"Okay, Josh," he finally said, "I guess, then, that's pretty much it, unless you have anything else." Picking up one of the documents he'd just signed, he added, "Perhaps you could give this to my secretary on your way out."

Ken Sullivan from H.R. called ten minutes later to say he couldn't believe it, but he'd been instructed to meet with Josh that morning to go over his termination agreement. The meeting took no more than twenty minutes, with Sullivan still in shock and most of the time spent on Josh's severance package: twelve months of full salary. It was the bare minimum the company could get away with, but Sullivan confided that Caldwell was adamant about not doing more.

"And there's one more thing," Sullivan said apologetically, "I don't know what happened between you and Caldwell, Josh, but he insists you clean out your desk and be out of the building by noon."

3

The Gift

March 10–November 17, 1987

It took Josh more than six months to land his first decent job offer, which was for an upper-mid-level position at United's big crosstown rival, CNA. It didn't compare with the opportunity he'd missed out on at United, however, and with no other prospects in sight, he began to toy with an idea he'd had before but never seriously considered.

His mother had died six years ago, and his father had passed away the previous December, leaving the Connecticut farm to Josh and Linda, Josh's older sister. Linda, who was married to an orthopedist and had two teenage daughters and a big house in West Hartford, assumed they'd put the farm up for sale. The sooner the better, she said, as Sheffield's real estate market was booming and they should be able to get a good price for the land.

Josh had no doubt that was true. Suburban sprawl had finally begun to inch its way into Sheffield, and there was no comparison between the property's value as a residential subdivision versus its worth as a farm.

The farm had become a shadow of what it had been. Once two hundred acres with seventy dairy cows, it had shrunk to a hundred acres and hadn't been operated as a dairy farm since 1958, when his father sold the herd and half the acreage. Josh's father had then gone to work part-time at the local hardware store and rented part of his remaining land to other dairy farmers who planted it in feed crops for their herds.

Still, Josh found he had a surprisingly strong emotional reaction against turning the farm into a housing development quite so fast, and he had admittedly procrastinated about putting it up for sale. Perhaps it was a sense of guilt, or perhaps he simply had fonder memories of growing up there than Linda did, but to him it wasn't just another piece of real estate. It was one of the oldest farms continuously owned by one family in Connecticut. Ethan Williams, the first member of the family to come to America, had carved it out of the wilderness more than three hundred twenty-five years ago. And it still had a wonderful old farmhouse, two barns, an apple orchard, and acres of open space in what *Money* magazine called one of the best small towns in New England.

Josh now found himself increasingly drawn to the possibility of buying his sister's half of the farm and moving back to Connecticut. He had initially dismissed the idea for a number of reasons. Sharon was a confirmed Chicagoan, had a million friends in the area, and would be loathe to move so far from her parents; she was their only child. His family had just moved into a new home ten months ago, and the kids were still getting used to their new surroundings. Although they loved visiting the farm, who knew how they'd adjust to living there? And what would he do in Connecticut? High-level job openings in the state's legendary insurance industry were scarce, and the search firm he was using hadn't come up with anything of interest there.

Yet the thought wouldn't go away, and in mid-September he happened to mention his possible interest in returning to Connecticut during a phone conversation with the banker who was handling his father's estate. An old friend of the family, Phil Levesque knew everyone in Sheffield's small business community.

"You ever think of buying an insurance agency?" Levesque asked.

"No," Josh replied, surprised by the question. "Why? You know a good one that's for sale?"

"Just so happens Bill Blake's about to put the Sheffield Agency on the market," Levesque said. "I'd think that kind of thing would be right up your alley, and we'd finance it in a second. Blake's built himself a real nice operation."

Josh couldn't believe he hadn't thought about buying an agency himself. He had always seen himself in a corporate role, and the idea of becoming a small businessman hadn't entered his mind. Good independent insurance agencies, moreover, rarely came on the market, and when one did the price could be prohibitive. In this case, the price seemed reasonable, and Levesque was literally laying the thing in his lap.

The obstacle of having to uproot his family remained, but the more he thought about Levesque's suggestion, the more sense it made. The agency could be a good business and a smart investment. It would allow him to move back to the farm, stay in insurance, get out of the corporate rat race, be his own boss, and work ten minutes from home. Living and working in Sheffield would, in short, be a whole new way of life, and he had to believe Sharon and the kids, once they adjusted, would be happy there.

Josh began researching the Sheffield Agency that afternoon and talked with Sharon about the idea long into the night. She was reluctant for all the reasons he'd thought about. They'd just gotten settled, she hated to leave the area, and then there were her parents.

It took several days of persuasion, but Sharon finally came around. It'd be especially hard on Matt, but the kids would adapt, she reasoned. Fortunately, her mother and father were in good health and loved to travel. And Sharon could see how much Josh wanted to do this. If he felt that strongly, she'd go.

By mid-September, Josh had inked the deal to buy Blake's insurance business, and the next day they put their house up for sale.

⌇

The movers arrived at 8:00 a.m. sharp on Saturday, November 14. It took four men the entire day to load the huge Mayflower trailer, but the driver finally squeezed in the last bicycles and baseball bats. Josh and Sharon stood together, watching everything they had accumulated over the past twelve years pull out of the driveway and start its eleven-hundred-mile trip east. Sharon wiped tears from her eyes and went back into the house to call her parents.

"All done?" her father asked when he heard her voice.

"All loaded and on its way," she answered. "Are the kids behaving?"

"They always behave over here," he said good-naturedly.

"How about Matt?" she asked. "Is he still down?"

"Yeah, playing his last soccer game this morning was tough, but I'm sure he'll be fine once you get him into school back there."

"I hope so," Sharon said.

Josh and Sharon checked the house one last time, then headed over to her folks for the night. The plan was for Josh to leave for Connecticut in their minivan Sunday morning, and for Sharon and the kids to fly there on Wednesday to join him.

⌇

It had been a hectic last two months, and Josh actually welcomed the long drive east as a chance to unwind. On Monday night he had stayed with friends in Manhattan and now was headed north on the Hutchinson River

Parkway toward Connecticut. The morning was clear, with a temperature in the fifties, and he figured he'd reach Sheffield shortly before noon. He planned to spend the afternoon unpacking the van and walking the property.

Normally cautious about money, Josh couldn't believe he'd just borrowed $2 million, including $700,000 to buy his sister's share of the farm and $1.3 million for the agency. Yet he'd never been more upbeat in his life.

He was in such high spirits coming out of the city that morning that he didn't even mind the construction delay approaching the New York–Connecticut line, where the Hutch became the Merritt Parkway, one of the oldest and prettiest highways in the country.

The Merritt had been built back in the 1930s to help relieve the congestion on the old Boston Post Road, one of the colonies' first major thoroughfares; it had been so clogged with carriages and post riders as far back as the 1700s that people had complained about it even then. The parkway had since been supplemented by I-95, but Josh thought anyone was crazy not to prefer it to the interstate. The Merritt had been designed to give motorists the feeling of driving through a park, and no one could afford to build another highway like it again. The state had planted thousands of native trees and shrubs along its course and built dozens of Art Deco–style bridges to allow it to pass over and under local roads. Even the bridges' motifs were distinctive, ranging from the state seal to historical depictions of the state's Puritans and Native Americans.

Josh put the van in cruise control, refilled his coffee cup from his thermos, and sat back, musing about his years growing up in New England. Not only had his memories grown fonder with time, but he realized he'd come to appreciate the region more and more with each passing year and wondered if he hadn't been destined to return all along.

New England for him was rolling hills and snow-covered mountains. Town greens and white-steepled churches. Family farms, dairy herds, and the old stone walls that stretched across the countryside.

It was the rocky coastline, sand dunes, and soft sandy beaches. Quaint seaports and harbors with their sport boats and lobster boats, sailboats and cruisers. Lighthouses and beach houses. The crash of the surf and the tang of salt air.

It was pre-Revolutionary inns and taverns. Historic halls, monuments, and battlefields. Old mill towns, covered bridges, and out-of-the-way antiques shops. Fleet blessings and fife-and-drum-corps musters.

And it was the food. The clambakes and lobster fests. Shad bakes and corn roasts. Pumpkins, cranberries, and, for three short weeks, the sweetest, most succulent strawberries on earth.

And, always in the background, the rhythm of the seasons, capped by the brilliant reds, golds, and russets of autumn.

Josh supposed he'd seen just about every part of New England. He'd fished and hiked in Maine, skied in Vermont and New Hampshire, and sailed off Rhode Island. He'd gone to concerts in the Berkshires, watched baseball in Boston, and combed the beaches on Nantucket and Cape Cod. For sheer beauty and variety, he knew of no other region in the country that even came close.

But his favorite state was Connecticut. Not only did it have most of the cultural charm and natural beauty of the rest of New England, but he considered it the best place to actually live.

Despite its small size, Connecticut was enormously diverse, extending from its heavily-populated central corridor to a host of small cities, towns, and villages that lay to the east and west. Economically, it was one of the wealthiest states in the nation. Culturally, it had everything from top-notch schools, colleges, and universities to first-rate restaurants, theaters, and museums. And the center of the state was just two hours from New York and Boston, putting the just about everything anyone could want within easy reach.

What especially attracted Josh at this point in his life was the overall tenor of life in the state. Despite its industrialization and waves of immigration over the years, there was still a streak of Yankee conservatism in Connecticut that made it especially appealing for raising a family. That conservatism, he knew, traced its origins back to his Puritan ancestors, who had passed on a culture of hard work, self-reliance, and moral values.

Josh had never taken the same interest in the family's history that his father and grandfather had, but it was impossible to go to school in Sheffield without learning something about the town's Puritan past.

The lack of a major port kept Connecticut relatively isolated during its early years, leaving Puritanism to shape virtually every aspect of Connecticut's growth. Each new town was organized around its independent Congregational Church, and as the congregations grew they sent out new shoots, settlers who established their own communities and churches, until today the state had a hundred sixty-nine towns that some likened to a hundred sixty-nine fiercely independent republics.

Everyone in colonial Connecticut paid taxes to support the church, and its elders set the moral standards, chose the state's political leaders, and determined what was taught in the schools. The state's first code of laws not only required observance of the Sabbath but outlawed drunkenness, swearing, and idleness, going so far as to prohibit "the Game called Shuffle Board" in "howses of Common Interteinement, whereby much precious time is spent unfruitfully and much waste of Wyne and Beare occasioned."

In 1818 Connecticut finally ended taxpayer support of the church, but the state's legislative system helped extend Puritan values deep into the twentieth century. The system kept power in the hands of the small towns by limiting each town or city to no more than two representatives in the lower house of the General Assembly, enabling the state's rural residents and their conservative views to dominate the state's politics right up until the 1960s. By then, less than 12 percent of the state's population could elect a majority in the state House of Representatives. It wasn't until 1965 that Connecticut gave equal representation to those living in its larger towns and cities.

Connecticut's English Puritans gradually became Yankee farmers, artisans, manufacturers, and merchants. The state's technological innovations helped spark the Industrial Revolution, and immigration gradually turned the population into the diverse society of today. But while time had transformed Connecticut, one could still feel the Puritans' influence in a multitude of ways.

You could see it in the state's architecture and the layouts of its villages, in its town meetings and the independent-mindedness of its local governments, and in the generally conservative tastes and manners of its people. You could see it in the quality of its schools, the number of its college graduates, and the productivity of its workers. And you could see it in the Yankee ingenuity of its modern-day tinkerers and craftsmen, who continued to rank among the country's most prolific inventors.

You could even see the remnants of Puritanism in the way today's residents handled their money. The thriftiest people in the country, New Englanders spent less on conspicuous consumption and had lower bankruptcy rates than other Americans.

Josh smiled at his musings. You had to give it to Connecticut, he told himself. It had rightfully earned one of its nicknames: The Land of Steady Habits. Josh was convinced that, other than marrying Sharon, coming back was the best decision he'd ever made.

∽

Josh left the Merritt Parkway just south of New Haven and took I-95 east toward Rhode Island. By 11:40 he was approaching the Baldwin Bridge, which spans the Connecticut River between Old Saybrook and Old Lyme.

The river, which takes its name from the Indian word *Quinecktecut*, meaning "long tidal river," originates a few hundred yards from the Canadian border and flows four hundred ten miles to Long Island Sound. It serves as the boundary between Vermont and New Hampshire, runs due south through the vegetable and old tobacco fields of western Massachusetts and northern Connecticut, passes below the glass towers of downtown Hartford, and turns southeast at Middletown for its final run to the sea.

The last twelve miles of the river provide one of the most scenic stretches on the continent, passing rock ledges and densely wooded hills in Deep River, Essex, and Lyme, then broadening into a succession of coves, inlets, and tidal marshes before emptying into the Sound. The Western Nehantic Indian chief Attawanhood, who took the Christian name Joshua, is said to have regularly sat atop the highest ledge, now known as Joshua Rock, watching his fellow tribesmen fish for salmon and shad.

Now eagles were beginning to return to the lower river to hunt in winter, and harbor seals played on its sandbars. Not to be outdone, hundreds of thousands of migrating swallows gathered over tiny Goose Island at sundown for several weeks each September, blackening the sky before diving in a spectacular, tornado-like funnel into the reeds below.

Josh knew the last stretch of the river well, having cruised it a hundred times in his father's twenty-two-foot Chris Craft, and they had camped and bow-hunted for deer on overnight excursions into the western hills.

He recalled how on September mornings, as the air turned cooler than the water, enormous billows of mist would hang over the river, shrouding it from anyone looking down from the adjoining hills. The spectacle was best on cool, clear mornings when, for someone looking east, the mist would sit just below the horizon and the sun would come up as a fiery orange ball from behind the dark blue hills. The rising sun would burn off the mist and as it arced across the sky would continuously change the hues of the river and the surrounding hills and marshes. The shifting colors and natural beauty of the area had drawn many of the country's leading impressionist painters to Old

Lyme during the early nineteen hundreds and continued to attract professional and amateur painters from around the world.

⤳

Once Josh crossed the river, he technically entered eastern Connecticut, a distinction he'd always considered as much psychological as geographical. No matter how you explained it, however, there was no question there was a different feel to the eastern third of the state. The early settlers in the Connecticut River Valley had viewed southeastern Connecticut as a dangerous frontier, and people subsequently tended to view eastern Connecticut as the most rustic part of the state, dominated by small towns and Yankee farmers and tradesmen.

Indeed, Josh had always considered eastern Connecticut to be the very heart of Yankeedom. So, apparently, had no less an authority than Mark Twain, who lived and wrote in Connecticut for years. It wasn't by accident, Josh thought, that Twain's quintessential Yankee—the inventive Connecticut mechanic who awakened in King Arthur's Court—had hailed from just east of the great river.

The first Europeans to arrive in the region were the Dutch; starting in the third decade of the 1600s they established a lucrative fur trade with the Indians up and down the Connecticut River and were soon sending beaver skins by the thousands back to Europe, where beaver felt hats were all the rage. A decade later, the English pushed the Dutch out, crushed the hostile Pequots, and settled the area.

Southeastern Connecticut gradually became a shipbuilding center, producing shipwrights, merchants, and sailors who took their place alongside the region's farmers, and eastern Connecticut became a hotbed of support for American independence. Hundreds of eastern Connecticut minutemen, including Colonel Israel Putnam, left their plows and rushed to Massachusetts to battle the British. Putnam became one of the heroes of Bunker Hill, issuing his famous command not to fire "until you see the whites of their eyes."

Eastern Connecticut produced Samuel Huntington, a signer of the Declaration of Independence and a president of the Continental Congress, the legendary patriot Nathan Hale, and the great Revolutionary War governor Jonathan Trumbull, who set up his "War Office" in the heart of eastern Connecticut and provided the Continental Army with much of the food and other supplies that enabled it to survive.

By the nineteenth century, New London had become one of America's great whaling ports, and the eastern part of the state became a major textile center as Yankee entrepreneurs built cotton and woolen mills and thousands of French Canadians, Irish, and other nationalities migrated to Connecticut to operate them.

Eastern Connecticut became part of the Underground Railroad that helped runaway slaves find freedom; Prudence Crandall set up her famous, if short-lived school in Canterbury to train African American girls to become teachers; and the region contributed thousands of young men and enormous quantities of materiel to help the North win the Civil War.

The New London–Groton area grew in importance throughout the twentieth century as the home of Electric Boat's submarine-building complex, a Naval Submarine Base, and the U.S. Coast Guard Academy. Beyond that area, though, most of eastern Connecticut remained rural and undeveloped. After textile manufacturing started moving south in the 1920s, the old mill communities began to decay, and Connecticut's main growth in population, manufacturing, and overall commerce occurred in the central and southwestern parts of the state. By the late 1980s, eastern Connecticut was a mixture of small and medium-size towns and small cities with wide gaps in wealth and income.

The one bond they shared was that eastern Connecticut had gradually become one of the last major green belts between Washington, D.C., and Boston, and most of the region's residents continued to view it as the most peaceful, charming, and livable part of the state.

◡⤸

Josh exited I-95 shortly after the bridge and headed north for the ten-minute drive to Sheffield on Connecticut 141. The countryside looked much the same as when he was a boy, with scattered houses, farms, and long stretches of woods.

Then he was there, crossing the town line, marked by the simple sign that read:

SHEFFIELD, CONNECTICUT
SETTLED 1659

Moments later he pulled up at the traffic light at Tedford's Corner, where 141 intersected Route 36, and was surprised to see the old gas station and bait shop on the southeast corner had been replaced by a strip shopping center that was still under construction. The only thing left was a faded, arrow-shaped sign that read SADROZINSKI FARM and pointed to the right. The last Josh knew, Sadrozinski had close to three hundred Holsteins on three hundred acres, making his place one of the biggest dairy farms in the area. Josh's father had sold Sadrozinski a hundred of those acres when he downsized the Williams farm back in 1958.

Continuing north on 141, Josh passed the Sheffield Fair Grounds, where a banner still proclaimed the fair would run from August 28 to 30. The three-day fair was the biggest event in Sheffield; as a kid Josh had spent practically every waking moment there, riding the whip and the ferris wheel, watching the ox and tractor pulls, and stuffing himself with fried dough and sausage sandwiches. He and his friends had been the first to sign up for the sack races, and as they got older they'd spent the evenings along the midway, checking out the girls, taking in the bands, and competing at the pitching and shooting booths for prizes.

Further on, he came to the turnoff for the Williams farm but instead of turning continued north toward the center of town, where he wanted to stop at the post office to pick up any mail that might be waiting for him. A mile and a half later, the road passed the newly expanded A&P supermarket; then it split at the beginning of the town green, encircling it in a big, elongated oval before coming together again on its way to Hartford. The green was graced by scores of white oaks and sugar maples, and thick carpets of leaves lay on the ground. At the southern end of the green, a Civil War monument stood next to a tall, white flagpole, and the American flag fluttered in the breeze.

Josh followed the road to the right, admiring the beautifully preserved historic homes across from the old common, some nestled up against the sidewalk, others set back from the road behind large lawns. The houses spanned more than three hundred years of the town's history, from the Ebenezer Stowe House, a seventeenth-century center-chimney saltbox, to a half-dozen later saltboxes, several late-eighteenth-century Federals, a Greek Revival mansion with graceful white columns, and two "newer" Victorians with their signature turrets, peaks, and porches.

The post office was next to a cluster of shops near the north end of the green, and Josh parked on the street and went in. He had gone to high school with the postmaster, Hal Rickert, who was behind the counter with one of his clerks serving the noonday crowd, which at the moment was down to a young woman and a stocky, middle-aged man with short, blondish-gray hair and tinted aviator glasses. Hal was just saying good-bye to the woman, and he lit up when he saw Josh.

"Red Williams!" Hal boomed, extending his hand. "Great to have you back. Welcome home, my friend."

The stocky man, who was just finishing up himself, looked over and asked, "Henry Williams's son?"

"Sure as hell is," Hal said, clasping Josh's hand with both of his.

"Well, I'm Bobby Kingman," the stocky man said, extending his hand to Josh. "You don't know me, but I knew your father."

"Nice to meet you," Josh said, shaking Kingman's hand. "How'd you know my dad?"

"Did business with him at the hardware store when I started buildin' in town," Kingman replied. "Real fine gentleman. I read you're movin' back to town and takin' over the Sheffield Agency. Good luck with everything."

"Thanks," Josh said.

"Matter of fact, let me give you one of my cards," Kingman said, reaching into his jacket pocket and handing Josh a business card. "I'm a builder and do a little real estate. Who knows, maybe I can throw a little business your way," he added with a wink.

"That'd be great," Josh said with an appreciative smile. The two men shook hands again, and Kingman waved as he went out the door.

"Seems like a nice guy," Josh said.

Hal shook his head and just laughed.

"Sorry," Hal said, "but I almost broke up when he gave you his business card. Kingman's the biggest con man in town. And he doesn't even live here. Lives down in Niantic. But he's built a couple of spec houses here and started that new shopping center you mighta seen on the corner of thirty-six and one forty-one."

"Yeah, I noticed it coming in this morning," Josh said. "Kingman's building that?"

"Like I say, he started it," Hal said dismissively, "but he's supposedly out of money and trying to sell it to another developer. Word is he paid too much for the land, and his two investors stand to lose their shirts.

"Kingman doesn't have any money of his own," Hal added, "but he's a genius at talking people into investing with him. Only problem is all his deals seem to go south."

Josh chuckled. "Just my luck to have him be my first prospect."

"Yeah, well, stay away from him," Hal said. "Guy's nothing but trouble."

~

Josh returned to his van and continued around the green until he was headed back on its other side. There was a modest amount of noon-hour traffic on the street and a handful of pedestrians on the sidewalk, including what looked to be several tourists enjoying the town. But the only really busy spot was the Sheffield Tavern, a restored eighteenth-century inn with a colonial-style restaurant and cellar taproom that were popular with locals and visitors alike. A plaque by the door boasted that the main structure went all the way back to 1739 and that President Andrew Jackson had stopped there during a visit to Connecticut in 1833. Two small children and their parents were inspecting the buckboard that was permanently parked in front of the inn, and Josh recalled fondly how he'd first climbed aboard it as a child.

He passed the town hall and then slowed down as he approached a handsome Federal-style colonial with entrances on three sides and a carriage house in back. The Sheffield Agency was located on the first floor of the main house; a family doctor had offices upstairs. Josh studied the house as he drove by, amused by the contrast between it and the sixty-story skyscraper where he'd worked for so many years.

Continuing on, he glanced up at the Congregational church, which sat on a rise overlooking the center of the green, its slender white steeple visible for miles and its chimes audible all the way back to the Williams farm. Built in 1755 on the site of the original meetinghouse, it was one of the oldest and most starkly beautiful Congregational churches in New England.

On an impulse, Josh swung into the driveway that ran between the church and the parsonage. The driveway led to a parking lot behind the church, then wound through a carefully manicured cemetery that dated back to the town's founding.

He had intended to visit his parents' graves later in the week, but it suddenly felt right to stop and pay his respects before going to the house where they'd lived most of their married lives. He parked and walked over to a pink granite headstone, the brief inscriptions on which read:

MARY KENT WILLIAMS   HENRY ALAN WILLIAMS
LOVING WIFE AND MOTHER   LOVING HUSBAND AND FATHER
FEBRUARY 9, 1912–APRIL 22, 1981   MARCH 2, 1910–DECEMBER 2, 1986

Josh dropped to one knee, resting his head in his hand and trying to remember his mother and father as they had been. The first images that came to him were of his mother waving as he and his sister boarded the school bus in front of the farmhouse, then years later his father sitting patiently in the passenger seat of their '52 Ford pickup attempting to teach him how to let out the clutch without hurling them both into the windshield. It was almost impossible to believe the years had gone by so fast.

Josh stood and looked around the quiet cemetery, where twelve generations of Williamses had been put to rest. It was remarkable, he reflected, how the family line had been maintained and how, even with all the migration to the cities and to the west, at least one male member had always stayed on the farm.

Each of those generations had their own lives, and it struck him how little he knew about most of them. Once, when he was eleven, he and his father had searched out every Williams headstone in the cemetery, and his father had described many of the family members who were buried there. Most had been farmers, but they had also served as soldiers, constables, and selectmen; several of the women had been teachers, and one had been the town's first librarian—the town's library was named after her. The truth, however, was that Josh hadn't ever really taken more than a passing interest in most of his ancestors when he was younger.

The only real exception was family patriarch Ethan Williams, who had fought in the Pequot War and helped found Sheffield. Josh was unaware of any specific stories about Ethan's exploits, but he'd always been fascinated by Ethan's musket, which hung over the kitchen fireplace. While there was no painting or other likeness of Ethan, Josh had visited the bronze statue of John Mason in Mystic and had always pictured Ethan as looking like the English captain, who was cast as a dashing soldier reaching for his sword as he strode into battle. In fact, however, Josh had no idea what Ethan had really been like.

The main reason he hadn't taken more interest in his ancestors, he supposed, was that he had been surrounded by so much history growing up that he'd tended to take it for granted. The farm went back to the mid-1600s. The current house was almost two hundred fifty years old and was full of antiques, stories, and memories. And in addition to a shelf of books on New England history, there were even some seventeenth-century family diaries. Josh had glanced through a couple of the volumes when he was in junior high but had quickly put them down because he found them difficult to read and boring.

Perhaps, Josh thought, he had rebelled in some way against learning more of the family's past, and maybe his early wanderlust was simply part of a desire for something new and his alone. If so, all he could say was that he'd outgrown those feelings. He had never felt closer to his roots than he did at that moment, nor had he ever felt more certain of where he belonged.

He looked around the cemetery one final time and could almost feel twelve generations watching him. It was as though they were reminding him he had been given a gift he was expected not only to enjoy but to pass on.

Josh left the cemetery and headed back south on 141, finally turning left on Stoddard Mill Road for the mile and a half drive to the Williams farm. The narrow country lane was bordered by crumbling stone walls and swaths of dogwood and mountain laurel whose blossoms turned the area into a picture postcard each spring. Josh passed two old farmhouses, then came up on a brand-new colonial that looked out of place sitting alone in a former pasture. A little farther on, the road crossed a stream that led to a pond and a few stone remains of an eighteenth-century gristmill that had given the road its name.

The Williams farm came into view from the top of the next rise, which looked out over a broad, undulating plain framed by rolling hills and the southern tip of Jepson Lake in the distance. The farm itself formed an almost perfect rectangle, its white farmhouse and red dairy barn and silo surrounded by acres of cornfields and pasture that rose and fell with the terrain. The whole scene reminded him again of how different this land was from the flat expanses of the Midwest, and he felt a brief shiver travel down his spine. No matter how many times he'd seen the farm from this spot, he'd never looked at it quite the way he was looking at it now. It was no longer just the family farm. It was his.

Two minutes later, he turned onto a gravel driveway that passed under a giant sycamore and then curved around to a courtyard behind the farmhouse. Bordered on three sides by the house, the dairy barn, and a five-bay garage, the courtyard was the epicenter of the farm, and the kitchen door that opened onto it was for all intents and purposes the only door anyone used. Anyone who came to the front door was a stranger.

Josh parked in the courtyard, grabbed one of his suitcases from the backseat and headed for the kitchen door, which he unlocked and pushed open ahead of him. The kitchen was slightly musty, but the floor and counters were spotless. Through habit he went directly to the sink, turned on the tap, and, after letting it run, drew a glass of water that he drained in several quick gulps. As always, it was the best water he'd ever tasted. He leaned back against the sink, surveying the familiar room. He was home.

Josh walked through the old farmhouse room by room. The house hadn't been lived in for almost a year, but he was pleasantly surprised that it still looked so welcoming, so much like the home it had been when his parents were alive. He and his sister had entrusted its temporary care to their father's longtime helper, Ben Chapman, who'd clearly been very conscientious. Linda had taken a few items, but for the most part the furniture, carpets, and pictures on the walls were just as their father and mother had left them. Josh and Sharon would have to decide what to keep and what to dispose of or store.

The house had been built in 1745 as a five-bay, two-and-a-half story colonial with twin chimneys, a center entrance hall, and a full second floor. It had replaced the original homestead built by Ethan Williams in 1660 and had been added to three times since. Josh's parents had totally renovated the interior in 1954 but had gone to great lengths to preserve the original floors, woodwork, and fireplaces, and had kept many of the original antiques.

After unloading the van, Josh wandered through the upstairs bedrooms, browsing family photographs and studying the half-dozen oil portraits of Williams ancestors that hung on the walls. The oldest and the one that always grabbed his attention was a 1720 painting of Ethan's grandson, Daniel. Everyone who saw the portrait said it was uncanny how much Josh and Daniel resembled each other through the eyes and in their almost identical jaw lines and reddish-brown hair. In fact, Josh's mother had always said that if you could dress the two of them the same way and give them the same haircuts, they could be twins. It was pretty interesting, Josh thought, that relatives born more than two hundred sixty years apart could look so much alike.

Josh paused at one of the bedroom windows and looked out over the courtyard to the big red dairy barn and a second, much older and smaller English barn that was partially visible behind it. The dairy barn, with its classic gambrel roof and silo, had been built back in 1919 to replace two other barns that could no longer accommodate the growing herd or meet the new health regulations for producing and handling milk, but it was now woefully out of date for that purpose and was being used for storage. The unpainted English barn, on the other hand, had been built sometime around 1740, making it the oldest structure on the property, and it was in such good shape the family had kept horses there right up until the time Josh left for college. In fact, Josh was hoping that with a little work on the stalls he could use it for horses again.

As Josh stood at the window, Ben Chapman's pickup truck pulled into the courtyard, and Josh realized it must already be two o'clock. Ben had worked as a helper around the farm for the better part of fifty years, and Josh had arranged to meet him that afternoon so they could walk the property together.

Ben was in his late sixties but could have easily passed for fifty. He had a leathery, permanently tanned face and looked fit in work boots, jeans, sweatshirt, and a dark blue baseball cap. He broke into a big grin when Josh came to the door and shook his hand warmly. Josh invited him in, but Ben declined.

"No, I think I'll just stay outside," Ben said with a shake of his head. "Don't want t' track the place up after all the time me and Mrs. Orvis spent gettin' it ready."

"You stop in town?" Ben asked, as Josh joined him in the courtyard.

"Yeah, I picked up the mail and stopped at the cemetery. I hadn't been there since they put Dad's name on the stone."

"Hard t' believe it's goin' on a year," Ben said, "and even more that it's been six years for your ma. They were both great people," he added, with a touch of genuine sadness.

For the next two hours, Ben led Josh around the farm, pointing out the major things that needed attention. The house needed painting, two of the garage doors were going to have to be replaced, the entire deck of the little bridge over Bixler Brook was rotting, and he was particularly concerned about the orchard, which Josh's father had increasingly neglected in recent years. The list, Ben added, didn't include any problems inside the house that Josh and his family might discover.

Ben commented on the condition of the soil, the prospects for extending the existing land leases, and a dozen other subjects, including the fickle New England weather, how Sadrozinski and the other dairy farmers in the region were doing, and how an increasing number of farms were switching over to growing sod and nursery stock, raising Christmas trees, and growing berries for the pick-your-own trade. Josh said he was interested in developing a strawberry field just west of the farmhouse and planting a couple of acres of corn, but wanted to put the main effort into rehabilitating the orchard he had always loved. The two men then slipped into a discussion about local politics and the town's current attitude toward development.

The biggest issue right now, Ben said, was whether a builder from Hartford should get approval for a twenty-lot subdivision just off Route 141 in the Sayerville section of town.

"How do you think it'll come out?" Josh asked.

"Hard t' say. Zonin' commission's very political right now, and half the town seems t' be against more houses. They say all they do is attract more families and drive up school costs and taxes."

"How do you feel?" Josh pressed.

Ben sighed. "Oh, I dunno," he said. "Sheffield's still one of the most rural towns in the state, and it'd be nice t' keep it this way. But you can't stop growth completely, and I s'pose another twenty houses ain't so bad.

"There's a new development just off Cedar Road that's worked out pretty well. Fifteen houses on five-acre lots, all in the three to four hundred thousand dollar range. The subdivision they wanna build off one forty-one's supposed t' be similar. I think if we can keep development t' that type of thing, we're probably okay. Just so long as they don't let 'em put in one a' them malls or build one a' them big incinerators or somethin'."

They were walking near the eastern edge of the property now, where the last glacier had deposited a giant, flat-topped boulder more than ten feet high and thirty feet wide, with several step-like grooves that virtually begged to be climbed. People once believed boulders like this had been deposited by Noah's flood, and colonial preachers had sometimes used them as pulpits. Josh had climbed this one a thousand times when he was a kid, and he and Ben couldn't resist clambering to the top, where they stood looking east toward Jepson Lake.

"You can see that new fifteen-house development from here," Ben said, pointing to an area near the southwestern tip of the lake. "They call it Deer Run. Backs up against the Northern Pequot Reservation."

"God, I forgot all about the reservation," Josh said. "It must be totally abandoned by now, isn't it? I'm not even sure there was anybody living there when I left Sheffield twenty years ago."

"Well, there's apparently still a coupla old-timers up there," Ben said, "but they gotta be close to ninety, so they ain't gonna be around much longer. I used t' see one of 'em walkin' along the road to or from town every once in a while, and I'd give 'im a lift if he was goin' my way. Nice old guy, but I haven't seen him lately."

"What do you think the state will do with the reservation when they're gone?" Josh asked.

"Oh, I'm sure the state's just waitin' for the last one t' die off, and then it'll close the place and add the land t' the state park," Ben replied. "Reservation's around five hundred acres, so it'll make a nice addition."

4

~

Two and a Half Years Later

May 18, 1990

It was four o'clock on a Friday afternoon, May 18. 1990—exactly two and a half years since Josh and his family had moved to Sheffield.

Josh was in his office finishing up a bit early in anticipation of their oldest son Matt's fourteenth birthday celebration that evening. It was an milestone after all they'd been through with him. Then, just to complicate things, Sharon called to say her Appaloosa mare, Lucy, was about to give birth. "I can't believe she picked this moment," Sharon said with a mix of excitement and exasperation, "but the sooner you can get home and give me a hand, the better. Otherwise we're never going to have this party tonight."

"Have you called the vet?" Josh asked, imagining Sharon frantically rushing around, trying to tend to everything at once.

"Yes, of course," she said. "He's driving into the courtyard right now."

"Okay, sweetheart," Josh said, beginning to stuff his briefcase. "Give me ten minutes."

As Josh walked to his car, he couldn't help but smile at the appropriateness of having a new foal on Matt's birthday. It was the horses, after all, that had turned Matt around.

The two younger children, Jacob and Sarah, had made the transition to Sheffield with ease, but Matt had fought the move from day one. Eleven and in the sixth grade at the time of the move, Matt was quieter and more introspective than his brother and sister, and spent the first several weeks after arriving in Sheffield brooding about having to leave his friends and enter a new school in the middle of the school year. Josh was certain at first that Matt would snap out of it, but instead he gradually became more withdrawn, his schoolwork suffered, and he even lost interest in sports, which had been his passion. His only real interest seemed to be hanging out with his one friend, Jimmy Potts, who was a year older and lived in the new house up the road.

Jimmy was a big, kind of goofy-looking, outdoorsy kid with a German shepherd named Hannibal. Unfortunately, Jimmy also had a penchant for trouble.

The first time they knew Matt was involved in that trouble was when a neighbor called to say someone with a BB gun had shot out the headlights on his pickup truck. He said he hated to call Josh, but his wife had seen Matt and the Potts boy in the area with some kind of rifle just the day before, and he wondered if Josh could check with his son. Matt denied it at first, then admitted Jimmy had a BB gun and they had been out in the fields shooting at birds and rabbits when Jimmy had shot at the truck. Matt swore he hadn't shot at the truck himself, but Josh was furious that he had been out with a gun shooting at anything, and Josh and Jimmy's father wound up marching the two boys over to the neighbor's house to apologize and make restitution. Josh prohibited Matt from seeing Jimmy for a week and made him promise he wouldn't pick up a BB gun again.

Just a month later Stan Sadrozinski drove into Josh's driveway with Matt and Jimmy in tow. He had caught them spray-painting several of his cows, and although Stan and Josh had become friends, he was visibly pissed. This time Josh kept Matt and Jimmy separated for a month.

Their final act, however, had been deadly serious. One day in August 1988, Sharon came home early from shopping with the two younger children and noticed the old matchlock musket was gone from over the kitchen fireplace. She was confused at first, then felt her heart jump when she realized who must have taken it. She told Sarah to watch Jacob and ran into the courtyard looking for Matt. She didn't see him anywhere and was about to call his name when she heard barking coming from the pasture on the other side of the dairy barn. Her first thought was that it was their Labrador retriever, Max, and that he might be with Matt. As she rounded the barn, she caught sight of Max and Jimmy's dog, Hannibal, romping in the field, and then of Matt and Jimmy standing together watching the dogs from about forty feet away. Except, she realized, they weren't watching the dogs at all. Instead, Jimmy was raising the matchlock to his shoulder as though getting ready to fire. She couldn't believe they had gotten the gun to work, but as she watched, the heavy weapon suddenly began to slip from Jimmy's grip and went off with a tremendous bang and cloud of smoke, sending a lead ball into Hannibal's brain. The dog, who'd come running toward Jimmy at the last second, dropped in its tracks, and the two boys stood in horror at what they had done.

Once again, Matt insisted Jimmy had been the instigator, reading about matchlock muskets in one of his father's gun books, melting down a lead fishing sinker to form the bullet, mixing the powder from ingredients in his chemistry set, and fashioning a makeshift wick. But it made no difference. It became clear the two boys had studied the gun book together, worked on the gun on several occasions when the rest of the family was out, and patiently waited until they were alone to fire it. They had even brought rags and a spray cleaner they thought would get rid of the smell of the burnt powder.

This time, the boys were prohibited from playing with each other at all, and Josh and Sharon despaired about what to do with Matt. But then things began to change. In the fall of 1988, Jimmy's family moved to Houston, and Josh bought the horses.

He acquired five of them: a pony for Jacob, a Morgan mare for Sarah, a Palomino gelding for Matt, Sharon's Appaloosa, and a second, larger Morgan mare for himself. The two younger children were thrilled, but Matt at first showed little interest in his horse, General. He only reluctantly took the riding lessons Josh arranged and begged off the family's weekend trail rides so often that Josh and Sharon finally gave up trying to get him to come. Even Matt, however, couldn't totally resist General, a beautiful golden Palomino with soft brown eyes and flowing white mane and tail. He gradually began to spend more time with General, started riding on his own around the farm, and ultimately rejoined the family's weekend rides.

By the spring of 1989, Matt and General had become inseparable, and Matt had written a paper for English class on the Palomino horse, tracing its history from ancient empires to the Spanish court and America's southwestern Indians. His grades were up, he was back into sports, and Josh and Sharon could only shake their heads in astonishment at his transformation. He had become a human being again.

With Matt's crisis behind them, Josh felt as he drove home that afternoon that he and his family had finally hit their stride. The kids were squared away. His business had taken off. He had finished the long list of repairs around the farm, brought in his first strawberry and corn crops, and was well along in rehabilitating the orchard. Through it all, Sharon had adjusted to her new surroundings beyond expectations. She initially missed her parents and friends, but eventually fell in love with the farm and the town. After putting her own touches on the old farmhouse, she had begun to think of it as her own. She'd become active in the Congregational Church, the PTA, and the

Democratic Town Committee, and with her outgoing personality, was already being asked to run for the board of education. After the first year, in fact, Josh had begun telling people she knew Sheffield better than he did.

⌒

Josh went directly to the English barn as soon as he got home, the sweetish mix of hay, leather, and the horses filling his nostrils as he stepped inside. The whole family was there with the veterinarian, Dr. Edmonds, who had just finished examining a newly born colt that was now lying on his side in the foaling stall. Josh watched unnoticed as the foal, no more than twenty minutes old, struggled to his feet, stood by himself on his wobbly legs, and began nursing from Lucy. It was a miraculous moment, and everyone burst into applause except the vet, who steadied the mare to make sure she wasn't spooked by the commotion.

Sarah's Morgan nickered in her stall, and when Sarah turned to look she saw her father and immediately rushed up to him, throwing her arms around his waist and hugging him with all her might.

"Daddy," she squealed, "isn't it wonderful!"

It was wonderful, and so were the dinner and birthday party that followed. There were balloons, ice cream, and a cake with fourteen candles, and although Sarah and Jacob could barely wait to get back out to the barn, they all managed to give Matt their cards and gifts in a way that clearly touched him.

About 8:30, Josh and Sharon put on their jackets and went out to the barn, where Sarah and Jacob were watching over the foal and his mother. Matt joined them a few minutes later, and the entire family stayed for the next half hour, talking softly and admiring the new arrival, after which they all walked back to the house together in the moonlight.

Josh and Sharon sat out on the porch talking before going back inside, and when they finally stood up Josh put his arms around her and held her.

"Happy?" he asked.

"Very," she replied, slipping her arms around his neck and kissing him on the lips.

Josh kissed her back and nuzzled her hair. It was days like this that you lived for.

When he got into bed, Sharon was already there reading, but before he could pick up his own book, she put hers down and began to talk about some of the things she wanted to do that summer and fall. She wanted to host a big Labor Day picnic at the farm, take a course in charcoal sketching from an artist in Chester, and see more of the summer theater productions at the local playhouses. In addition, she said, she had decided to run for the school board next year.

"So what do you think about all that?" she said playfully as she turned off her light and stretched out on her stomach next to Josh.

"I think it sounds terrific," he said, picking up on her ebullient mood and reaching over to turn off his own light. He turned back toward her, propped himself on an elbow, and leaned down and kissed her ear. "I also think you'd make a great politician," he added.

"Um-hum," she murmured, "who's the politician?"

He didn't answer, but instead began gently massaging her shoulders, gradually working his way down her long, graceful back to her narrow waist.

Sharon sighed and turned on her side, wrapping herself around him. They slowly made love, taking their time the way she liked it, and fell asleep in each other's arms.

5

Out of Nowhere

May 19, 1990

Josh got up at his usual 6:30 the next morning and went to the kitchen, where Sarah had left a note saying she was already up and had gone out to the barn. She had also brought in the morning newspapers, including *The Day*, published in New London, and the *Norwich Bulletin*. He began skimming the headlines as he sat down with his orange juice and cereal.

Both papers led with stories about German reunification, but it was a headline just below the fold in *The Day* that grabbed his attention: "State Must Negotiate on Casino Plan."

According to the story, a U.S. District Court had given a local Indian tribe, the Mashantucket Pequots of Ledyard, a first-round victory in its efforts to open a gambling casino next to the bingo hall it already operated on its reservation. The court had ordered the state to negotiate a compact with the tribe governing the conduct of the casino games, and the tribe's chairman, Richard "Skip" Hayward, had reacted by praising the decision and promising to run a facility that would be "a good neighbor for our community and an economic boon for all of southeastern Connecticut."

The casino plan, the paper explained, was "one of dozens of similar proposals developed since passage of a 1988 federal law allowing tribes to conduct gambling." Under the law, tribes could "offer any type of gambling allowed in the state," and since Connecticut let charities hold "Las Vegas Nights" where games like blackjack, roulette, and dice were permitted for fund-raising, the Mashantuckets contended they should be able to have a casino of their own.

The state, the article said, had argued the law did not apply in Connecticut's case and was considering whether to appeal.

Josh was stunned. The federal government was going to force Connecticut to permit an Indian tribe to build a Las Vegas-style casino in Connecticut? In rural eastern Connecticut? Twenty miles from his farm? Just because the state allowed charities to hold Las Vegas Nights? A casino was totally out of keeping with the region, and the judge's ruling seemed absurd.

Moreover, he had to assume that if the government let the Mashantuckets build a casino, other tribes would rush to do the same thing. And if casinos ever got going in southeastern Connecticut, their potential would be enormous.

The only casinos in the Northeast were in Atlantic City, which drew from a huge market extending from New York City to Washington, D.C. Southeastern Connecticut stood to tap an equally lucrative market reaching from New York to Boston. The idea of the region becoming Atlantic City North seemed preposterous, but if the court ruling held, what was there to stop it?

Josh reached for the *Bulletin* for anything further on the ruling, but there was only a relatively brief story on the first page of the second section that added little to what he'd read.

A potentially huge development like this coming seemingly out of nowhere was more than unsettling. It was clear from both articles, however, that the legal battle over the casino had been underway for some time. Yet Josh hadn't known anything about it, and he doubted that 99 percent of the people in Connecticut had been aware of it either.

What the hell was going on? Josh wondered. And who could he talk with to get some answers?

He began running through names in his head, then remembered Brad Merriweather, a Norwich attorney who had served in the state legislature and now lived in town. Sharon had become friends with Brad's wife, Janet, and Josh occasionally saw Brad at the Old Lyme racquet club, where they both played tennis.

It was just 7:00 a.m., so Josh decided to spend some time with the horses and give Merriweather a call in a couple of hours.

He glanced at *The Day*'s headline one more time. He thought he might be overreacting, but something told him he wasn't. The whole thing just felt bad. He stood up and carried his half-eaten breakfast to the sink. He had lost his appetite.

◥

Brad Merriweather was on his way out the door when Josh called a little after 9:00, but he invited Josh to drop by later that afternoon.

The Merriweathers had built a house on six acres near the northern edge of town, and when Josh arrived, Brad was out in back trying to pull up a tree stump with his tractor. He managed to dislodge the ornery stump with one final tug, and then shut off the engine, wiped his brow, and climbed down to greet his guest.

In his late forties, Merriweather was a rugged five nine, had thick dark hair, and in his overalls and T-shirt looked like a farmer rather than a trial-room lawyer. But he had a reputation as one of the sharpest criminal attorneys in the state and was a partner in Norwich's top law firm.

According to Sharon, Brad had spent several years in the state attorney general's office before entering private practice and had subsequently been elected to the state House of Representatives. About four years ago, he'd stepped away from politics to commit full time to his legal work. Nonetheless, the buzz was that he still had his hands in things up in Hartford, and he was often sought out for political advice.

Brad took Josh into the kitchen, where he popped open two cans of Budweiser and suggested they go to his study to talk. He was sorry, he said, that Janet was out because he knew how friendly she and Sharon had become and he was sure she would have liked to say hello.

After some brief tennis talk, Josh turned to the casino by saying he'd been surprised by the story in the morning papers and was hoping Brad might be able to give him some insight into what was happening and what it might mean for the region.

"I don't know where I've been," Josh said, shaking his head, "but I didn't even know a casino was under consideration."

"Don't kick yourself too hard," Brad replied, "because I guarantee you're not the only one. This whole casino thing's been simmering for more than a year now, but most people in Hartford gave it so little chance of going anywhere that almost no one, including the press, has been paying much attention.

"The fact is, neither side has had any interest in publicizing this case. The Indians felt they were winning and didn't want to rock the boat, while the state screwed the whole thing up and was just praying it would somehow go away."

Josh frowned. "What do you mean, the state screwed it up?"

"It's complicated," Brad replied, "but let me give you the basics.

"If you remember your Connecticut history," Brad began, "the English got together with the Mohegans and Narragansetts and pretty much wiped out the Pequots in the Pequot War back in the 1600s.

"When the war was over, the settlers gave most of the surviving Pequots to the other two tribes, who tried to incorporate them in their own villages. Over time, though, many of the Pequots slipped away and reassembled at different locations under their own leaders.

"Connecticut finally recognized the two largest Pequot groups, the Mashantuckets and the Easterns, as separate tribes and gave them their own reservations in what are now Ledyard and North Stonington. Then the colony recognized the Northern Pequots as a third tribe and set up a reservation for them here in Sheffield in 1686."

"How many Pequots were left after the war?" Josh asked.

"Nobody knows for sure," Brad said, "but the total population of the three reservations was probably never more than a few hundred.

"In any event, most of the Pequots moved off the reservations during the next two hundred years to find work, and small numbers of poor whites, blacks, and other Indians filtered in and out of the reservations, mixing with the Pequots who stayed. By the early 1900s, the old Pequot culture had become so diluted that it had almost completely disappeared and the three reservations had become little more than shelters for a handful of poor luckless souls with mixed ancestries.

"Then in 1973, the last person living on the Mashantucket Reservation— a feisty seventy-eight-year-old grandmother named Elizabeth George— passed away.

"Eliza George," Brad continued, "had clung to the reservation all her life, living in a run-down old farmhouse and driving off intruders with a shotgun. As she got older, one of her greatest hopes was that she might be able to persuade some of her grandchildren to move onto the reservation in order to keep it out of the state's hands when she died. But the grandchildren were typical white mainstream Americans who had never been part of the tribe, and most of them had little interest in their grandmother's reservation."

"So Eliza's death could have easily been the end of the tribe," Josh interjected, finding himself increasingly drawn into the story.

"And it would have been," Brad replied, "if it weren't for Eliza's eldest grandson, Skip Hayward, who came to see the reservation as a place where family members might build homes and open businesses. In 1974, Skip persuaded some of his relatives to form a corporation to pursue those goals, but a year later an Indian issues lawyer named Tom Tureen approached him with a better idea—to reestablish the Mashantuckets as an Indian tribe and file land claims that could lead to federal recognition and to compensation for reservation land taken from the tribe over a hundred years ago."

"Just a second," Josh interrupted again. "I just want to be clear. Are you saying the Mashantuckets had been recognized by Connecticut as an Indian tribe but had never been recognized as a tribe by the federal government?"

"That's right," Brad said. "The federal government began making treaties with Indian tribes following the creation of the United States, but it didn't interfere with relationships the original thirteen states already had with their tribes. As a result, neither the Mashantuckets nor any other Connecticut tribe ever entered into a treaty with the U.S. government that would have provided federal recognition."

"What's the advantage of being federally recognized?" Josh asked, realizing more and more that he knew next to nothing about Indians.

"There are a lot of advantages," Brad replied. "To begin with, it gives tribes access to federal programs for housing, health, and education, but even more important, it gives them 'sovereign nation' status."

"And what does that do for them?"

"Basically, it turns them into semi-independent countries and establishes a government-to-government relationship between the tribe and the United States."

"Aren't Indians American citizens?" Josh asked, obviously puzzled.

"Oh, sure," Brad said. "They're American citizens, and Indian tribes are subject to whatever federal laws Congress chooses to apply to them. But sovereignty adds some very important rights. It lets them set up an autonomous tribal government, lets them place their reservation lands in federal trust, and lets them operate businesses on tribal land that are exempt from federal and state income taxes, local property taxes, and most state and municipal laws."

"You mean like building and zoning codes?" Josh asked.

"Yeah, building codes, environmental regulations . . . that type of thing. And now the courts have ruled that federal recognition also opens the door to tribes being able to go into the gambling business."

Josh pursed his lips and nodded. "I can see why Hayward might want to convert from a state to a federal tribe," he said facetiously. "But it can't be that easy, can it?"

"No, it's not," Brad said. "There's a unit in the Department of the Interior called the Bureau of Indian Affairs that has seven specific criteria for determining whether a group is a true Indian tribe and qualifies for recognition. For example, the petitioning tribe has to be able to prove its members descend genealogically from a historic Indian tribe. And it has to be able to show it's existed as a distinct and uninterrupted community from historical times to the present."

"Jesus, how'd the Mashantuckets ever get recognized then?" Josh asked. "I mean, you just said there was no one left on the reservation when Eliza died and Skip Hayward's generation had never been part of the tribe."

"The short answer," Brad said, "is that they did a political end run around the BIA and went directly to Congress for recognition."

"How were they able to do that?" Josh asked.

"That's where Tureen comes in," Brad replied. "Despite the fact that the State of Connecticut could have taken back the Mashantucket Reservation and terminated the Mashantuckets as a state-recognized tribe after Eliza died, it hadn't done so, and Tureen drew up a new tribal constitution containing provisions for adding new members to the tribe. Then in 1976 he filed a federal lawsuit on behalf of the Mashantuckets against the owners of eight hundred acres of former Mashantucket land he claimed the state had sold illegally back in the 1800s. Tureen based the claim on a 1790 federal law that prohibited the sale of Indian land without federal approval, and he demanded the land be returned to the tribe.

"As intended, the suit created a nightmare for the property owners by casting a cloud over their titles, and they ultimately joined the Mashantuckets in urging the state's Congressional delegation to help work out a settlement."

"Which I assume it did," Josh said, appreciating the pressure it must have put on Connecticut's Congressional delegation to solve the problem.

"Right," Brad replied. "The Connecticut delegation pushed through a special act of Congress in 1983 that gave the tribe federal recognition in return for dropping the lawsuit. The act also threw in $900,000 the Mashantuckets could use to buy land that lay within a designated settlement area.

"Even then," Brad added, "the deal nearly fell apart because Hayward never produced the necessary evidence to establish that the current Mashantucket Pequots were a genuine tribe of Indians rather than simply a collection of individual would-be Indians. In fact, President Reagan initially vetoed the bill for that reason, but he finally signed it when it became clear the bill's backers had the votes to override him.

"So basically what you're saying," Josh said, "is that the tribe outfoxed the federal government."

"Totally," Brad said. "But that was only the beginning."

Brad excused himself for a moment and got up and went into the kitchen for a couple more beers.

⁓

"Did Connecticut have any laws about who qualified as an Indian?" Josh asked after they settled in again. "I mean, there's got to be some blood criteria for qualifying as an Indian, doesn't there?"

"As a matter of fact," Brad replied, "at one point there was. In 1961 Connecticut passed a law requiring a person have at least one-eighth Indian blood in order to make the cut, but the legislature changed the law in 1974 to let state-recognized tribes set whatever qualifications they chose. The rationale was that if the one-eighth requirement stayed in place, it wouldn't be long before no one qualified."

"So, theoretically, if a tribe said one percent was enough, I could be one percent Indian and ninety-nine percent Norwegian and still legally qualify as an Indian? Is that right?" Josh pressed.

"Actually, according to the state law, you don't have to have any Indian blood at all to qualify as an Indian. You just have to meet the particular Indian tribe's criteria. In the Mashantuckets' case, Hayward set qualifications that required members to be related to Pequot descendants living on the reservation in the early 1900s. That both addressed the genealogy issue and apparently limited members to his own extended family."

"So what happened after Congress granted the Mashantuckets recognition?" Josh asked.

"Well, I'm afraid that's when the state made its crucial mistake," Brad said. "After negotiating a settlement with the feds, the Mashantuckets negotiated a companion settlement with the state that avoided giving Connecticut regulatory authority over activities the tribe had a right to conduct on the reservation. Based on that agreement, the tribe moved to open a high-stakes bingo operation, which it claimed the state couldn't block because it allowed non-profit groups to conduct bingo and other games of chance."

"Didn't the state fight it?" Josh asked..

"It tried to," Brad said, "but by the time the state woke up and realized its mistake, it was too late. The whole issue wound up in federal court, where the judge ruled that although Connecticut retained legal authority for criminal and civil matters on the reservation, it had abdicated its authority to regulate activities there that were legal elsewhere in the state. As a result, the tribe went ahead and opened its bingo hall in 1986.”

“Okay, that’s bingo,” Josh said. “But now we’re talking about a full-blown casino. What made that possible?”

“Congress again,” Brad answered.

“In 1988, Congress decided gaming was a chance for impoverished tribes to lift themselves up by their bootstraps and passed the Indian Gaming Regulatory Act, which gives federally recognized tribes the right to conduct any kind of gambling on their land that’s allowed in the state where they’re located. The Mashantuckets saw the act as an invitation to graduate from bingo to casino gambling, and in 1989, they applied to the state to open a casino in accordance with the new federal law. Since the state already allowed charity casinos, the Indians argued it had no choice but to comply with their request. The state says that’s ridiculous because the Las Vegas Nights law was never intended to permit real casinos, but as you can see from this morning’s papers, the U.S. District Court’s siding with the Indians.”

“I assume the state’s going to appeal,” Josh said, inflecting the words as a question.

“I’m sure it will,” Brad replied, “starting with the U.S. Circuit Court of Appeals. Given the way the case has gone so far, though, I don’t see much chance of getting a reversal. The state could then appeal to the U.S. Supreme Court, but I don’t see much hope there, either. In fact, I doubt the Supreme Court would even hear it.”

“What happens then?” Josh asked.

Brad drained the last of his beer.

“Look, Josh,” he finally said, “I’m probably not the best guy to ask, because I may be overly pessimistic. But I have to tell you, I’m very concerned about where this thing could go. There’re twenty-five million people within a two- or three-hour drive of here, so it’s very likely the Mashantuckets’ casino will be a huge success. The one limitation is that the state’s Las Vegas Nights law doesn’t permit slot machines. But I’ll give you odds that once the tribe opens its casino, the state’ll make a deal to allow slots in return for a percentage of the profits. I can smell it. The state simply won’t be able to resist the money.

“And if Connecticut does permit slots,” he continued, “I think you’ll see gambling explode here. You'll have every real and make-believe Indian tribe in the state trying to get federal recognition so they can open a casino, and you'll see pressure begin to build immediately to legalize non-Indian casinos. Furthermore, even if the state doesn't give non-Indian casino developers licenses in their own name, it's virtually certain that the big Las Vegas casinos will team up with the Indians one way or another to get in here."

"How big you think casino gambling could get in Connecticut?" Josh asked.

"That's my point. Once this thing gets going, there's really no limit. You've got five other state-recognized Indian tribes in Connecticut in addition to the Mashantuckets, and I'm sure every one of them, plus another half-dozen would-be tribes, have their eyes on a casino. So it's perfectly conceivable Connecticut could wind up becoming the second-biggest casino market in the country after Las Vegas."

"What about southeastern Connecticut?" Josh asked. ""How many casinos do you think they could build here?"

Brad shrugged. "Hell," he said, "Indian tribes alone could potentially build four."

Josh stared at the tiny motes of dust in a shaft of afternoon sunlight. Twenty-four hours ago he'd been on top of the world. Now some off-the-wall ruling about an issue that he hadn't even known existed was casting a shadow over every major move he'd made in the last three years—uprooting his family, changing careers, and sinking every cent he had into the farm and his business. Casino gambling was about as far from what he had come back for as he could imagine, and if Brad's scenario played out, there was no way he was going to stay.

"What about the Northern Pequots here in Sheffield?" he asked.

Brad shook his head. "That's probably the one tribe you don't have to worry about. They've been moribund for seventy years. I can't imagine them making a case for recognition."

"Isn't there anything the state can do to stop the Mashantuckets?" Josh pressed.

"Yeah, there is one thing. The state could repeal the Las Vegas Nights law. The tribes would fight it, but there's a good chance repeal would stop 'em in their tracks."

"Is anybody working on that?" Josh asked.

"A few legislators have talked about it," Brad said, "but there's no real support for it yet. Remember, the casino issue's still in the courts, and most people aren't even aware of it."

As he drove home, Josh kept thinking it was inconceivable that a newly-resurrected Indian tribe could succeed in turning Connecticut upside down. And yet that seemed to be exactly what was happening.

⌒

Bobby Kingman sat at his kitchen table that Saturday morning drinking a cup of coffee and reading the same newspaper articles about the proposed Mashantucket casino that Josh was reading six miles away. Only Bobby's reaction was entirely different. He was jealous.

A week shy of forty-seven, Bobby was a man in perpetual motion, but so far it seemed he was doing little more than spinning his wheels while the rest of the world passed him by.

The problem, Bobby was convinced, was that his life had been pretty much a series of bad breaks, beginning with his father walking out on the family when Bobby was five. The son of a bitch had simply split one day, and they had never heard from him again. Bobby and his mother had had to move to a cheap apartment in the Niantic section of East Lyme, and his mother, who had developed a drinking problem, had worked as a motel clerk to support them.

Bobby wanted to go to college, but the family had no money for luxuries like that, so he went to Vietnam, fighting off gooks at Long Bin during the Tet Offensive and laying ambushes along the Ho Chi Minh Trail. When he came home, he entered the local technical college but quit and started working construction to make some money. After a few months, he decided he couldn't stand reporting to assholes who weren't nearly as capable as he was and set up a home-improvement business of his own.

He made a little money on a few projects but gradually decided his real forte was persuading investors to join him in putting up spec houses, building strip shopping centers, and refurbishing old buildings. He got his real estate license and succeeded in raising money for a half-dozen projects, but for one reason or another, most of them had flopped. Now he was back to doing home-improvement jobs and hoping something better would turn up.

Along the way, Bobby had married a nurse from New London named Heidi Goodwin, and they had two sons in as many years. The marriage had become increasingly strained as Bobby became more and more absorbed in trying to make a go of his various ventures, and he and Heidi began to argue constantly about money. Even then, Bobby believed, they probably could have stayed together if she hadn't caught him with another woman two years ago and divorced him. Heidi and the boys kept the house, and Bobby found himself back in a cheap apartment.

He had a girlfriend of sorts, and he tried to do something with his kids every other weekend, but between his personal and business setbacks, he had to admit his life currently sucked.

Bobby threw a half cup of good coffee into the sink and, still dressed in his T-shirt and shorts, went back to his bedroom, glanced absently at a stack of still unopened cartons, and flopped down on the disheveled bed. Shit, he thought, at some point his luck had to change. After all, he was smart, he had good ideas, and he had always had a God-given knack for winning people's confidence. All he needed was a break.

But the breaks always seemed to go to others. The story about Skip Hayward and the Mashantuckets' casino was a perfect example. Like Hayward and probably hundreds of other people in southeastern Connecticut, Bobby had a Pequot ancestor somewhere in his past. Or so Bobby understood. Bobby's mother never talked about their Indian heritage, but her estranged sister, Mavis, supposedly still visited an uncle who lived on the Sheffield Pequot Reservation. That made the guy Bobby's great uncle, but Bobby had never met him, had never been on the reservation, and had never had the slightest interest in going there. In fact, he assumed his mother had purposely tried to dissociate herself from her Indian ancestry, and he had always been glad she did. With all its problems, the last thing the family needed was for people to think they were descended from a bunch of Indians.

Yet Skip Hayward was clearly making a fortune from his Indian ties. He had miraculously turned his family into an Indian tribe and was raking in millions with his bingo hall. Now he was going after a casino and the courts were backing him. Not only that, but based on what Bobby had heard, Hayward was pulling the whole thing off despite the fact he was as white as Bobby was.

Bobby had always assumed that the demand for bingo was limited, and that Hayward had pretty much cornered the market. But a casino was an entirely different story. It could be absolutely huge, and if the Mashantuckets were allowed to build a casino, he had to assume any other Connecticut tribe that could get federal recognition could also build one. He had read somewhere that the Mohegans were also trying to get recognition, and who knew how many other Connecticut tribes were trying to do the same?

There had to be a way he could use his Indian connection to get a piece of the action, Bobby thought. But first he had to understand exactly what that connection was. And the best way to do that, he figured, was to talk to his Aunt Mavis. There was no point calling her this weekend because it was his turn to be with the kids, but he decided he'd definitely get over to see her as soon as he could. Cashing in on his Indian ancestors was obviously a long shot, but just thinking about it gave him a boost, and he got out of bed to get dressed.

6

~

Respite

May 19–September 4, 1990

Sharon was surprised at how troubled Josh appeared to be as a result of his meeting with Brad Merriweather. She understood his concern about the proposed casino but thought at this point he was way overreacting.

Not that Sharon had any love for gambling. Growing up in Chicago, she had associated gambling with the mob and the infamous local gambling and bookie joints that, it seemed, were always being raided by the police, and she had been turned off by the side trip she and a girlfriend had made to Las Vegas during a visit to Hollywood in the early seventies. The whole Strip was so tawdry it was laughable, while the image of people hunched over long banks of slot machines, mindlessly feeding them their hard-earned money, was pathetic. She couldn't imagine anything more out of character with eastern Connecticut.

"Still worrying about the casino?" she asked, walking into the library a few days later and catching Josh staring out the window at the nearby hills.

"That obvious, huh?" he replied, without turning around.

"Fraid so," she said, placing her hands on his shoulders and gently kneading the muscles in his upper back with her thumbs.

"Don't you think you might be overdoing it just a bit?" she continued, as she felt him begin to relax. "I mean, Brad's admittedly got a much better feel for the situation than I do, but nobody can possibly know at this point how things will play out. For all we know, the courts may still block the casino, and even if the Indians do get to build it, there's no guarantee it'll be a success."

"True," Josh acknowledged. "Brad's painting a worst-case scenario. But I hope there's one thing he's right about."

"What's that?"

"The Northern Pequot Reservation over there in the hills," he said, pointing in its general direction. "The Northerns have been on that reservation for more than three hundred years, but when I asked Brad if he thought they could ever qualify for a casino, he said the tribe had effectively been dead for so long that he couldn't imagine it happening."

"So is that what you've been doing . . . standing here worrying about a nonexistent Indian tribe? What am I going to do with you, Josh?" she asked, slipping her arms around him and giving him an affectionate squeeze.

Josh turned to face her. "Sorry," he said. "I don't mean to be so pessimistic. It's just that we've sunk everything we have into this place—personally and financially—and if they ever did build a casino here, there's no way I'd want to stay."

"I understand," Sharon replied, "but why agonize over something that even Brad says isn't going to happen?"

"Good point," Josh acknowledged.

"In fact, the more I think about it," Sharon went on, "the more I have to question whether casinos could ever get the kind of hold on Connecticut that Brad's talking about. I just have to believe that people here are too smart to let it happen."

Josh thought about that for a moment, then shook his head and smiled. "Not going to let up, are you?"

"What do you mean?"

"Trying to cheer me up."

"Okay, you caught me red-handed," she said, "but at least I made you smile."

For the time being, there was very little further movement on the Mashantucket casino. The state appealed the case to the U.S. Circuit Court of Appeals, but a ruling wasn't expected until September, and in the meantime the pleasant late-spring weather gradually lifted Josh's mood. Remarkably, there was almost no talk about the casino in the press or around town, and he almost began to think the whole thing might just go away.

The summer proved to be the best the family had ever had. Matt was growing up fast, but was still close to the rest of the family. Sarah, now eleven, was the family spark plug and organizer, and Jacob, going on seven, was now old enough to join in just about everything.

Josh and Ben Chapman had doubled the sweet corn and strawberries they'd planted the previous year, and they'd made enough progress with the apple orchard that this year's crop promised to be the best in a decade. The strawberries looked so good by early June that Josh and the kids opened a small farm stand on Route 141 for the short season, then reopened it when the first corn and apples were ready in August. The kids helped pick and haul the crops, Matt and Sarah took turns manning the stand, and all three got to keep the money it brought in. When they weren't working, they rode their horses, fished for bass and pickerel at the millpond, had friends over, or, in Matt and Sarah's case, rode their bikes to the town beach up at the lake to hang out and swim. Sharon started her art classes, began going out mornings to sketch scenes around the farm, and managed to get Josh to take her to several summer theater productions.

There was only one untoward event all summer, and even that seemed to draw the family closer together.

Josh took off the second Monday in July so that he and Sharon could take the kids hiking through Devil's Falls State Park. The park, which bordered Jepson Lake and the Indian reservation, contained seventeen hundred acres of some of the most rugged terrain in the region, including deep ravines, massive rock outcroppings, and a cascading waterfall, all hidden under huge oaks, beech trees, and broad stands of cedar, hemlock, and pine.

The temperature was already pushing into the mid-eighties when they arrived about 10:00, and the parking lot was almost empty. Josh picked up trail maps at the ticket booth, and everyone stood around studying them at the beginning of the main trail. They decided to head for the waterfall first and then climb to the top of Lookout Hill, which the map said was the highest point in the southern half of the county. The kids initially ran up ahead, and Josh and Sharon walked behind, keeping an eye on them and feeling the coolness of the forest settle around them. Sharon took Josh's hand as they passed a cedar swamp and a spectacular display of white and pink rhododendrons that grew in immense tangles under the trees.

"This is really beautiful," Sharon said. "I could spend the whole day walking these trails. How come you never took us up here before?"

"I don't know," Josh said. "I guess we've just been so busy with the farm and the horses that I really hadn't thought about it."

"Did you come up here as a kid?" she asked.

"Yeah, once in a while," Josh replied, "but really not that much. This place used to be a lot rougher before the state fixed up the trails, and as interesting as the park is, it's never really attracted that many locals. Kinda like New Yorkers never visiting the Statue of Liberty, I guess."

They reached the waterfall about twenty minutes later and stood together on a slab of rock watching the water tumble seventy feet into a large shallow pool and then run off into a stream that eventually flowed into the Connecticut River.

"Would you believe that this bedrock we're standing on goes back hundreds of millions of years to when Europe, Africa, and America were all connected?" Josh asked.

"How do you know that?" Matt asked.

"Because I read they've found the same rock in northwestern Africa."

"That's amazing," Matt said, and each of the kids bent down and felt the rock.

"In fact, this whole area is really pretty interesting," Josh continued. "The park's always been kind of a dark, mysterious place for some people, and it's inspired lots of myths and old wives' tales. If you look hard, you can see the entrance to a small cave just behind the falls. Some of the early settlers believed the cave was a witches' lair, and according to an old Puritan legend, those potholes there near the base of the falls were made by the devil himself."

"Where?" Jacob asked wide-eyed, straining to see.

"Right there," Josh said, squatting down by Jacob and pointing to the area in front of the falls.

"Actually," Josh said, "the potholes were made by tiny stones that got caught up in swirling eddies, but the story got going that they were made when Satan was walking along the streambed one day and accidentally got his tail wet. He supposedly got so mad that he stomped up the falls, carving out the potholes with his flaming hooves."

"So, is that how the park got its name?" Sarah asked.

"Yeah, apparently," Josh answered. "And for all anyone knows, it may have been one of your ancestors who came up with the story."

Sarah rolled her eyes at the thought of one of her forebears concocting such a ridiculous tale. "Do you think our ancestors really believed in all that supernatural stuff?" she asked.

"Well, I doubt anyone took that particular story seriously," Josh replied, "but just about everybody believed in the devil and witches in Europe back then, and the Puritans were no different. They believed life was a struggle between good and evil, and if you think about it, you can imagine how alone and vulnerable they must have felt over here in the wilderness. So if you put yourself in their place, you might have believed in the devil and witches too."

"Anyway," Josh said, trying to lighten things up, "the witches' lair looks empty this morning, so I think we can sneak by and go on up the trail."

Jacob shot his mother a conspiratorial grin, and they all started out again, each of the kids, including Sarah, stealing a final look at the cave as they went.

The main trail led steadily uphill from the falls, finally ending at the top of Lookout Hill. Everyone was breathing hard and perspiring by the time they got there, but it was worth it. An opening in the forest afforded a spectacular panorama to the south and southeast, taking in most of the lake and stretching all the way down to the Sound. Josh pointed out the general direction of New London and Niantic, but from six hundred feet the towns below were largely hidden by an endless canopy of trees.

"You know, it's amazing," he said. "If you looked down from this hill a hundred fifty years ago, you'd have seen almost nothing but farmland. But once Connecticut's farmers started moving west, the woods took over again, and from up here you'd think this whole region was nothing but trees. In fact, one of the least-known facts about Connecticut is that it's sixty percent woodland, making it one of the most heavily forested states in the country."

They sat on the rocks admiring the view and resting for a while, and then started down the hill, passing two teenage couples who were laughing and panting on their way up.

Once down the hill, the family veered off onto a secondary trail that led to the lake, almost immediately running into a flock of wild turkeys and then passing a lone eight-point whitetail buck that stood staring at them from the edge of a small pond. A few minutes later, Josh and Sharon stopped to try to catch a second glimpse of a bushy-tailed, black and brown animal that had darted out from behind a tree and disappeared into a patch of ferns. At first, Josh thought it might be a large mink, but then wondered if it might be a fisher, a secretive, weasel-like animal that had recently been reintroduced into Connecticut after being gone for more than fifty years.

They finally gave up looking and started out again just in time to see the three children stop suddenly about eighty feet up ahead and hear Sarah let out a scream. Josh and Sharon looked at each other and immediately started running toward them. When they reached them, Josh could barely believe his eyes.

Two large coyotes had somehow managed to fell a young deer about twenty-five feet into the woods, and the deer was struggling to get up as the attackers tore at its hind legs and throat with their sharp white fangs. Jacob watched in terror, while Sarah clung to Matt, crying and refusing to look. Desperately Josh looked around for a stick or a rock and finally found a fallen branch that he heaved into the melee, brushing one of the coyotes and hitting the other squarely on the head. Momentarily confused, the coyotes turned to look in Josh's direction, while the deer, its neck covered in blood, lurched to its feet and bounded away. Having lost their prey, the coyotes stared menacingly at the intruders, studying them with their yellow slant eyes. With the deer's blood still dripping from his snout, the closest coyote snarled and took a step toward Josh, who held his ground and motioned for the rest of the family to cluster behind him.

As he watched the lead coyote, Josh remembered the coyote he had seen coming out of his cornfield the previous summer and how it had retreated back into the corn as soon as it saw him. The two coyotes today, however, were much bigger, and if animals could smell fear, these could certainly smell it now.

"Shout and clap your hands to try to scare them off," Josh called over his shoulder, and simultaneously began scanning the ground for anything he could use against the coyotes if they attacked.

As everyone clapped and yelled, Josh spotted a football-size rock about seven feet away and began to gauge whether he could get to it before the coyotes could get to him. But before he could decide whether to go for it, the lead coyote began to slowly turn away, and the two animals slinked off quietly into the woods.

"Thank God," Sharon sighed and put her head on Josh's shoulder, while the two youngest children hugged him, positively giddy with relief and ecstatic at the deer's escape.

"Nice goin', Dad!" Matt said excitedly, patting his father on the back. "I saw you lookin' at that rock, but I'm sure glad we didn't need it."

No one, though, was more relieved than Josh, who silently cursed himself for trying to save the deer without any thought of the risk to his family. But there was no point in stopping to explain his blunder now. Not amid all the celebrating. The incident had made him an instant hero, and he suggested they call it a morning and head back to the car for their picnic cooler and an early lunch.

By the time they'd all sat down at one of the picnic tables, even Sharon seemed to have regained her composure, and the kids had excitedly told their versions of what had happened a dozen times.

"Well, one thing's for sure," Josh said to the kids as they ate their sandwiches. "You're in a very select group, because I've never known anyone who's seen coyotes take down a deer the way you did this morning. I've talked to farmers and hunters who've seen the remains of deer coyotes have gotten to, but I've never met anyone who's actually seen coyotes kill one. Every once in a while you'll hear of a coyote going after a lamb or snapping up a chicken or a pet, but when it comes to meat, they usually feed on small wild animals and insects."

"Do you think they were able to get to the deer because it was so young?" Sharon asked.

"Could be," Josh said, "although it was bigger than the coyotes, and even the young ones are incredibly alert."

"Or maybe it was sick and couldn't run fast," Jacob suggested.

"That's probably more likely," Josh agreed.

"Are there a lot of coyotes in Sheffield?" Sarah asked.

"I really don't know, honey," Josh replied. "They're very elusive animals who usually stay away from people and hunt at night, so it would be very hard to get an accurate count."

"Do you think there are a hundred?" Sarah pressed.

Josh chuckled. "I doubt it," he said. "From what I understand, coyote families usually stake out a pretty big area for themselves and keep other coyotes out, so there can't be that many of them. I do know, though, that there were never any coyotes in Sheffield until about thirty years ago."

"How'd they get here?" Matt asked.

"They migrated from the West," Josh said. "A hundred years ago the only coyotes in the United States were west of the Mississippi River, but as more and more of their enemies, like wolves and mountain lions, got killed off, they began to multiply and gradually work their way here."

"So are our coyotes the same as those in the West?" Matt asked.

"They're all part of the same species," Josh said, "but the eastern coyotes interbred with wolves and evolved into bigger animals as they came east. From what I know, western coyotes usually don't go more than thirty pounds, but both coyotes this morning looked liked they weighed at least fifty."

"Did you think they were really going to attack us?" Sarah asked.

"I honestly didn't know," Josh answered, seeing his chance to come clean. "I've never heard of coyotes attacking people in New England, but I was asking for trouble. I made a mistake spoiling those two coyotes' dinner without thinking they might come after us, and for a minute it sure looked like they were considering it."

"But if you didn't throw the branch, they would've killed the deer," Jacob said, obviously troubled by the dilemma.

"You're right, Jacob," Josh said, "but in a situation like that I should have thought about our family first. For all I knew, those two coyotes could have been rabid, and I certainly wouldn't have wanted to have to fight 'em off with our bare hands, would you?"

"No way!" Jacob responded.

"I didn't think so," Josh said and affectionately ruffled his son's hair.

"Anyway," Josh added, "I think the lesson for all of us today is simply to be careful with wild animals, because you never know when they might turn on you. In fact, that's going to be even more important in the future, because other animals like bears and moose are already coming into northwestern Connecticut, and you can bet they'll be showing up here before long."

"Are you serious?" Matt asked.

"Absolutely," Josh said. "And you can add bobcats to the list as well. If you count the park and the lake, Sheffield's ninety-five percent undeveloped, and we're eventually going to get any type of animal that comes into the state.

"But that's one of the things that makes this town so special," Josh said cheerfully. "I mean, I'd rather have a couple of bears and coyotes than have a thousand people driving up and down our street, wouldn't you?"

Everyone laughed at the idea of a thousand cars on Stoddard Mill Road, and with that they cleared the table and started for home.

The entire family took in the Sheffield Fair at the end of August, and Josh and Sharon and the kids marked the unofficial end of summer with a Labor Day picnic at the farm for their friends and neighbors. Everyone in the family felt a certain wistfulness as the last guest left that evening, and Jacob didn't want to go to bed because he was afraid summer would be over when he woke up the next morning. It didn't happen quite that fast, but the weather did begin to turn cooler that night, and by Tuesday morning there was already a whiff of autumn in the air.

7

~

Roots

September 4, 1990

The summer wasn't nearly as idyllic for Bobby Kingman. His problems had begun back in March with a dispute with a woman who had hired him to put an addition onto her kitchen. He'd finished 80 percent of the job when the customer caught him substituting cheaper materials for some of those he'd promised. Though he offered to reduce his price, the woman wound up suing him and winning $3,000 in small claims court. Then when Bobby couldn't make the payments on his pickup truck, the dealer repossessed it, and it took Bobby two weeks to scrape up the cash to get it back.

The whole episode absorbed so much time that Bobby had fallen behind on his other jobs, and he had to work evenings and weekends to keep the rest of his customers pacified. There were already so many complaints against him at the Consumer Protection Department that he was afraid one more would cost him his contractor's license.

With so many distractions, Bobby hadn't ever gotten around to sitting down with his Aunt Mavis to ask her about their Northern Pequot connection, but over the Labor Day weekend he finally found time to give her a call.

He hadn't seen much of Mavis since she and his mother had had a falling out some thirty years ago, but he had stopped in at the funeral home when her husband died a few years back, and he knew she'd appreciated it. She seemed genuinely pleased when she heard he was interested in learning about their Indian ancestry, and she invited him to her home in Waterford to talk about it.

Mavis, now seventy-one, had aged considerably since Bobby had seen her last, but she was still a bundle of energy. She'd made a coffee cake and laid out a complete genealogy chart for him before he arrived.

"You know," Mavis confided, "your mother never wanted to talk about our Indian ancestry, but I think it's fascinating and something to be proud of. In fact, I have an uncle who lives up on the Northern Pequot Reservation, and I still go up and visit him regularly."

"Yeah, I remember hearin' about him," Bobby said. "What's his name, again?"

"Ray Summerwood," Mavis replied.

"Boy, he's gotta be gettin' on by now," Bobby commented.

"Would you believe he's ninety?" Mavis said, "but he's in good health, and he and another old timer who lives on the reservation kinda take care of each other."

"Has Ray always lived on the reservation?" Bobby asked.

"He grew up there," Mavis explained, "but he joined the Navy in World War I and after that lived in New London and worked at one of the local marinas up till the mid-sixties. Then he decided to come back to the reservation and retire."

"He ever get married?" Bobby asked.

"No, so he really doesn't have anybody but me," Mavis said. "But he's very self-sufficient, and I think he's really content living out his life where he was born.

"I used to try to get up there once a month," Mavis continued, "but I go more often now that he's older. The man who's up there with him is a couple years younger, but they don't have a car or a phone or anything, and I worry about them. So either my daughter Leigh or I stop there every week now just to bring them a few groceries and check on things.

"It's amazing, though, how little they need. They still do a little fishing and hunting and grow most of their own fruits and vegetables. It's actually pretty neat when you think about it."

"So you really spend quite a bit of time on the reservation."

"I do, but I'm glad to do it," Mavis said, "Ray's a very sweet man, and I feel responsible for him.

"And besides," she added, "I enjoy going up there because of the family ties and the history and everything. Leigh and I also take care of the cemetery on the reservation. Our ancestor, Rachel Amos, who the whole family's descended from, is buried there."

"She must be on this genealogy chart, then," Bobby said, sliding closer to Mavis so that they could look at it together.

"She's right here," Mavis said, pointing to the first entry. "Leigh and I did the research ourselves."

The chart showed nine generations, beginning with Rachel Amos, who died in 1803. Bobby was listed in the eighth generation, his sons in the ninth.

"Unfortunately," Mavis said," we don't know much about Rachel because there is only one surviving reservation overseer's report prior to 1800 and only three surviving reports from 1800 to 1809. But we do know that the 1800 report lists Rachel and her seventeen-year-old daughter, Fanny, as living on the reservation, and that the 1803 report lists her as having died and been buried on the reservation in that year.

"We also know that Fanny took up with a white man by the name of John Skerret, and that she and Skerret are listed as the parents of a baby son named Robert Skerret in the 1804 report."

Bobby ran a finger over his lower lip. "How do you know Skerret was white?" he asked.

"Because that's the way he's identified in the overseer's report," Mavis said.

"How are Fanny and the baby identified?" Bobby asked.

"They're not identified as anything," Mavis said. "They're just listed with everyone else living on the reservation. The only people specifically identified by race in that report are Skerret and a black man."

"Was it common for non-Indians to live on the reservation?"

"It was fairly common, especially after the American Revolution. The state actually put welfare recipients on the reservations at times, and other indigent people drifted on and off. That apparently was the case with John Skerret, because he seems to have only stayed for a year or so and then disappeared."

It was the story of his life, Bobby thought bitterly, remembering his own father.

"What happened to Fanny and Robert?" Bobby asked.

"That, fortunately, we've got a lot more information on. As you can see from the chart, Fanny then married an Indian named George Pinawee, and they had a son who died when he was still a boy. George died in 1850 and Fanny stayed on the reservation until she died six years later."

"And Robert?" Bobby asked, studying the chart, the top portion of which read:

RACHEL AMOS, ? – 1803
|
FANNY AMOS, 1783 – 1856
          &   &

JOHN SKERRET, ? – ?   GEORGE PINAWEE, ? – 1850
| |
ROBERT SKERRET, 1805 – 1884   AARON PINAWEE, 1807 – 1815

"Robert left the reservation and settled in New London, where he married a white woman," Mavis said. "Each successive generation then took white spouses, and as you can see, Rachel's line continued right through today. We're all related to Robert, Fanny, and Rachel."

"Do you think either Rachel or Fanny were full-blooded Indians?"

"It's impossible to tell, Mavis replied. The first specific mention of race for either of them was in the 1810 reservation overseer's report, where a new overseer listed Fanny, George Pinawee and their son as Indians."

Bobby did a quick calculation in his head. Even if Fanny were 100 percent Indian, that meant that Bobby was only one-sixty-fourth Indian. And if Fanny was less than 100 percent, he was much less than that.

"How many livin' descendants does Rachel have?" Bobby asked, seeing there were too many to count.

"We've come up with fifty-seven," Mavis said, "although who knows how many we may be missing."

"And do most of them live around here?"

"Nine live out of state, but the rest live in Connecticut and most of us are in this area."

"Are there any other surviving family lines in addition to Rachel's?" Bobby asked.

"Just one, the Joberts. They come from a Northern Pequot named Attawan, but there are only two descendants left. One of them, Louis Jobert, is the man who lives on the reservation with Ray, and the other is Louis's sister, who lives up in Colchester."

"And that's it?"

"As far as we know, that's it. Remember, the Northern Pequots were a very small tribe. There were probably never more than fifty or sixty of them from the beginning. Some were killed fighting for the colonists in the Revolutionary War, and others joined the Brothertown Indian movement after the Revolution and ended up in upstate New York or Wisconsin with other Indians who went there to get away from the white man and preserve their culture."

Bobby was impressed. His aunt was a walking encyclopedia on their family and the tribe.

"Do you know many of the descendants who live around here?" he asked.

"I know them all," Mavis said brightly, "because I visited or talked to them on the phone when we were putting together the genealogy chart. We also have this little group called the Northern Pequot Sewing Society.

"There are only three of us," she said, "but the society's existed since 1850, when some of the Pequot women off the reservation began getting together to make clothes and blankets for those who still lived there. It's just a social thing—all we really do is collect a little money for the cemetery and have a picnic for any of the descendants and their families we can get to come. But the picnic's fun. The kids swim in the lake and Ray welcomes people back as chief."

"Ray's the chief?" Bobby asked, surprised there still was a chief.

"Well, it's just ceremonial," Mavis said, "because there's really nothing for him to do except maybe write a letter or sign something every once in a while and send it to Hartford."

"If you'd like to visit the cemetery," Mavis said hopefully, "I'd love to show you Rachel's tombstone. And I could introduce you to Ray while we're there. I know you'd like him."

"Yeah, I might do that," Bobby replied. "This genealogy stuff's really pretty interestin'."

8

New Blood

September 5, 1990–March 31, 1991

On September 5 the casino burst back into the news. This time the *Norwich Bulletin* carried the story at the top of the front page. "Court Clears Way for Ledyard Casino," the headline read. According to the story, the Second U.S. Circuit Court of Appeals in New York had upheld May's lower court ruling that Connecticut must enter into negotiations on a gambling compact with the Mashantuckets. Instructed by the court to cease its delaying tactics, the state essentially acknowledged defeat and in October agreed to a mediated settlement that gave the Mashantuckets almost everything they wanted.

The settlement instantly became national news, with the *New York Times* reporting that the Mashantuckets were "the first American Indian tribe east of the Mississippi to reach a gambling agreement under a federal law signed in 1988, and could be the first in the nation to actually begin full casino-style gambling." Connecticut officials, the article noted, were "not happy about any of it," but had been "compelled by federal court order" to reach a gambling compact with the tribe.

It was the same old story, Josh thought: the state was against the casino but powerless to do anything about it. The hopelessness of the situation was highlighted further by the race for governor that fall, in which a Democrat, a Republican, and an Independent all vied to succeed retiring Democratic Governor William O'Neill but in which none of the candidates seemed to have any better ideas than O'Neill for blocking the Mashantuckets. In the end, the voters elected the Independent, former U.S. Senator Lowell Weicker, who had played a key role in helping the Mashantuckets obtain federal recognition in 1983.

In one of O'Neill's last acts before leaving office, the state appealed September's casino ruling to the Supreme Court, but by then virtually no one thought the appeal had a prayer. In fact, when Josh ran into Brad at the racquet club in early March, Brad said the casino now looked so certain that the tribe had supposedly just sewn up a $60 million loan to finance it.

"Who they getting it from?" Josh asked as he and Brad changed into their tennis clothes in the locker room. "One of the big investment banks?"

"That's what I would have thought," Brad replied, "but from what I hear, it's coming from a Chinese-Malaysian billionaire named Lim Goh Tong. They say he controls a conglomerate that owns a resort casino called Genting Highlands in Malaysia, just outside Kuala Lumpur. The place is supposed to be one of the biggest casinos in the world, and the word is Lim's been looking for a chance to pick up an American casino for years."

"He must be pretty positive about this one to put up that kind of money," Josh responded.

"No question," Brad said. "His willingness to bet sixty million bucks on the Mashantuckets is the best indication yet of where this whole thing can go."

Josh just nodded at Brad's comment, but it stuck with him for the next hour and a half as he struggled through his singles match. He had beaten his opponent the last three times out, but this time he lost in two sets.

⤳

Bobby Kingman followed up his September visit to his aunt with a visit to the state's Indian Affairs Coordinator at the Department of Environmental Protection in Hartford.

He felt a little awkward walking into the guy's office without ever having actually been on the Northern Pequot Reservation, but he figured the most important thing at that point was to find out how the federal recognition process worked. He could see the Northerns had stopped functioning as a tribe a long time ago, but it seemed to him that if the Mashantucket Pequots could resurrect themselves, then the Northern Pequots should be able to do the same.

He quickly found out the situation was infinitely more complex than that. The difference between what the Mashantuckets had done and what the Northerns would have to do, the coordinator explained, was enormous.

The Mashantuckets, Bobby learned, had managed to get recognition through an act of Congress, but the Northerns would have to go through the Bureau of Indian Affairs, and the BIA had a daunting set of requirements for granting recognition. Even if you could get through the process, it could take ten or twenty years and could cost millions of dollars to hire the experts you'd need to prove your case. If Bobby wanted additional advice, the state coordinator recommended a nonprofit legal services organization in Washington that specialized in Indian issues, but it seemed pointless to pursue things any further.

Discouraged, Bobby never bothered to call Mavis back. Then in late March he happened to hear about the Chinese-Malaysian billionaire, Lim something or other, and he got excited all over again.

If a big-time player like Lim was willing to put up sixty million bucks to build an Indian casino in Connecticut, Bobby reasoned, you knew the market had to be huge, and you had to assume other investors would quickly begin looking for other tribes to partner with.

And that gave Bobby an idea.

Lim, Bobby reflected, was investing *after* the Mashantuckets had been recognized and were eligible to pursue a casino. But right now there were no other federally recognized tribes in Connecticut. Therefore, Bobby thought, he might be able to attract an investor who'd be willing to front the Northern Pequots the money they needed to hire the experts necessary to get recognized. After all, that was Bobby's forte—attracting investors.

Energized, Bobby called the legal services people in Washington to discuss his interest in finding an investor who might back the Northern Pequots, then called Mavis. He apologized for not having gotten back to her but wondered if she'd still be willing to take him up to the reservation to meet her uncle and see Rachel's grave.

"Of course," Mavis said, quickly forgetting her disappointment when she hadn't heard back from him. "I think of you every time I go up there, and it's wonderful you're still interested."

⤳

Mavis agreed to pick Bobby up in front of the Sheffield Town Hall at 9:30 on Saturday morning, March 31.

Bobby got there a few minutes early and sat in his pickup, studying a map of the town. The reservation had a good mile of frontage on Jepson Lake and was bordered on the north by the state park and on the south by Deer Run and the Standish farm—making it potentially one of the most picturesque spots around.

The obvious problem, however, was access. At its closest point, the reservation was only about three-quarters of a mile from the state highway, but the only way to get to the reservation was by way of Cedar Road, a narrow back road that ran from the highway to the entrance to the state park. Putting a casino on the reservation would clearly require getting access to the state highway by either building a new connector to the highway through the Standish farm or reconstructing a part of Cedar Road for that purpose. Either solution, Bobby was sure, would involve a battle with the town.

The drive to the reservation took less than ten minutes. Mavis took Lake Street to Cedar Road, then continued along Cedar for about two miles until they came to a dirt road on the left that led off into the woods. The area was posted with no-trespassing notices, but there was no plaque or sign indicating they were entering an Indian reservation.

"You'd think the state'd have some kind of marker or somethin' to let people know the reservation's here," Bobby commented.

"Actually, the state did have a small sign years ago," Mavis said, "but kids or somebody must have taken it down, and no one's ever bothered to put one back up."

The dirt road wasn't bad at first, but it deteriorated into a stretch of bumps and potholes as it wound uphill.

"Jesus," Bobby said as they rocked and bounced along, "thank God I skipped breakfast this morning. I had no idea the land was so rough in here."

"Yeah, I'm afraid there' a lot of ledges and ravines in this section," Mavis said, keeping her eyes on the road and a tight grip on the steering wheel. "And, unfortunately, another thirty percent of the reservation's really nothing but wetlands. But that's probably why the colonists gave this particular land to the tribe in the first place."

"I'm sure you're right," Bobby said, appreciating her cynicism.

"But the lake front's pretty," she went on, "and the land gets a lot better in another sixty yards or so."

Eventually they arrived at a broad, flat meadow where two old house trailers and several dilapidated shacks came into view. The roofs of two of the shacks had completely collapsed, and the rusted hulk of a 1947 Chevy rested nearby.

"Welcome to the Northern Pequot Tribal Nation," Mavis said. "It's not much, but I'm afraid it's all that's left."

Bobby thought it looked like Appalachia but didn't say anything.

Mavis pulled up to the second trailer just as a rail-thin man with wisps of snow-white hair opened the trailer door and stepped out to meet them.

"I've brought you a visitor," Mavis called out cheerfully as she and Bobby got out of the car, and proceeded to introduce Bobby to her uncle.

The old man had gray eyes flecked with green, and one eyelid sagged slightly. He eyed the newcomer suspiciously at first, but he relaxed when he found out Bobby was a relative.

"I guess that makes you my grandnephew," Ray Summerwood said cordially when Mavis explained the connection.

"Bobby's very interested in his genealogy," Mavis said, "and I wanted him to have a chance to meet you and see Rachel's grave. Then I was hoping you might have time to tell him a little about the reservation."

"Yeah, I'd really love to learn more about the tribe," Bobby said, flashing his most ingratiating smile. Up close, Bobby could see that the old man's face was so lined and weather-beaten that he could have been just about anything, but he was surprised the man didn't somehow look more like an Indian.

Ray said he was glad Mavis had brought Bobby up, and went back inside to get a coat so he could walk down to the cemetery with them.

"Where's Louis?" Mavis asked when Ray rejoined them.

"Probably restin'," Ray replied. "Did somethin' to his ankle the other day huntin' squirrels, and it's really been botherin' him. We can go over and see him when we get back."

The three of them set off for the cemetery, which was at the far end of the meadow.

It was a perfect morning, crisp but sunny, and Bobby caught glimpses of the lake sparkling through the trees. Too bad they'd turned the upper part of the meadow into such a dump, he thought, because the rest of the area was really very pretty.

The old Indian burial ground contained forty-one gravestones spread out irregularly over about a third of an acre. Mavis and Leigh hadn't been in yet to clean up the winter debris, but it was obvious the cemetery, which was enclosed by a low stone wall, was being cared for. The earliest markers were simply rough fieldstones with no inscriptions, while those put in place after 1800 tended to be small sandstone or slate tablets bearing the name of the deceased and the dates of his or her birth and death. The last person to have been buried on the reservation, Ray explained, was his father, who died in 1952.

Some of the inscriptions were so badly weathered that Bobby found them impossible to read, but Rachel Amos's inscription was still clearly legible. It simply gave her name and the date of her death: June 3, 1803.

Louis was up when they got back and invited everyone into his trailer, where they sat down at the tiny kitchen table while he made tea. Looking around the cramped space, Bobby could see there was no electricity or running water. The only nods to modernity were an ancient gas stove and a couple of small propane heaters.

Louis was a fairly large man with a broad face, close-cropped, steel-gray hair, and a slightly swarthy complexion that made him look more Indian than Ray, and he immediately impressed Bobby as the more dominant personality. He wanted to know all about Bobby and his relationship to Mavis, and then he and Ray spent almost two hours taking Bobby through the history of the tribe and the reservation.

The main reason tribes like the Northern Pequots had broken up and scattered so early, they explained, was that the colonists hadn't given them enough land to subsist on, and the young men had had to leave to earn a living.

"And not only that," Louis said, "but as small as the reservations were in the beginning, the colonists gradually whittled away at most of them over the years. This reservation, for example, started out at six hundred acres, but the state sold off a hundred acres in the 1830s to raise money to help support the people livin' here. So it was kinda like makin' an animal eat its own tail to survive."

"That's right," Ray interjected, "and naturally the part the state sold off was the best farmland on the entire rez. The family that bought it farmed it for more than a hundred fifty years and then sold it to developers who turned it into that fancy subdivision next door."

Bobby listened attentively to the history of the place and expressed particular interest in such things as when Ray had become chief, who some of the other chiefs had been and how many people had lived on the reservation since the turn of the century. Ray and Louis both seemed to be genuinely enjoying the discussion, and Bobby could feel them warming up to him as it progressed.

The Pequots, Louis recalled proudly, had once been the most powerful tribe in New England. And they had attained that status, he added, because of both their martial skills and their production of wampum, which was increasingly used as a form of currency once the Europeans arrived.

"In fact, lemme show you somethin'," Louis said, going to a cupboard and coming back with an Indian hatchet and wampum belt he said had been handed down through his family.

"These were the two great symbols of Pequot strength," Louis said proudly, laying them on the table in front of Bobby.

Bobby hefted the hatchet briefly but was much more interested in the wampum.

"How the f…," he started to say, but caught himself. "How'd they make these?" he asked, examining the small, cylindrical purple and white shell beads that had been drilled lengthwise and strung together.

"The Pequots cut them from whelk and quahog shells they found along the shores of Long Island Sound," Louis explained, "and then drilled each one and strung it with gut or hemp. And the incredible thing is they did it all with stone tools until the Europeans arrived with metal ones."

"These purple ones are really beautiful," Bobby said, touching the highly polished darker stones.

"Yeah, they're from the hard-shelled clams, or quahogs, that go into chowder. The quahogs can give you purple, white, or purple and white banded beads, whereas the whelks are softer-shelled snails and only give you white."

"What did the Indians originally use wampum for?" Bobby asked.

"They believed shells came from the spirit world," Louis explained, "and that the shell beads had great spiritual power that could help in everything from fighting and hunting to fending off illness and finding a wife. Chiefs used wampum to show their status. Shamans took it as payment for their services. Powerful tribes like the Pequots took it as tribute from lesser tribes, and powerful sachems received it from lesser sachems. And all the tribes used it for things like sealing treaties and ransoming prisoners."

"But then you said it was also used to buy and sell goods after the white man came—right?" Bobby asked.

"Right," Louis replied. "The coastal Indians used wampum to acquire European goods, and the European traders then used it to buy furs from the interior Indians."

"It was an incredible time for the Pequots," Louis added, "because they were literally minting money. And the more metal knives and drills the Europeans provided them, the faster they minted it."

Louis shook his head and let out a little ironic chuckle. "And all we have left now is a few acres and a picnic each July—isn't that right, Mavis?" he said, reaching over and patting her hand.

"And I thought you loved the picnics," Mavis said, feigning disappointment.

Louis smiled. "I do," he assured her. "And in fact," he added, "I want to be sure you invite Bobby and his two sons to the next one. We could use a little new blood around here."

On the way back from the reservation, Bobby said he'd like to take Mavis to lunch at the Sheffield Tavern in appreciation for all her time. When they got there, he asked for a window table and ordered a bottle of wine with their meal.

Mavis seemed to enjoy the attention and really opened up over lunch, talking about the family, her late husband, and how much her life had changed since he'd died. Bobby listened patiently and sympathetically, and then turned the conversation back to the reservation as they lingered over dessert.

"I wanna thank you again for showin' me the reservation and introducin' me to Ray and Louis this mornin'," Bobby said. "It was really interestin' to listen to those old guys talk about the tribe's history and to think about how we're connected to all of it."

Mavis smiled and watched her nephew pour the last of the wine into their glasses. "I'm really glad you enjoyed it," she said, "and that there's finally someone else in the family who's interested."

"What's amazin' to me," Bobby continued, "is how those two old guys have been able to survive up there all by themselves all this time. What's sad is the poverty and the fact the state'll obviously close the reservation once they die."

Mavis sighed. "I know. It is sad," she agreed. "And the other thing is, I have no idea what will happen to the cemetery once the state takes the place over."

"You know, I've been thinkin' about the whole situation," Bobby said, "and I'm just wonderin' if it wouldn't make sense to try to get some of the descendants together to build up the tribe and try to get the federal government to recognize it. That way you could keep the reservation open and get the government to provide some money to fix the place up. The Mashan-tuckets managed to get recognized, and they say the Mohegans are tryin' to do the same over in Montville."

"Actually," Mavis said, "Leigh and I've talked about it, but it could never happen here."

"Why not?" Bobby asked with a puzzled look.

"Because," Mavis said, "you can't compare us to the Mashantuckets or the Mohegans. The Mashantuckets made a special deal with Congress that we could never do, and the Mohegans are the biggest tribe in the state. They've got hundreds of members, not to mention a church and even their own little museum."

Mavis picked absently at the tablecloth.

"All we really have," she continued, "are two old men trying to live their lives out in peace and quiet—that and a few descendants who have no asso-ciation with the tribe other than to come to a picnic once a year. And even then, I have to just about beg 'em to come.

"The truth is," she added, "there may still be two people living on the reservation, but the tribe died a long time ago. There's simply nothing left of the old culture—no language, no songs, no dances, no crafts, no customs, no anything."

"But I thought you told me you had a ceremony where Ray welcomes everybody back to the reservation each year?"

"Bobby," Mavis said with an air of exasperation, "that takes about twelve seconds. The only reason people come to the picnics is to eat hot dogs and hamburgers and swim.

"I mean, don't think it's like some big Indian powwow or something. The people who come are just normal, everyday people. They wouldn't know the difference between a rain dance and the bunny hop."

"Come on," Bobby insisted, "you've got a lot more here than you realize. You've got an Indian reservation, you've got an Indian cemetery you main-tain, and you've got an Indian chief. You've also got this women's group—the sewin' society—that's met for a hundred forty years, and descendants who come together every year on the reservation. Then there's you and Leigh, who go up regularly and take care of the tribe members who live there.

"I've been lookin' into this, Mavis, and these things are important. Genealogy, social and political continuity—these are the things the government's lookin' for when you apply for recognition."

"But it's much more complicated than that," Mavis insisted. "The Mohegans have been trying to get recognition for years without any success, and there's no way we could put together an application that even came close to theirs."

"I'm not so sure you're right," Bobby objected.

"Bobby," Mavis said, "you don't understand. We'd have to submit thousands of pages of evidence proving the tribe had met all kinds of criteria for the past three hundred years, and even if it had, we could never afford to hire the kind of people you'd need to do the research and put together an application."

"What if I could come up with the money?" Bobby asked.

"How could you do that?"

Bobby played with his unused coffee spoon, then looked up and said, "Well, I'm certain there are investors who'd put up the money if we'd agree to let them go in with us on a casino."

Mavis's expression froze. "Oh, I see," she said cynically. "This is not about genealogy. This is about a casino. That's why you came to me. You want to do what the Mashantuckets are trying to do."

Bobby put up his hands in mock surrender.

"I knew you'd think that," he said, "and it's partially true. I think a casino could give our family the financial security none of us has ever had. But I'm also interested in our roots, and it's clear that a casino is the one thing that could save the reservation and revive the tribe."

Mavis studied Bobby carefully.

"I mean, wouldn't you want that?" Bobby asked earnestly.

"Yes," Mavis finally said, "but I'm not sure I could live with the idea of turning the reservation into a casino. It's almost . . . sacrilegious."

"Look," Bobby said as gently as he could, "it's not just the Mashantuckets who are gonna build a casino. Tribes all over the state and all over the country are gonna be doing it in order to better themselves. That's why Congress is allowin' tribes to open casinos—to help them take control of their lives. It's probably the only decent thing the white man ever did for the Indian."

Bobby leaned closer and touched Mavis's hand.

"You know, when we were standin' up there by Rachel's grave, I was thinkin' what it must have been like on the reservation the day they buried her," he said. "Those people had nothin'. No money, no decent place to live, no future. Don't you think every one of 'em would have given anythin' to get the kind of opportunity the government's offerin' Indians today? You can't turn down that kind of gift without at least thinkin' about it."

"I *am* thinking about it," Mavis said. "But I just can't see how it could ever work."

"Mavis, you have to be more positive."

"It's not just that," Mavis said. "Even if the tribe qualified, I can't believe Louis would ever allow a casino on the reservation."

"Why do you say that?"

"Because I know him. He's very religious. He was brought up a Baptist, and even though he doesn't go to church anymore, he reads the Bible every night and has very strict morals. He won't even allow beer at the picnics, which is one of the reasons we can't get more people there. So I can't imagine how he'd ever agree to gambling."

Bobby winced. "What about Ray?"

"Ray might not be opposed," Mavis said. "But he'd never go against Louis, and you couldn't ever expand the tribe without their agreement. They are the tribe."

"Would you at least talk to Louis, and see if he'd be willin' to sit down with me and discuss it?" Bobby asked. "He seemed reasonable enough."

"Bobby, you don't know him. He's a kind, interesting person, and I could see he liked you. But he's an old man who's set in his ways. The more I think about it, the more certain I am how he'll react."

"Please, Mavis," Bobby pleaded. "This is too important to simply let it drop. The only way we can do this is if we work together. And if we succeed, I swear you can have whatever money you need to protect the reservation. You'll be able to preserve the burial ground, do research on the tribe's history, even hire experts to revive the language—whatever you want. But you've got to talk to Louis and convince him at least to listen."

Mavis stared at her plate, uncertain.

"Please, Mavis," Bobby repeated. "This could be the biggest opportunity the tribe's ever had. Otherwise Ray and Louis are simply gonna die and it'll all be forgotten."

Mavis finally looked up. "All right," she said. I'm due back at the reservation on Tuesday. I'll see if I can talk to both Ray and Louis then, and after I get home I'll give you a call."

Bobby's relief was almost palpable.

"Thank you," he said. "I know you're not lookin' forward to talkin' to them, but it'll all work out. You'll see."

9

The Big Money

March 31–April 19, 1991

Nothing ever went smoothly, Bobby thought, following his lunch with Mavis. He had won her over, but now Louis was the problem. Christ, Bobby told himself, the guy should jump at the chance to turn that junkyard into something. Furthermore, the son of a bitch was eighty-eight years old and should be willing to step aside for others. Clearly, however, Louis had no intention of doing that, and you couldn't just sit around and wait for him to die. With Bobby's luck, the man would live to a hundred.

Bobby could only hope that Mavis could sweet-talk Louis into cooperating. God knew, both Louis and Ray owed her big-time for everything she'd done for them.

The weekend dragged by, and Bobby became increasingly edgy as Tuesday, April 2, approached. He thought several times of calling Mavis to give her another pep talk but pulled back each time he started toward the phone. She had given him her commitment, and he didn't want to give her a chance to back off. By Tuesday afternoon, he couldn't concentrate on work and knocked off early to make sure he was home when she called.

He jumped when he finally heard the phone just after 5:00 and answered it on the second ring. He could tell almost immediately from Mavis's tone that the meeting hadn't gone well.

"I'm sorry, Bobby," he heard her say, "but I'm afraid Louis turned me down flat. He's unalterably opposed to gambling and said a casino would desecrate the reservation."

"Are you sayin' he wouldn't even talk about it?" Bobby asked.

"He listened at first," Mavis said, "but then he just cut me off. I've never seen him get so upset."

"What about Ray?"

"I thought he seemed interested at first," Mavis said, "but when Louis blew up, he backed off. He'd never challenge Louis."

"How about if we wait a few days and then you and I go up and to talk to Louis together?"

"I'm sorry, Bobby, but I don't think that'd be a good idea. Louis is angry at me for bringing you up in the first place. He thinks you're just an opportunist and told me to tell you he never wants to see you on the reservation again."

"All right, relax," Bobby said, recognizing the meeting had really shaken her up. "You made a gallant effort, and I'm sorry it was so difficult. Let's just let things cool off, and then you and I can sit down together and talk about it. Maybe we'll still be able to work somethin' out."

∽

Bobby was almost ready to chuck the whole casino idea when he picked up a message from his answering machine on Monday, April 15.

The message was from the Washington legal services lawyer he had spoken with over the phone. When Bobby reached him the next morning, the lawyer said he had had a call from a major real estate developer in New York named James Grimaldi who was interested in finding a Connecticut tribe he could help shepherd through the recognition process in return for an interest in a potential casino. The lawyer said he'd talked to Grimaldi about the Northern Pequots, and Grimaldi would like to speak with Bobby.

Bingo! Bobby thought. He'd been chasing penny-ante investors half his life, and now the big money was chasing him.

He called Grimaldi's office immediately and didn't have to wait more than twenty seconds before the man himself came on the line.

After some brief introductions, Grimaldi explained he had heard good things about the Northern Pequots, and he and an associate might be interested in an investment in the tribe if Bobby was interested.

"From what I understand," Grimaldi said, "I think we might be able to be very helpful to each other."

"Well, I have to be honest and tell you that we're considerin' a number of possibilities," Bobby replied, "but I'd certainly be happy to talk."

"Good. Is there any chance you might be able to come to New York this Friday?" Grimaldi asked.

"You mean the nineteenth?" Bobby asked, quickly checking his kitchen calendar. If the guy wanted to see him that fast, he had to be serious.

"Yes, unless of course you'd prefer to set up something later."

"Give me a minute while I check my book," Bobby said, cradling the phone against his shoulder and briefly flipping through an old magazine on the counter. "Yeah, I think I could do the nineteenth."

⤵

Bobby drove down to New York City in his pickup truck, leaving his apartment at 5:30 a.m. to give himself plenty of time to make his 10:00 appointment with Grimaldi. He figured that, with the early start, he should be able to make the drive in three hours, but he hadn't been to the city for at least ten years, and the last thing he wanted was to risk being late for potentially the most important meeting of his life.

As it turned out, he soon began wishing he had left even earlier. I-95 moved well through New Haven, but the traffic began to build around Bridgeport and then slowed to a crawl all the way from Stamford into the Bronx. By 9:00, he was still inching along the FDR Drive on the east side of Manhattan and beginning to sweat. Finally, he gave up and turned off at Sixty-Third Street, fought his way crosstown to Park Avenue, then headed down Park to the address Grimaldi had given him on Park Avenue South.

Grimaldi Development Corporation was located on the forty-ninth floor of a new office tower that was hard to miss, but finding a parking garage with a vacancy was another story. He finally found one and hoofed it three blocks back to Grimaldi's building, getting there in time to squeeze into an elevator just as its doors were closing at one minute to ten. He tried to smooth out his suit on the way up but decided that was pointless. The suit was fifteen years old and suffered from more than a few wrinkles. What concerned Bobby was whether Grimaldi was expecting him to look like an Indian. If he did, he was certainly in for a surprise.

The elevator stopped, and Bobby stepped out into a hallway with office suites at either end. He took a deep breath and headed toward the one with Grimaldi's name over the door.

A knockout Asian receptionist in a low-cut blouse greeted him warmly when he gave his name, then promptly deflated him by saying Mr. Grimaldi was running about fifteen minutes late. "If you'll have a seat," she said, "I'm sure he'll be with you shortly."

Bobby was tempted to make a crack about how he had just busted his ass to be on time, but thought better of it and instead asked for the key to the men's room. When he came back, he thanked the receptionist politely, stealing a closer look at her cleavage, then took his time perusing the framed photographs and renderings of Grimaldi's projects that hung on the walls. They consisted primarily of office buildings and shopping malls on Long Island and in Fairfield County, Connecticut, although his most recent project appeared to be the big new office tower where their meeting was about to take place. Most of the photos included a tall, handsome man about Bobby's age who, along with a group of dignitaries, was holding a spade or helping cut a ribbon. Bobby recognized Governor Cuomo and Senator D'Amato from New York in two of the photos, and Connecticut's Governor O'Neill in another.

"Mr. Kingman?" Bobby finally heard a woman say, and he turned to see a willowy, six-foot-tall blonde addressing him. "I'm Greta Lindstrom, Mr. Grimaldi's assistant," the young woman said and shook his hand. Mr. Grimaldi is free now if you'd like to come with me."

Bobby thought that would be a great idea but settled for admiring her long, perfect legs as he followed her to Grimaldi's office, her high-heeled crocodile pumps clicking along the hall ahead of him. Without even meeting Grimaldi, it was clear he not only had powerful friends but a taste for stunning women as well.

Greta Lindstrom stopped at a corner office, where she knocked discreetly and then slowly opened the door. As she ushered Bobby in, a tall, athletic-looking man with wavy black hair, deep-set eyes, and a pencil-thin mustache came out from behind his desk to greet him. He was impeccably dressed in a gray pinstriped suit, light blue shirt, and burgundy tie, and he looked to Bobby as though he had just stepped out of a magazine ad.

"Mr. Kingman, it's a pleasure to meet you," he said, extending his hand. "I'm Jim Grimaldi, and I'm so pleased you were able to come to New York this morning."

Bobby returned the warm greetings, relieved that he didn't see any hint of surprise at his non-Indian appearance. Obviously the guy must have already checked Bobby out. Either that or he couldn't care less what Bobby looked like as long as he thought Bobby controlled an Indian reservation.

Bobby insisted Grimaldi call him by his first name and looked around the office.

"What a fabulous view," he enthused as he focused on the dazzling panorama provided by the office's floor-to-ceiling windows. The Empire

State Building loomed before him, reflecting the sun, and looking to the left, he could see all the way to the World Trade Center and the entrance to New York Harbor.

"A little perk for putting up the building myself," Grimaldi explained modestly.

The office itself was furnished with an elegant wood-and-steel desk and matching credenza, and the mahogany-paneled back walls were either hung with artwork or lined with bookshelves displaying books, photos, and various plaques and memorabilia. A stunning blue-and-gold Persian carpet covered the floor, and as Bobby got acclimated, he noticed several modern sculptures strategically placed around the room.

Grimaldi directed his guest to a sitting area and sat down opposite him, his back to the windows so Bobby could look out; a moment later the blonde returned with a china coffee service for two. As he watched her pour and add cream and sugar, Bobby wondered if he could ever figure out how to dress or live like this. These people looked more like movie stars than anyone he'd ever encountered.

Grimaldi, who was disarmingly open, said he'd been in the real estate development business for twenty-two years and explained the kind of projects he specialized in. His biggest current project, he said, was a new shopping mall on Long Island, but he was also looking at a major potential opportunity in Stamford, Connecticut, once the economy improved.

"And how about you, Bobby?" Grimaldi asked. "I understand you're also in the real estate and construction business."

"Yeah, I also do a little shopping center development," Bobby replied. "In fact," he added, unable to resist the opening, "if you ever do one of your projects up our way, I'd certainly be interested in having a chance to get involved."

Grimaldi nodded appreciatively. "I'm not planning anything along those lines at the moment," he said, "but as I indicated on the phone, a colleague and I are interested in the possibility of working with your tribe to build a casino in Connecticut, and we understand from your Washington attorney that you may be looking for a partner. If that's the case, we think we'd be ideal."

"Can you tell me why you're interested in us as opposed to any of the other Connecticut tribes?" Bobby asked.

"Of course," Grimaldi said with an appreciative smile. "In fact, let me explain how we're approaching the entire Indian casino market.

"My associate and I are convinced Indian gaming's about to explode, and we're in the process of selecting two or three tribes around the country that we want to help get in the business and succeed. We particularly like Connecticut because of its strategic location, and we think that once the Mashantucket court case is resolved, things are going to begin to move fast there."

Bobby nodded in agreement.

"The challenge we're facing in Connecticut," Grimaldi continued, "is that the Mashantuckets are the only tribe that's federally recognized right now, and they've already made a deal with somebody else. The Mohegans look like the next tribe to be recognized, but for reasons we don't need to get into, they don't appear to be an opportunity for us."

Bobby was tempted to ask why, but decided it was better just to let Grimaldi keep talking.

"That leaves four state-recognized tribes, but there are a couple of reasons we're particularly interested in you. For one thing, you're a good half hour closer to New York than the Mashantuckets and fifteen minutes closer than the Mohegans, which gives you an advantage over both of them. Most important, though, we think your tribe probably has the best chance of the remaining tribes to be recognized."

"Why do you think that?" Bobby asked, suddenly fearing there must be some huge misunderstanding.

"Mainly because you've had Northern Pequots living on the reservation continually for over three hundred years, and there don't appear to be any divisions or disputes within the tribe.

"I am right about that, aren't I?" Grimaldi asked pointedly.

"Absolutely," Bobby assured him. "We've been very fortunate that way."

"Well, that's critical," Grimaldi emphasized. "Divisions can really complicate a tribe's bid for recognition and drag things out forever."

Bobby nodded. "Very true," he said.

"So that's pretty much it," the developer concluded. "If your situation is as clean as it looks and you can expand the tribe the way your lawyer says you intend to, we think you're probably our best bet. "Of course, we've got to get to know you better and make sure there aren't problems we don't know about. But short of that, we think we can get you through the recognition process relatively fast."

"What do you think it'll take to do that?" Bobby inquired.

"Probably ten or twelve million dollars," Grimaldi answered matter-of-factly.

Bobby felt the adrenaline rush. "And you're willin' to invest that kind of money?" he asked, trying not to show his excitement.

"If you're the right tribe, we'd be willing to invest whatever it takes," Grimaldi said. "We'd pay for all the historians, genealogists, and lawyers you'd need to prepare your application, not to mention help you win the friends and influence the people you'd need to get it approved in Washington. We'd also provide funds to help you expand and strengthen the tribe. And, I should add, Mr. Kingman, that we would make sure that you personally would receive a sufficient salary to enable you to focus your undivided attention on the project."

Grimaldi paused to let the full impact of what he was offering sink in. "You might say we'd provide the total financial package," he concluded.

"And what would you expect in return?" Bobby asked, eyeing Grimaldi carefully.

"It's very simple," Grimaldi said. "We'd be willing to provide the money in exchange for the exclusive right to negotiate a casino development and management contract with the tribe that gives us forty percent of the casino's net profits for the first twenty years. We'd negotiate the final contract when the tribe received recognition, and we'd also require that the tribe waive its sovereign immunity so we'd have the right to go to court if the tribe didn't perform."

Bobby thought about that for a moment. It was a huge percentage, but Grimaldi and his partner would clearly be shouldering all the risk, and without a wealthy, long-term investor, the tribe would never be able to see the project through.

"How successful do you think a casino in Sheffield could be?" Bobby asked.

"We'll know better once the Mashantucket casino goes into operation," Grimaldi answered, "but we're very optimistic. If we can get you up and running in nine or ten years, and assuming Connecticut allows slots by then, which we're certain it will, we think you could do three to four hundred million dollars in gross gaming revenues the first year."

"Gross gaming revenue?" Bobby asked uncertainly.

"It's how much players bet, lose, and leave behind in a casino," Grimaldi explained. "In other words, it's simply a more refined term for total customer losses," he added with a hint of a smile. Revenue from things like food and beverage, lodging, entertainment, and retail would be extra."

Bobby looked out and studied the antenna atop the Empire State Building, as though he had to think about the proposal. It was almost surreal, sitting high above midtown Manhattan and listening to astronomical numbers like these.

Bobby tried to control his breathing. "Well," he said, looking back at Grimaldi, "that's an interestin' offer, but obviously we'd have to get to know more about you, too."

"Of course," Grimaldi said reassuringly, and picked up a folder that he handed to his guest. "Hopefully this material will be a good start."

Bobby glanced through the file but decided there was no point in beating around the bush.

"So if our tribe were interested in workin' with you, Jim, how would we proceed?"

"Why don't we do this," Grimaldi said. "I'd like to come up to Sheffield with my colleague next week to see the reservation and meet some of your people. Then we can talk some more."

"Uh, I'm afraid I'm gonna be away most of next week," Bobby lied, scrambling to find an excuse to keep Grimaldi from coming up quite so soon, but not wanting to risk putting him off too long. "But I'd be happy to have you up the week after."

"Fine," Grimaldi said, checking his calendar. "How about May first?"

They shook hands on it.

10

~

Clearing the Way

April 19–May 1, 1991

As pumped as Bobby was when he left Grimaldi's office, he had no illusions about his ability to do the deal unless he could win Louis over or at least neutralize him. And now he had only eleven days to do it. It was all enormously frustrating. Here he was on the verge of the biggest score imaginable, and he was being blocked by an old man living in a pathetic little trailer on a decrepit Indian reservation.

Bobby considered trying to organize the tribe's descendants without Louis's cooperation, but he dismissed the idea because it would clearly create exactly the kind of division and controversy Grimaldi wanted to avoid. In fact, if Bobby couldn't work something out with Louis, he wouldn't even be able to show Grimaldi the reservation because Louis would chase them off, and Bobby'd never see Grimaldi again.

Furthermore, there was no way he was ever going to get Mavis to help him recruit other descendants to do something either of the old men opposed. She seemed so fragile after her bout with Louis that Bobby was even reluctant to ask her to talk to him again. If Bobby put too much pressure on her right now, he worried he might lose her altogether. And that'd be a disaster, because she was the linchpin in the entire enterprise.

Bobby consequently decided early Sunday morning, April 21, to take the bull by the horns—go up to the reservation himself, try to talk some sense into Louis, and hopefully solidify his relationship with Ray at the same time.

Bobby shaved, stopped at a convenience store to pick up several boxes of tea as a kind of peace offering, and got to the reservation just after 9:00. He encountered only a couple of cars on Cedar Road, and there was no one in sight as he turned onto the dirt road leading up to the meadow. The road felt even worse in his pickup truck than it had in Mavis's car, and he attempted to steer around each pothole in order to avoid breaking an axle. If he could ever get his hands on the reservation and some money, he swore, the first thing he was going to do was fix the goddamned road.

It was a pleasant morning, and Louis was standing in the doorway when Bobby pulled up and stopped in front of his trailer. The old man had presumably heard the truck coming but had never seen it before and had no idea who was intruding on his privacy.

The moment Bobby got out of the truck, however, Louis's face flushed. He asked angrily what Bobby was doing there.

"I just wanted to bring you a little somethin' to thank you for your hospitality the other day," Bobby said, holding up a plastic bag containing the tea. "And I was hopin' you and I and Ray might be able to talk a little more."

"Ray's down at the lake," Louis said curtly, "and I told Mavis to tell you to stay off the reservation. I have no interest in your damn casino. Now get out before I get my gun!"

"I just want to talk for a few minutes," Bobby protested, taking an initial step toward the trailer.

"I warned you," Louis said and started back inside, limping noticeably on his bad ankle.

Bobby quickly followed him into the trailer.

Just as Bobby came through the door he saw Louis pull a .22 rifle out of a closet in the kitchen and start to aim it at him. Bobby instinctively grabbed the rifle and yanked it out of Louis's hands, sending the old man crashing against the sink in the process.

Bobby tried to help Louis up, but he seemed to be unconscious. He knelt down and checked his pulse and heart. Both seemed okay, but Louis had a nasty cut on his temple, and Bobby assumed he must have a concussion.

Jesus, Bobby thought, he couldn't believe it. The damn fool had come at him with a gun, and now everything was in ruins. Plus Bobby could very easily wind up in jail.

Bobby fought off a momentary surge of panic, then steadied himself and went to the door of the trailer and looked out. There was no sign of Ray. He went back to check on Louis. He still wasn't moving.

As Bobby's eyes fell on the stove, the idea came to him in an instant. He had watched Louis make tea, and it had occurred to Bobby then how dangerous the old gas stoves were since the gas jets worked even if the pilot lights were out.

He didn't hesitate. He wiped down the gun with his handkerchief and put it back in the closet, then made sure that all the trailer's windows were closed and that the door closed snuggly. He found two candles in holders and placed them on the kitchen table. He lit the candles, blew out the stove's two pilot lights, turned both burners on, and set them to high. After taking a quick last look at Louis, he exited the trailer.

He looked around again to make sure Ray wasn't returning, then got in his pickup and drove halfway down the dirt road, where he stopped, turned off the engine, and cranked down his window to listen. The wait seemed interminable. He figured it could take as much as a half hour for the propane gas to build up to the point where the candles would ignite it, and in the meantime anything could happen. Louis might regain consciousness, Ray might return, or the gas might leak from the trailer and never explode.

As it turned out, it took less than twenty minutes. The explosion shattered the morning silence, jolting Bobby and sending flights of startled birds into the air. Bobby immediately turned the ignition, threw the truck into gear, and drove as fast as he dared down the remainder of the rutted road. The explosion was so loud he was certain it must have demolished the entire trailer.

Bobby saw no traffic when he reached Cedar Road, and he headed south toward the state highway. He kept checking his rearview mirror, but on the whole he was amazed at how calm he was. You do what you have to do, he kept telling himself. Besides, Louis had brought it on himself.

Now he simply had to be sure nobody had seen him.

～

Mavis called Bobby Sunday evening with the terrible news. Louis Jobert had been killed that morning in a gas explosion that destroyed his trailer. People over at Deer Run had heard the explosion and reported it to the state police, who investigated and called her a little after two. She had gone up to the reservation immediately, but the trailer was a mangled wreck; some pieces had been thrown a hundred feet from the site.

"Oh, Bobby, it was the most horrible thing I've ever seen. They wouldn't even let me look at Louis because they said he was so torn apart," Mavis said, bursting into tears.

"I'm so sorry," Bobby said, trying to console her. "I know how much you liked him. Is Ray all right?"

"Yes, thank God," Mavis said. "He was down at the lake when he heard the explosion and came up as fast as he could, but there was simply nothing he could do. He was wandering around in a daze when the first trooper got there, and it apparently took several hours before they could get him to identify what was left of Louis's body. He was a little better when I got there, but he's absolutely devastated, and I'm not sure how long he can hang on without Louis."

"Where are you and Ray now?" Bobby asked.

"He's alone in his trailer, and I've just come back to the house to get some things so I can go back up there and stay with him tonight. I tried to get him to come here, but he refused, so I'm going there."

"Would you like me to go with you?" Bobby offered.

"No, no, I'll be all right. It's just that it's such a tragedy for both of them," she said, and began crying again.

Bobby let her collect herself, then asked if they had any idea how it happened.

"The fire marshal said it was the old gas stove," Mavis replied, regaining some of her composure. "They think Louis may have been asleep, and the stove somehow leaked gas that one of pilot lights set off. But they don't really know."

Mavis paused for a moment as though there were something else she wanted to say.

Bobby waited, his antennae searching for any hint that she might be suspicious.

"Bobby," she finally said, "I know you were disappointed with Louis, but you've got to forgive him and come to the funeral with me. We're going to bury him on the reservation Wednesday morning, and other than his sister, he has no family."

"Of course I'll go to the funeral," Bobby replied. "I know how close you were to Louis, and I want to do anythin' I can to support the tribe."

⌣

Bobby was enormously relieved by his conversation with Mavis, and he felt even better when he read the brief accounts of the explosion in the local papers Monday morning.

The stories, virtually identical, stated that an eighty-eight-year-old man living on the Northern Pequot Reservation in Sheffield had been killed Sunday when an explosion evidently caused by a defective gas stove ripped through his house trailer. The stories identified the victim as Louis F. Jobert, one of the last two remaining residents of the reservation, but gave no additional information other than the name of his surviving sister. There was obviously very little interest in an old man dying in a weekend accident on an obscure Indian reservation.

The next thing Bobby had to do was to inform Grimaldi about the accident and get him to delay his visit for a couple of weeks. He wasn't looking forward to the call, but he desperately needed to buy time, and he certainly didn't want Grimaldi to hear about Louis on his own and get nervous. The key to everything now was to get Ray to back the casino, and the key to Ray was Mavis. But Bobby obviously wasn't going to be able to broach the subject with either of them until after the funeral.

Bobby put in the call to Grimaldi just after 4:00.

"You hear the news?" Grimaldi asked as soon as he came on the phone.

"Which news?" Bobby responded, thinking momentarily that Grimaldi must have heard about Louis's accident.

"The Supreme Court announcement. We just got the word from Washington. I thought that's why you were calling."

"What happened?" Bobby asked.

"The Court declined to hear Connecticut's appeal of the Mashantucket casino case. It completely removes the last obstacle to Indian casinos in the state."

"That's fantastic," Bobby said.

"Yeah, it's a great thing for all your tribes up there. As we discussed in New York, this should really get things moving in Connecticut. We think the Mashantuckets should be able to open within a year, and the Mohegans shouldn't be more than three years behind.

"It also puts some pressure on us to decide whether we're going to work together," Grimaldi continued, "so the sooner we can make that decision the better. We're still on for May first, right?"

"Well, that's actually why I called," Bobby said. "I'm afraid we had some sad news on Sunday. Louis Jobert, one of our two elders, was killed in a propane gas explosion up on the reservation, and it's really shattered the community."

"How'd it happen?" Grimaldi asked, the concern immediately evident in his voice.

"The fire marshal says it was apparently a defective gas stove. The explosion destroyed his entire house trailer."

"I'm very sorry," Grimaldi said, "but what are you saying? You want to postpone the meeting?"

"I'm afraid we're gonna have to," Bobby answered, "just for two or three weeks. We're all pretty shaken up, and the community's gonna need a little time to recover."

"Well, I can certainly appreciate that," Grimaldi said sympathetically. "But I have to ask if you think this could in any way affect your efforts to rebuild the tribe and pursue our potential project."

"Absolutely not," Bobby replied stoically. "It just strengthens my determination to move forward, and I know that's gonna be the effect on everybody."

"Good," Grimaldi said, and they proceeded to talk about dates.

As Bobby put down the phone, he breathed another sigh of relief. The call had gone better than he could have hoped.

⤚

Thursday morning was cool and overcast as the tiny funeral cortege, consisting of three cars, a hearse, and Bobby Kingman's pickup truck, made its way across the meadow on the Northern Pequot Reservation and came to a halt at the old burial ground. The driver of the hearse and his helper got out and opened the back doors to their vehicle, while Bobby and six others gathered around the minister from the Sheffield Baptist Church and awaited directions. In addition to Mavis and her daughter, Leigh, the group included Ray, Louis's sister, Verna, and two women who looked to be in their seventies who came with Verna in Leigh's car. According to Mavis, the two women were the other members of the sewing society and direct descendants of Rachel Amos.

The two funeral home employees slid the simple pine coffin from the back of the hearse, and Bobby and Ray came over to help carry it into the cemetery, where they laid it gently beside a freshly dug grave. The entire group then stood silently as the minister led them in prayer and conducted a brief service, speaking warmly of Louis's noble heritage and the faith that had sustained him. Occasional gusts of wind whipped little swirls of leaves around the gravestones as the minister delivered his eulogy, and at one point Bobby reached out and steadied Ray out of concern he might collapse. In five minutes, the whole thing was over, and Bobby and the minister helped lower the casket into the ground.

Bobby was disappointed that Mavis and Leigh hadn't been able to get a few more people to show up, but following the service he made a point of talking briefly with Verna and both of his newly discovered relatives, and he lingered with Mavis and Ray for a moment after everyone else had gone. Mavis finally helped Ray into her car, then stood talking with Bobby before getting in herself.

"Ray's agreed to stay at my house for the next few nights as long as I bring him back here by Saturday," she said, "so we're going to stop at the trailer and pick up a few of his things. Maybe you could come over and have supper with us Friday night if you're free."

"Definitely," Bobby said, giving her a warm smile. "Anythin' I can bring?"

"Just yourself," she answered, and then hugged him and began to cry. "Thank you, Bobby," she said through her tears. "Thank you for forgiving Louis, and thank you for coming today. You have no idea how much it means to me."

Bobby drove back through the meadow behind Mavis but kept going when she stopped off at Ray's trailer. He slowed down just long enough to glance at the wreckage of Louis's trailer, recalling the tension of waiting halfway down the road to hear if the candles and propane would do their job. Well, he hadn't needed to worry. Except for the undercarriage there was almost nothing left. A moment later he saw a dump truck enter the meadow from the dirt road. It was the gravediggers coming back to fill in Louis's grave.

⤙

Bobby decided he'd wait until after the weekend before bringing up the casino with Mavis again, but after that he intended to move as quickly as possible to reorganize and expand the tribe. His first priority was to get his aunt firmly on board and then to recruit Ray. He'd have to consult with Mavis, but the next logical step after that would be to get the two other members of the sewing society together in order to pitch them on his vision. Once he had a core group, he felt certain the lure of casino profits would attract as many other descendants as he needed to round out the tribe.

Bobby accomplished step one in an emotional meeting with Mavis on Tuesday, April 30. She was willing, she finally said, to do whatever Bobby thought best for the reservation and the tribe, and they agreed to go up to the reservation to see Ray together the following afternoon.

Before they could go, however, the unthinkable happened.

⤙

Virtually every politician in Connecticut had indicated a willingness to abide by the Supreme Court's decision on the Mashantucket casino, and the Court's refusal to hear Connecticut's last-ditch appeal was regarded by practically everyone as having settled the matter once and for all.

On the very day Bobby was meeting with Mavis, however, Connecticut's new governor, Lowell Weicker, suddenly launched an all-out campaign to block the Mashantucket casino, charging it would attract organized crime, prostitution, and drunk driving.

"Casino Plan Threatened by Weicker," the lead headline in *The Day* declared the next morning.

Weicker, the paper reported, had asked the legislature to pass an emergency bill repealing the "Las Vegas Nights" law and thereby "closing the casino door to both charitable groups and the Indians. The Governor said he was certain "nobody ever contemplated that Las Vegas Nights were an invitation to casino gambling."

Bobby had no idea what Weicker's chances were of getting the legislature to go along, but he could see the situation was serious because the Mashantuckets went ballistic. Their lawyer called Weicker's action "outrageous," while tribal chairman Skip Hayward accused the Governor of trying to break a treaty just as the white man had broken hundreds of other treaties with the Indians down through the ages.

The bottom line appeared to be that there was now going to be a pitched battle in the state legislature, and if the Governor won, both Bobby and the Mashantuckets could presumably kiss any hope of a casino good-bye.

Bobby's first reaction was that he was jinxed. No matter what he did, things seemed to turn against him. This time, however, he not only stood to lose the opportunity of a lifetime, but if the casino went down, he would have killed a man for nothing.

~

II

Firestorm

May 1–14, 1991

Governor Weicker's proposal to repeal the state's Las Vegas Nights law was the first hopeful news Josh had heard about the casino in a year, and he called Brad Merriweather as soon as the story broke to get Brad's take on the Governor's chances.

It was too early to tell, Brad said, but why didn't Josh stop in Saturday morning, when he should have a better fix on things.

This time, Brad was on the phone in his study when Josh arrived, and Janet Merriweather invited Josh to have a cup of coffee with her in the kitchen while he waited for Brad.

"He's been talking with some of his old colleagues from the House all morning about the casino," Janet said, "and now he's on the phone with somebody from the Governor's office. I haven't seen him so involved in an issue since he left the legislature."

Brad finally came into the kitchen shaking his head. "I might as well be back at the Capitol," he said. "I've spent more time this week on politics than on my practice."

"Don't let him fool you, Josh," Janet said. "He loves it."

Brad smiled and went over to the counter to pour a cup of coffee. "In small doses, sweetheart. In small doses."

Janet winked at Josh. "I think I've heard that before," she said, and then excused herself to go shopping with their eleven-year-old daughter.

Brad came back to the kitchen table and sat down opposite Josh.

"The Governor's proposal has created an absolute firestorm," he said as he eased himself into his chair. "The State Senate's scheduled to vote on repeal in ten days, and if the Senate approves it, it'll go to the House a few days later. I've agreed to help line up some votes for the Governor, but I've got to say this looks like it's gonna be even tougher than I thought."

Josh frowned. "Are you saying the Governor might not be able to pull it off?"

"Right now, I'd say it's fifty-fifty at best."

"But why?" Josh asked. "I'd have thought that with the Governor coming out swinging like this, he'd win in a walk."

"There's no question he's rallying the anti-casino side," Brad said, "but he's coming in awfully late. The Mashantuckets are almost at the finish line, and besides that, you've got to remember that Weicker's a third-party governor who just whipped both the major parties in an election. Neither the Democrats nor the Republicans have any love for him or any incentive to go out of their way to help him."

"Okay, I can understand all that, but what about the big picture—opening the flood gates to casino gambling? I mean, isn't that what this is all about?"

"The problem," Brad replied, "is that you and I see the Governor as being on the side of the angels on the casino, but the Mashantuckets are positioning themselves the same way. They're promising to create thousands of new jobs, pump millions of dollars into the economy, and take people off the welfare rolls. At the same time, they're saying they're going to build their little casino off in the woods where it won't bother anybody and are going to put in every possible safeguard to minimize any problems."

"The job part kills me," Josh said. "Here's Connecticut with its history of engineering and technology, and these people want to train thousands of croupiers and cocktail waitresses. I mean, where's this country headed? Who's going to be left to invent and build anything of real value?"

"Josh, I can't argue with you, but right now a job's a job. Remember, we're going into the second year of a recession. There are thousands of people in this state who don't have jobs, and there are thousands more worried about theirs."

Josh started to react, but Brad kept going.

"And I'm afraid the Mashantuckets have two more things going for them as well."

"Just two?" Josh interjected.

Brad ignored the sarcasm. "And, unfortunately, they're the kind of emotional issues that can swing a vote like this," he continued.

"And they are?" Josh asked, unable to imagine what could be left.

"Sympathy and guilt," Brad said. "The feeling that the state's screwed the Indians royally over the years and is now trying to do it again."

Brad took a sip of coffee.

"You see the Kevin Costner movie *Dances with Wolves* by any chance?" he asked.

"Sure. It won the Oscar this year. Half the state must have seen it."

"Well, that's part of the problem," Brad said. "Everybody and his brother have just been watching white soldiers beat the shit out of a bunch of Indians. Now here comes this poor little tribe from southeastern Connecticut that just wants to do what Congress says they have a right to do and open a little gaming parlor up on their reservation. But just as these poor Indians finally get to the point where they're ready to build it, *wham!* The state comes in and breaks another white man's promise by reneging on the compact."

"Christ, Brad, you yourself told me that based on the BIA's rules, it's questionable whether the present-day Mashantuckets even qualify as a tribe."

"True, but most people know next to nothing about the current Mashantuckets. The important thing," Brad said, "is that the legislature thinks they're a continuation of the same tribe the state virtually wiped out hundreds of years ago, and there're going to be a lot of legislators who feel the state owes them one."

At that point, the phone rang, and Brad got up to answer the kitchen extension. It sounded to Josh as though it were another one of Brad's political friends calling about the vote. Brad finally said he'd call him back and returned to the table.

"Just to show you how complex this thing's getting," Brad said, "that was a state rep from Danbury I served with in the House. He says the Mashantuckets are not only trying to milk the sympathy and guilt angle, but now they're accusing the anti-casino people of racism."

"You mean against Indians?" Josh asked, just wanting to make sure he wasn't missing something.

"No," Brad said, "against blacks."

"Blacks?" Josh blurted. "I thought Hayward and his family were white!"

"Hayward and his closest relatives are white," Brad said, "but there's evidently another side of the family that's predominantly African American, and people from that side are increasingly joining the tribe."

"I didn't know that," Josh said.

"There's no reason you would know it," Brad replied, "and there's no reason why most of the legislators would, either. Except that the tribe and their lobbyists are trying to make an issue out of it by claiming that part of the opposition to the casino is nothing but prejudice against blacks. The rep who just called says they're already making inroads with the Black Caucus in the legislature, and they hit him with the argument last night."

"So you mean to tell me that this whole casino's being spearheaded by a white guy who's created a new Indian tribe and is trying to win votes by claiming the state's prejudiced against blacks? I don't believe this," Josh said. "This story gets more incredible all the time."

"And more complicated," Brad added, "which is what makes the vote so hard to predict."

"Actually," Josh countered, "given everything you say the tribe has going for it, I'm wondering why you think the governor has even a fifty-fifty shot at getting the legislature to back him?"

"Because I think that if we can get the public to understand what's at stake here, we can put enough pressure on the legislature to win," Brad replied. "The biggest problem we're facing is that the casino's been treated almost exclusively as a legal issue up to now, and there's very little time to get people riled up and turn it into a political one.

"In fact," Brad added, "that's one of the things I wanted to talk to you about. Our state rep, Reid Dowling, is leaning to the Mashantuckets, and I thought that since Sharon campaigned for him she'd be a good person to try to push him back our way."

"That son of a bitch!" Josh exploded. "He lives in this town, and you're telling me he's leaning toward the casino?"

"Wait a minute," Brad said, trying to clam Josh down. "This actually presents an opportunity. If the Senate votes for repeal, it'll set up a final battle in the House, and right now the pro-casino people are expecting Dowling to vote with them. So if we can switch Dowling, it'll be like picking up two votes. And two votes could conceivably swing this thing."

"I absolutely can't believe Dowling's that stupid," Josh said, still furious.

"Do you know him personally?" Brad asked.

"Yeah, I know him. I even voted for him."

"I thought you were a Republican?" Brad said.

"I am, but the guy had this great spiel about preserving the area's rural character, and I couldn't go against Sharon. I even gave him money."

"That makes it even better," Brad said.

"What do you mean?" Josh asked.

"My original thought was that Sharon should talk to him, but it would actually be better if you both did."

"Why? Sharon's the politician, not me."

"Because the two of you are the perfect team. Sharon's on the Democratic Town Committee and campaigned for Dowling, and you're a prominent Republican businessman who supported him."

Josh looked skeptical.

"Remember," Brad said, "this is Dowling's first term, and he's a Democrat in a normally Republican district, so he needs every vote he can get. You may not be able to persuade him, but I guarantee he's going to listen to what the two of you have to say."

"Do you know why he's leaning toward the casino?" Josh asked, genuinely puzzled.

"He's telling friends he thinks the casino could help jump-start the region's economy by creating jobs and boosting tourism," Brad replied. "But as you probably know, he owns a travel agency in New London, and the cynics are saying his real interest is boosting his own business."

"Well, he can go back to his travel agency full-time if he votes for the Mashantuckets," Josh said, "because he'll never get reelected in this district. Not in a million years. The district's nothing but small towns, and the last thing any of them want to see is a casino anywhere near here."

"That's presumably why he's holding back on giving the Mashantuckets a final commitment," Brad said. "What he's obviously hoping is that the Senate votes against repeal and the issue never gets to the House. That way, he gets the casino, but he never has to vote on it."

"So why not wait until we see how the Senate votes before approaching him?" Josh asked.

"Because the Senate and House votes could come so close together we might not have time to get to him. Besides, if he's really still on the fence, it's important you and Sharon talk to him before he makes up his mind."

Josh thought about that for a moment.

"Okay," he finally said, "how do you suggest we do this?"

"It's easy," Brad said. "Just have Sharon pick up the phone and tell him the two of you'd like him to drop by the house to talk about the casino. He won't like the subject, but he'll come. And when he gets there, simply tell him you're interested in his views and how he plans to vote."

"You think he's going to come right out and tell us how he's going to vote?"

"No," Brad replied. "But that's fine. All you want to do is deliver your message—which should be that the casino is a bedrock issue for you and Sharon, and neither of you could ever support anyone who voted for it.

"Remember, you've got to make it absolutely clear to him that there's no compromise on this. Dowling's main interest right now is in gauging the political cost of voting for the casino, and the important thing is that he leaves understanding he's going to lose you and others like you if he supports it."

⌐⌐

Sharon was livid when she heard about Reid Dowling. She was surprised the casino had gotten as far as it had, but once the Governor came up with a plan for stopping it, she assumed the legislature would rush to support him and Dowling would be one of those in the lead. Suddenly both assumptions were out the window. If somebody like Dowling was inclined to vote for the casino, she reasoned, then the Governor's proposal had to be in trouble and she clearly didn't understand the state as well as she thought she did.

What was so dismaying was that she thought she knew Dowling.

He was young and energetic, had a nice family, and seemed so right for the town and for eastern Connecticut. He'd won a seat on the town's Board of Finance in 1989, and had then volunteered last year to run against a crusty old Republican state rep who was so entrenched he hardly bothered to campaign. No one thought Dowling had a prayer, but he'd campaigned tirelessly and pulled off one of the biggest upsets in the state in the 1990 elections.

Sharon had been especially impressed by Dowling's concern for protecting eastern Connecticut's open spaces and preserving its small towns and their way of life. She'd heard him give the same speech over and over about how the state had to come up with policies to slow urban sprawl and fund farm preservation, and she had watched him gradually win over people as he went door to door throughout Sheffield.

Sharon consequently took on the task of confronting Dowling as a personal challenge, calling him at home Sunday afternoon, May 5, and asking him to stop in at the farm Tuesday evening. She then began reading through the file on casino gambling Brad had prepared, and when she finished she dug out one of Dowling's 4-by-8-inch campaign cards.

The card had a picture of Dowling on the front along with a headline and copy that read:

DOWLING

FOR

STATE REPRESENTATIVE

Reid Dowling will work hard to protect
our environment and preserve the character
and values of our small towns and villages.

Below that was a list of several Dowling proposals, and the back gave his biography and the address of the polling places in each of the district's five towns.

Sharon turned the card over again and studied Dowling's photograph. Thirty-six years old, with earnest blue eyes and wavy brown hair, Dowling was smiling directly into the camera. She guessed she'd handed out a couple thousand of the cards, and the longer she looked at his picture the angrier she got.

⌒

Reid Dowling kissed Sharon on the cheek as he came in the kitchen door and apologized for being late. He was sorry, he said, but things were particularly hectic right now between the legislature and his business and he'd been running behind all day.

"Same old Reid," Sharon said with a smile, "always trying to fit in one more appointment. Well, you don't have to apologize to me," she assured him, and went over to the counter, where she shooed their Labrador out of the way and took down three coffee mugs from a shelf.

The dog ambled over to Dowling.

"Beautiful dog," Dowling said. "What's its name?"

"Max."

Dowling bent down and rubbed Max's neck. "I think he likes me. Don't ya, fella."

"He likes everybody," Sharon said.

"Oh," Dowling said, with a touch of disappointment.

"You still take yours black?" she asked.

"You remember!" he beamed, straightening up and leaving Max to wonder what suddenly happened to his ardent admirer.

"How could I forget after all those coffee hours?" she replied, and placed the mugs on a tray with a small plate of cookies.

"Yeah, there were a lot of 'em, all right, but it was all those nights in people's living rooms that won it for us," Dowling said fondly. "Can I carry that?" he offered, pointing at the tray.

"No, no, just grab the plate over there by the breadboard," Sharon said breezily. "It's a turkey sandwich. I figured you'd be hungry."

"How'd you know?"

"Wild guess," she replied.

Josh and Jacob were watching television in the library when Sharon and Dowling came in, and they both immediately got up and shook hands with the state representative. Dowling made a big fuss over how much Jacob had grown, and wanted to know if he and his own seven-year-old, Michael, were still good friends. Oh, yeah, Jacob said, Michael cracked him up with his jokes, and they were on the same team in slow-pitch this year. Jacob then scooted off, and the three adults sat down around an antique maple coffee table.

Sharon and Dowling spent the first few minutes exchanging reminiscences about the campaign, and then Josh asked how he liked the job now that he'd won it.

"It's like the old saying 'Be careful what you wish for,'" Dowling said, polishing off the last bite of his sandwich. "But, seriously, I love the challenge. And I want to thank you both again for all your help. I never would've made it if it weren't for friends like you—and especially you, Sharon," he said warmly. "You were fantastic."

"It's easy to support somebody you believe in," Sharon responded.

"That's true," Josh said. "You really sold me with that talk you gave at the library on the area's future."

"And that's why I called," Sharon said with a slightly troubled frown. "We're concerned about the casino, Reid, and were hoping you could give us some insight into how the vote's likely to go."

Josh watched Dowling carefully and was impressed that he didn't miss a beat.

"Well, right now it looks like the vote's gonna be very close in the Senate, and if the bill makes it to the House, I think it'll be very close there, too. In fact, if it does make it to the House, I have to tell you honestly that I haven't decided yet myself how to vote."

"Really?" Sharon said. "I'm surprised. I'd have thought you'd be the last one to want to see a casino anywhere near here."

Dowling nodded. "True, but I'm afraid this whole casino issue's a lot more complex than it might look. I mean, even the vote's complicated in that it's not a straight up or down vote on the casino itself, but a vote on whether to repeal the Las Vegas Nights law. Churches and charities raise a lot of money from Las Vegas Nights, so just for starters, you have to ask whether it's worth penalizing them in order to block the casino."

"How do you feel about the casino itself?" Josh asked.

"Well, the big negative, obviously, is that it'll expand gambling in the state," Dowling replied. "The Republicans got us into gambling in the early seventies, and now we've got the lottery, dog tracks, jai alai, off-track-betting parlors, and high-stakes bingo, and I'm concerned about adding a casino to the mix. Casinos can be a lot of fun, but I know there are some people who can't handle them, and that creates problems for everyone from the gamblers and their families to the social agencies that have to help pick up the pieces.

"Overall, though," he continued, "I doubt the type of thing the Mashan-tuckets are planning would have that much of a negative impact. The casino they're proposing is really pretty modest, and its potential is limited because they can't have slot machines. And slots are the big draw."

"You don't think the state might permit slots once the casino's up and running?" Josh asked.

"Not a chance," Dowling said dismissively. "The Las Vegas Nights law prohibits them, and half the legislature's against the casino now even without slots."

"What about crime?" Josh asked.

"It's a concern," Dowling acknowledged, "but I don't think it's as big a problem as the Governor's trying to make it. If Connecticut had a history of organized crime it'd be one thing, but we don't, and the Mashantuckets have agreed to have the state police stationed at the casino and to do what-ever else it takes to insure a clean operation. So I really think the Governor's exaggerating the issue and in the process ignoring a lot of others."

"For instance?" Sharon inquired.

"Well, the big one's obviously jobs. Connecticut's in a recession, and de-fense jobs are disappearing. The casino could create two thousand new jobs, pump up the construction trades, and spur tourism, which could bring mil-lions of dollars into the state.

"But there are major legal and fairness issues as well," Dowling continued. "The courts have ruled that the tribe has the right to open a casino based on the Las Vegas Nights law, and the state's already negotiated a gambling com-pact with the tribe. So the first question is whether repealing the Las Vegas Nights law would actually stop the casino or, as a lot of experts believe, would come too late to nullify the courts' decision. And even if repeal could stop the casino, the second question is whether it'd be fair for the state to back out of a deal it's already negotiated—especially with a tribe it tried to wipe out hundreds of years ago."

Dowling paused and reached for a cookie. "So I think you can see this isn't going to be an easy vote," he added, trying to coax as much sympathy as possible for his predicament.

Sharon gave him a moment to bite into his cookie, but otherwise showed no intention of letting up.

"How about the environmental impact?" she pressed.

Dowling put the rest of the cookie down and drank the remaining two swallows of his coffee.

"Well, the biggest problem would obviously be traffic," he said, "and the only way to solve that is with better roads and mass transit. But the most important thing, in my opinion, is that gaming and entertainment are clean industries, and they're a heck of a lot better for the environment than smokestacks and nuclear power plants, which we certainly have our share of."

"What about other tribes building casinos?" Josh asked. "If the Mashantuckets get one, the papers say the Mohegans could be next."

"I doubt the Mohegans will ever build a casino," Dowling responded. "They've had a recognition application in for fourteen years, and it's never gone anywhere. And besides, even if the Mohegans or any other local tribe ever got recognized, I think the Mashantuckets would have pretty much cornered the casino market by then. I mean, how many casinos could eastern Connecticut support?"

"So it sounds like you really are torn," Sharon ventured.

"I really am," Dowling said, grimacing to underline his dilemma. "How do you both see it?"

Josh began to answer, but Sharon broke in.

"Excuse me, honey, let me give it a try," she said, all traces of her earlier smile now gone.

"Reid," she began, "you and I are friends, and it's important we be up front with each other. Josh and I both understand that casinos have their place, but we think it'd be a huge mistake to bring them into Connecticut. And spare me the BS about casino gambling being a clean industry. You know it spews out its own toxic waste just as smokestacks spew out theirs."

Dowling started to respond, but Sharon cut him off.

"We also think it's naive to believe that the Mashantuckets won't expand their casino way beyond what they're talking about now, that other tribes won't build casinos, and that the big non-Indian casino developers won't get in on the act.

"Furthermore," Sharon declared, "I don't buy the economic arguments. It's true the casino will create jobs, but those jobs will come from other people's losses.

"And one more thing," she added, clearly now on a roll. "It may be true that the state can't ultimately block the casino by repealing the Las Vegas Nights law, but you of all people have an obligation to at least go down fighting."

"Sharon," Dowling finally broke in, "I don't necessarily like gambling any better than you do. But it's already here. It's all around us. The state takes in over a hundred million dollars a year from it. Don't you think it's a little hypocritical for the state to approve gambling as long as the money goes to the government, but to argue it's bad for people if the proceeds go to an Indian tribe?"

"You talk about hypocrisy!" Sharon flared. "Nobody's more hypocritical than the casino industry. They don't even want to use the word 'gambling.' Instead, they call it 'gaming,' as though it's some kind of . . . of . . . innocent Edwardian dalliance rather than a scheme to fleece as many people as possible."

Sharon feigned a laugh. "What a joke," she said derisively. "And the biggest joke of all is the way the casinos portray themselves as family entertainment centers. Some family entertainment! The kids get dumped in the nursery while mommy and daddy go off and blow the mortgage money."

Sharon fixed Dowling with a withering stare.

"And then you talk about being fair to the Mashantuckets! Well, how fair is it to give them a license to do what the rest of us would be put in jail for? How about being fair to the rest of us and protecting the state from this whole disgusting scam?"

Sharon stopped to catch her breath.

"Sharon," Dowling said, "believe me, this is more complicated than. . . ."

But Sharon interrupted him again.

"Reid," she said, "Josh and I came back to eastern Connecticut with our kids for a reason. We came back because of the quality of life here. I didn't work my tail off for you because I'm on the town committee. I supported you because I believed you were sincere about what you said in your campaign. But if we can't agree on something as basic as this, then I was obviously dead wrong."

Sharon paused, then continued in a softer tone.

"We need your help on this, Reid. Josh and I both think you could have a bright political future. But I have to tell you there's no way on God's earth we could ever support you again if you desert us now."

Dowling took a deep breath and stared down at the remainder of his half-eaten cookie.

"Okay, I get the message," he said somberly. "Let me finish thinking this thing through and see where I come out. All I can say is that if the bill does come to the House, I promise I'll think very hard about how you both feel. The last thing I want is to lose either one of you."

Sharon and Josh thanked Dowling for coming and walked him to the door.

"What do you think?" Sharon asked as they watched his car leave the courtyard.

"I think you just ruined your friend's evening," Josh replied, looking at his wife as though he'd just seen a side of her he'd never witnessed before. "I've never seen you that wound up."

"I'm sorry," Sharon said. "I didn't mean to take over, but ... he was so smooth. I just couldn't let him get away with it."

"Sorry? You were terrific! All I could think the whole time you were going at him was that you should be the one up in Hartford instead of him."

"No, seriously," Sharon insisted. "What do you think he's going to do?"

"Obviously he's leaning toward the casino," Josh said. "But I know you shook him up. I could see it in his face. He was absolutely stunned."

⌒

Josh and Sharon telephoned Brad that night to give him a blow-by-blow account of the meeting with Dowling.

"Perfect," Brad said, chuckling over Dowling's quandary. "Dowling must've thought he'd been hit by a freight train. Which is exactly what we want ... give him something more to think about before he makes his decision."

11:20 a.m. Thursday, May 9

Brad called Josh at the office late Thursday morning to say he had just heard the Senate had begun debate on the repeal bill and could vote as early as noon. The lobbying on both sides, he said, was fierce, but the Governor had managed to switch a key Republican vote that morning.

"Who switched?" Josh asked.

"Ted Lovegrove from Fairfield. He's no fan of Weicker, but the Governor's arguments about money laundering and crime apparently swayed him."

"So how does it stack up now?" Josh asked.

"Looks like fifteen to fifteen, with six undecided," Brad said. "So stay tuned. I'll call you as soon as I know the result."

12:55 p.m. Thursday, May 9

Brad called again just before 1:00. The Governor had won. The Senate had voted to repeal the Las Vegas Nights law by one vote, eighteen to seventeen, with one senator absent. The bill now would go to the one-hundred-fifty-one-member House. Hopefully, the tide had turned.

Friday morning, May 10

The vote was front-page news in all the local papers the next morning. "Senate Passes Ban on Vegas Nights—Close Vote Gives Weicker Weapon Against Casinos," the *Hartford Courant* proclaimed.

The opposing sides had clashed on a wide range of issues, according to the accounts, but concerns that casinos could seriously damage the state ultimately won out. If Connecticut wasn't careful, Senator James Fleming warned his colleagues, the state could become "the Atlantic City of New England."

9:30 a.m. Saturday, May 11

Brad called Josh and Sharon on Saturday morning to fill them in on the aftermath of the Senate vote. He said the House vote could come as early as Tuesday, but the Mashantuckets were concerned the momentum was now against them and were trying to get a delay. The Senate vote had given the anti-casino forces a huge boost, he said, but the latest line on the House vote still had the Mashantuckets slightly ahead.

7:00 p.m. Tuesday, May 14

Brad phoned again on Tuesday evening. The Mashantuckets had managed to get a two-day delay, and the House vote was now scheduled for Thursday afternoon, May 16. If anything, the outcome now appeared more in doubt than ever, and it looked as though the deciding battle would be fought on the House floor. Since they now had enough notice, Brad suggested, why didn't he, Josh, Sharon, and Janet drive up to the Capitol together on Thursday to watch it unfold?

12

Flashback

May 15, 1991

Josh had become so wrapped up in the casino war raging in Hartford that he almost forgot about the reception he and Sharon had been invited to in honor of the 1661 Ebenezer Stowe House Wednesday evening. The Stowe House had just been completely restored by the Sheffield Historical Society, which was hosting a reception at the house followed by a presentation at the town hall entitled "Sheffield in the Seventeenth Century."

Josh hadn't been in the Stowe House for years, and he hadn't ever really taken much interest in it. He'd always tended to think of it as simply another old house like his own. Whether it was the hype surrounding the restoration or just his mood that evening, he had a very different reaction this time around.

He and Sharon took a stroll around the modest grounds before going in, and Josh found himself increasingly fascinated as he studied the house's design and construction. The ancient structure had a stern, almost fortress-like appearance, with a distinctive hewn overhang, dark, unpainted clapboard siding, small casement windows, and a reinforced oak door. The house had been built almost a hundred years before his own, and if he concentrated hard enough he could picture Ebenezer Stowe coming back from a day in the fields and bolting that heavy door against the wild beasts and Indians who still roamed the area.

As Sharon started up the front steps, Josh hung back for a moment, trying to imagine he was Ethan Williams coming to call on his neighbor, and for a fleeting second he had the sensation that he actually was Ethan waiting for Ebenezer to come to the door and invite him in.

"Come on, Josh," Sharon finally said, holding the door open and breaking his concentration. "Are you just going to stand there, or are you coming in?"

"Sorry," Josh said, snapping back to the present.

Stepping inside was literally like stepping back more than three hundred years. The house was a typical early saltbox, with two rooms both upstairs and down and a lean-to kitchen in the rear, but in this case everything had been painstakingly restored, from the original hand-hewn walls and floors to the original fireplaces, and each room had been carefully fitted with period furniture and furnishings. In each room docents dressed as seventeenth-century Puritans explained its particular treasures, from a three-hundred-fifty-year-old spinning wheel and rare corner cupboard to the original butterfly hinges that were still in use on many of the doors. The prize attraction was Ye Greate Kitchin, dominated by a massive stone fireplace and equipped with a magnificent collection of early-colonial kettles, pewter, and woodenware.

Josh and Sharon lingered in the kitchen, sipping wine and examining the exhibits, then headed upstairs to see the bedrooms, whose highlights included a feather bed and a prized early Connecticut painted blanket chest. Feather beds, one of the docents explained, were one of the few comforts a Puritan was likely to allow himself—although, she added, Ebenezer Stowe had written that he once threw one into Jepson Lake to kill the bedbugs that were tormenting him and his wife.

Just before 8:00 everyone walked over to the town hall for the presentation by the town historian, Charlotte Dodson, a pert, fiftyish community-college professor who was known for her lively lectures. Using slides of sketches, she took the audience through the founding of Sheffield, then devoted most of her talk to the period leading up to and including the great Indian uprising known as King Philip's War. Although one of the most important events in New England history, the uprising was something you rarely heard or read about, and Josh became increasingly absorbed in Mrs. Dodson's account of how it had impacted Sheffield and Connecticut.

Connecticut's settlers had pretty much relaxed after the Pequot War, she explained, and the colonists and Indians in New England had lived in peace right up through the founding of Sheffield in 1659. Tensions between the colonists and the Indians began to grow again after 1665, however, as more new towns like Sheffield were established, and the Indians lost more and more of their land and autonomy. By 1675, the Wampanoags, of Plymouth and eastern Rhode Island, had had enough, and their grand sachem, Philip, encouraged a loose coalition of New England tribes to fight back.

"Ironically," Mrs. Dodson noted, "Philip's father, Massasoit, had played a key role in helping Plymouth Colony survive and is famous for having joined the Pilgrims in the first Thanksgiving. But it quickly became clear that the son was determined to erase his father's mistake. On June twenty-fourth, Philip and his men drew first blood by killing ten colonists at Swansea, and from there the conflict escalated into the bloodiest war Americans have ever fought in terms of its casualty rate."

"My God," Sharon whispered to Josh, "I've never even heard of that war."

"Don't feel bad, half the people in Connecticut never heard of it either," he whispered back, and then refocused on Mrs. Dodson's narrative.

Connecticut reacted to the Swansea attack by sending forty soldiers to New London and Stonington to protect the area against the Narragansetts, who it was rumored were about to join the Wampanoags. The rumor initially proved false and the war spread instead across most of modern-day Massachusetts and northern Rhode Island, as well as up the coast to present-day Maine. Nevertheless, fear of a Narragansett attack remained high, and every town in eastern Connecticut went on alert, mustered their militias, and ordered that each home be locked down at night.

"Here in Sheffield," Mrs. Dodson said, "the town fathers put fifty-nine-year-old Lieutenant Ethan Williams in charge of the local militia, and assigned Williams and Ebenezer Stowe to draw up plans for the town's defense."

Josh thought of Ethan's musket hanging over the mantle, and in his mind's eye he could see his ancestor sitting in Ebenezer Stowe's kitchen poring over hand-drawn maps with several other men.

Philip's alliance concentrated its attacks against the least-defended English villages, killing and scalping colonists, burning their homes and meetinghouses, and destroying their crops and cattle. This time the Indians were equipped with muskets, giving them equal or sometimes greater firepower than the colonists as they swooped down on isolated settlements or ambushed colonial patrols. They massacred fifty-eight English at Deerfield, Massachusetts, set the heads of dead soldiers on poles along the road at Northfield, and rampaged through Springfield, just north of the Connecticut border.

After the attack on Springfield, wild rumors swept Connecticut claiming the Narragansetts were now preparing to attack southeastern Connecticut in earnest, that five thousand Indians were planning to invade Connecticut from New York, and that hostile Indians had been spotted between Hartford and Sheffield. The Connecticut colony hurriedly established night watches in all of its towns and ordered the local militias to guard workers in the fields and patrol the main roads.

Josh once again pictured Ethan, this time lying in wait along the Hartford road with a contingent of militia at midnight, guarding the town against a possible attack. He could almost feel the cold steel of the musket in Ethan's hands and see the narrow dirt road in the moonlight.

The colonial government in Hartford, Mrs. Dodson continued, mobilized more and more men, including young Jonathan Stowe and Francis Sayer from Sheffield, and recruited both Mohegans and Pequots to help crush the uprising.

Certain that the Narragansetts were finally about to join the uprising, the colonists declared war on the tribe in November. They assembled a one-thousand-man force, including three hundred Connecticut whites and a hundred fifty Connecticut Indians, and attacked more than a thousand Narragansetts in a fortified village located on a frozen swamp near present-day Kingstown, Rhode Island. The colonial force wiped out hundreds of men, women, and children in a fierce battle that became known as the Great Swamp Fight. The attack left the village in flames, but also killed or wounded more than two hundred English, including at least eighty Connecticut men. The surviving Connecticut troops limped back toward home, some freezing to death in driving snow before finding shelter in homes and meetinghouses in eastern Connecticut.

"Sheffield," Mrs. Dodson said, "briefly turned its own meetinghouse into a hospital, and the town scrambled to collect food, rum, and other provisions for the battered army."

As she spoke, she put up a slide showing a sketch of a large room with a pulpit, mattresses, and several wounded soldiers being tended to by men and women in Puritan dress.

Josh thought of a field hospital he'd visited in Vietnam, then envisioned himself at the meetinghouse on the screen, helping load a young soldier from a wagon onto a litter and carrying him inside. The soldier's left cheekbone had been shattered by a musket ball, and Josh could see the unconscious boy's pitiful face clearly as he and another man transferred him onto one of the mattresses. The sense of being at the meetinghouse lasted for only seconds but was so vivid it felt more like a flashback than something he was imagining. He forced himself to shake it off, then cast a quick glance around the lecture hall to be certain where he was. It had to be the wine, the historic old house, the memory of Vietnam, and the power of Mrs. Dodson's story.

When Josh finally refocused on the screen, he realized Mrs. Dodson had already moved on to a new slide. She was explaining how Philip had moved his winter quarters to a camp near Albany, New York, to try to recruit additional Indians and strike an alliance with the French. Instead of joining Philip, the powerful Mohawks attacked him, driving him back into New England with nothing to show for his efforts.

Despite their setbacks, Philip and his Indian allies redoubled their attacks. Most of the colonial towns along Narragansett Bay were abandoned. Providence was sacked. Refugees streamed into Boston, and one Indian raiding party made a quick strike into northern Connecticut, killing a colonist near Windsor and burning houses in Simsbury.

Fortunately for the colonists the onslaught gradually lost steam. The Indians began to run low on food and gunpowder, and as their losses mounted, their morale sagged. In the meantime, the colonists pressed their counterattacks and by the spring of 1676 had killed or captured thousands of Indians and gained the upper hand. In April they captured and executed the Narragansetts' chief, Canonchet, and in August they shot and killed Philip himself.

The killing of King Philip, Mrs. Dodson concluded, finally brought the war to an end, but the cost had proved horrific. In all, the Indian alliance destroyed or damaged more than a third of the English settlements in New England and killed or wounded probably close to two thousand colonists. Even these numbers paled against the price paid by the Native Americans.

"No one will ever know the exact numbers," Mrs. Dodson said, "but if you add the total number of Indians who died as a result of the war to those who were shipped out as slaves or left of their own volition, the war probably cost southern New England's Indians more than half their total population."

In the question-and-answer session after the lecture, someone asked Mrs. Dodson what she thought would have happened if other Indian tribes had joined the Pequots in fighting the English in 1637 instead of waiting to fight them in King Philip's War almost forty years later.

Mrs. Dodson thought there was no question the Pequots and their allies could have pushed the colonists back into the Atlantic at that earlier point, and that the colonists knew it. As it was, many colonists gave up and sailed back to England prior to 1650, and a widespread Indian war before that time could have easily led to a mass exodus of colonists and discouraged others from coming.

"I think it's impossible to understand the first colonists unless one understands that they lived with the risk of being driven out every day," she said.

"The Puritans," she added, "were enormously conflicted about the Indians. On the one hand, they viewed themselves as more virtuous and humanitarian than other Europeans, and they saw it as their responsibility to educate the Indians and convert them to Christianity. But at the same time, they viewed the Indians as unpredictable savages, and I'm still shocked when I go back and read the early texts by how brutal and uncompromising they were in their determination to eliminate the Indian threat.

"One of the deepest fears of many Puritans," she stated, "was that the wilderness might ultimately turn them into savages themselves, and one can certainly argue that at times it did."

"How different," another person asked, "do you think America would be today if the early English colonists had been driven out of New England?"

"Given the role of New England in shaping the United States," Mrs. Dodson replied, "it could have been enormous. Longer term, however, there's no reason to think it would have stopped the tide of European migration to America. It would have slowed it, presumably shifted it, and possibly changed its composition, but it certainly wouldn't have halted it. It was simply one of the great tides of history."

The last question of the evening came from Josh, who asked Mrs. Dodson if she could give them a brief history of the Northern Pequot Reservation in Sheffield.

She replied that the local reservation was an interesting topic that few people ever showed much interest in, but with all the publicity being given to the Mashantucket Pequots, she had to believe she was going to start getting more questions about it.

The Northerns, she explained, were by far the smallest of the three groups of Pequots that reassembled after the Pequot War, and one of the most remarkable aspects of their history was that the state agreed to give them a reservation despite their small size. Although the reasoning behind the state's thinking was unclear, it appeared the Northerns had won favor in Hartford by particularly distinguishing themselves in fighting for the colonists in King Philip's War, and it seemed likely that Connecticut had granted them a reservation as a reward. The reservation's population had declined rapidly after 1800, and by 1900 there were only five people living there.

"After the fatal trailer explosion there last month," Mrs. Dodson concluded, "it now looks like there may be just one."

13

⌒

Down to the Wire

May 16, 1991

The Governor's office mounted an all-out blitz against the casino as the House vote neared, lobbying some legislators four and five times and distributing a flier highlighting the problems casino gambling had brought Atlantic City.

"Since 1978," the flier stated, quoting from Ovid Demaris's *The Boardwalk Jungle*, "violent crimes have doubled, tripled, and quadrupled. Pacific Avenue, only a block away from the Boardwalk, is crawling with hookers, pimps, pickpockets, drug pushers, car strippers, and thieves. Loan sharks are having a field day, and muggers attack people in broad daylight."

The Mashantuckets denounced the flier as misleading and attacked the Governor for pandering to people's worst fears. The tribe planned to open "a modest gaming facility" that in no way compared to Atlantic City or Las Vegas, they insisted.

Despite the escalating charges and countercharges, the contest appeared dead even on the night before the vote. As House Speaker Richard Balducci told the press, it looked like a "jump ball."

What Josh found disappointing was that eastern Connecticut wasn't leading the charge against the casino. He could understand how other areas of the state might not feel particularly threatened by the casino at this point, but he was dismayed that more people in eastern Connecticut didn't recognize it as a threat to their region. Instead, they seemed to be as split on the issue as the state was as a whole.

According to Brad Merrriweather, House members from eastern Connecticut were evenly split, with four Representatives, including Reid Dowling, still on the fence. The previous Sunday, the minister at the Sheffield Congregational Church had worked the upcoming vote into his sermon, criticizing the idea of letting gambling get a further grip on Connecticut, but Sharon heard that the pastor at the Episcopal Church had spoken of the need to bring a measure of economic justice to Connecticut's long-suffering Indians. Even southeastern Connecticut's two daily newspapers were split on the issue.

Clearly, Josh thought, the casino issue was proving far more complex than he'd ever expected. As Dowling had pointed out, the vote wasn't structured as a simple yes or no vote on casino gambling. Instead, legislators were being asked to repeal a popular law in order to put up a last-minute roadblock to the casino that many thought was too little, too late. In addition, there were a multitude of other reasons to vote against repeal: being fair to the Indians, obeying the courts, creating jobs, helping churches and charities, opposing racial prejudice, and even sticking it to an arrogant third-party governor.

Josh was afraid there was another reason, too. The Connecticut he had so strongly fixed in his mind was obviously changing. He was beginning to fear that legalized gambling, let loose in the early 1970s, was working its way into the fiber of the state, and large numbers of people were simply more apathetic toward casinos than he had ever dreamed.

Attitudes about gambling, after all, were changing all across America. Once a mob-infested vice, gambling was becoming mainstream. And Connecticut, it appeared, just happened to be one of the states in the lead. Or maybe Connecticut didn't just happen to be in the lead. Maybe the state was like a long-sheltered teenager suddenly exposed to the temptations of the big city and unable to resist them.

⌇

The Merriweathers picked up Josh and Sharon at 1:00 p.m. on Thursday, May 16, for the forty-five-minute drive to Hartford. The giant sycamore in front of the Williams house had just begun leafing out, and Max raced to the end of the driveway to see everyone off.

"So, how's it look?" Josh asked hopefully as they got underway.

"Still too close to call," Brad replied, "but I'm concerned the momentum's begun to shift to the Mashantuckets."

"Why, what's happened?" Josh asked.

"It looks like the two-day delay they engineered is helping them. They're not only picking up more support from minority and liberal legislators on the race issue, but they've made additional inroads among conservative Republicans who are anti-regulation and anti-Weicker."

Josh shook his head in frustration. "Talk about strange bedfellows."

"Not only that, but this charity-fund-raising thing is really beginning to bite. At least a dozen House members have told me they've been deluged by last-minute calls and telegrams from churches, charities, and civic groups urging that the Las Vegas Nights law not be repealed."

"You don't sound very optimistic," Sharon commented.

"Sorry," Brad said, "but I don't like what I'm hearing."

"What's happening with Dowling?" Josh asked.

"At least that's one positive thing," Brad answered. "So far, it looks like he's still on the fence."

⌢

The Connecticut State Capitol overlooks Hartford's Bushnell Park, a thirty-seven-acre oasis of rolling green lawns, winding paths, and hundreds of rare and native trees just a few minutes' walk from the city's center. Built in the 1870s out of New England marble and granite, the Capitol's setting and grand Victorian Gothic style make it one of the most magnificent state-houses in America.

It was a perfect spring afternoon in Hartford, warm and sunny, and Josh studied the ornate features of the Capitol as he and Sharon and the Merriweathers climbed the gradual hill leading up to the north entrance. The gold dome was brilliant against the blue sky, and the American and Connecticut flags flew from separate poles atop the east and west wings. Josh couldn't help but feel a moment of exuberance at the splendid scene. This was what great public buildings were for—to instill a sense of pride in citizens, to create a touch of awe and respect for the government, and to make you feel the people inside knew what they were doing. He just hoped the people inside knew what they were doing today.

Before going inside, Brad stopped for a moment and pointed out some of the high-relief scenes that ran around the facade of the Capitol, the first of which depicted Captain John Mason and his Mohegan and Narragansett allies defeating the Pequots. It was one of the signal events in Connecticut's long history, and Josh couldn't help but feel a momentary rush at the thought that one of his ancestors was there.

Inside, the rotunda was teeming with people. Brad briefly left his little group in the North Lobby while he checked on the status of the House proceedings. When he came back he said he thought there was just enough time to give them a quick tour of the first floor.

They began at the model of the *Genius of Connecticut*, a winged, angelic woman who was meant to embody the spirit of the state. The original of the statue had once crowned the Capitol dome.

They paused at the model of the Civil War flagship *Hartford*, whose commander, Admiral David Farragut, issued the stirring order "Damn the torpedoes, full speed ahead."

They passed into the Hall of Flags, which displayed battle flags of Connecticut regiments from the Civil War to Korea.

They stopped at an exhibit entitled *Connecticut: The Constitution State*, which explained how the "Fundamental Orders" adopted by the state in 1639 became the first known written constitution to embody the principle of representative government.

Finally they came to the statue of Connecticut's greatest hero, Nathan Hale, the twenty-one-year-old, Yale-educated teacher who'd taught in a one-room schoolhouse not more than ten miles from the Williams farm. With the outbreak of the Revolutionary War, he'd been commissioned as a captain in the Continental Army, and in 1776 he volunteered to cross enemy lines to gather critical information on British troops and intentions. Hale was captured and hanged. Before going to the gallows he uttered the unforgettable words "I only regret that I have but one life to lose for my country."

As the little group headed up one of the grand stairways to the House visitors' gallery, Josh found it hard to believe that the main discussion in these halls over the past two days had revolved around craps, hookers, drug pushers, and pimps.

⁓

Josh and his companions entered the crowded visitors' gallery and found four seats on one of the back benches. The floor debate was just about to get underway.

"This is quite a spectacle," Sharon whispered as she looked around the ornate chamber and scanned the roughly hundred fifty legislators below.

The gallery overlooked the chamber from the front, so that visitors could look down directly into the faces of the members as they sat behind tiered rows of small desks or rose to speak. Democrats sat to the right, Republicans to the left, with the former in the majority. Electronic tally boards were mounted on the side walls, and nine massive chandeliers and a dozen matching sconces added a warm glow to the chamber's intricately carved walnut paneling.

Sharon spotted Dowling and quietly pointed him out just as a Democrat from New Haven named Stolberg stood and began to speak into a handheld microphone.

"Mr. Speaker," Representative Stolberg intoned, "it has been the policy of the state of Connecticut not to allow casino gambling."

The proposal to repeal the Las Vegas Nights law, he said, "is an effort to remain true to that commitment. It is in no way anti-Indian, but rather an attempt to stop the exploitation of all Connecticut citizens by predatory gambling interests."

Stolberg's expression hardened.

"For the gambling industry to extend itself into one casino in Connecticut and then in all likelihood into others would, ladies and gentlemen, change the nature of our state, and I ask you to look forward to see whether a Connecticut moving dramatically in that direction is the Connecticut that you want our children to grow up in."

"Stolberg," Brad explained in a stage whisper, "is the floor leader for the repeal bill. Now he's yielding to Larry Anastasia, the chairman of the Public Health and Safety Committee, who's the floor leader for the other side."

"Mr. Speaker," Representative Anastasia began, "I rise in opposition to the bill."

Anastasia hit hard at the damage repeal would do to charitable organizations, and at the fact there was no guarantee it would stop the casino, but Josh was surprised he said virtually nothing in defense of the casino or the Mashantuckets.

"So when do they march out the pro-casino arguments and start trying to hang the guilt trip on us?" Josh whispered to Brad.

"Give it a second. Here comes Kevin Rennie, one of the conservative Republicans against the bill."

"So this is Armageddon," Rennie began, "where the world ends not with a bang, but with the whirling of a roulette wheel?

"Do you believe that the destiny of our entire state, or even one part of it, hangs on our willingness to smite the Pequot Indians? In a state that allows and promotes the Daily Number, Play Four, Instant Lottery, LOTTO, off-track betting, jai alai, dog racing, and casino nights? Can anyone claim that one more addition to that list will mean the end of life as we know it, every virtue replaced by a vice?

"Is obeying a federal law really going to bring, as one list claims, mobsters, union racketeering, prostitution, AIDS, tuberculosis, and the destruction of wetlands? A revised list will undoubtedly include the return of leprosy and the extinction of the snail darter."

Laughter rippled through the hall.

The fact of the matter, Rennie continued, was that the state had foolishly refused to believe that the federal Indian Gaming Regulation Act applied to Connecticut.

Now, faced with the consequences of its own policies, he charged, the state was trying to make up for its mistakes by yanking the rug out from under the Mashantuckets, who were only trying to play by the rules the white man had set.

"Where's the fairness?" he demanded.

"In the nineteenth century, the trail of tears for the American Indian led to Oklahoma and its reservations, but today here in Connecticut it runs from the Senate to the House of Representatives, staining this building. Let it end here, and let it end today!"

The gallery erupted in applause, and Josh realized for the first time that most of the spectators in front of him had to be Mashantuckets and presumably members of other tribes.

"Do you think we've got any speeches that good?" Josh asked.

"I doubt it," Brad replied. "Kevin Costner must have written that one."

The anti-gambling forces counterattacked in full force. They assured the chamber that the Attorney General had, in fact, opined that repealing the Las Vegas Nights law would eliminate the legal basis for casino gambling in Connecticut. They argued that the vote today was not about being for or against Indians, but about whether to expand gambling to an entirely new level in Connecticut. And they warned that the casino would prey on problem gamblers, exploit low-income people, and burden the state with increased crime and social problems.

Moreover, they cautioned, the legislature shouldn't be swayed by misplaced sympathy for the Mashantuckets.

"This is not an impoverished tribe," Representative Farr declared. They already had a high-stakes bingo parlor, and "if they get this casino, their per capita income will exceed Kuwait's."

Representative after representative stood to speak as the debate progressed, and Brad checked "yes" or "no" beside each name on a small scorecard.

At the moment, Representative Rapoport was praising the Mashantuckets for intending to use the money from the casino to buy back additional acreage of their ancestral land, to build new housing, and to create health services. According to their plan, he emphasized, "Not a penny of the proceeds will go to individual Indians."

Josh leaned over to Brad. "You think that's true?"

Brad just smiled and replied that Rapoport might believe it, but he was sure none of the Mashantuckets sitting in the gallery did. In any case, he said, it was irrelevant. "If the casino goes through, the Mashantuckets may well become the richest group of people in the world, and they can spend the money any way they damn please."

Deputy speaker Janet Polinsky was now in the speaker's chair, and at this point she recognized Representative Parker from Hartford.

"Okay, now you're going to hear from the Black Caucus," Brad said softly.

"Madam Speaker, I rise to oppose the bill," Parker declared, "and I ask myself what shall we tell our children who are white and black and yellow and brown and red? That is the question before us today.

"I'd like them to know that on this spring day of May 16, 1991, I voted with the Native Americans. And I'd like them to know that much like other minorities across this country who use the law of the land for redress, they won. And now we want to change the rules.

"I ask all of my colleagues on both sides of the aisle to have the courage of that movie I saw, *Dances with Wolves*, to stand and be counted today for a sovereign nation that is asking you to help them improve the quality of their lives."

Sharon and Josh had been watching Reid Dowling intermittently, but Dowling had made no move to speak, and there was nothing in his behavior that indicated which way he was going to vote. At Brad's suggestion, Sharon had written Dowling a one-sentence note saying she and Josh were in the gallery and were counting on him. After reading it, Dowling looked up at the gallery briefly, but Josh thought they were buried too far back to be seen.

Representative Maddox now had the floor.

If the Mashantucket casino were approved, he warned, other tribes would almost certainly follow with their own casinos, and that would put pressure on the legislature to open up the state to non-Indian casino developers as well—all because of a simple technicality the legislature now had an opportunity to fix.

He hated to think of the human costs the casinos could bring, Maddox said sadly.

"I am absolutely amazed at the busloads of senior citizens that go to Atlantic City. They have a neat sign up down there that really struck me: 'We cash Social Security checks.'" Perhaps, Maddox suggested, if the House voted for casino gambling today, Connecticut could go New Jersey one better and allow its casinos to take food stamps as well.

Finally, Reid Dowling rose to speak.

"Madam Speaker," Dowling began, "this is my first term in this House, but no matter how long I am here, I doubt I will ever have to cast a more difficult vote.

"I would greatly prefer not to expand gambling in Connecticut. But Congress has legislated and the courts have ruled that the Mashantuckets have the right to build a casino on their reservation, and I believe that instead of battling the Pequots the way we did three hundred fifty years ago, we should seek to work with them to make the best of it.

"There may be problems, but there can also be benefits.

"Many of you know that I am committed to protecting the quality of life in our small towns. But we can't protect our quality of life without jobs, and right now eastern Connecticut desperately needs new jobs. One of the most promising ways for us to create new jobs in this state is by promoting tourism, and the proposed casino could help create thousands of environmentally friendly jobs in this fast-growing industry.

"So, in an effort to make the most of a difficult situation, Madame Speaker, I urge my colleagues to make peace with our ancient adversaries and vote against repeal."

Josh looked at Sharon and then at Brad and Janet, but there was nothing to say. Brad just shook his head and made another check on his scorecard.

Josh couldn't focus on the few remaining speeches, because all he could think of was the evening they had spent with Dowling and how they'd fooled themselves into thinking they had a shot with him. Brad said there were still a good number of votes he couldn't predict, but it looked as though the anti-casino side was going to fall at least a dozen votes shy. They needed a miracle to win.

At last, the Speaker called for a roll-call vote, and the members of the House began to punch in their votes, which immediately appeared on the two electronic tally boards. It was close at first, and Josh began to hope against hope, but soon it became clear the bill was going down. The final tally on the boards was eighty-four to sixty-two against repeal. Brad said the vote was actually closer but some members changed their votes toward the end in order to be with the winning side.

But the final margin didn't matter. Josh and his companions headed glumly for the exit, while most of the people in the gallery cheered and hugged and congratulated each other on their historic victory.

Sharon cast one final glance in Dowling's direction and saw him exchanging congratulations with another rep who had spoken against the bill. "Traitor," was the only word she could think of as she walked out the door.

14

"What America Is All About"

February 1992–February 1993

The Mashantuckets opened their new casino, named Foxwoods, on February 15, 1992, nine months after their victory in the state legislature. Not even they could believe its success.

Despite heavy rain, fifteen thousand people from as far away as Maine and Maryland visited the casino the first day. They included veteran gamblers, novices, singles, couples, sightseers, busloads of seniors, and carloads of young men. Traffic was backed up for nearly a mile in both directions on Route 2, the seventeen-hundred-car parking lot was overflowing by mid-morning, and some gamblers abandoned their cars in fields and along back roads to walk to the casino through the rain and mud.

People were packed three and four deep at the poker tables, craps tables, roulette tables, blackjack tables, baccarat tables, pai gow tables, and the big-six money wheel, waiting their turn to bet. Cocktail waitresses couldn't keep up with the drink orders, and so many customers were still gambling at the scheduled 4:00 a.m. closing time that management decided to stay open around the clock.

But opening day was just a taste of what was to come.

The crowds continued to pour in, and on July 15, just five months after Foxwoods' grand opening, the Mashantuckets unveiled plans for a massive, two-phase expansion that would create a 2.5-million-square-foot complex with 130,000 square feet of gambling space, a hotel and convention center, indoor trolleys, shops, theaters, restaurants, a man-made lake, and a heliport. The expansion, the Mashantuckets declared, would make Foxwoods the biggest casino in the Western Hemisphere, bigger even than Donald Trump's Taj Mahal in Atlantic City.

In a front-page story, *The Day* reported that Foxwoods was expected to do between $120 and $140 million in gross gaming revenue its first year, that attendance was already averaging more than 10,000 people a day, and that the casino now employed some 3,200 people.

Al Luciani, the professional manager from New Jersey the Mashantuckets had hired to run Foxwoods, told reporters he had never seen anything like it.

"This is an incredible success story," Luciani marveled. "This is truly what America is all about."

⤳

Foxwoods' explosive start quickly attracted the attention of other casino investors and developers.

The most prominent was Steve Wynn, born in Connecticut in 1942 and now the most flamboyant and influential casino developer in the country. Wynn had turned the Golden Nugget into the first luxury hotel in downtown Las Vegas, had built the Atlantic City Golden Nugget in 1979, and in 1989 had taken the concept of a resort casino to new heights with the construction of the Mirage in Las Vegas. The Mirage was modeled on a tropical resort, had a massive atrium filled with ten thousand tropical trees and plants, live sharks that swam in a huge aquarium behind the registration desk, white tigers that roamed behind a glass wall, and a giant volcano that erupted every fifteen minutes in front of the entrance.

In March 1992, a month after Foxwoods opened, Wynn flew to Connecticut to begin a campaign to get the state legislature to legalize non-Indian casinos and to permit slot machines, which he contended were essential for any commercial casino coming into the state.

Wynn's arguments were simple and compelling. Connecticut needed jobs. It needed tax revenue. And it needed to rejuvenate its biggest cities, which he called "boring." If Connecticut would only legalize slots, he declared, he would be willing to help the state begin to solve its problems by building a fabulous casino and entertainment complex in Bridgeport, one of the state's most troubled cities and just an hour from Manhattan.

Even gambling skeptics had to see his proposal made sense, Wynn contended. After all, the state had already approved casino gambling for the Indians, who were starting to make a fortune. The trouble was, Foxwoods' gambling profits were tax exempt, and Connecticut had screwed up by never working out a deal with the Mashantuckets that gave the state a piece of the action. So why not open up the state to non-Indian casinos and tax those like any other business?

A tireless promoter with movie-star good looks, Wynn pressed his arguments in public meetings, in hearings, in interviews, and in television and newspaper ads. He won over the majority leader of the State Senate, and flew a group of key legislators to Las Vegas on his private jet for an all-expenses-paid weekend so they could study the Mirage firsthand. He extolled the virtues of gaming, flew in fifty of his casino employees to spread the gospel at a Bridgeport job fair, and asked the public to sign cards urging their legislators to approve non-Indian casino gambling.

⤜⤳

Josh and Sharon had grown increasingly close to the Merriweathers in the months since their disappointing visit to the State Capitol, and Josh once again looked to Brad to help him keep up with the shifting sands of casino politics in Hartford.

Brad watched Wynn's Connecticut offensive with a clinical eye, calling it the most dazzling and expensive lobbying effort in the state's history. If the Puritans were still around, he joked, they'd be convinced that Satan himself had come to Connecticut to tempt the state. But, Brad said, there was still a chance Wynn might fall short, because the Governor distrusted him and the legislature was deeply divided over whether to extend the right to open casinos to non-Indians.

Wynn's campaign steadily gained momentum throughout the year, however, and by December was the main topic of conversation throughout the state, including at the holiday party Sharon and Josh threw the Sunday before Christmas.

The family went all out for the occasion. Sharon brought in a caterer for the first time in her life, she and Sarah decorated the house with boughs and mistletoe, and Josh and the kids cut down a sixteen-foot blue spruce that they put up in the courtyard and strung with hundreds of white lights. The first guests arrived just after five, and the party soon overflowed into the library and halls, the decibel level gradually rising as the bartenders refilled glasses, someone banged out "Jingle Bells" and "Here Comes Santa Claus" on the upright, and Sharon finally called people into the dining room, where the buffet table was laden with platters of sirloin, turkey, and salmon.

Josh wanted to stay away from the topic of Steve Wynn or anything else connected with gambling, and he figured he was safe when he stopped to mingle with several guests who were talking football. The group included

Brad and a professor named Jim Pritchard who taught management and public policy at Yale. As luck had it, the subject turned to politics soon after Josh
arrived and Pritchard asked how the group felt about Wynn's proposal for
Bridgeport. The consensus was against building more casinos in the state.

"How about you, Professor?" Brad asked. "How do you feel about it?"

"Well, I was never in favor of bringing casinos in here in the first place,"
Pritchard said, "but now that we're letting Indians build them, it's pretty hard
to justify keeping non-Indians out. In fact, I'd argue we'd be much better off
bringing in a couple of tax-paying non-Indian casinos than leaving the market
entirely to Indian casinos that pay nothing. And Wynn's proposal for Bridgeport looks to me like a pretty good way to start."

"So are you telling me Wynn's even got the Ivy League behind him now?"
Josh asked, draping a friendly arm around Pritchard's shoulder.

"Hey," Pritchard responded, raising a hand in self-defense, "I can see I'm
in the minority here, but from a practical standpoint Wynn's proposal could
be a huge opportunity for Connecticut—not only could it help revive Bridgeport, but it could mean hundreds of millions of dollars in casino taxes. The
first casino built that close to New York City will outdraw any casino in the
country, and I can't think of anybody better than Wynn to pull in the crowds."

"Remind me never to invite you back," Josh said with as much good
humor as he could muster, but Brad, who Josh suspected had had one too
many eggnogs, appeared genuinely annoyed.

"You know, Professor," Brad said, "I don't doubt Wynn's casino would
pull in the crowds, but I have to say it's pretty goddamn pathetic if the best
idea we can come up with to save Bridgeport and raise revenue is to encourage
people to gamble. I'd have thought good public policy should be more about
protecting people from the gambling industry than partnering with it to exploit them."

"Look," Pritchard shot back, "I'm not saying bringing Wynn in here is an
easy choice. I'm simply saying it's the realistic one. Connecticut can either
build a casino in Bridgeport or it can wait for New York to build one in
Queens or the Bronx."

⌐↩

Josh took the family skiing in Vermont over the long New Year's weekend,
and two days later Sharon's mother and father came east to take care of the
kids while he and Sharon flew to the Florida Keys just ahead of a snow-

storm. The Florida trip was their first vacation alone since moving to Sheffield.

It was a magnificent six days in the sun, with nothing to do but swim, sail, relax, and enjoy each other. They sat on the terrace of a small, out-of-the-way café their last night, sipping daiquiris and watching the sun set over the Gulf, and they promised each other they'd try to carve out a week for themselves every winter from now on.

The question that wouldn't go away, however, was whether they should stay in Sheffield.

On the one hand, Brad Merriweather's pessimistic view of what was to come seemed to be materializing all too fast. Foxwoods was growing by leaps and bounds. The Mohegans and several other Connecticut tribes were moving toward federal recognition. And now the powers in Hartford appeared close to opening the state to Steve Wynn, which could easily lead to other non-Indian casino developers coming in behind him.

On the other hand, neither Josh nor Sharon was ready to leave, and for the moment at least, Sharon seemed to feel even more strongly than Josh about giving it more time. She knew what the town and the farm meant to him, she said. She had adopted both as her own, and it would break her heart to leave now.

For now, therefore, they decided to stay.

"There's only one caveat," Josh added as a graceful sailing yacht passed in the distance. "If the state caves in to Wynn and it looks like there'll be a mad scramble for casinos across the state, we'll leave. We'll sell the business and the farm and simply move somewhere else. No one's got deeper roots in Sheffield than I do, but I'll never let the past keep us here if it becomes time to let go."

$$\backsim$$

By the time Josh and Sharon got back home on January 11, it appeared that time might come sooner than later. Steve Wynn had managed to pick up additional support over the holidays, and it now looked almost certain the legislature would back him.

Then the situation took another sudden turn.

On January 13, Governor Weicker pulled the rug out from under Wynn by announcing he had just signed an agreement with the Mashantuckets giving them exclusive rights to operate slot machines in the state in return for 25 percent of their slots win, or a guaranteed minimum of $100 million a year. If the state were ever to legalize slot machines for anyone else, it would release the Mashantuckets from the agreement, and they could keep all their slot machine profits for themselves.

"The Governor," Brad Merriweather told Josh that evening, "thinks the agreement is a coup, because it'll not only plug a hole in the state budget, but it'll also block Wynn, who'll never be able to top the Mashantuckets' hundred-million-dollar guarantee."

Furious at the Governor, Wynn promptly counterattacked, proposing a grandiose scheme to build casinos in both Bridgeport and Hartford that would guarantee Connecticut $140 million a year in state and local taxes. The public gaped and supporters cheered, believing Wynn might just pull it off. But it soon became clear that after almost a year of trying to batter down Connecticut's doors, Wynn's luck was running out. Despite his bold assurances, there was growing skepticism about his ability to generate the promised $140 million and as interest in his proposal waned over the succeeding weeks, he gradually gave up.

Neither Josh nor Sharon were sure how to react. Wynn had been stopped, but the press predicted that giving slots to the Mashantuckets would take gambling in Connecticut to new heights. Slots, it was pointed out, were by far the biggest draw at most casinos, typically accounting for a good 70 percent of their take.

Equally disheartening, the Governor's slots deal meant that the state and the tribe, once implacable foes, were now totally in bed with each other. The more the public lost to the slot machines, the more the state treasury stood to take in.

Nonetheless, Josh and Sharon couldn't help but take some encouragement from the fact that Connecticut had succeeded in turning back the first attempt to introduce non-Indian casinos into the state. With Wynn at least temporarily stopped and the actual impact of slot machines still uncertain, they reaffirmed their decision to stay put for now and wait to see what would happen next.

15

The Northern Pequots
Rise Again

May–August 1993

It was the beginning of May, and Josh had heard almost nothing further about the Northern Pequots since the fatal trailer explosion on their reservation two years earlier. He'd been leaving for church that Sunday morning and heard the thud. It hadn't been until late afternoon that Ben Chapman stopped over and filled him in.

Ben was one of the volunteer firefighters who had responded to the explosion, and he said the only other person living on the reservation at the time was the same old man he'd occasionally given a lift to over the years. The man had been so broken up by his friend's death that he'd told Ben he didn't think he could continue to live on the reservation, and Josh had no idea whether he was still there or not.

Josh had subsequently driven past the reservation from time to time, but he had never been able to see any signs of life from the road, and he had gradually stopped worrying about the Northerns, or whatever might be left of them, ever becoming a player in the casino game.

As far as he knew, the only thing of note that had happened on or near the reservation since the explosion was that a New York developer had bought the Standish farm, a two-hundred-twenty-acre parcel that bordered the state highway to the south and the Deer Run subdivision and the reservation to the north. The realtor who handled the transaction told Josh that although she'd never met the developer, her understanding was he wanted to warehouse the land for another subdivision.

Josh was shocked, therefore, when he flicked on the 11:00 p.m. news the first Monday in May and heard the TV anchorwoman begin to talk about the tiny Indian tribe in the town of Sheffield that could be one of the next groups to build a casino in eastern Connecticut. And he was doubly shocked when the screen switched to the tribe's chief—a stocky, middle-aged man with a fringed buckskin jacket, bolo tie, and long, blondish-gray hair pulled into a ponytail that hung down his back. It took Josh a second to recognize the man because of the hair and the way he was dressed, but Josh couldn't miss the tinted aviator glasses. It was Bobby Kingman, the real estate promoter Josh had been warned away from on his first day back in Sheffield.

Kingman, the anchorwoman said, would be holding a news conference tomorrow at 9:00 a.m. to formally announce his tribe's bid for federal recognition.

⌒

Bobby had never held a press conference in his life, but he felt a cool confidence as he prepared to speak before the dozen or so reporters, photographers, and TV cameramen who gathered at the Sheffield Tavern Tuesday morning. After checking his notes one final time, he cleared his throat and began to speak.

He was pleased to announce, he said in a firm voice, that the Northern Pequot Tribal Nation, of which he had been elected chairman and Chief for Life, had applied to the Bureau of Indian Affairs for federal acknowledgment as an Indian tribe that traced its lineage back to the original Northern Pequots.

"Our tribe," Bobby said, "has been based in Sheffield since 1686, when Connecticut provided us with our reservation, and we currently have fifty members. Two of those members, I'm happy to say, are with me this mornin' —Ray Summerwood, who recently stepped down as chief, and Mavis Dostin, our vice chair and historian." Bobby gestured toward a frail, white-haired old man and a nervous-looking woman who appeared to be in her seventies. The old man was wearing a jacket similar to Bobby's, but otherwise there was nothing to suggest that either he or the woman were descended from Indians.

"We've been workin' nearly two years to put together our application," Bobby continued, "and have compiled more than twenty thousand pages of material documentin' our tribe's history."

He went on to read a brief statement about the tribes' past, then opened the floor to questions.

"Are you planning to build a casino?" the reporters clamored almost in unison the instant he finished.

"One at a time, please!" Bobby pleaded. "I think you were first," he said, pointing to a woman he recognized from one of the Hartford channels.

"It looks as though we all have the same question, Mr. Kingman. Are you looking to open a casino?"

"We're studyin' it," Bobby replied. "At the moment, casinos look like the best bet for helpin' us become self-sufficient, but our first goal is simply to obtain recognition for the tribe."

"How about land claims?" a newspaper reporter wanted to know. "Do you intend to make any land claims?"

"We're considerin' them," Bobby responded, "because we believe some of our land was taken illegally, but we haven't made a decision yet."

"How much land are you talking about?" the reporter asked excitedly.

"I'm sorry, I can't comment on that right now," Bobby begged off.

"Do you have a financial backer?" someone else asked.

"Yes," Bobby replied, "fortunately we do, because we never could have afforded to put together our application without one."

Their backer, Bobby explained, was James Grimaldi, a highly successful New York real estate developer.

"What's your deal with him?" still another voice called out.

"That's confidential at the moment," Bobby said, "but we'd obviously look to partner with him on any business venture we undertake."

"Does that include a casino?" two questioners asked simultaneously.

"Yes," Bobby replied. "But so far Mr. Grimaldi's only role has been to help us hire the experts needed to complete our recognition application."

"Can you tell us who the experts are you've brought in?"

"Sure," Bobby replied, looking for the index cards on which he'd written the names. "We have Mrs. Faye Gilman, a genealogist from Boston, Professor James Royster, a historian from NYU, and Professor Harold Locke, an anthropologist from the University of Rhode Island. I have copies of their resumes for anyone who'd like them.

"I should also add that we've retained Rigby and White as our legal counsel, which, if you check, you'll find is one of the top law firms in Washington on Indian affairs.

"Oh, and one other thing," Bobby added. "I meant to mention that Mr. Grimaldi's purchased the Standish farm adjacent to the reservation for the benefit of the tribe."

The only zinger came at the very end of the press conference.

"I understand, Mr. Kingman, that you never showed an interest in your Indian heritage until recently. If that's so, can you tell us what changed your mind?"

Bobby smiled as though anticipating the question.

"I figured somebody'd ask me that sooner or later," he replied good-naturedly.

"The truth is I've always been aware of my Indian heritage, but I was reluctant to talk about it when I was growin' up, because I thought the other kids would make fun of me. You know how it is . . . you want to fit in and be part of the crowd. The last thing you want is to be singled out as bein' different."

Bobby looked repentant.

"Well, I'm afraid that was me. But I began to become interested in my genealogy as I got older, and fortunately, I have a wonderful great-uncle and a dear aunt who've helped me appreciate my ancestors." Again he gestured to Ray and Mavis.

"You know," he added, looking directly into the cameras, "I think I'm like a lot of Americans in that more and more of us are takin' an interest in our roots. Mine happen to go back to the Northern Pequots, and I can tell you right now, I'm thrilled by this chance to do somethin' for my people."

⌒

The Northern Pequots' announcement hit Sheffield like a bunker-buster bomb.

Many of Sheffield's newer residents had never even heard of the Northern Pequots before the fatal accident on the reservation in April 1991, and most of the older residents had simply taken the report of the accident as confirmation there was virtually no one left there.

Almost everyone, therefore, was shocked to learn they had a functioning Indian tribe in their midst, and that it had already lined up the money to build a Las Vegas–style casino in their town.

The town hall was deluged with calls from angry residents demanding to know what the town planned to do to block the casino, and there was wild speculation as to whose property the Indians might file land claims against. The newspapers were flooded with letters asking how many casinos Connecticut could afford before they ruined the state, and how the government could allow a defunct Indian tribe to destroy their community.

Others charged that the whole thing was an elaborate fraud, ridiculed the Northerns as a "casino tribe," and in some cases went after Bobby Kingman personally, picking up on the fact that he had never previously shown a shred of interest in Indians and dismissing him as a con artist with a history of failed schemes designed to bilk suckers out of their money.

Sheffield's first selectman, Jim Clark, said a project even half the size of Foxwoods would overwhelm the town's roads and services, and Sheffield's state representative, Reid Dowling, who had supported the Mashantuckets in the famous 1991 Las Vegas Nights vote, declared his unequivocal opposition to a casino in town.

"There is no way I am going to stand by and let a bunch of pretend Indians and a New York developer trash Sheffield," Dowling said on television. "I want to assure everyone in my district that I'll fight this thing to the end."

The initial frenzy lasted about a week, then gradually began to subside as calmer heads pointed out that the Northern Pequots might never succeed in gaining recognition and that, in any case, the Bureau of Indian Affairs was so swamped with recognition applications that it could be ten years before the Northerns' application was even considered. By then, it was pointed out, market conditions might have changed to the point that they wouldn't support another casino in Connecticut.

Nevertheless, anxiety continued to run high as the town came to the realization it now faced years of uncertainty before the casino question was resolved.

❧

Bobby took the initial uproar in stride. Some of the personal attacks stung, but the last thing he wanted to do was to respond in a way that risked further inflaming the community. He had succeeded in breaking the story on his own terms, and his goal now was to let things calm down while the tribe's application made its way through the BIA.

Steve Wynn's campaign to build casinos in Bridgeport and Hartford had given Bobby a bad scare by threatening to divert gamblers away from eastern Connecticut, but Bobby's plans had otherwise gone almost exactly as envisioned.

The keys had been to get Mavis back on board after Louis's death and then to persuade Ray to stay on the reservation and become the nucleus of the reconstructed tribe.

Mavis had been relatively easy to persuade because of her gratitude to Bobby for attending Louis's funeral and her desire to keep the reservation out of the state's hands, but it took considerably more work to convince Ray, who remained emotionally crushed by Louis's death and extremely uneasy about his ability to continue living on the reservation alone.

Bobby and Mavis finally persuaded Ray to stay by promising to move onto the reservation part-time themselves, and Bobby used the tribe's new war chest to purchase three brand-new mobile homes for Ray, Mavis, and himself; he also brought in gas generators for electricity and set up a construction trailer as a temporary tribal office. In the meantime, the lawyers drew up a new constitution for the Northerns, and Mavis began taking Bobby around to the homes of Rachel Amos's other descendants, where he spent hours laying out his plans for expanding the tribe, gaining recognition, and building a casino on the reservation.

Most of the descendants were initially skeptical, in some cases totally dismissing the possibility of ever reviving the old tribe, but in the end it was difficult for even the biggest skeptics to pass up the possibility of millions in profits. Within two months, Bobby had recruited twenty new members to the tribe, and once Foxwoods opened, he easily increased the number to the fifty he mentioned at the press conference.

The only thing Bobby was uncomfortable about was the partner Jim Grimaldi had brought into the deal—a billionaire real estate and casino mogul from Miami named Paul Ivy. Ivy, who was in his early sixties, had made his money with huge shopping malls and office parks up and down the East Coast, had an interest in half a dozen casinos in the Caribbean, and was a major political contributor who could supposedly help the tribe in Washington.

Bobby had met the Miami partner only once, during a visit Ivy had made to the reservation with Grimaldi two years earlier, and he had seen right off the bat that Ivy could be a challenge to work with. Physically, he was a barrel-chested, bull of a man with a big, shaved head that made him look like a professional wrestler, and he had an aggressive, blunt-talking personality to match. At the same time, however, the man was an elegant dresser who tended to make even Grimaldi look plain, and he had a certain old-boy charm that he seemed to be able to turn on and off at will. Bobby figured the odd mix of toughness and almost courtliness had to be part of what had driven him to the top. The effect was to keep you off balance because you never knew what was coming next, and Bobby noticed that it seemed to intimidate even Grimaldi. Ivy hadn't neglected to lay on the charm with Bobby, but he'd also made it clear he was putting in most of the money for the Northerns' recognition bid and was the one calling the shots.

Still, Bobby couldn't really complain, because it appeared that Ivy and Grimaldi had so far invested more than $5 million in the project. A big part of that had gone to the researchers and lawyers who'd written the tribe's recognition application, but the two men had also funded the tribe's reorganization, provided the new mobile homes and other improvements on the reservation, and put Bobby, Mavis, and Mavis's daughter, Leigh, on the payroll. Bobby alone was pulling down a cool $150,000 a year, which was almost three times what he'd ever made in his life. In addition, Ivy had just hired one of the hottest lobbying firms in D.C. to help push the tribe's application, and Bobby had no idea how much money Ivy was spreading around Washington to win friends for the project.

∽

One of Bobby's ideas for reviving the tribe was to turn the annual Northern Pequot Sewing Society picnic into a major event. He and Mavis had managed to draw most of the tribe's new members to the picnic in 1992, and this year he was planning a full-scale powwow in late August to celebrate the tribe's resurgence and raise its profile among other Indians.

Bobby invited tribes from throughout the Northeast to participate and hired an Indian medicine man from Michigan to bless the event. He used his new-found money to pave the dirt road leading up to the reservation, set up giant open tents, and marked out a circular performing area in the heart of the meadow for the hundreds of Indian dancers, singers, and drummers scheduled to attend.

Bobby advertised the powwow heavily and distributed free tickets to the local schools. To his delight, close to a thousand onlookers were in attendance when members of a western Pennsylvania tribe, dressed in their magnificent regalia, their colors flashing and flags flying, led in the rest of the performers during the grand entry. Tom-toms pounded and the dancers swooped and glided in a great circle to kick off the festivities.

Bobby cheered every performance, from the Grass Dance and the Chicken Dance to the Smoke Dance, the Jingle Dance, and the Eastern War Dance. He donned a custom-made Northeast Woodland Indian vest to help present prizes. And, in between, he wandered through the tents and concession area introducing himself and examining the Indian jewelry, war clubs, and paintings the vendors had on display. He bought a painting of Sitting Bull, ate buffalo burgers, and posed for photographs with each of the dancing and singing troupes in all their splendor. That evening he personally lit a huge ceremonial bonfire, and the different troupes took turns singing and chanting ancient tribal songs as the flames leapt skyward, illuminating the meadow and the woods beyond.

When they finished, Bobby asked Quiet Eagle, the Michigan medicine man, to come forward and give the final blessing. As Quiet Eagle approached, however, a girl from one of the troupes called out to ask if the Northerns wouldn't first sing one of their traditional songs.

Bobby, who had just started to whisper something to the man next to him, looked up at the girl as though he had been hit by a stun gun.

"No, no," he said instinctively, trying to smile and wave off the request. "Really, sweetheart, that's very nice, but this is your evenin', not ours."

"Pleeez," the girl persisted, and others around her began to take up her plea. Within seconds, all the troupes were cheering and clapping rhythmically for the Northerns to sing.

Bobby hesitated and glanced at Mavis, who was staring daggers at him, shaking her head and mouthing "no."

The clapping intensified, someone started beating a tom-tom, and Bobby finally threw up his hands in capitulation.

"All right, give us just a minute," he said, and motioned for the other Northerns to come over and gather around him. Mavis buried her head in her hand as the visiting Indians let out a cheer.

After a panicked huddle that seemed to last forever, the Northerns finally stood in a group and sang "Take Me Out to the Ball Game." It was the only song Bobby could get them to agree on.

It was all incredibly embarrassing, but Bobby figured what the hell. If they got the casino, it wouldn't make any difference. And if they didn't, nobody'd ever remember the Northern Pequots anyway.

16

The New Girl in Town

May 4–September 12, 1993

Josh and Sharon's decision to stay in Sheffield for the time being was based on the assumption that they could pick up and leave whenever they chose. However, the Northerns' May 4 announcement meant that option was now out the window.

Every cent Josh had was tied up in either his business or the farm, and the possibility of the tribe building a casino less than two miles from his kitchen door meant no buyer would touch the farm until the casino question was resolved. The farm was too far from a main road to have commercial value, and its proximity to the potential casino totally destroyed its residential appeal.

It was now assumed the Northerns intended to make land claims against the homeowners in Deer Run, which had once been part of the reservation, then expand the reservation by adding both Deer Run and the Standish farm. That would give the tribe more than eight hundred contiguous acres, extend the reservation to the state highway, and set the stage for a massive casino complex.

With no prospects for selling the farm in the near future, Josh turned his attention to expanding his business as a way out of his financial predicament. The insurance agency was doing well, but if he could grow the business faster, he could sell it in two or three years for enough to be able to leave Sheffield whether or not he could find a buyer for the farm.

Economics weren't the only consideration, however. In addition, he felt a steadily building anger at being forced from his home and a growing determination to fight.

In the meantime, the introduction of slot machines fueled a whole new surge of growth at Foxwoods.

By spring 1993, the Mashantuckets had installed more than fourteen hundred of the machines. As Josh looked at a newspaper photo of the endless rows of slots and their players, he recalled an old photo he'd seen showing nineteenth-century workers operating row after row of weaving machines in one of the great textile factories that once dotted the region.

The similarity was uncanny. Most of the people in the two photos were women, and everyone appeared to be totally absorbed in their work. One difference, Josh mused, was that one group was making money while the other was losing it; a second was that the casino owners were clearly making bigger profits than the factory owners had ever dreamed of.

The slots attracted a new type of customer, and by the summer of 1993 the casino's financial results were again blowing past all expectations. According to a confidential earnings report obtained by *The Day*, Foxwoods had gaming revenues of $35 million in June alone, including an astounding $20 million from slots after just a few months. Apparently, it was reported, Foxwoods was now making more money than the Electric Boat Division of General Dynamics, which was the largest submarine builder in the world and the region's biggest employer.

Indeed, gaming analysts believed Foxwoods was making more money than any casino in either Las Vegas or Atlantic City, and Marvin Roffman, an analyst from Philadelphia, went even further.

"I would venture to tell you," Roffman told the newspaper, "that this casino is now the most profitable in the world."

Even that was only the beginning. On September 3, 1993, the Mashantuckets opened their second gambling hall, along with a new retail concourse, and they announced they would soon open the new hotel, theaters, and nightclub they had been building for the past twelve months.

The expansion brought the total amount of gambling space to almost a hundred forty thousand square feet, putting Foxwoods within reach of soon becoming not only the most profitable but also the largest casino on earth.

∽

Josh's efforts to build his business got a big boost late that summer when his friend Bob Duncan approached him about buying the Duncan Agency in Norwich, which was close to twice the size of Josh's operation. Duncan, who was sixty-six and eager to retire, had let the business slip in recent years, and wasn't earning what he should be based on his volume. Duncan's agency still had a solid reputation, however, and he had built a large book of Workers' Compensation policies by signing up scores of small companies as well as a number of sizable Connecticut manufacturing firms with facilities around the country. It was Duncan's most lucrative line of business and a market Josh currently wasn't in.

Josh saw the acquisition as a way to both enter an attractive new market and nearly triple the size of his agency overnight. Duncan expressed a willingness to be paid out over ten years, and by September he and Josh were in serious discussions.

In fact, September 1993 was turning out to be one of the busiest months ever for the entire Williams family. Now eighteen, Matt was a senior at Southeast Regional High, was a starting midfielder on the school soccer team, and, with the help of his father, had just bought his first car, an '86 Plymouth. Sarah, who was almost fifteen, had moved up to the high school from the Sheffield Middle School, and nine-year-old Jacob was in fourth grade at Sheffield Elementary. Josh and Sharon had begun to visit colleges with Matt and, after winning a two-year term on the Sheffield board of education in 1991, Sharon was getting ready to run for reelection.

On top of everything else, it was apple harvest time.

❧

The farm's orchard of several hundred trees produced primarily Macintosh, Cortland, and Red Delicious apples, and for the past two years the family had done a land-office business selling them at the farm stand. They began picking the Macs in late August and worked right up to the end of October, but September was their busiest month. This year the Macs and the Cortlands were particularly crisp and juicy and in heavy demand. Ben Chapman hired two part-time pickers during the week, and it was an old Williams tradition for the whole family to go out about three o'clock on Sunday afternoons and pick as many bushels as they could before supper.

The Sunday suppers were typically among the most enjoyable times the family had together, and on those evenings Josh and Sharon made an extra effort to draw out the kids on what was happening in their lives. This was beginning to get harder to do as Sarah and Matt got older, and the second Sunday in September proved the most challenging instance yet.

Slender, with short auburn hair and freckles, Sarah was a bit of a tomboy who loved the outdoors and especially riding her chestnut mare, Honey. Josh had selected Honey for her gentleness, but the horse, a graceful mid-size Morgan, could run and jump with the best of them, and Sarah delighted in challenging Matt to races and jumping contests, just as she'd always challenged him in everything, from Monopoly to touch football. She still couldn't quite outrace him, but she had gradually established herself as the family's top horseperson, winning ribbons in horse shows all over eastern and central Connecticut. There was nothing Josh enjoyed more that watching her ride, and he only hoped she wouldn't lose interest now that she was starting high school.

A late bloomer, Sarah was taking a keen new interest in boys and her social life, and her desire to impress a new girlfriend led to an argument with Matt. He drove her to school each morning and she saw no reason he couldn't give her friend a ride as well. Given that Sarah was already taking the bus home after school because of Matt's soccer games and afternoon practice, she thought stopping by her friend's house in the morning was the least he could do to compensate.

Matt was on a ladder picking Macs when Sarah complained again that he was just being pigheaded about giving her friend a ride. "It's not going to kill you to leave two minutes earlier in the morning," she said, looking up at him.

Matt looked down and shook his head. "I told you a hundred times I'm not going a mile out of my way every morning to get your friend. So get off it!" he said, and went on picking.

Sarah waited for him to come down, then tried again. "Please. It's not that far out of the way."

"What'sa matter?" Matt taunted. "You already tell her I'd do it and now you can't deliver?"

At that, Sarah got so mad she took a swing at him. Matt stepped away just in time, and Sarah lost her balance and fell down, knocking over a basket of apples.

"Nice going, Sarah," Matt said. "Now you can pick 'em up."

"Pick 'em up yourself," Sarah shot back, scrambling to get back on her feet.

"You knocked 'em over," Matt said, laughing and watching to see whether she'd come at him again.

"Go to hell," she retorted, and refused to talk to him for the rest of the afternoon.

The tiff spilled over to the supper table when Sharon reminded Matt and Josh that they had to finish up their college visits.

"At a minimum, we've still got to do Bowdoin and Colby," she said.

Everybody looked at Matt. A lean, handsome kid, he'd shot up to six feet in the past year and was one of Southeast's best all-around athletes.

"How about the weekend after next?" Josh suggested when Matt didn't respond. "We could drive up to Maine Friday night and get an early start Saturday morning."

"What do you think, Matt?" Sharon prodded.

Matt grimaced. "I don't know, Mom. I don't think my grades are gonna be that great this semester, and I'm wondering if it really makes sense to keep looking at schools like those. The more I think about it, the more I think I want to go to UConn."

"I thought you wanted to go to a small liberal arts school?" Josh said with a puzzled look.

"Yeah, I know, Dad, but I'm still not sure what I want to major in, and I think I'd have a lot more choices at UConn."

"Look, Matt," Josh said, "that's your decision. UConn's a good school, but what's this about your grades? You know this is a critical semester."

"I know, Dad." Matt said. "I'm trying."

"What's the problem?" Josh pressed. "School just started."

"That's true, but even after two weeks I can see that things are gonna be tougher than I expected."

"What are you having trouble with?" Sharon asked.

"Right now, physics and calculus," Matt said. "But it's not just that. I've got five advanced courses, plus soccer, and I promised Miss Woodlack I'd try out for *The Sound of Music* this fall. It's just something different I'd really like to do. So there's a lot more pressure this semester, that's all."

"Well, maybe you're going to have to give up soccer if it's that serious," Josh said.

Matt didn't say anything.

"How about if we look into a tutor?" Sharon suggested.

"Yeah, I guess," Matt said.

"I may know somebody," Josh said. "He's a science teacher I play singles with once a week at the club. I don't know about calculus, but I know he teaches physics and does some tutoring."

"What's his name?" Sharon asked.

"Clayt Conner. Lives here in town but teaches at Ledyard High. Really sharp, nice young guy, and a heck of a tennis player. You want me to give him a call?" Josh asked, looking from Matt to Sharon.

Matt and Sharon both agreed.

"I don't believe this," Sarah interrupted, shaking her head.

"You don't believe what?" Josh asked.

"I don't believe you're all falling for this," Sarah replied.

"You know darn well," she said, looking at Matt, "that the real reason you're so stretched and all of a sudden want to go to UConn is because of your new girlfriend."

"You've got another new girlfriend?" Jacob asked.

"Yeah, but this one's serious," Sarah said. "He's with her all the time. She's the reason he doesn't have time for anything else."

"You don't know what you're talking about," Matt retorted.

"Yeah, right," Sarah said sarcastically. "I know you drove her home twice this week, even though you don't have time to drive me."

"Okay, that's enough, Sarah," Sharon said. "Sorry, Matt, but you know you can't keep anything from your sister now that she's at the high school."

"Do you have someone new?" Sharon asked casually.

"Well, yeah, kinda," Matt answered reluctantly.

"Do we know her?" Sharon asked.

"No, she just moved here this summer."

"What's her name?" Sharon asked.

"Kayla," Matt replied with a sigh of resignation.

"Kayla what?" Jacob asked.

Matt stared daggers at Jacob.

"Timko," he finally replied.

"What year is she?" Sharon asked.

"She's a senior," Matt said.

"Where's she from?" Josh asked.

"New Jersey," Matt answered.

"Oh," Josh said. "Does her father work at Pfizer?"

"No, Dad," Matt said with a flash of defiance. "They're from Atlantic City, and her father works at the casino, but I don't know what he does there, okay?"

Josh and Sharon were both taken aback by the sharpness of Matt's reply.

"What's she like?" Jacob asked, breaking the awkward silence.

"She's a real fox," Sarah answered for him. "All the guys are hitting on her."

"Well," Sharon said, ignoring Sarah and now trying to get off the subject as gracefully as possible, "we'd love to meet her. It's got to be hard to start your senior year in a new town."

꙳

Josh and Sharon talked about Matt at length in bed that night. They were caught off guard by his sudden interest in UConn but agreed that the bigger issue was his grades.

"What do you think is really going on with him?" Josh asked. "You think it's the girl?"

"I honestly don't know," Sharon replied. "I can understand he's feeling a lot of pressure because of everything he's got on his plate, but I'm troubled by the fact he's kept this Kayla so quiet. He's always been open about his girl-friends, and it can't just be that he didn't want us to know about her father. Matt knows how we feel about the casino, but he can't believe we'd be op-posed to the girl because her father works there."

"Look," Josh said, "let's see if we can find a tutor, and then I'll sit down with Matt and make sure he understands we have no interest in trying to pick his girlfriends. Knowing his track record with girls, though, I doubt this thing with Kayla will last that long."

17

Casino Town

September 14, 1993

Josh had a full schedule on Tuesday, September 14. He started with an insurance company breakfast in Willimantic, visited a prospective client in Colchester, then rushed back to Sheffield for the weekly Rotary luncheon. From there, he planned to drive to the Duncan Agency in Norwich, and after that head down to Ledyard Center, where he'd arranged to meet Clayt Conner after school to discuss his tutoring Matt.

Although he still had to examine the Duncan Agency's books, Josh had already decided to buy the agency if he could get it for the right price. He was convinced he could improve Duncan's business by consolidating it with his own, and Bob Duncan was proving to be an easy person to work with. He was a big, friendly bear of a man who loved to play golf and schmooze, and it seemed he was involved in every civic and charitable event in Norwich. Josh could see why he'd been so successful in building his business, and he could also see how he could have let it slip as he began spending more time at his Florida condo.

Duncan had just returned from lunch when Josh arrived, and they spent the first ten minutes talking sports before getting to the business at hand, which was to sit down with Duncan's office manager and bookkeeper, Marge Hanlon, to begin going over the financials.

"You're gonna love Marge," Duncan said. "Been with me for twenty years and is absolutely my right arm."

"You're lucky to have somebody like that," Josh said. "You think she'd stay?"

"I'm sure she would," Duncan said, buzzing Marge to come in. "This is her life. She's fifty-five, never married, and lives with her sister up in Sprague."

There was a polite knock on the door, and a stout woman with gray hair pulled back in a bun walked into the room, carrying several file folders and a ledger. She struck Josh as a bit formal, but she had a pleasant smile and looked very professional in her white blouse, gray slacks, and blue blazer. Josh thought she handled herself very well as she took him through the financials for the past three years and the results through June of the current year. She was clearly much more familiar with the numbers than Bob, and Josh could easily see how she'd become indispensable to him.

When they finished, Marge gave Josh a set of documents she'd prepared for him, and it was agreed Josh would call to set up a second session once his accountant had gone through them.

⌒

Josh left Duncan's office a little after 3:00 and drove to Ledyard, where he was meeting Clayt at 3:30.

The traffic got heavier as soon as Josh reached Route 2A, one of the main routes to Foxwoods, and became bumper-to-bumper in places as the road wound through the little village of Poquetanuck in the town of Preston. If the traffic was like this on a Tuesday afternoon, Josh wondered how people ever got out of their driveways on the weekends.

Josh had followed the newspaper reports about the developing friction between the Mashantuckets and the neighboring towns of Preston, Ledyard, and North Stonington, but he was amazed at the number of signs that had blossomed opposing the tribe's efforts to expand its reservation by purchasing land outside its designated settlement area and, in effect, "annexing" it by placing it in federal trust. The signs popped up the moment he entered Preston, then seemed to double and even triple in number as he left 2A and crossed into Ledyard. Hundreds of signs nailed to trees and pounded into lawns delivered the same defiant message:

NO ANNEXATION
NOT ONE ACRE!

The three towns had first become riled over annexation back in February, when the Mashantuckets applied to the BIA to take two hundred forty-seven acres outside their settlement area into trust, where they could develop it free of state and local regulation and taxes. Residents feared that if the tribe's annexation bid were successful, it could use its enormous gambling profits to buy and annex virtually any land it chose, and the towns had banded together to fight the application.

Allowing tribes to annex land in the West, where there were wide-open spaces, was one thing, the towns argued, but allowing them to take scarce land that was already an integral part of an incorporated town was an entirely different matter. Furthermore, the towns claimed, the whole idea behind annexation was to enable poor tribes to obtain enough land to become economically self-sufficient, and the law certainly shouldn't apply to wealthy tribes like the Mashantuckets.

The reaction to the tribe's two-hundred-forty-seven-acre trust request was nothing, however, compared to the way the towns reacted to a proposal the Mashantuckets made to the towns in July.

Encouraged by Foxwoods' phenomenal success, the Mashantuckets offered the three towns $5 million each if the towns would permit the tribe to buy up to seven thousand acres of additional land that it could add to its federal trust holdings without town opposition. The land in question represented 15 percent of the entire town of North Stonington, 12 percent of Ledyard, and 5 percent of Preston, and included 376 single-family homes. The tribe provided a map showing the boundaries within which it wanted to acquire the land and gave the towns thirty days to respond.

Predictably, the proposal boomeranged the instant it went public.

The immediate reaction was confusion, fear, and anger. Residents lined up at their town halls to look at copies of the tribe's map to see if their property had been targeted, and they stopped each other on the streets, in stores, and in churches to express outrage at what they saw as a blatant land grab. Some panicked homeowners called the tribe to sell, but most vowed to resist.

The Mashantuckets, townspeople charged, were trying to bribe the towns into giving up their own sovereignty. They were trying to use an outdated federal law to annex town land and drive people out of their homes. And they were trying to get out of paying taxes despite being richer than God.

Over the next month, residents flocked to emergency meetings to find out how they could fight the Mashantuckets' proposal, and new grass-roots groups formed to lead the resistance. They were the ones responsible for the NO ANNEXATION signs Josh saw everywhere as he drove to his meeting with Conner.

༄

Josh reached Ledyard Center a few minutes early and decided to make a quick stop at the community store. Pulling in, he parked one space down from a new Mercedes 500E with its windows open and its speakers pumping rap across the parking lot, the electric drums hitting him full-force as he opened his door and stepped onto the pavement. The two black teenagers inside rocked with the beat, and as Josh reached the store's entrance, he felt the aggressive thump-thump of a second stereo entering the lot. Looking back, he saw a silver BMW pull up next to the Mercedes and two black and two white kids pile out.

Josh turned and went into the store, where he picked up two small items for Sharon. He could still hear and feel the stereos inside the store. "Little loud out there," he commented to the clerk as he checked out.

The woman rolled her eyes. "Mashantuckets'" she said, glancing through the front window to the parking lot. "Same kids pulled in just about this time yesterday and started hangin' out. Owner let it go because he didn't want to start somethin', but then finally had to call the cops because customers were complainin'."

"What happened?" Josh asked.

"Nothin', because the kids took off before the cops got here. But he just now called 'em again, so we'll see what happens."

The woman put the two items in a bag and handed it to Josh. "Problem is," she added, "the tribe's got so much money, the kids think they can do whatever they want. And if you complain, the parents accuse you of bein' prejudiced."

When Josh left the store, the teenagers, in baggy pants and turned baseball caps, were peering under the hoods of the Mercedes and BMW, apparently comparing engines and seemingly oblivious to the earsplitting noise. As he unlocked his car, a police cruiser turned into the parking lot, and he saw two of the kids reach in their front seats and turn off the stereos. The cruiser pulled up on the other side of the BMW, and an older, heavyset cop got out and approached the kids. None of them looked up.

"Engine problems?" the officer asked.

No one answered at first, and then a chunky black kid with a New York Mets cap slowly looked back over his shoulder at the cop. "Why? You a mechanic?" he asked.

Everyone snickered.

"You one of the drivers?" the officer countered.

"Yeah, why?" the kid answered.

"Can I see your driver's license?"

"For what? I ain't done nothin'."

"The store owner says you and your friends are disturbing the peace and interfering with his business."

"How we doin' that?"

"Blasting your music and taking up his parking spaces."

The kid turned to his friends and spread his hands. "You hear any music?" They shook their heads.

"Your license," the officer said again.

"Jesus, man," the kid finally said, and fished it out of his wallet. "Can't you guys ever stop hasslin' us."

The cop looked over the license. "This is a New York license," he said. "You planning to stay in Connecticut?"

"Yeah, whadaya think?" the kid answered as though it was the dumbest question he'd ever heard.

"Then you've got thirty days to get a Connecticut license," the officer said, handing back the New York license. "Now I want you all to get in your fancy cars and get outta here. This is the second complaint we've had in two days. If I get one more I'm gonna write summonses for all of you."

The kid stood defiantly for a moment and then shrugged. "Okay, you want us out of here, we'll go, but I'll tell ya right now—a couple more years and we're gonna own this town."

Josh watched the teenagers go, then drove to a nearby pizza restaurant to meet Conner. Clayt was sitting in a booth when Josh arrived, and he stood when Josh approached. A tall, slender black man in his mid-thirties, Conner wore wire-rim glasses and was dressed in a sports coat, tie, and khakis; he reminded Josh of a professor he'd had at Stanford. The two men greeted one another with the easy manner of friends who had spent hours trying to beat each other's brains out on the tennis court.

"We still on for Saturday afternoon?" Clayt asked.

"Damn right. I gotta get back at you for last week," Josh said, still smarting from the way Clayt had come back from love-four and beaten him with an overhead smash that had almost put a hole in his chest. "I've still got a welt from your last shot."

"I had to do *something* to end it," Clayt said, flashing an infectious grin. "You've been beatin' me regularly for the last couple of months."

Josh smiled. It was an exaggeration, but he had been having a pretty good run, and beating a younger guy like Clayt was better than beating a dozen guys his own age.

Besides being one of the top players at the club, Conner was one of the most interesting people Josh had met since coming back to Connecticut. They rarely had time to talk about anything but tennis and sports, but Josh had read a story about Conner a while back that described his role as both the manager of an inner-city youth program in New London and a science teacher at an overwhelmingly white suburban high school. The gist of the story was that the kids in both places loved him. According to the article, Conner was on a crusade to get minority kids to stay in school, had helped dozens of them to get into college, and was passionate about trying to bridge the gap between the hip-hop and civil rights generations.

They ordered Cokes, and Josh proceeded to fill Clayt in on Matt and his problems, including his new girlfriend. Clayt listened quietly and, after a few questions, said he'd be happy to work out a schedule for tutoring him in physics and calculus a couple evenings a week. Matt, Clayt observed, sounded like a pretty normal kid who was simply a little overextended and probably just needed a bit of extra help to get on track.

"So," Josh remarked when they finished with Matt, "it looks like there's a real battle going on over annexation. I couldn't believe the number of signs as I drove in."

"Yeah, I'm afraid the town's going through a lot of turmoil right now," Clayt replied. "It's too bad, because when I started teaching here, Ledyard was a quiet place with good, stable neighborhoods, one little shopping center, and one of the best school systems in this part of the state."

"You're not saying all that's changed already?" Josh asked.

"No, of course not. But it's changing fast, especially the closer you get to the reservation. A lot of families have moved out, and there are 'for sale' signs all over the place."

"People just don't want to live near the casino?" Josh asked.

"That's part of it, but it's more complicated than that. It's the whole atmosphere being created by the casino, the tribe, and all the new casino workers and tribe members coming in."

"How big's the tribe now?" Josh asked.

"They say they'll have over three hundred members by the end of the year," Clayt replied. "But it's not just the numbers, it's who they're bringing in. I mean, it's no secret that most of them are poor, inner-city blacks who never dreamed Congress was going to turn 'em into Pequot Indians. You can guess the town's reaction, and my problem is I can see it from both sides."

Josh's immediate instinct was to back away from the racial issue, but Clayt seemed to have no inhibitions about discussing it.

"On one hand, it's a fabulous story," Clayt continued. "Here's a bunch of people, many of them earning the minimum wage or on welfare, and suddenly they're brought into the tribe and given new houses on the reservation or in the most expensive part of town, along with a multi-million-dollar community center, jobs, hundred-thousand-dollar stipends, free education and health care, trust funds for their kids, and a chance to make something of their lives. But on the other hand, you've suddenly got this influx of people with a street culture that's totally alien to the town.

"And it's not just the townspeople who are having a hard time adjusting. Some of the white Mashantuckets are complaining that the blacks are nothing but freeloaders, that they want to take over the tribe, and that they've created serious drug and security problems on the reservation."

"And I assume the black Mashantuckets have their own complaints," Josh said.

"Oh, sure. They've got their own list, but their biggest concern is the way Hayward and his white relatives are cutting up the pie. A lot of blacks, and especially the newer arrivals, are complaining they're being treated like second-class citizens and not getting a fair shake on the money, jobs, and houses that are being handed out."

"Is that true?"

"I'm sure some of it is. Although I have to say it's pretty hard for some poor stiff makin' three hundred dollars a week in New London to be very sympathetic. In fact," Clayt said with a chuckle, "some of the complaints are hilarious. My wife was just telling me about how the tribe helped one guy down in New York get out of jail, brought him up here, and gave him a job and a three-hundred-fifty-thousand-dollar house only to have him gripe that the job didn't pay enough and the house wasn't big enough. I mean, you can't make this stuff up."

Josh thought about the scene he'd just witnessed at the community store. "How does all the easy money affect the kids?" he asked.

Clayt took a drink of his Coke.

"Pretty much the way you'd expect. Most of the Mashantucket kids have pocket money, and some will come right out and tell you they've got a fortune waiting for them and don't see any reason to bust their butt studying. We're seeing more and more disciplinary problems, and some of the older kids are dropping out of school completely just to hang out and cruise around town in their parents' Mercedes."

"But it's not just the money. Part of it's the parents, and I'm convinced another factor is that a lot of these kids face a real identity crisis once they get here. I mean, think about what it's gotta be like for a bunch of inner-city black kids to suddenly be dropped onto an Indian reservation in a white town next to a glitzy casino that they supposedly own a piece of. Who exactly are they supposed to be? Are they supposed to be street or Indian, or act white?"

"How do the other kids react to the Mashantuckets?" Josh asked.

"Depends. Some keep their distance, some suck up to them because of their money, and others are just curious or treat them like anybody else. But it's interesting. Kids are sharp. They say the Mashantuckets act like they're 'entitled,' which pretty much nails it."

"How about relations between the town and the tribe on things other than annexation? Do they work together on anything?"

"Not much," Clayt said. "Basically it's a very antagonistic relationship. The Mashantuckets claim the townspeople opposing them are jealous bigots who are against Indians and blacks, and are trying to block them at every turn. And the townspeople feel the Mashantuckets are fakes who are here solely for the money. In fact, people say that if the casino ever hit hard times and the members stopped being paid to be Indians, the whole tribe would fall apart overnight."

"Where do you see things going from here?" Josh asked.

"Well, the one bright spot is the tribe's starting to use some of its money to get members to stay in school, go back to school, go to college, or do whatever else it takes to get an education. So as that begins to kick in and both sides begin to realize they have to live and work together, you gotta hope things will improve."

Clayt continued, "The tougher problem for the town and the whole region is the gambling. If Foxwoods keeps expanding and the Mohegans and Northerns build casinos, then this whole area's gonna become one big casino town. And that'd be a disaster. Especially for the low-income people I work with. The casinos are just one more way to take away what little they have. And, of course, the other thing is the message this whole gambling culture we're creating is sending the kids—that it's all about luck and getting something for nothing instead of hard work. It's exactly the opposite of what I'm tryin' to teach 'em."

Clayt looked at his watch. "Afraid I gotta go. You know, if you're interested in this annexation issue, you really ought to come over to the high school Saturday morning. The town's so up in arms the head of the Bureau of Indian Affairs is flying up for a hearing."

Josh reached for his wallet and put down a ten-dollar bill. "Good idea," he said. "You goin'?"

"Nah, I hear enough about the Mashantuckets during the week. Besides, I want to go over to the club and use the ball machine Saturday morning. Gotta get ready for a match with this dude who says he's gonna kick my ass."

"Yeah? Guy any good?"

"Kinda over the hill, but even old guys can be dangerous."

They both laughed and walked out together.

18

⌒

The Hearing

September 14–18, 1993

Bobby Kingman was pleased with the way things had progressed since the Northerns announced their recognition bid in the spring.

Sheffield had returned to at least a semblance of normal, and Bobby had continued his efforts to rebuild the tribe, expanding the new tribal council and holding the big summer powwow. In addition, Grimaldi reported they were beginning to make inroads in Washington. He said their lobbyists had now had two encouraging conversations with a high-level political appointee at the Department of the Interior about the tribe's application, and Paul Ivy had personally talked with an influential western Republican senator who served on the Senate Indian Affairs Subcommittee and who'd agreed to make calls on the Northerns' behalf.

Even more important, Grimaldi intimated they were beginning to get support from the White House as well. The new president, Bill Clinton, had opposed Indian casinos when he was governor of Arkansas, but once he became a presidential candidate he made a concerted effort to win Indian votes and raise money from casino tribes. By the time of the Democratic presidential convention in 1992, Clinton had moved to neutral on the issue, and recently Grimaldi had sent Bobby an article in which Clinton was quoted as praising Indian gaming as "a positive economic development tool for Indian tribes."

Grimaldi attached a Post-it to the clipping that read simply: "Another of Paul's good friends!"

The one cloud on the horizon was the increasingly bitter dispute over annexation in the towns of Ledyard, Preston, and North Stonington. Bobby was afraid it would inflame anti-casino sentiment in Sheffield at a time when the town was still settling down from the shock of the Northern Pequots' May announcement, and he was furious at the Mashantuckets for stirring up a hornets' nest with their ham-handed annexation tactics.

Bobby became even more concerned when he read that the top official in the BIA, Assistant Secretary of the Interior for Indian Affairs Ada Deer, was breaking bureau precedent to come to Ledyard for a public hearing on the Mashantuckets' latest trust request. According to *The Day*, Deer's visit had been arranged by the region's congressman, Sam Gejdenson, and local anti-annexation groups were hoping the visit meant the BIA was reconsidering its normally automatic approval of trust applications.

The last thing Bobby wanted to see was any sign the BIA was beginning to bend to public pressure in Connecticut on annexation, because the Northerns were counting on being able to annex the Standish farm once they were recognized, and anything that weakened their ability to do so could be disastrous for them. Their intention was to use the farm to build an access road from the state highway to their current reservation, but unless the tribe annexed the farm, the town could conceivably use its zoning and other regulatory powers to block the road indefinitely.

Bobby called Jim Grimaldi on September 14 to give him a heads-up on the BIA visit and was surprised when Ivy himself called back a couple of days later. Up to that point, Ivy had let Grimaldi handle virtually all the direct dealings with the tribe and had remained almost totally invisible. At first, Bobby had thought the lack of direct contact with the man was a little strange, but he'd gradually learned from Grimaldi that this was Ivy's typical MO: take financial control of a project and then run it from the background. So the moment Bobby heard Ivy's voice he began imagining the worst about Secretary Deer's visit.

"Chief!?" Ivy's slightly clipped, gravelly voice came on the line. "Paul Ivy here.... Right, it has been a while, but Jim tells me things are moving along well up there. Tribe's growing, and the town's settled down a bit. Just what we want, so keep up the good work!"

"Thanks," Bobby said. "And I hear from Jim that we're makin' progress in D.C. as well."

"Yeah, we're doin' okay, but the reason I called is this Deer visit."

"You think it could be a problem?" Bobby asked.

"I did at first, but we checked it out, and it's apparently just a public relations stunt to help the Congressman. The towns think he's too close to the Mashantuckets and are furious with him for not coming out against annexation. He says he's neutral and is evidently trying to prove it by bringing Deer up to hear the towns' side."

"And that's the only reason Deer's coming—to help Gejdenson?" Bobby asked.

"Looks that way," Ivy said, "because the BIA's telling us she has absolutely no intention of turning the visit into a public hearing. They're saying it's simply an off-the-record informational meeting and that they couldn't legally use any of the testimony even if they wanted to."

"That's certainly not the way the Congressman's spinnin' it," Bobby said, "so I gotta assume the townspeople are going to be even more pissed at him when they find out that's all it is."

"You're probably right," Ivy replied, "but hopefully it won't affect us. As far as I can tell, the BIA seems pretty determined not to be influenced by the locals."

"That's a relief."

"Big relief," Ivy said. "But just the same, I want you to go to the meeting Saturday to say hello to Deer and make sure there's not something we're missing. I got a barrel of money tied up in this thing, Chief, and the one thing I can't stand is surprises."

"Understood," Bobby said. "I'll go."

"Good. Anything more we need to discuss?"

"I don't think so."

"Okay, then, take care of yourself," Ivy said, and signed off as quickly as he'd come on.

Bobby sat staring at the phone. At one time, he would have resented Ivy telling him so bluntly what to do. But not now. The game was getting trickier, and he needed Ivy's money, contacts, and involvement more than ever.

⸺

Bobby arrived in Ledyard Center just after 10:00 on Saturday morning and was immediately caught up in the traffic headed for the high school.

There were lines of cars approaching the school from two directions, and several hundred vehicles already filled the front parking lot and spilled onto the grass along the two access roads leading up to the modern, low-slung building. Three police cruisers were parked in front of the main entrance and another behind the school, where Bobby finally parked.

According to the morning papers, Congressman Gejdenson had asked residents not to bring signs, placards, or written material into the auditorium, but anti-annexation activists were holding up NO ANNEXATION—NOT ONE ACRE signs out on the sidewalk, and others were passing out signs and buttons and literature to everyone coming in. One of the handouts was an 11-by-17 sheet of paper with two maps of Ledyard. The first map was labeled "Before

Annexation" and the second "After Annexation." The second map showed a large chunk of the town broken away and marked "Mashantucket Pequot."

A state trooper and a young Ledyard cop were stationed at the door as townspeople filed in, and when Bobby finally entered the auditorium he saw it was already packed. Shaking his head at the turnout, he quickly made a bee-line for the stage to greet Secretary Deer before the program began.

Bobby was conscious of additional police officers standing along the sides of the auditorium as he walked down one of the two aisles, but nobody appeared to be paying any attention to them; instead people were busy greeting neighbors, settling in, and talking among themselves. Yet another policeman blocked the stairs leading to the stage, but Bobby, who was dressed in his usual buckskin jacket, identified himself as Chief Kingman of the Northern Pequot tribe, and the officer let him through.

Bobby had never met Ada Deer, but he'd read a brief article about her and knew she was a Menominee Indian from Wisconsin, where she'd grown up in a one-room log cabin. She was said to be passionate about helping Indians overcome years of poverty and neglect, and Bobby couldn't imagine she had much sympathy for all these white suburbanites who had come out to protest the Pequots trying to take back a few lousy acres.

Deer, who looked to be in her late fifties, was a large woman with big glasses and streaks of gray running through jet-black hair. She wore a dark business suit and turquoise and silver jewelry.

"Excuse me, Secretary Deer," Bobby said extending his hand. "I'm Bobby Kingman, chairman of the Northern Pequots, and I just wanted to welcome you to Connecticut and tell you what a fantastic job you're doing."

The head of the BIA looked at him quizzically for a moment, taking in his blue eyes and long, blondish hair, but then smiled graciously and thanked him for the kind words. She'd love to have a chance to talk with him, she said, but unfortunately the program was about to start.

No problem, Bobby said; he just wanted to say hello and wish her the best, after which he headed back up the aisle in search of an empty seat. Looking up, he saw a huge white banner hanging from the back balcony that read "Thanks for Coming, Ada!"

Bobby found a seat just as Congressman Gejdenson took the mike. In his mid-forties, Gejdenson was already the dean of the Connecticut House delegation because of his years in office, but there was speculation that his failure to back the towns on annexation could cost him the next election. Nevertheless, Gejdenson hewed to his official neutrality, praising Deer for her willingness to come to Connecticut and expressing hope the towns and the tribe could come up with a compromise.

"It won't be easy," he declared, "but even the Israelis and the PLO signed a peace accord this week."

Bobby thought it was a good line, but it quickly became clear the crowd had little patience with the Congressman and simply wanted to hear from Deer.

When Deer finally stood to speak, however, she quickly dashed any hopes she was there to offer the towns encouragement. She told the audience in a clear, pleasant voice that she was in Connecticut to listen to their concerns, but that the comment period on the Mashantuckets' application to take the two hundred forty-seven acres into trust was already over and that everything said today was consequently off the record. Moreover, she said, there was no basis for treating Connecticut or well-to-do tribes any differently than any other tribe when it came to their trust requests.

"Putting land into trust is a very routine process that is undertaken by tribes and the bureau all across the country," she pointed out. "What is going on here is no different than what is going on anywhere else."

Nonetheless, Deer stated, she wanted to assure everyone that the decision on the Mashantuckets' request would be handled fairly, and she hoped the towns and the tribe could work out a compromise. She was encouraged that this could happen, she said, because she detected "hope and healing in the skies around us."

The audience's honeymoon with Deer ended instantly. Bobby could literally feel the disappointment spread through the crowd.

"What bullshit," the man next to him grumbled.

"Money talks," a woman behind him said.

"A charade," another muttered. "She must think we're all idiots."

Bobby, on the other hand, couldn't have asked for more. The only part of the meeting that made him uneasy occurred when two women from North Stonington rose to read an emotional plea to the Assistant Secretary.

Foxwoods, they told her, taking turns reading from a prepared statement, was destroying the peacefulness, stability, and quality of life of their communities.

So far, the first woman said stoically, they had shouldered all of it: "the traffic, the crime, the garbage thrown on our roads, the men using our yards as toilets, and the loss of countless numbers of our friends and neighbors, who are giving up, selling now, and leaving while the getting is still good.

"The one thing we cannot accept, however, is annexation, because it threatens to literally dismantle our towns and destroy our ability to govern ourselves."

"Assistant Secretary Deer," the second woman concluded, "you know the law regarding trust acquisitions, but what you may not know is the human impact the threat of annexation is having here.

"We therefore ask you to recognize the uniqueness of our situation, and say no to annexation!"

There was dead silence at first, and then the great majority of the crowd rose en masse, cheering, clapping, and waving NO ANNEXATION signs in an outpouring of pent-up emotion.

Assistant Secretary Deer looked on impassively as the demonstration continued, but Bobby had to wonder how long the BIA could hold its ground against a community as worked up as this one. He also couldn't help wondering how much time he had before Sheffield began to rev up its fight against the Northerns.

While things had remained relatively quiet in Sheffield over the summer, Bobby believed that was only because a decision on the Northerns' recognition application was so far in the distance and little had been done yet to organize the opposition to the casino. So far it appeared the town was leaving the fight entirely in the hands of Jim Clark, its first selectman. Clark was a crafty politician, but he had to be close to seventy-five years old, and Bobby doubted he had either the energy or the sophistication to wage a particularly effective campaign against the kind of money Ivy was willing to spend. Bobby figured it was therefore just a matter of time before someone else emerged to mobilize the opposition.

As Bobby followed the crowd out of the auditorium, he spotted Josh Williams maybe sixty feet ahead of him. He hadn't talked to Josh since that day in the post office almost six years ago, but it immediately occurred to him that Josh was exactly the kind of guy he worried about. He presumably had both the smarts and the organizational experience to pull the town together against the Northerns and their casino, and the Williams name still carried a lot of clout among the old-timers in town. Bobby had no way to know what Josh was thinking, but he was obviously sufficiently interested in Ledyard's battle with the Mashantuckets to have come over from Sheffield, and he clearly bore watching.

~

19

Ol' Blue Eyes

September 19–November 17, 1993

Virtually all of Sheffield's local officials had come out against the potential Northern Pequot casino, but Josh was uneasy that the town wasn't moving faster to formulate a strategy to stop it. His sense was that the town's first selectman, Jim Clark, was getting too old to lead the charge and that it was essential to begin pushing back against the tribe before it gained further momentum. He was particularly concerned that the town hadn't made any effort to hire a legal expert who could help plan its defense and instead was relying entirely on its long-time town attorney, Justin Pierce. Pierce was great at mortgage closings, a colleague cracked, but his only experience with Indians was rooting for the old Boston Braves.

Actually, Josh believed the town was going to need two strategies: one to try to block the Northerns from receiving federal recognition and a second to throw up as many obstacles as possible to their ever building a casino if they were recognized.

Increasingly impatient, he had begun to toy with the idea of forming a citizens' group to prod the town into more action, but he'd become so immersed in trying to expand his business he hadn't followed through. After seeing and hearing what he had in Ledyard, he decided he couldn't wait any longer.

His first step was to meet with leaders of the groups opposing the Mashantuckets to learn as much as he could from their experience, and his second was to make an appointment with a Washington law firm that Brad Merriweather recommended. Brad offered to do whatever he could to help, but said that if the town were going to stop the Northerns it was going to need a firm that specialized in Indian issues and knew its way around the federal government.

Josh originally planned to go to Washington on November 17 but had to postpone the trip because of, of all things, an invitation to Foxwoods.

Foxwoods was bringing in Frank Sinatra to inaugurate its new fifteen-hundred-seat Fox Theater beginning November 17, and Bob Duncan called to invite Josh and Sharon to dinner that evening, followed by Sinatra's opening-night concert. They were calling it the biggest entertainment event ever to hit eastern Connecticut, Bob raved, and he just happened to have four tickets.

Josh was in such an anti-casino mood that he almost declined, but he was in the final stages of buying Duncan's agency, and he hated to say no. Even then, however, he might have begged off if it weren't for Sharon.

"Why not," she'd said. She'd love to see Sinatra, and it was probably the only benefit they'd ever get from the casino.

"You sure?" Josh asked.

"Positive," Sharon said. "It'll be fun. I can wear that black evening dress I've never worn."

⤺

The newspapers were full of stories on Sinatra's approaching visit. At seventy-seven, he missed an occasional note, but he was a legend and could still pack 'em in. He was booked for five consecutive performances, and they were all sold out, with tickets ranging up to $200, a record for eastern Connecticut.

Sinatra was scheduled to come in with an entourage of fourteen people in addition to his thirty-five-piece orchestra and to stay in one of the three Presidential Suites at the top of the casino's new three-hundred-twelve-room luxury hotel, which was opening simultaneously with the Fox Theater. The papers reported that his suite included a fireplace, a Jacuzzi, and a grand piano, and a hotel spokesman commented that if the crooner just wanted to relax, all he had to do was pour himself a Jack Daniels from the bar and gaze out over the peaceful countryside.

Local radio stations played Sinatra's songs, music stores promoted his newest CD, and Foxwoods piped his hits over its sound system. *The Day* published a marvelous photo of a young Frank Sinatra being greeted by the mayors of Norwich and New London during a visit to open a local movie theater in 1949. Now, forty-four years later, Foxwoods was bringing him back for a rare encore.

On the evening of the concert, Josh and Sharon met Bob and Doris Duncan at their home in Norwich and drove together in Bob's Lincoln to Randall's Ordinary, a seventeenth-century country inn in North Stonington. The inn was famous for colonial dishes prepared over an open hearth and served by waiters and waitresses in colonial attire. Josh had taken the family there a couple of years ago, and afterward they'd roamed the property, taking in the gardens, barns, and farm animals.

A cold drizzle was falling when the two couples arrived, and Sharon recalled the cozy setting as they entered the inn and were seated by the innkeeper near one of the hearths. Bob ordered champagne for everyone and toasted their deal, which they now hoped to close on December 31. They sipped their champagne and chatted, nibbling fire-roasted popcorn.

"Have you been to Foxwoods?" Doris asked.

"No," Sharon said. "This'll be our first time."

"Well, you're in for a treat," Bob said. "The place is fantastic."

"Do you go there often?" Sharon asked.

"Not that often," Doris replied. "We've been there what, dear, maybe a dozen times?"

"Yeah, probably," Bob said. "We'll have dinner and then pop into the casino, maybe win or lose a hundred bucks, and go home. Doris likes the slots, although I prefer the table games."

"So I take it you think the casino's been a good thing?" Josh asked.

"Hell, it's been terrific," Bob answered. "Look what it's done for this area. It's already pulled us out of a recession. It'll have over nine thousand employees by the end of the year. It's boosting tourism. It's sending a hundred million dollars a year to Hartford. And it's breathing some life into eastern Connecticut for a change.

"I mean, think about it—the reservation was just woods three and a half years ago, and now you've got a hundred thousand visitors a week coming here. With the new theater, the place'll be off the charts."

Josh could see Sharon was about to jump in with a different view, but he squeezed her knee in a plea to cool it. This was supposed to be a social night out, and Josh saw no point in getting into an argument with Bob when he was trying to buy the man's business.

"And another thing," Bob added, warming to his subject, "all these moralizers who claim to be so upset by casinos clearly have no understanding of American history. Hell, the Indians were the biggest gamblers ever to come down the pike. They bet on everything from dice to lacrosse, and bet everything from their horses and dogs to their wives. The colonists built a lot of their town halls and colleges with lotteries. George Washington used lotteries to help build the District of Columbia. And in the Old West just about everybody gambled, from gunfighters and dance-hall girls to sheriffs and preachers. So I think people are getting a little carried away when they start complaining that a single casino's going to corrupt eastern Connecticut. God, this state may have been founded by Puritans, but people have gotta loosen up. Know what I mean?"

As though on cue, the waitress arrived in her white bonnet and apron, saving Josh from having to respond, and began serving the entrees—Lobster Newburg, cranberry duck, and two venison stews. Bob ordered more champagne, Sharon asked Doris about her grandchildren, and no one mentioned gambling again for the rest of the meal.

The food was superb, and everyone was in high spirits when they finally left the cheerful, bustling inn and headed out into the soggy November night.

Bob Duncan took a left out of the restaurant parking lot and headed northwest on Route 2 for the five-mile drive to Foxwoods. Searchlights promoting Sinatra's visit bounced off the clouds up ahead, and as the car rounded a curve, Foxwoods' new hotel and casino complex suddenly rose up out of the countryside, illuminating a long line of cars, pickups, and buses waiting to get in. Bob finally fought his way to one of the valet stations, and they all got out and went in via the main entrance.

The new Fox Theater was part of an indoor theater theme park consisting of glittering marquees and three and four-story-high building facades designed to create the impression of an old-fashioned theater district. Hundreds of ticket holders jammed the square in front of the theater, while gaggles of gawkers watched from the sidelines.

Inside, it could have been an opening night in New York, London, or Paris. The ladies wore evening dresses and their best jewelry, the men dark suits and in some cases tuxedoes. As Sharon looked around, she marveled at the contrast with the drab and tedious Wednesday night town committee meeting she was missing back in Sheffield.

Then he was on. Sinatra. Ol' Blue Eyes. The Chairman of the Board. Strutting across the stage in a black tuxedo, singing "Come Fly with Me," and lifting everyone with his magic. For the next hour he dazzled the audience with his favorites: "My Way," "The Lady Is a Tramp," and "Strangers in the Night," drawing shrieks and applause. "Chicago" gave Sharon goose bumps, and when Sinatra closed with "New York, New York," the city's name spelled out in lights behind him, the audience rose in a standing ovation.

Sinatra responded in kind, thanking everyone. "You know," he told the crowd, "the guys who wrote all the good songs have either died or gotten drunk." The audience loved it, erupting again in applause and finally bringing him back for an encore.

Afterward Bob insisted on giving Josh and Sharon a tour so they could see how fast Foxwoods was expanding.

He led them down a long shopping concourse lined by huge plate-glass windows on one side and faux-nineteenth-century New England storefronts on the other.

Sharon quickly saw that other than the theatergoers who stayed to gamble, the people surging up and down the concourse were as motley an evening crew as she had ever seen. In fact, she might as well have been at the local mall. Most of the patrons seemed to be dressed in T-shirts, jeans, stretch pants, or warm-up outfits, although none looked particularly athletic. Even at that late hour, a number of parents were pushing children in strollers or carrying babies in backpacks or front carriers, and at one point she spied a mother breast-feeding her infant on a bench along the concourse as the crowd streamed by.

The concourse became more crowded as they approached a replica of a town square, where a sea of people stared up at a twelve-foot sculpture of an Indian preparing to shoot an arrow into the sky.

"That's the Rainmaker," Bob said excitedly, "and if we timed this right, it should be just about ready to go off!"

The Rainmaker knelt on top of a rock ledge, bow drawn tight, ready to fire his arrow through a huge, pyramid-shaped skylight into the heavens. As the crowd watched, a laser arrow suddenly shot skyward. Lightning flashed, thunder rumbled, an eagle screeched, drums beat, voices chanted, and rain began to fall from above. Mist rose from the rocks, and the ethereal voice of an Indian elder sounded from the great beyond as a rainbow appeared.

"Fantastic, isn't it?" Bob enthused. "The whole thing's run by computers, and that Indian alone's more than two tons of molded urethane. You'd think you were in Vegas, wouldn't you?"

"Pretty spectacular," Josh agreed.

Bob then steered them into a cavernous, smoke-filled hall packed with gaming tables and long banks of slot machines.

"This is the original casino," he said, raising his voice over the din.

The hall was a mob scene, with people pressed around the blackjack, craps, roulette, and other tables, playing the slots, or simply wandering through. Purple- and green-clad dealers dealt the cards and spun the wheels as cocktail waitresses in matching Pocahontas tunics pushed their way through the crowd. Bob gave the group a running commentary on the games they were passing, but by the time they got to the slots, the bleeping, clacking, and calliope music was so loud he gave up trying to be heard.

Most of the slot players, Josh noticed, seemed to be in their fifties, sixties, and seventies, and three-quarters of them were women. Most played with intense concentration, dropping coins into the machines as fast as they could, pressing the electronic start buttons rather than pulling the handles in order to speed up the action, and mechanically filling their buckets with coins each time they won. A number of women, Josh realized, were playing two machines at a time, turning with smooth, practiced motions from one machine to the other each time the spinning icons in their windows came to a stop.

"So, what do you think?" Bob asked when they finally emerged back on the concourse.

"It's huge," Sharon replied.

"Yeah, that's why some people actually like the new casino better," Bob said. "It's more intimate."

Sharon, Doris, and Bob took a restroom break while Josh sat down on a bench to wait.

"Hi," he said to a teenager who was sitting alone. "Howya doin'?"

"Pretty good," the kid answered. He was wearing a high school jacket and looked about sixteen.

"Did you go to the Sinatra concert?" the boy asked.

"Yes, we did," Josh replied. "He was terrific."

"Yeah, I thought I might spot him, but he must have gone in and out the back."

"You been over here before?" Josh asked.

"Oh, yeah," the boy said, "I come over on Wednesdays with my mother and father, and hang out while they play the slots."

"Doesn't that get kinda boring?"

"Nah. It's a pretty neat place. I usually meet a few friends, and we go over to the arcade or cruise the concourse lookin' for chicks.

"Sometimes," the boy said, "I just like to watch the people. You wouldn't believe some of the weirdos you see here. And they're always adding new stuff. Next month they're opening the Cinedrome and Turbo rides, which'll be awesome."

"You can't go in the casinos, though, even with your parents, right?" Josh asked, thinking about Matt.

"No. You gotta be twenty-one, which sucks. But you can play bingo when you're eighteen."

Just then, Josh saw Sharon, and took his leave to join her.

"Who's your new friend?" she asked.

"You're kidding!" she gasped when he told her the boy came to the casino regularly with his parents. By the time she looked back, the boy was walking off with two other teens.

Bob took everyone over to the new casino, which had murals on the ceiling and felt more like a nightclub. The room was only half the size of the first casino, but according to Bob, it had seventeen hundred slots as opposed to fourteen hundred in the first hall, and the noise was twice as deafening. What really caught Josh and Sharon's attention, however, was a woman who was attached to an IV bag suspended from a pole on wheels. The woman was walking slowly, pushing the pole with one hand and clutching a bucket of coins in the other. Sharon gaped as she watched the woman and her male companion speed up in an effort to grab two machines that had just been vacated thirty feet up ahead.

"God, can you imagine wanting to play those machines that much?" Sharon half-yelled into Josh's ear. He just shook his head and didn't even try to answer.

Josh's ears were still ringing when they finally got to Bob's car, and the buzzing didn't completely stop until they reached Norwich, where he and Sharon got into their own car for the drive back home.

The rain was now coming down in sheets, making it difficult to see through the windshield, and for the next five minutes they focused all their attention on retracing their route out of town.

"So, did you enjoy the evening?" Josh asked when they finally reached the highway and the rain slowed down.

"I loved Sinatra," Sharon said. "But no matter what it costs, Josh, promise we'll leave before we ever let them build something like that next to the farm."

"Promise," he said, and thought again of the massive casino lit up like a giant ocean liner in the Ledyard cornfield. He couldn't help wondering what the original Pequots or Ethan Williams would have thought.

20

The Breakup

November 18–December 22, 1993

As the holidays approached, Josh raced to wrap up the Duncan deal. Sharon, who had won reelection to the school board in early November, became embroiled in contentious hearings on whether to build a new middle school, and her Appaloosa, Lucy, bore a second colt. Jacob got the lead role in his school play. Sarah made the high school swim team. And Matt began the new basketball season as one of Southeast's starting forwards.

Josh had had a one-on-one with Matt back in September in which he made it clear he expected him to knuckle down academically; he also brought up his new girlfriend, Kayla Timko. He said he and Sharon were looking forward to meeting Kayla, but he hoped Matt wouldn't allow her to distract him from his studies.

Matt had promised to do his best to get back on track and claimed his sister had exaggerated how much time he was spending with Kayla. He acknowledged he was more serious about her than any of his previous girlfriends, but said he still had a lot of competition for her and it simply wasn't time yet to bring her by the house.

Josh had been reasonably satisfied with the conversation, although as the fall progressed, the results appeared to be decidedly mixed.

Academically, Clayt Conner's tutoring seemed to be paying off, and Matt had begun doing better in both physics and math. On the negative side, he seemed to be spending more time than ever with Kayla, and it was clear to his parents that he was in no hurry to have them meet her. The first time they saw her was when Sarah pointed her out at a soccer game. Kayla was standing with two other girls at one end of the bleachers; from what Josh could see she was stunningly attractive, with shoulder-length dark hair and a drop-dead figure that was hard to miss in tight jeans and a sweater. She was obviously popular, because every time Josh looked, there seemed to be at least one or two guys chatting her up.

That, unfortunately, was exactly what bothered Matt every night as he lay in bed thinking about her. She was too popular. Even after they started going together, he couldn't help feeling jealous any time he saw her talking to any of the other guys who'd been after her.

The one he was most concerned about was Greg Elliot, who was the basketball team's point guard and clearly hadn't completely given up. Greg was a cocky smart-ass with a cutting sense of humor, and Matt had always felt uneasy around him. Greg's family, moreover, was loaded, and one of the things that especially bothered Matt was that Greg had a '93 Ford Mustang, the hottest car at school, and had driven Kayla home several times the first week of school.

In addition to having to worry about Greg, Matt was concerned about what his parents would think of Kayla when they met her. He knew from the start they wouldn't be thrilled with Kayla because of the way she looked and dressed and made herself up, not to mention her connection to the casino. His parents would be very pleasant, Matt was sure, but they'd be wondering the whole time about why he couldn't have stayed with Courtney Meyers, who was on the honor roll and was one of the stars on the girls' track team. His mother thought she was terrific.

But Matt felt the comparison was unfair. Kayla might not be a standout student, but it wasn't because she wasn't smart or ambitious. He'd never met anyone who seemed so sure of what she wanted out of life. She planned to have her own business someday in the travel or hospitality field, and she had taken a job as a hostess at the Sheffield Tavern, where she was working twenty hours a week in order to make enough money to attend the local community college.

Matt finally took Kayla home to meet his parents in late October. They didn't stay long, but it turned out better than he'd hoped. His mother and father were very cordial, Sharon showed Kayla briefly around the house, and she and Josh accompanied Matt and Kayla out to the barn to show Kayla the horses. Kayla, Matt thought, was very polite and even demure, and he breathed a quiet sigh of relief when they finally got back to his car and headed out.

By early December, Matt had blown off most of his friends to spend as much time as possible with Kayla, was at her house at least a couple of evenings a week, and was driving her to and from her restaurant job whenever he could.

Matt simply couldn't get enough of her. She was not only the most gorgeous girl he'd ever met, but she was more mature than any of the other girls at school. He loved talking with her. He loved to be seen with her. And he loved her body. When he thought about lying in the front seat of the car with her, parked on a dirt road near the farm, both half undressed, kissing her mouth and her breasts and sliding his hand down between her warm thighs, he wanted her so much his whole being ached. And the fact she wouldn't let him go any further added to the ache.

The basketball season posed a new challenge for Matt because of the amount of time it meant he had to spend with Greg Elliot. Southeast had been picked to win their division, and Matt was doing his best to work as smoothly as he could with Greg. But every time he looked at him he thought of their competition for Kayla.

The friction finally flared into the open the day before the pre-Christmas home game against Winthrop, Southeast's biggest rival.

Matt was on his way to his next class when he rounded a corner and saw Kayla talking and laughing with Greg in the hall. She saw him out of the corner of her eye and turned to face him, at first with a smile. Her smile vanished when she saw the look on his face.

"Don't you have gym next?" he asked sullenly, without acknowledging Greg. As he asked the question he made a quick gesture with his head toward the other end of the building, where the gym was located. "I mean, aren't you gonna be late?" he said, trying to soften his tone.

Kayla hesitated, then looked at her watch. "Yeah, you're right," she said, managing another smile. "See ya, Greg," she said, "and you're picking me up tonight . . . right, Matt?" she called back as she started down the hall.

"Yeah, nine-thirty," he called back, and turned and left without looking at Greg.

Greg didn't react, but it was obvious Matt was rattled, and Greg rubbed it in after practice that afternoon in the locker room.

"What's the matter, Williams?" Greg said as they stood at their lockers dressing. "You didn't like me talkin' to your girlfriend this morning?"

Matt ignored him.

"You know, you better be careful, Williams, or next thing you know, she'll be asking me to drive her home again. And I wouldn't blame her, given that piece of shit you drive."

Matt could feel the other players looking at him.

"At least I'd know what to do with a piece of ass like that," Greg added loud enough to be sure everyone could hear.

Matt looked around slowly, then suddenly lunged at Greg, who was shorter but more muscular, grabbing him by the shoulders and slamming him against his locker. Two teammates immediately separated them, but the coach blamed Matt for making the first move and made him apologize and shake hands.

Matt was furious he had taken the brunt of the blame, and the more he fumed on the way home, the more wronged he felt by everyone, especially Kayla. By the time he picked her up at work that night, he was bristling with righteous indignation and determined to insist she not let Greg get between them again.

Matt had mapped out exactly what he was going to say, but when Kayla got in the car, everything went wrong. She brushed off her conversation with Greg in the hall. When Matt pressed her, instead of offering an apology, as he expected, she became angry and called him immature.

"My God, Matt," Kayla said, "I was just talking to him. It wasn't like he was fucking me or something."

Matt absolutely lost it. "Goddamnit, you know I can't stand it when you talk like that!" he yelled. "Obviously, you don't care what happens to us anymore. And if that's the case, then as far as I'm concerned, it's time we split."

"Fine!" Kayla retorted as Matt pulled up to her house. "I don't have time to deal with your jealousy, anyway," she shouted, getting out of the car and slamming the door behind her.

Matt knew at once it was over. Even if they ever made up it would never be the same. He couldn't believe he'd let it happen.

Sharon and Josh were out when Matt got home that night, and he rushed off to school so fast in the morning that the next time they really saw him was at the basketball game that afternoon.

⏤

The gym was packed solid for the game and the stomping and cheering shook the stands as the Southeast Panthers, in blue and white, loped out onto the court for their warm-ups. Josh and Sharon sat just behind the Southeast bench, caught up in the growing excitement. They had both come out of their seats screaming when Matt scored the go-ahead basket to win two evenings before, and they were hoping he'd have another big game today.

Matt, however, was just hoping to get through the afternoon. He hadn't slept for more than an hour the previous night, and he had never felt so depressed and hopeless. He dreaded having his parents see him play this afternoon. Even worse, he had caught a brief glimpse of Kayla as she filed in with one of her girlfriends. He'd assumed she'd come to the previous home game to see him; now, with his confidence shot, he was wondering if it had actually been to see Greg.

Southeast got off to a fast start, but they let down late in the game and were only up by one with a minute ten remaining. Matt was having a horrendous afternoon, with only three points and a single rebound. Greg Elliot, on the other hand, was on fire, with eighteen points and seven assists.

The teams exchanged quick buckets, and with twenty-three seconds left, Southeast inbounded the ball to Greg Elliot. He dribbled across the half-court line, stopped, and held the ball over his head, trying to set up a final play to score two more points and, with virtually no time remaining, effectively ice the game. With seven seconds left, he found an opening and fired a crisp pass to Matt, who was at the foul line, back to the basket.

They had practiced the play a hundred times. Matt was supposed to fake right, then feed the ball to Greg coming around on his left so that Greg could drive in for a layup. But it was a stupid call. If they could just keep possession of the ball for another seven seconds, the game would be over. Clearly Greg just wanted to cap his night with some last-second heroics.

Matt caught the pass, feinted right, then turned left just in time to see Greg streaking around him, anticipating the pass. But there was no way Matt could let Greg make the final basket. Not after what had happened with Kayla. And not with his parents and the entire school screaming at the top of their lungs as the seconds ticked down.

Instead of feeding Greg, Matt pivoted back to the right and went up for a turnaround jump shot.

Josh and Sharon and the entire crowd held their breath.

As he went up, Matt had a clear look at the hoop. His shoulders were square to the basket, and the shot felt right as the ball left his fingers and started on its flight.

But it wasn't to be. Matt watched in dismay as the shot bounced off the rim. Instinctively he went for the rebound in a superhuman effort to retrieve the ball and atone for the shot and his failure to feed Greg.

He never got to the ball. Instead he committed his fifth personal foul, and Josh and Sharon watched him go to the bench, where he draped a towel over his head as Winthrop's six-five center sank two free throws to hand Southeast its first loss of the season.

It was Matt's third disaster in twenty-four hours. The coach wouldn't look at him. The rest of the team ignored him. And what was worse, the story behind why he hadn't passed to Greg would be all over town by evening.

~

21

Gearing Up for a Fight

January–December 1994

Josh closed the Duncan deal on December 31, 1993, and flew to Washington, D.C., four days later to meet with Rick Pugliese, an attorney with Kane and Shapiro, an old-line law firm that had recently expanded its environment and natural resources practice to include federal Indian policy.

It was drizzling as the plane descended into Washington; thin rivulets of water pulsed across the plane's window and gave the great white city a muted, gray look. Quite a difference, Josh thought, from his first visit almost thirty years ago, when he had flown down with his mother, father, and sister to visit the city during spring break. He had been fifteen, and he vividly recalled looking out the window on a crystal-clear day as his father pointed out the cherry blossoms and the magnificent central esplanade that swept past the White House to the Capitol and the Supreme Court Building. He had been studying the branches of government in school, and it had been a thrill to think he was actually seeing all three at once in real life. Yet at the moment, Josh thought bitterly, all three branches of government seemed to be aligned in promoting policies that were threatening to destroy his town and his way of life.

~

Rick Pugliese looked nothing like the young, buttoned-up Washington attorney Josh expected after talking with him on the phone. Instead, he was in his mid-fifties, heavy and rumpled, with a shock of unruly dark hair and a mustache and small goatee that somehow didn't go with his broad, puffy face. His desk was buried in paper, leaving just enough room for a battered brown briefcase that was lying open and stuffed with additional documents. Josh's first reaction was that he must have walked into the wrong office, but once he got over the surprise, he took an immediate liking to the man. Pugliese had an easygoing, down-to-earth manner together with an impressive background that gave Josh hope he had found someone who truly might be able to help him. Originally from Arizona, Pugliese had worked on Indian matters for a Phoenix law firm and had then come to Washington to work at the Interior Department, dealing with issues involving both the Bureau of Indian Affairs and the National Park Service. He had joined Kane and Shapiro just over a year ago to specialize in those areas.

"How familiar are you with what's happening in Connecticut?" Josh inquired, sipping from the large Styrofoam coffee cup Pugliese had placed in front of him.

Not that familiar, Pugliese admitted, but he had read the news clips Josh had sent him on the Northern Pequots and believed he could get up to speed quickly if they were to work together. Obviously, he said, everyone connected with Indian country knew about the Mashantuckets and Foxwoods, but the BIA's main focus had always been on western states with large Indian populations rather than on New England.

"Based on the clips, how strong a case do you think the Northerns have for recognition?" Josh asked.

"On the surface, I'd say it looks pretty thin," Pugliese replied. "But I'm not the one who's going to make the decision. The BIA is, and I think you've got to be concerned about a couple of things. One is the basic bias the BIA brings to recognition decisions, and the other is how much political pressure the Northerns' investors are able to bring.

"I don't know how much you know about the BIA," Pugliese continued, "but it's an anomaly in the federal government. It's responsible for the government's relations with more than five hundred fifty Indian tribes that have signed treaties with the United States, and it's the only agency in the entire government set up to benefit a specific ethnic group."

Pugliese explained that most of the treaties involved tribes giving up land in return for the United States' promise to provide them with certain health, education, and welfare benefits in perpetuity, and that the BIA did everything from operating schools and police departments on many reservations to handling the leasing of agricultural and mining rights on tribal lands.

"The BIA also gives heavy preference to hiring Indians," Pugliese said, "to the point that over ninety percent of its twelve thousand employees are Indians. The BIA's rationale is that Indians know Indian problems best and that Indian people desperately need jobs, but it means the BIA is not only run for Indians, it's also run by Indians.

"So I think you can see what you're up against," Pugliese said. "The BIA's mission is to help Indians, and if they think the Northerns have even a half-decent case for recognition, and if the tribe's backers are able to apply some political heat, then you have to assume the BIA will lean heavily in their direction."

"But how far can the BIA lean?" Josh asked. "I mean, my understanding is that tribes have to meet very specific criteria to get recognized."

"Well, unfortunately, there's a lot of misunderstanding about that," Pugliese said. "What isn't generally understood is that the criteria are essentially internal guidelines rather than requirements embodied in law, and the BIA has considerable latitude in how it interprets and applies them."

"So what do we do?" Josh asked.

"You've got two options," Pugliese said. "One is to simply sit back and let the BIA make a decision on the Northerns' application. The other is to exert as much counterpressure as possible by identifying weaknesses in the application and using them to try to persuade the BIA that the tribe doesn't meet the guidelines.

"The pluses of the first approach are that it costs you nothing in terms of time or money, and you may well get the same result you would if you challenged the application. The negative is that you may miss coming up with something that could block the tribe's recognition."

"What do you think it'd cost for the research and legal work we'd need to seriously challenge their application?" Josh asked.

"Hard to say," Pugliese replied, "because there are so many variables, but let's say roughly a half a million dollars over the next three years."

"That's a lot of money to come up with," Josh said, "but let's say we could do it. How would we start?"

"The first thing we'd do is file a request under the Freedom of Information Act for copies of the Northerns' application," Pugliese said. "We need that to get going, and it could take months to get the BIA to release it. And at the same time we'd begin lining up a genealogist and a historical researcher to help us review it.

"All we need is a client," Pugliese said with a sympathetic smile.

"And all *we* need," Josh said, "is the money."

᠆᠆᠆

Josh's first priority after returning from Washington was to consolidate his newly expanded business, which he renamed the Williams agency, but he simultaneously began following up on his plans to create a local anti-casino group.

He spent virtually every spare moment for the next three weeks recruiting members. By the end of January he had pulled together a core group of twenty people who met at his home to found a grass-roots organization they christened Citizens Against the Casino.

For starters, CAC named Josh president and chose Carol Zajak, an attractive thirty-five-year-old blond dynamo and popular teacher at Sheffield Elementary, as vice president. It then set out to collect a thousand signatures on a petition opposing the casino and, at Josh's recommendation, agreed to ask the town to allocate $175,000 in its upcoming budget to cover the first-year costs of hiring the legal and research assistance necessary to begin building a case against the Northerns' recognition.

Going door to door and manning a card table at the supermarket, CAC collected the thousand signatures in less than week, and two days later Josh and Carol met with Jim Clark, Sheffield's septuagenarian first selectman, to press their case for the $175,000.

A farmer with snow-white hair, a big square jaw, and a folksy manner, Clark made no bones about being more comfortable behind the wheel of one of the town's snowplows than conducting a budget meeting. At the same time, he was a shrewd politician who knew two-thirds of the people in town by their first name and had managed to be elected to ten straight two-year terms.

Clark was initially leery of CAC, seeing it as one more group he now had to deal with in trying to run the town, but he also recognized its potential in helping fight the Northerns. Privately, he also felt more comfortable with "Red" Williams as the head of CAC than he would have with some newcomer who had no roots in the town. Josh's father, Henry, had been a good friend, and Clark had known Josh when he was growing up.

Saying he appreciated CAC's concerns, Clark initially insisted he was moving as fast as he could to stop the casino. He had already secured "interested party" status in connection with the Northerns' recognition application, he explained, and he was planning to ask the Board of Finance for an initial $30,000 to hire outside counsel. True, it wasn't as much as CAC wanted, but the town was already facing a big tax hike in its 1994–1995 fiscal year, and the Finance Board would be reluctant to spend more to oppose the Northerns until it had a better feel as to when the BIA might begin to consider their application.

"Gettin' more money from the board right now's like pullin' teeth," Clark said. "But look," he added, "nobody'd be happier to have more ammunition to fight the tribe than me, and if you're sayin' this new group of yours will get behind me on the $175,000, then I'll see what I can do."

CAC immediately went to work on the Finance Board, visiting each of its five members individually and laying out the case for the additional money. At first, three of the members said there was no way they could support such a large request, but two new developments helped turn things around.

In March, the BIA approved the Mohegans' long-stalled recognition petition, and the Mohegans unveiled plans to build their own casino and convention center in the Uncasville section of Montville, less than ten miles from the Williams farm. Then, seven weeks later, the Mashantuckets, who had vowed never to block another tribe from Indian gaming, agreed to share their slots monopoly with the Mohegans, thereby guaranteeing that the Mohegans' new complex would be built on a scale equal to Foxwoods. Under the new agreement, both the Mashantuckets and the Mohegans agreed to pay 25 percent of their slots revenue to the state and reserved the right to stop their payments if the state allowed another casino to be built in Connecticut without their approval.

Under growing pressure from CAC and alarmed by the speed with which the Indian gaming tsunami was now rolling across eastern Connecticut, the board ultimately voted unanimously to approve the $175,000 appropriation.

⁓

No one was more delighted with the Mohegans' good fortune and the latest slots deal than Bobby Kingman. The Mohegans' recognition meant the BIA was looking favorably on Connecticut's Indians, and the slots agreement set an important precedent for extending the same deal to other tribes.

Moreover, Jim Grimaldi told Bobby in late April that the political environment in Washington had never looked more promising, and when Bobby picked up *The Day* on April 30, he had to agree. The front page carried a photo of Mashantucket chairman Skip Hayward presenting an Indian sculpture to President Clinton during a ceremony on the South Lawn of the White House.

Hayward was in Washington to attend a historic meeting between the President and more than two hundred tribal leaders from around the country, but it appeared that Hayward was receiving top billing. The paper noted that the President called Hayward by his nickname and that Hayward had a few moments alone with Vice President Al Gore before a breakfast the Mashan-tuckets hosted for tribal leaders in the ballroom of the Washington Sheraton, where Gore was the guest of honor. Hayward held Tipper Gore's hand during the opening prayer and later introduced the Gores as "the people who will someday occupy the White House as first family."

Indeed, it sounded as though much of the conference centered around Hayward and gambling. Whatever may have happened in the past, the President told the tribal leaders, America's new goal for the nation's Indians was self-determination, and he praised Indian gaming for helping to meet that objective.

"Indian gaming operations give tribes a competitive edge," the President declared, "and you've had precious few."

Bobby looked at the photo of Hayward again and shook his head in wonderment. Hayward looked no more Indian than Bobby did, yet there he was standing next to the President of the United States like he was Geronimo.

As promising as things seemed, Bobby didn't want to jinx himself by becoming too optimistic. Now he had to worry about this new group called CAC and its founder, Josh Williams, who was emerging as the leader of the local opposition. CAC had forged an alliance with the First Selectman, had raised more than $10,000 in contributions, and was responsible for goading the town to appropriate $175,000 to fight the tribe. Admittedly, it was nothing compared to the $6 million Bobby estimated Ivy and Grimaldi had now spent, but Bobby was keenly aware of the weaknesses in the tribe's application and was becoming increasingly uneasy about CAC's obvious intention to try to pick it apart.

⌒

The peaceful tableau at the White House contrasted sharply with the growing turmoil in the towns surrounding Foxwoods.

Week after week, the headlines told the story:

TASK FORCE HEARS LITANY OF COMPLAINTS
AGAINST MASHANTUCKETS

TRAFFIC, CRIME WORRIES CAUSE SLIP
IN SUPPORT FOR FOXWOODS

POLICE NAME SUSPECT IN 3 STABBINGS—
TRACE KEY CHAIN TO MASHANTUCKET

NORTH STONINGTON CLUB MANAGER CHARGED
IN PROSTITUTION RING

A NEIGHBORHOOD IS CHANGED FOREVER—
LEDYARD RESIDENTS SELL EN MASSE TO TRIBE

GROWING GAMBLING CULTURE ATTRACTING TEENS

There were so many stories that they began to blend together, although one from *The Day* stuck in Josh's mind longer than the others. It concerned a man named Lindell Killebrew, who the newspaper said had lost his last few hundred dollars playing a $1 slot machine at Foxwoods the previous week, and was camping in the parking lot of North Stonington's Dew Drop Inn while waiting for his next disability check. He was peacefully escorted off the property by a state trooper, but told the paper he planned "to return to Foxwoods with his new check and play the $5 slots."

⌇

Back in Sheffield, the Williams Agency had a strong spring and summer. More than two hundred people visited the farm to pick their own strawberries. Josh engineered the hiring of Kane and Shapiro when the town's new budget took effect in July. And Josh and Sharon breathed a sigh of relief when Matt went off to UConn in early September.

Matt had gone into a deep funk after his breakup with Kayla and the basketball fiasco, and hadn't really come out of it until the summer. He seemed increasingly eager to go off to college, however, and all the early reports indicated that college life was the right tonic for him.

Apple-picking season wasn't as much fun without Matt, but the family gradually adjusted. The weather was gorgeous, with a skein of sunny days and crisp nights. The swamp maples began turning red slightly earlier than usual, waves of Canada geese honked as they flew south, and the countryside gradually came alive in a blaze of color. One of Sharon's sketches won first place in a local art show and CAC began publishing a monthly newsletter about the struggle against the potential casino.

The Bureau of Indian Affairs finally released a copy of the Northerns' recognition application just before Christmas, almost six months after the town's lawyers had requested it, but even then the BIA refused to provide key sections of the petition. In all, it released just under twenty thousand pages of material, including a current membership roll, historical reports, meeting minutes, copies of laws, land deeds, newspaper articles, obituaries, and internal documents, but it withheld almost six hundred pages of information primarily relating to living tribe members. The BIA claimed the latter material represented confidential commercial and financial information and personal histories that did not have to be released under the Freedom of Information Act.

Kane and Shapiro immediately appealed the BIA's denial of so many documents but advised the town that it now had all it was going to get.

~

22

A Second Chance?

January–November 1995

Matt had done his best to get into the swing of college life, staying on campus all but one weekend right up until Thanksgiving of 1994. He'd studied hard, played intramural soccer and basketball, and worked out regularly, trying to build himself up. He'd hit it off with his roommate, a football player from Norwich, and toward the end of the first semester he had begun to take an interest in a girl he met in English Lit.

But he still couldn't get Kayla out of his mind.

What bothered him most was that he might have misjudged her. Despite the fact that a half-dozen guys had made a play for her following the split, she hadn't taken up with any of them, and he couldn't help but wonder what might have happened if he'd tried to make up.

He hadn't, however, and Matt had told himself a million times that it would have been foolish even to try. She was simply too hot and he was too jealous. He heard from friends that she'd enrolled at the community college in Norwich that fall, and he had no doubt she already had a new circle of admirers.

The last thing Matt ever expected was the chance encounter he had with Kayla shortly after New Year's 1995.

He had taken a part-time job at the drugstore during the long UConn holiday break and was stocking shelves the first week in January when he felt a tap on his shoulder.

When he looked around, there was Kayla, dressed in a parka and with a shopping basket in her hand.

"Hello, Matt," she said cheerfully. "I saw you from across the store and just wanted to say hi."

Matt was so flustered he wasn't sure whether he should shake hands or kiss her after all this time.

"Well, at least you can give me a kiss," she said, offering her cheek and solving the problem for him.

"You look terrific," Matt finally managed to say.

"So do you," Kayla said, "but I thought you were up at UConn."

"I am," he said, "but we're still on midyear break."

"How do you like it up there?"

"I do . . . I mean I'm getting used to it," he replied, trying to regain some of his composure and wanting to remind her that the whole reason he was there was because of her.

"Did you make the soccer team?" she asked.

"'Fraid not," Matt said, wondering whether she really thought he was that good. "Those guys are a little over my level. How about you? I heard you were at Three Rivers."

Yes, she said, she'd bought a car and had been driving to Norwich three days a week to get her associate degree in travel and tourism. The big news, though, was that she was working as a receptionist at Foxwoods' new hotel and was about to move into a house with four other girls in Norwich so she could be closer to work and school.

"I'm so excited about the job," she bubbled. "The hotel's fabulous, and there's a chance to get into management if I stick with it."

It sounded exciting, Matt said, and he was very happy for her.

"You know, Matt," Kayla said tentatively, "we're having a housewarming party Sunday night with a bunch of friends, and I'd love to have you drop over if you're free."

Matt looked at Kayla as though he wasn't sure he had heard her right. She was even more beautiful than he remembered, and he could still smell her perfume from the brief kiss. Suddenly all the months of analyzing and rationalizing went out the window.

"Sure," he said, "I'd love to come."

⌒

The house Kayla and her girlfriends were renting was a big old Victorian built in the 1800s by one of Norwich's wealthy mill owners. It was a good thing it was so big, because there had to be sixty or seventy cars parked along the street, in the driveway, and up on the lawn.

Inside, the downstairs was packed with partygoers. Couples danced in the living room to music from two oversize speakers, and the place smelled like beer and tobacco smoke tinged with pot.

Matt didn't see Kayla, and he wandered into the kitchen, where he filled a plastic beer cup from one of two large kegs, then walked around the house looking for her. He finally spotted her talking to two guys in the dining room and stood by the doorway waiting for her to notice him. When she did, she lit up immediately, excused herself, and came over and greeted him with a peck on the lips.

Kayla explained that probably half the people at the party were from Fox-woods, since both she and one of her housemates, Amy Carlson, worked there. The crowd was older than Matt had expected, with many in their early and mid-twenties. As Kayla took him around, he was amazed at how many people she knew. Most important, it didn't appear that she was with anyone.

When Kayla finally went off to circulate, Matt stood talking with Amy's boyfriend, Tim Paxton, a seasoned but surprisingly young-looking card dealer who'd already been at Foxwoods for almost three years.

"How'd you get into the business so young?" Matt asked him.

"Pure luck," Tim said, taking a final drag on his cigarette and stubbing it out in an empty beer cup. "I got in when Foxwoods first opened and you only had to be eighteen because they didn't have slots. Then when they got slots and raised the age to twenty-one, they grandfathered me."

"What kind of hours you work?"

"Usually six p.m. to two a.m., five nights a week, but it varies," Tim said.

"You don't mind the late hours?"

"Nah, I'm used to it, and it leaves the day free, which is great because I'm going full-time to Three Rivers for my accounting degree. But the main thing's the money."

"I didn't realize the pay was that great," Matt said. "From what you hear, I thought the biggest attraction was the benefits."

"Well, for most of the older guys that's true," Tim said. "But for somebody like me who's single and trying to put himself through school, the money's pretty good. Our base is four dollars an hour, but our 'toke rate,' which is based on tips and the winning percentage of the house, typically runs about twelve an hour. So, all in all, I average around sixteen bucks an hour plus medical and things like free uniforms and meals."

"What do customers usually tip?" Matt wanted to know.

"Five dollars a session is pretty standard," Tim said. "But the tips can be a lot bigger if a player's having a good run. And you need a few of the bigger ones to make up for the occasional stiffs who don't leave anything."

"Do you keep your own tips?"

"No, we pool the tips and divide 'em based on the hours worked," Tim said. "So if a player's not dropping with you, you hope he's at least dropping with the dealer next door."

"Did you know anything about casinos before they hired you?" Matt asked.

"Are you kiddin'?" Tim replied. "I didn't know shit. But they teach you everything. You train eight weeks for blackjack, for example, and thirteen for craps."

"Do you specialize in any particular games?"

"Not really. I get into pretty much everything. Like last night, I started with blackjack, moved to showdown poker, and then wound up dealing acey-deucy in the high-stakes pit, where the minimum's a hundred dollars a bet."

"Sounds pretty intense."

"It is, but they give you regular breaks," Tim said, "It's important to stay fresh because the last thing you want to do is misdeal or make some other mistake. A dealer's supposed to be flawless. You make a mistake and players can go nuts."

"You ever have to throw anybody out?" Matt asked.

"Not recently," Tim said, "but it happens. In fact, there was a situation at a table next to me just the other night. Guy started yelling and getting very confrontational, and security had to pick him up by the elbows and hustle him out."

"What'd they do to him?" Matt asked.

"Who knows. Probably blacklisted him from ever coming back. But that's obviously exactly the type of thing you want to avoid. The best dealers are the ones who can create an atmosphere that keeps everybody happy and coming back. That's really the job: keeping people happy while they lose their money."

Matt laughed. "How do you manage to do that?" he asked.

Tim shrugged, as though trying to think exactly how to explain it.

"It's really an individual thing," he said. "Everybody's got their own style, and it depends to some degree on the game. But take blackjack. I just try to make everybody comfortable, get people bantering back and forth, and try to develop a little rhythm where they start getting into the game and having fun.

"The other thing is, I try to be as empathetic as I can. I celebrate with my customers when they win and commiserate with them when they lose."

"So you don't try to win for the house?" Matt asked, surprised.

"Hell, no," Tim said. "The house doesn't need any help. Except in a very few instances, the odds always favor the casino. If you count everything—craps, poker, slots, you name it—Foxwoods keeps around nine percent of everything that's gambled. All I do is run the games and try to give people a good time."

"And nobody does that better than you! Right, Tim?" Kayla interjected, coming over at that moment and giving him hug and a kiss.

"How would you know?" Tim said jokingly, slipping his arm around her waist and flashing his best smile. "You're too young even to get on the floor."

"I don't have to see you in action to know," Kayla said. "Everybody says you're the best."

Matt felt the same surge of jealousy he'd felt a year earlier, but this time he was smart enough not to show it.

He was disappointed he didn't get to spend more time with Kayla, but they did have a few minutes together at the end of the party, and she walked him to the door to say good night.

"Thanks for coming, Matt," she said. "It was really nice to see you again. I don't know if you're involved with anyone, but if you're not why don't you give me a call when you're going to be back from school some weekend. I work most nights, but maybe we could do a movie on a Friday evening or something."

Matt was so elated he hardly noticed the road as he drove home.

Two days later, a snowstorm covered Sheffield with four inches of wet, sticky flakes that clung to the trees and roofs and brought the kids out to make snowballs and snowmen. It was vintage Connecticut, just the way the state liked to depict itself in the tourist brochures.

As 1995 began, however, it looked as though casino gambling was well on its way to becoming the state's new image.

Foxwoods began the year with nine thousand employees and more than a half billion dollars in slot machine revenues alone. The Mohegans were rushing to build their own casino. And at least half a dozen other actual or would-be tribes were pursuing federal recognition.

Then the state's newly-elected Republican governor, John Roland, added to the casino frenzy by reviving the idea of permitting a private developer to build a casino in Bridgeport. There was only one catch: since the Mashantuckets and Mohegans would not have to pay the state part of their slots revenue if the state permitted another casino without the tribes' okay, the Bridgeport casino would have to provide the state with enough new revenue to offset the lost slots payments from the two Indian casinos.

It was an enormous hurdle, but the lure of a casino within an hour of New York City continued to be so great that at least ten developers, including Steve Wynn and Donald Trump, immediately jumped into the fray.

ꙅ

The barriers to casino gambling in Connecticut now seemed to be crumbling so fast that Josh began to wonder if there was any point in continuing to resist the Northern Pequots' effort to build a casino in Sheffield. Nevertheless, he continued to do what he could to keep the pressure on the town to oppose the Northerns, and in late January First Selectman Jim Clark recognized Josh's growing influence by appointing him to a new six-person Casino Task Force created to work directly with the town's Washington law firm and the genealogist and historian the town had hired.

The task force, which included Sheffield's three selectmen and three public members, met for the first time in early February 1995, bringing in the town's team of lawyers and researchers to get their initial take on the reams of material the BIA had released just before Christmas.

In addition to Rick Pugliese and a second attorney from Kane and Shapiro, the team included Martin Stertz, a history researcher from the University of Massachusetts who had worked on other recognition cases, and Gladys Greene, a highly regarded genealogist from New Haven who had once worked for the BIA. All four agreed the application's main weakness appeared to be its failure to prove the Northerns had continued to function as a tribe for most of the twentieth century, but they cautioned it would take another month for them to fully evaluate all the material the tribe had submitted and be in a position to begin their own research.

Mrs. Greene also said that, based on her initial review, she found it curious that the tribe hadn't been able to come up with more information on its key ancestor, Rachel Amos. Rachel, Mrs. Greene noted, was documented as having lived on the reservation in 1800 and having been buried there in 1803, but there was no documentation regarding her lineage.

The reason this was so important, she explained, was that forty-nine of the tribe's fifty members based their claim to Pequot ancestry on being descended from Rachel; the only other member was Louis Jobert's eighty-five-year-old sister.

"My intention," Mrs. Greene said, "is to zero in on Rachel, because if we could show she didn't have Pequot blood, the tribe's case for recognition would collapse."

꙰

Like Josh, Bobby Kingman was discouraged by the renewed attempt to put a casino in Bridgeport, although once again his concern stemmed from a fear that a Bridgeport casino would intercept gamblers from New York and southwestern Connecticut who would otherwise come to Sheffield. In fact, Bobby feared that if the state gave the green light to building a casino in Bridgeport, Paul Ivy and Jim Grimaldi might lose interest in Sheffield altogether. Bobby also was increasingly worried about the progress the town had made in organizing to fight the tribe, and he was particularly concerned about the personal crusade Josh Williams seemed to be on to block the tribe's recognition.

Nevertheless, like Josh, Bobby pressed on.

One of his main goals was to continue to legitimize the tribe in the eyes of the BIA and other Indians. Toward that end, he presided over regular monthly meetings of the Northerns' Tribal Council, worked on arrangements for the tribe's third annual powwow—this time inviting tribes from across the United States—and joined with other Pequot descendants to demand the removal of Captain John Mason's bronze statue from the site of the Pequot fort Mason had burned in 1637.

Bobby had actually never heard of the statue until 1991, when a member of the Eastern Pequot Tribe asked the Groton Town Council to remove the monument because it glorified the massacre of his ancestors. He charged that the statue was a "tombstone" for the Pequot people, and a group called the Southeastern Coalition for Peace and Justice formed to get rid of it.

In response, the town of Groton formed the John Mason Statue Committee to look into the issue. After listening to all sides, it recommended a compromise in which the statue would be left up, but the plaque would be changed from one that lauded Mason for his leadership in saving Connecticut's colonists to one that made no mention of the Pequot War and instead simply described Mason as a Puritan soldier who had become deputy governor of the state.

The statue's backers immediately ridiculed the proposal, pointing out it would be like trying to describe George Washington without mentioning that he was America's commander in the Revolutionary War. The whole idea, they insisted, was nothing but historical revisionism and political correctness gone berserk. Rather than trying to rewrite history, some suggested, the committee should consider putting up a second statue in tribute to the gallant Pequots.

In the end, Mason's defenders proved far less effective than his opponents and the Groton Town Council recommended moving the statue from its site in the Mystic section of town to the new Indian museum being planned by the Mashantuckets next door to Foxwoods.

The recommendation instantly set off a new round of fireworks, with Mason's supporters declaring it would be the ultimate historical irony for Connecticut's earliest hero to be carried off by a suspect Indian tribe and placed alongside America's biggest casino so that legions of gamblers could gawk at him.

Even the great gambling state of Connecticut balked at the idea, and the state Department of Environmental Protection, to whom the final decision was entrusted, held a hearing in February 1995 before making a final determination.

Outraged that the state was still considering leaving Mason where he was, the statue's opponents converged on Hartford to lambaste the state for its insensitivity to the feelings of the Pequots' descendants. No one expressed greater dismay than Bobby Kingman, who attended the hearing with his Aunt Mavis. He spoke on behalf of his entire tribe, he declared, in demanding that the state move the statue.

"I know," Bobby told the DEP panel, "a lot of people say that what happened, happened. History is history and all that.

"But we don't celebrate slavery or murder just because they're part of history, and there's no reason why we should celebrate John Mason by allowing him to stand over the graves of our murdered ancestors. It's just too painful for our people and the spirits of those who've gone before us.

"We insist that the statue be taken down now!" Bobby almost shouted. "And if it has to be displayed anywhere, we agree it should be at the new Mashantucket museum, where visitors can learn about the people and the culture Mason tried to wipe out."

Bobby sat down to ringing applause from the statue's opponents, and Mavis told him afterward she was certain he'd won a lot of friends in Indian country. In fact, she said, he ought to print up his remarks and send them around to other tribal chiefs throughout New England. Bobby thought that was a brilliant idea, and he decided he might even go and take a look at the Mason statue before it came down. He just hoped it was marked on the map, because he had no idea exactly where it was.

One of the people who could have given Bobby directions was Matt, who had visited the Mason statue with his family and who had always been impressed by the fact that one of his ancestors had fought with Mason in the Pequot War. Even if he'd known about the dispute over the statue, however, he wouldn't have had time to give it much thought, since the second semester at UConn was now in full swing and his main interest other than school was what to do about Kayla.

Matt really didn't know what Kayla had in mind when she suggested they get together, and he had decided to take things very slowly this time. He consequently waited three weeks before calling her. She seemed happy to hear from him, and they made a date to have a bite and see a movie together the second Friday in February.

When Matt picked her up at her house, he was disappointed to find she'd invited her housemate, Amy, and Amy's boyfriend, Tim, to join them. As it turned out, they all had a good time, and he realized it actually made things a little more comfortable the first time around. Amy said it was good to see Kayla get out and enjoy herself because she worked so hard, and they all agreed to go out together again.

Two weeks later the four wound up going to a party together instead of a movie, and in March Kayla invited them all to a concert at Foxwoods that her father had given her tickets for. By early April, Matt had gone out with Kayla four times, but it had always been with Amy and Tim or a larger group, and Kayla had kept it strictly platonic. As a result, Matt began to suspect Kayla simply wanted an escort and picked him because she considered him relatively safe as long as they didn't get too close. That possibility didn't do much for Matt's ego, but the truth was he liked her friends, and it was worth driving down from UConn just to be near her. Then in late April he was glad he had been patient.

They had gone to another party, and Kayla had asked him to drive her to her parents' house in Sheffield for the night so she could do some shopping with her mother the next morning. It was the first time they'd been alone in a car since they'd started seeing each other again, and Matt took the back way to Sheffield, passing the dirt road where they used to park.

"Wasn't that our old dirt road?" Kayla asked.

"I didn't think you remembered," Matt said.

"Of course I remember." Kayla said, giving him a playful punch on the arm. "I always liked that road."

"Enough to go back?" Matt ventured.

"Sure," Kayla said. "It's early."

"Are you serious?" Matt asked, looking over at her in the semi-dark.

"Why, aren't you?"

Matt stopped the car, turned around, and headed back to the dirt road, which was essentially two tracks that disappeared over a little knoll. He followed the tracks just beyond the knoll so the car was hidden from the main road and pulled up under the same tree they had parked under several times before.

Matt left the motor running, and they both unfastened their seatbelts and slid next to each other on the Plymouth's bench seat.

There was one thing he wanted to say, he told her nervously, and that was that he'd never forgive himself for the way he'd behaved the night they'd broken up. He'd never gotten over her, he said, and he wanted to apologize.

Kayla said she also was sorry for what had happened. But she had to tell him that her life had changed a great deal since then.

She was determined to have the career she had always dreamed about, and she was working as hard as she could toward that goal—going for her degree, working full-time at the hotel, and still trying to find a little time for herself. Consequently, she told him, she wasn't ready for another relationship that would tie her down.

But she was still attracted to him, she said, caressing his cheek and running her fingers over his lips, and she'd love to continue seeing him occasionally on weekends if he'd like. With that, she pressed against him and gave him a long, soft kiss.

Seeing her only a couple of times a month wasn't what Matt wanted at all, but it was a start, and she felt so good and smelled so delicious in his arms, he wasn't going to argue. He began unbuttoning her coat, and within minutes they were stretched out on the seat together, their clothes all over the car and his fingers probing the wetness between her thighs. It was as though nothing had ever changed—except that this time Kayla, who had maneuvered on top of him, sat up, fitted him with a condom from her purse, and, rising slightly as she straddled him, took him inside her. Matt tried to sit up, but she gently pushed him back and began to slowly and rhythmically move against him, gradually quickening the pace until he began to thrust so hard he felt he might go through her. Kayla stayed with him, arching her back to drive him deeper, and then let out a soft, almost inaudible moan as she came. With one final effort, Matt grasped her hips and exploded in a burst of passion more intense than he'd ever imagined.

As they lay exhausted, locked together on the car seat, Matt knew he'd do anything in the world not to lose her again.

～

As 1995 progressed, the contest to see who would build a casino in Bridgeport gradually narrowed down to four men.

There was Steve Wynn, the chief cheerleader for gaming in America or, depending on your viewpoint, the snake oil salesman who had been trying for three years to get a foothold in the Land of Steady Habits.

There was Donald Trump, the brash New York real estate entrepreneur and author of *The Art of the Deal*, who already had investments in Trump's Castle and the Taj Mahal in Atlantic City. By building in Bridgeport, he stood to win twice—by siphoning off New York–area gamblers who would otherwise head to the Indian casinos in eastern Connecticut, and by stopping a competitor from attracting New Yorkers who were currently inclined to patronize his properties in New Jersey.

There was Lim Goh Tong, the enigmatic Chinese-Malaysian billionaire who had bankrolled Foxwoods and whose casino holdings included properties in the Bahamas and Australia, in addition to his huge Malaysian resort. Lim and his Mashantucket partners were determined to stop any private casino developer from coming into Bridgeport.

And then there was Solomon Kerzner, known alternatively as "The Sun King," "the richest man in South Africa," and the "Bugsy Siegel of the bush veld." Kerzner was the developer of South Africa's Sun City, the internationally famous resort casino that had become such a symbol of apartheid that Bruce Springsteen and other recording stars produced an anti-apartheid album in which the chorus sang "I ain't gonna play Sun City." Despite the tarnished image of Sun City and allegations of bribery against him in another case, Kerzner had managed to spread out around the world and now owned thirty-five properties from the Indian Ocean to the Bahamas, where he was completing an over-the-top resort casino with a spectacular outdoor aquarium and glass-walled pedestrian tunnels that gave guests the sensation of walking on the bottom of the sea.

Attracted to Connecticut by the success of Foxwoods, Kerzner had taken a 50 percent stake in the partnership hired by the Mohegans to develop and manage their casino, whose opening was now just a year away. Like Lim and the Mashantuckets, Kerzner and the Mohegans were prepared to do everything possible to keep private developers like Wynn and Trump out of Bridgeport.

It was uncanny, Josh thought, just how accurate Brad Merriweather had been five years ago in foreseeing what was now happening. It was as though everyone and everything in Connecticut had become pawns in some kind of giant international chess match.

Josh even had a dream in which he and Sharon and the kids were all alone in the south pasture, which suddenly turned into a giant chessboard. They had to run and weave and duck to avoid the rooks and bishops and knights that kept darting and slashing and pouncing from the corners and sides. Finding it harder and harder to run, Josh was about to be overtaken by a castle when he abruptly woke up in a cold sweat.

As prescient as Brad had been, however, he never could have predicted the twists and turns in the spectacular bidding war that erupted for the right to build the Bridgeport casino.

Wynn and Trump quickly emerged as the odds-on favorites to win the state's nod, promising to build billion-dollar projects that would generate more than enough tax revenue to make up for the Indians' slots payments. Wynn touted his reputation as a visionary, while Trump claimed he was the better businessman, boasting that he had bought the Empire State Building and that Wall Street was "in love with Donald Trump."

Then, as the bidding became more intense, Trump suddenly dropped out, leaving Wynn the apparent victor.

By summer, however, Governor Rowland was having growing misgivings about Wynn and losing the Indians' slots payments, and in still another dramatic turn of events, he invited the Mashantuckets to enter the bidding for

Bridgeport.

The Mashantuckets, who until now had been among those leading the fight against a Bridgeport casino, instantly did a one-eighty. They began touting the benefits of a casino for the beleaguered city and submitted their own proposal.

Wynn and the Mashantuckets went at one another hammer and tongs, and on October 3 the Governor ended the guessing game about who would win by choosing the tribe's bid. But before the Mashantuckets could celebrate, Sol Kerzner and the Mohegans played their trump card. They wanted in on the Bridgeport bonanza along with the Mashantuckets, they told the Governor, or they'd withhold their own slots payments once they got their casino up and running.

Infuriated by the Mohegans' threat to torpedo the deal, the Governor and the Mashantuckets refused the Mohegans' demand, and the legislature, already deeply divided over the Bridgeport casino, killed the entire project in November.

The Pequots railed privately at the Mohegans, who, they charged, had stabbed them in the back once again, just as Uncas had three and a half centuries ago.

23

Confrontation

January 1996

Bobby and his partners had breathed a sigh of relief when the latest effort to build a casino in Bridgeport collapsed, and they received a second piece of good news in January 1996. The Republican senator who had been pushing the Northerns' recognition application told Ivy he was optimistic it would be placed on the BIA's "active list" by midyear.

It was enormously encouraging, because the BIA was supposed to make a preliminary decision on a recognition petition one year after it went on the active list, followed by a final decision eight months later. Bobby couldn't believe the decision-making process would move that fast, but getting on the active list, and getting on so soon, would be a giant step forward.

Bobby only wished things were going as smoothly in Sheffield. There were rumors that the town's consultants, who had been researching the Northern Pequots for a full year now, had come up with information damaging to the tribe's case, and the selectmen called a special town meeting for late January for the town's Casino Task Force to report its findings.

Interest was so great that some four hundred people jammed the town hall on a frigid Monday evening to hear the report firsthand. Bobby and Mavis rounded up as many tribe members as possible to attend, and by the time the meeting got underway, thirty-four of them were sitting or standing together in a group at the back of the cramped hall. While most were dressed like everyone else in the room, several were in beaded Indian shirts, one woman arrived in an Inuit-style fur parka, and a heavyset man wore a headband and a Sioux war shirt. Bobby was in his usual buckskin jacket, and Mavis, who had increasingly embraced her role as tribal historian and vice chair, had her hair in two long braids and wore a colorful Indian shawl. As First Selectman Clark walked to the lectern to start the meeting, Bobby and

Mavis unfurled a six-foot paper banner that read "Northern Pequot Tribal Nation" and taped it to the wall behind their group.

Clark ignored the banner and began by identifying the other five members of the Casino Task Force, along with the town's genealogist, historical researcher, and Washington attorney, all of whom sat side by side at a long folding table at the front of the room. Clark explained he'd like to start by describing the steps the Task Force had taken to analyze the Northerns' recognition application and then turn the meeting over to Attorney Pugliese to describe the Task Force's findings. He assured everyone that once Pugliese finished, they'd have a chance to ask questions.

⌇

Pugliese sat studying the audience while the First Selectman spoke. It was his third visit to Sheffield, but his first opportunity to attend a town meeting or see any of the Northern Pequots in person.

Truth be told, he had accepted the Sheffield assignment with some ambivalence, since although he had worked both sides of Indian cases, most of his work had been on behalf of Indians and he felt most comfortable representing their interests. It was a preference that went back to the start of his career in Phoenix, where he'd worked primarily on cases involving large tribes in and around Arizona, like the Navajos, Apaches, and Pueblos, and then developed further once he joined the Interior Department and began to expand his focus to tribes in California and the Northwest. He had not only come to feel a deep empathy for Native Americans; he'd developed an equally deep disdain for the way the government had treated them, constantly changing its policies, adopting contradictory ones, and breaking more treaties than anyone could keep track of.

Congress had tried to protect Indians with the Nonintercourse Act in the late 1700s, prohibiting the sale of Indian land without federal approval, then in 1830 passed the Indian Removal Act, which forced thousands of Southeast Indians to move to reservations west of the Mississippi. It had outlawed, and then legalized, the practice of their native religions. And it had sent their children away to boarding schools, only to later close the schools and send the children home.

The government's shifting policies and infamous neglect had contributed to Indians having the highest rates of poverty, unemployment, and disease of any group in America. Joblessness on many western reservations ranged between 50 and 80 percent. Health-care expenditures for Indians were less than half of what the government spent on health care for federal prisoners. And to make matters worse, it looked as though the BIA had mismanaged and lost track of billions of dollars in Indian trust funds that had been amassed from timber, oil, and mineral leases on Indian lands and that could have been used to help Indians get on their feet economically.

At the same time, Pugliese believed it was a mistake to try to solve the problems of Indian country by letting tribes open casinos and making Indians the instrument for spreading casino gambling across the United States. His feelings began with a mild aversion to gambling, but he had become increasingly concerned it would eventually create a backlash against Indians, would weaken their sovereignty by forcing them to negotiate compacts with their states, and in the end would do little for most Indians, while a tiny fraction struck it rich.

Nevertheless, he was incensed that phony Indians and billionaire developers were cashing in on something meant for legitimate tribes. The deeper he had gotten into the Sheffield assignment, the more certain he had become that he was up against the most egregious example of this type of cashing in he had ever seen. He had been prepared to believe the Northerns might have Pequot roots somewhere in their past even if they didn't qualify as a tribe, but when he saw them, he wondered even about that. Other than a single old man who was so weathered he could have been anything, none of the Northerns' facial features suggested even a hint of Indian blood, while the Indian clothes some of them sported struck him as ludicrous. He particularly kept looking at the Sioux war shirt, which he was certain he had seen in a mail-order catalog. It symbolized just how far the whole whacky phenomenon of newly formed tribes seeking casinos had come.

Only in America could things get this screwed up, Pugliese thought to himself as Clark concluded his remarks and began to introduce him.

Clark took the audience through Pugliese's résumé, emphasizing his government experience and the fact that he had been dealing with Indian issues his entire career. "He's one of the top experts in the country on Native American issues," Clark said, "and we were lucky to be able to get 'im."

Seemingly impressed by his credentials, the crowd settled back and listened attentively as Pugliese took them through the Task Force's findings.

He began by carefully explaining that the BIA's rules required petitioning tribes to meet a number of specific criteria, including that they be able to prove their continuous existence as a social community from historical times to the present and that they be able to show they had maintained a functioning tribal government during the entire period.

Pugliese paused and looked deliberately out at the audience, including the Northerns gathered at the back of the room.

"Based on our review," he stated, "we believe there's insufficient evidence of community for the past seven decades and insufficient or no evidence of political governance for most of the last century. Consequently, we believe the Northerns do not meet two of the most important criteria for recognition and we've prepared a ninety-five-page submission to the BIA urging rejection of the tribe's petition."

Bobby was doing a slow burn as he listened to Pugliese. The tribe's petition might have weaknesses, but this was too much.

"Furthermore," Pugliese said, "our genealogist, Gladys Greene, believes there's a serious question as to whether the current tribe's key ancestor, Rachel Amos, was even a Northern Pequot. If she wasn't, that alone would disqualify the tribe from recognition."

This was the first time Bobby had ever heard anyone question Rachel's genealogy, and he now absolutely seethed with hatred for the goateed Washington lawyer. Mavis glanced over at Bobby and could see he was literally turning red. She instinctively put her hand on his thigh to try to calm him down before he popped out of his chair and did or said something foolish.

Bobby surprised her by quickly regaining his composure. He waited for Pugliese to finish, then calmly walked to one of the microphones that had been set up for questions.

"I wonder, Mr. Pugliese," Bobby began after identifying himself, "if you could tell us how much the town has now spent on your firm and the other consultants to fight the tribe's application?"

Jim Clark motioned that he'd take the question and replied that, as had been reported at the last selectmen's meeting, the sum was approximately $260,000 through November.

"Two hundred sixty thousand dollars," Bobby repeated slowly. "Over a quarter of a million dollars. I gotta tell ya," he said, shaking his head as though he couldn't believe the number, "I find it pretty amusin' that the town's spendin' all this money and all this time on our tribe now, when you wouldn't give us the time of day for the last three hundred years.

"Well, you can dig up every technicality you want to try to prove we didn't survive. But you can see from the tribe members with me tonight that we did survive!" he said proudly, gesturing to his companions behind him. "And we survived despite three hundred years of poverty, hostility, and neglect— during which you took our land, belittled us, ignored us, and hoped we'd disappear."

Bobby's voice choked with emotion. "I can't wait to see your evidence about our social and political continuity," he went on. "But I'm not the least concerned, because we had some of the top experts in the country help us with our petition, and we and they are confident of approval."

Bobby paused for effect, then continued. "However, there's one thing I do take great offense to."

The people sitting farthest away were now craning their necks to see him.

"And that's your insinuation we're not related to the Pequots who settled here. We've submitted proof of our bloodlines, and you obviously have no evidence to the contrary, or you'd have submitted it to the BIA."

With that, the other tribe members burst into applause, causing Josh to rise and head for the nearest microphone in order to respond.

"I'd like to say for the record," Josh began, "that we have great respect for the historic Northern Pequot tribe. But based on the BIA's standards, it's clear that that tribe no longer exists."

"Liar!" one of the tribe members shouted. "Bigot!" a second yelled. "Indian hater!" a third hollered. There was a moment of stunned silence followed by a smattering of boos and catcalls directed at the back of the hall.

"Furthermore, Mr. Kingman," Josh said, ignoring the exchange and raising his hand to quiet everybody down. ". . . furthermore, it's awfully hard to take seriously your complaints about the town's efforts to block your application for federal recognition. If your group were simply seeking recognition for historical and cultural reasons, I think everyone in town would be happy to leave the decision to the government. But we all know that's not what this is all about. This is about using recognition to build a casino, and I want to be sure you understand we're going to fight you every step of the way."

Bobby glared at Josh as virtually the entire room erupted in cheers and applause.

⬱

Bobby stewed over the town's one-sided opposition to the tribe's recognition, and especially to Josh Williams's personal put-down. It was one thing for the town to be opposed to the casino. Bobby understood that. But it was another thing to have to sit there and listen to his genealogy being challenged.

There was no question that a big part of the problem was Williams. He had organized the opposition much more effectively than the town's elected leaders would have done on their own. Unfortunately, there was no obvious way to get at him. His family had been in town forever, people liked him, and his farm's location near the reservation gave him a personal stake in stopping the casino that wasn't likely to be easily overcome.

To Bobby's knowledge, the man had no particular vices. He apparently didn't drink or gamble or play around, the usual chinks in anyone's armor. Yet, Bobby thought, everybody had their weaknesses. If he could soften Williams even a little, it had to help in a close fight.

He obviously had to be careful in the way he approached it, but he felt he at least had to try.

～

Josh was standing just outside his private office, talking to his secretary, when Bobby sauntered through the insurance agency's front door on Friday afternoon, January 31. Bobby could see Josh do a double take, then say something to the woman and start toward him. Good, Bobby thought, he'd caught Williams off guard, and it was going to be pretty hard for Josh not to agree to spend at least a few minutes with him.

"Mornin', Josh," Bobby said cheerfully.

"Hello, Bobby," Josh said politely, extending his hand, "what brings you here this morning? Still developing shopping centers?"

"No, no, don't have much time for that anymore," Bobby replied, shaking his head and smiling, "but I do have somethin' I'd like to talk to you about if you've got a minute."

Josh hesitated, then nodded and invited Bobby into his office. He offered his visitor a chair, then sat down behind his desk.

"I'm sorry about that little exchange we had the other night," Bobby began, frowning as though he truly regretted what had happened. "I want you to know I understand your bein' against the casino. I know your family helped found the town and you want to protect it. But our people have been in town a long time, too, and believe me, the last thing we want to do is hurt it."

"I'm afraid we've got pretty big differences on what's good for Sheffield," Josh replied stiffly.

"Yeah, I know," Bobby said. He leaned back in his chair and crossed his legs. "But I hoped that if we could get to know each other a little better, we at least might be able to turn down the volume in town. I mean, hell, we all have to live here while this thing is being settled, right? And if the casino does go through, we gotta work together to try to make the best of it for everybody. There's no sense lettin' things degenerate into an all-out war where neither side wants anything to do with the other. Know'm sayin'?"

"So what have you got in mind?" Josh asked, eyeing Bobby skeptically.

"Well, I thought you and I might be able to sit down together every couple of months or so and just talk about things. Then maybe if we were able to make a little progress, we could ask one or two people from each side to join us. I mean, people fight over issues all the time, but it doesn't mean they can't talk to each other and try to work things out. Especially in a small town like this."

Bobby paused as though hoping for a positive response, but Josh simply sat with his fingers steepled against his lips, watching his visitor.

"I was even thinkin'," Bobby continued, "that to show there's no hard feelins, the tribe could do a little business with your agency. We got three mobile homes and a van up on the reservation right now, and a dozen families in the area that got to get their insurance somewhere. Then if things worked out for us and you were interested, you'd have a leg up for the casino's business."

Josh still didn't respond.

"But that's not the important thing," Bobby added quickly. "The important thing is that we begin to talk."

Josh finally shifted in his chair and shook his head as though he couldn't believe what he was hearing. "Do you really have that low an opinion of me?" he asked. His tone was a mixture of disbelief and disgust.

"Whadaya talkin' about?" Bobby asked, seemingly baffled.

"To think you can walk in here and bribe me?"

"Whoa ... slow down for just a minute, will ya, Josh? If you think that's what this is about, then you got the wrong idea. I came here to see if we could start a dialogue for the good of the town. Doin' some business with you is just somethin' I brought up as a goodwill gesture ... just an olive branch, that's all. But if you're that sensitive to doin' business with Indians, then maybe there's an even bigger problem here than I realized. I always assumed a lot of the opposition to the tribe is bias against Indians, but I never figured that included you."

24

Blindsided

February–December 1996

Josh took Bobby Kingman's January 31 visit as a sign of weakness, and he became reasonably upbeat as the winter progressed. It was beginning to look as though the town might actually have a shot at blocking the Northerns' recognition bid, and the Williams Agency, which was now into its third year, was exceeding expectations. Another twelve months and he should be able to sell the agency for roughly twice what he had put into it, which would let him walk away from Sheffield any time he chose without first having to sell the farm.

Josh had been particularly successful in expanding the book of Workers' Compensation business he'd inherited from the Duncan Agency, and Workers' Comp now represented the fastest-growing and most profitable part of the Williams Agency's revenue.

In the meantime, he and Sharon were increasingly aware of how fast the kids were growing up. Sarah, who had announced she wanted to be a doctor, was already a junior at Southeast and beginning to think about college; Jacob was in his first year of middle school and getting tall and lanky like his brother; and Matt, in his second year at UConn, was already halfway out of the nest.

Keeping Matt involved with the family was consequently becoming harder and harder. To Josh and Sharon's disappointment, he'd taken up with Kayla again the previous spring, and they could only hope he wasn't headed for a repeat of the emotional disaster he'd experienced the first time around. Fortunately, it seemed the new relationship was at least less intense than the first. As far as they could tell, Matt saw Kayla only two Friday nights a month. His usual routine was to return to Sheffield from UConn on those weekends, but otherwise he stayed on campus while the university was in session.

Matt explained that Kayla was too busy getting her degree and working full-time at the hotel for them to see each other more often, but other than occasionally mentioning they were going to a movie or to a party, he said little about her, and Josh and Sharon decided not to interfere. Matt was now going on twenty and doing well at UConn, and they were simply going to have to trust him.

⌒

Matt had just left to return to UConn on Sunday evening, March 17, when Josh got an unexpected call from Dave Drier, his senior salesman in the Norwich office. Drier apologized for the noise in the background, but said he was calling from his car phone as he watched a massive fire engulf a large apartment building in Waterford that the Williams Agency had recently insured. Drier said he'd heard about the fire on the radio and had rushed over there immediately. Fortunately, the building was a newly converted mill and no one had moved in yet, but the fire had gotten up in the rafters between the ceiling and the roof and spread quickly through the whole structure.

"There're three departments on the scene," Drier said, "but it looks like a total loss."

"How much is it insured for?" Josh asked, forgetting the exact amount.

"Nine point one million," Drier replied. "The Pittsfield has the policy."

Josh attended a scheduled meeting in Sheffield early Monday morning, then drove to the Norwich office to make certain the loss was being handled properly. As soon as he arrived, he could sense something was wrong.

Dave Drier shot up from his desk the moment he saw Josh and followed him into his private office.

"Josh," Drier said before Josh could even hang up his coat, "I'm afraid we got a problem."

In his early fifties, Drier was overweight with thinning gray hair and a somewhat pasty complexion. At the moment, though, he was paler than Josh had ever seen him.

"It's the mill," Drier said. "There's no policy on it."

"What do you mean?" Josh stared at him. "You just told me last night the Pittsfield has the policy."

"Yeah, I thought they did. I sold the policy. The owner thinks he bought the policy. And we've got a copy of the binder we sent him spelling out the coverage. But the Pittsfield says they never issued a policy."

"That's impossible!" Josh responded.

"I know, Josh, but I've been talking to the Pittsfield for the last half hour and they're positive. They never issued a policy on the mill, and they never even had any communication with us about it."

"But you sold it."

"Yes, damn it," Drier said, raising his voice in frustration. "We both know I sold it. Christ, it's the second-biggest apartment deal we've ever done."

"All right, calm down," Josh said, sitting down on the edge of his desk and motioning for Drier to take a chair.

Drier sat down, grateful for the change in tone.

"What's the date of the binder?" Josh asked.

"February 26, 1996," Drier replied. "It's just a few weeks old."

"It's agency bill, right?" Josh asked, using the term the industry used when the agency did the billing instead of the insurance company.

"Yes," Drier answered.

"Then the insured must have at least sent in a down payment on the premium," Josh pressed.

"Maybe so, but there's no record of it," Drier said. "The only thing I can find is the copy of the binder."

"Who issued the binder?" Josh asked.

"Marge," Drier answered.

"Well, what does she say?" Josh asked as though it was the most obvious question in the world.

Drier shrugged helplessly. "She didn't come in this morning, Josh, so I couldn't ask her. I called her at home, but there's no answer."

"Did you try her sister at the bank?"

"Yes," Drier said. "But she said Marge left very early this morning and she assumed she was at work. She says she has no idea where else she could be."

Josh went around and sat behind his desk. He looked at the pile of papers awaiting his attention, then stared at Drier. "Dave," he said, "is there something going on with Marge?"

Drier considered the question. He gazed skyward, as if some answer were written on the ceiling. "Not that I know of," he finally said. "She might have been a little moody lately, but it's certainly nothing that's affected her work. I mean, she works harder than anybody. She's always the first one in every morning and the last one out at night. Hell, I can't even remember the last time she took a vacation."

Josh looked at his watch and then looked out the window. "It's nine forty-five," he said. "If we don't hear something by ten, I'm going to call the state police and report her missing."

❦

Marge Hanlon still hadn't appeared by noon, and there was no word from the police. In the meantime, Josh went over everything with Drier again and talked with the Pittsfield Insurance Company himself. He then began to lay out all the possible explanations for and consequences of what had happened. He was handicapped for the moment because he couldn't go back and talk to the mill owner without panicking him, but several things seemed clear.

The Williams Agency had sold a commercial package policy covering the converted mill and sent the insured a binder confirming the coverage.

However, there was no record of the agency having received a down payment from the insured and there was no copy of the policy in the files.

Therefore, Marge Hanlon had either made some kind of innocent mistake in handling the policy and booking the down payment, or she had committed fraud by diverting the insured's check to her own account.

Either way, The Pittsfield would be required to honor the policy sold to the building's owner because Josh's agency was an authorized agent of The Pittsfield and had bound coverage on behalf of the insurer.

And finally, if Marge had embezzled the insured's down payment, the Williams Agency would be responsible for reimbursing The Pittsfield for the amount of that payment.

Fortunately, the agency's fidelity bond covered employee fraud losses up to $100,000, but what worried Josh was that the missing down payment could be just the tip of the iceberg and that Marge could have been embezzling from the agency for months or even years. If that turned out to be the case, it could prove to be very costly to Josh, since any losses over $100,000 would come directly out of the agency's pocket.

❦

Josh had his secretary get him a sandwich at 1:00, then holed up alone in his office hoping against hope that Marge would appear with a simple explanation that would make the whole crisis disappear. He was unable to concentrate on anything but Marge and the missing policy, constantly glanced out the window for any sign of her car, and held his breath as he reached for the phone each time it rang.

The first call he received regarding Marge's whereabouts came in at 3:55 p.m. He had assumed it would be from either Marge's sister or the police, but it came from neither. Instead it came from a woman named Valerie Taylor at Community and Family Services. Mrs. Taylor said that Marge Hanlon was in her office. Marge had asked her to call and arrange for the two of them to come over to the agency and meet with Josh after it closed.

"Is Marge all right?" Josh asked.

"Marge is safe, Mr. Williams," Mrs. Taylor replied.

Josh resisted asking additional questions. From the woman's voice, he could tell she wasn't going to say anything more. He thanked her and suggested she and Marge come over at 4:45. By then, he said, the staff would be gone. The woman agreed.

Josh took a deep breath and walked into the outer office, where he announced he had just heard from Marge and she was okay. "She'll be in later this afternoon," he said, doing his best to manage a smile. All five employees in the office appeared relieved, although it was clear they were all waiting for him to tell them something more. Instead, he simply suggested everybody knock off after a trying day. He'd said he'd talk to them all in the morning.

Drier hung back as the others gradually left, but Josh assured him he could handle things by himself, and Drier, too, was gone by 4:15.

Once everyone had left, Josh returned to his office and slumped in his chair, staring absently out the window. All he could do now was wait.

⌒

Josh stood when he saw the car pull into the driveway and went to the front door to let the two women in.

Marge was accompanied by a petite, dark-haired woman who looked to be in her early forties and who introduced herself as Valerie Taylor. Josh greeted them politely, but he noticed immediately that Marge avoided eye contact and looked ten years older than when he'd seen her last. When he brought them into his office and took their coats, he also noted that Marge's clothes, which were always so neat, were badly wrinkled and that she clung to the smaller woman as though she were scared to death.

Josh invited them to sit on the couch and pulled up a chair across from them.

"As I explained over the phone, Mr. Williams," Mrs. Taylor began, "I'm an associate director of Community and Family Services. Marge came to our office this morning seeking help, and I've been working with her to try to help her deal with an extremely serious problem. Unfortunately, that problem involves your insurance agency as well. Marge asked me to arrange this meeting so she could explain it to you."

Josh glanced at Marge, but she was staring at the floor.

"I'm going to let Marge speak for herself, Mr. Williams, but there's one thing I'd like to say before she begins. What she's about to say is going to be very upsetting to you, but it's taken a great deal of courage for her to come in here this afternoon, and I hope you'll hear her out. Then perhaps we can talk about how we can work together to deal with the situation."

"Are you ready, Marge?" Mrs. Taylor asked gently.

Marge nodded almost imperceptibly, then looked up with the most anguished expression Josh thought he had ever seen.

"I'm sorry, Josh," she began, her voice trembling. "I've been stealing from you and our clients to gamble at the casino. I'm *so ashamed*," she said, and burst into tears.

Josh had prepared himself for the worst, but he was still staggered by the admission. It was incredible, he thought as he watched Marge, how blind he'd been. He'd continued to depend on her to run the Norwich office's day-to-day operations, just as Bob Duncan had, never imagining anything like this could ever happen. But then, why would he? And why hadn't anybody noticed anything?

Slowly, the story emerged.

Marge had never been to a casino before she and her sister visited Foxwoods shortly after it opened, just to look around. They'd wandered through the casino, watching people play the various table games, but none of it had any appeal for them and they'd left after a short time.

Then, she said, she and her sister had gone back for dinner after the casino put in slot machines, and they'd both played the slots for the first time. Her sister wanted to leave after five minutes, but Marge thought they were fun and stayed for almost half an hour until her sister finally dragged her away.

Marge hadn't been able to get her sister to go back, but she'd returned to Foxwoods for lunch with a couple of girlfriends about a month later, and they'd all played the slots afterward. This time, everybody had a good time, and they had begun going to Foxwoods together once a month just for a night out.

The problem started, she said, when she went to Foxwoods alone on a

Friday night and then began to go there regularly on Friday nights, just to relax and have something to look forward to at the end of the week.

"I thought it was really a good outlet for me," Marge said. "The casino's bright and alive and cheerful. The employees are friendly, they bring you free wine, and you can even earn points for playing. Not only that, but it's safe, because they have all that security."

Josh nodded, picturing the setting.

"The big thing, though," Marge continued, "was that I really enjoyed the slots. I don't have a family, and the truth is all I really do is work. Everybody depends on me. Mr. Duncan basically had me running the agency, and since you bought it, the pace has gotten just that much faster. I found that when I played the machines I could forget about everything. It like . . . puts you in a trance where you don't have to think, and no one's constantly calling your name and asking you to do something."

"How'd you do at first?" Josh asked. "Did you win?"

"No, not really," she said. "I wanted to win every time I pushed the button. And I got a rush at first when I did win. It makes you feel important, like you've accomplished something. I even thought that if I kept playing I might win one of the jackpots.

"But the main reason I played at first was simply to escape, and I didn't mind spending a little money to do it. I started with the twenty-five-cent machines, and you really can't lose much. It was simply the price of admission, like a dinner tab or a movie ticket.

"The trouble began when I started going on Saturdays and Sundays as well, and especially when I began playing the more expensive machines. Once I started playing the dollar and five-dollar slots, I could easily lose two hundred dollars in a weekend, and the more I played the more I lost.

"Then there was the weekend I lost a thousand dollars for the first time. It was a tremendous shock, and all I could think about that next week was winning it back."

"I take it you didn't, though?"

"No, I never won it back," Marge replied weakly. "Instead, I started going to the casino on Wednesdays after work, so I was now going four times a week and playing the ten- and even the hundred-dollar machines.

"That's when I really began to lose. I simply couldn't control it. I went through my entire savings, more than ninety-five thousand dollars, and maxed out my two credit cards. Then I began looking for other places to get money.

"The first thing I thought of was borrowing from my sister. But I couldn't because I couldn't bear the thought of her learning about my gambling."

Marge stopped and took a deep breath.

"And that's when I thought of the office," she said, barely able to finish the sentence before again dissolving in tears.

Josh got up and brought her a box of tissues and a glass of water.

Marge took several moments to compose herself and finally managed to continue. "As you know, half of our business has gone to direct bill, where the insurer bills the customer directly and the customer sends his premium payments directly to the insurance company. But we still bill the rest ourselves through agency bill, and those customers still send their checks to us, after which we forward the payments to the insurance company minus our commission."

That had led her to the agency's Workers' Comp business, she said, where she was responsible for generating the invoices sent to their clients, as well as collecting the money and remitting it to the insurance companies that wrote the policies.

In Workers' Comp, she explained, the agency's clients paid a deposit premium at the beginning of the policy term based on their payroll at the time, then were either billed an additional sum or sent a refund at the end of the term based on whether they had gained or lost employees. Consequently, she said, she had picked those companies that were growing the fastest and had simply inflated the invoices at the end of the term, skimming off the excess for herself.

"Didn't any of our clients catch on?" Josh asked incredulously.

Marge closed her eyes and shook her head. "Most of them were used to constantly increasing costs and simply trusted me to get them the best policy at the best price," she said. "If they did question the bill, I just blamed it on the market and their rate of growth, and agreed to look for something better. What I hoped at first was that I'd hit it big at the casino and would be able to pay the money back in the form of a premium refund the following year."

"How long have you been doing it?" Josh asked

"A little over two years," Marge answered.

"So does that mean you started before or after I bought the agency?"

"Right after," she replied.

Josh stared at her and asked the big question. "And how much money have you've taken?"

Marge looked down and answered in a voice barely above a whisper: "About a million dollars."

"A million dollars?!" Josh repeated, as though he must have misheard her.

"Maybe a little more," she said, looking up at him as though praying he wouldn't hate her. "I honestly don't know exactly. After a while, I lost count."

Josh felt as though he'd been hit in the face with a baseball bat. He faltered, but then steadied himself, not wanting to show his devastation and possibly cause her to shut down. That was the last thing he wanted at this point. It was essential he learn everything possible while she was willing to talk. If she had chosen to go to a lawyer instead of coming in with Mrs. Taylor, it could have taken months to learn the details of what she had told him so far.

"And what about the apartment house that burned down last night?" he asked. "Did you issue a binder and keep their down payment?

"Yes," Marge answered. "The apartment owner sent in a five-thousand-dollar down payment and I couldn't resist it. But my intention was to pay it back in a couple of weeks because I was scared to death that something might happen to the apartment building before I could activate the policy.

"And of course that's exactly what happened," Marge said ruefully. "I did okay at first, but then lost most of the money and was desperately trying to win it back when the apartment building burned down. When I heard about the fire on the news last night, I knew it was all over for me. You'd discover almost immediately what I'd done and from there you'd find out about the Workers' Comp money as well. I was so depressed and humiliated that I got in my car and tried to drive off the Mohegan-Pequot bridge.

"But there was no way to do it!" she blurted, shaking her head and burying her face in her hands. "I couldn't even kill myself, because there was no place to drive off the bridge!"

Mrs. Taylor stepped in at this point. She stroked Marge's shoulder.

"As I said," Mr. Williams, "Marge came in to see me this morning. She told me she drove around for an hour after the bridge incident trying to decide what to do next. She finally went home for a couple of hours and then drove to our office and waited in her car for the office to open.

"I think you can see she's lost control of her life. She's become a pathological gambler in that she can't resist her impulses to gamble despite the consequences. We're beginning to understand it's a neuro-biologic illness, just like alcohol or drug addiction."

Mrs. Taylor opened the slender portfolio case she'd brought with her and extracted a folder she handed to Josh. "These are some of the latest articles about gambling addiction," she said. "I thought you might find them helpful in trying to understand what's happened."

Josh glanced through the folder, scanning the articles' titles.

Mrs. Taylor paused to give him a moment to absorb the material then continued, "It's estimated there are two million adults in the United States who qualify as pathological gamblers, which means they have five or more symptoms from a list of ten used to diagnose the illness. The list includes things like preoccupation with gambling, repeated unsuccessful efforts to cut back or stop gambling, borrowing or stealing to support the habit, or loss of a job or a significant relationship because of it. Another four million adults are considered to be 'problem gamblers' because they have three of the symptoms, and millions more are at risk of becoming addicted as easy access to gambling spreads.

"We've been seeing a flood of new cases in Connecticut since Foxwoods opened because the equation is very simple: the greater the availability of gambling, the greater the number of gamblers. And the greater the number of gamblers, the greater the number of pathological and problem gamblers.

"And one of the saddest things," Mrs. Taylor said, "is the number of middle-aged women who are being hooked on slots. They particularly like playing the slots because it allows them to gamble in isolation, but what they don't realize when they start is that modern slot machines are the most addictive form of gambling ever devised. The newest machines are literally addiction-delivery devices that use fast action to mesmerize people and keep them playing. We call them the crack cocaine of gambling, and unfortunately, each new model is more technologically sophisticated than the last."

"And you're telling me states are depending on these machines for revenue?" Josh asked angrily. "My god, how can they justify it? It's not only morally corrupt, it's . . . it's criminal. I mean, come on—how's it any different than if the government were to partner with the tobacco companies to push cigarettes or if it were to let restaurants keep serving tainted food that was making people sick? Is the gambling industry that powerful that nobody's willing to do anything about it?"

"I suspect you know the answer as well as I do," Mrs. Taylor answered matter-of-factly. "Once Congress opened the door to casinos, partnering with them became a way for states to raise revenue without having to increase personal taxes, and now states like Connecticut are so hooked on the easy money that nobody wants to rock the boat. 'It's a trade-off' is the way the politicians put it. But I'm afraid politics isn't my field, Mr. Williams. My role is simply to try to repair the damage after it's done. And, unfortunately, the damage is far greater than almost anyone imagines.

"What we do know," Mrs. Taylor continued, "is that half the people in Gamblers Anonymous admit they've committed a crime connected to their gambling, and it's estimated that the total cost of gambling, including, debt, crime, and treatment, is already nearing half a billion dollars a year in Connecticut."

"The other thing that I'm afraid is pretty obvious," Mrs. Taylor concluded, "is that the casinos are creating a whole new class of criminals in states that never had casinos before, including people like Marge who've been in positions of trust and have led exemplary lives."

Josh sat back, more frustrated than he had ever felt in his life. It was as though some devastating pathogen had been loosed on the region, but instead of trying to contain it, government was hell-bent on spreading it.

"So what do you suggest we do next, Mrs. Taylor?" he asked. "You've obviously been through this before."

The social worker paused before answering. It was always one of the most important moments in her job.

"You have every right to call the police and throw this into the legal system, Mr. Williams," she said. "There are several cases in the local courts right now where gamblers are being prosecuted for stealing from their employer, and the number keeps rising. But if I can play the role of mediator, I do have a suggestion."

Josh waited without responding.

"The one hopeful thing is that Marge has finally admitted she has a gambling problem and has agreed to enter a treatment program. That's the first step toward recovery, and I sincerely believe the best option for both of you would be to try to work out an agreement for her to repay you as much as she can over time without going to court. If she honors her agreement, it could avoid a lot of damaging publicity, as well as a great deal of additional misery for everyone."

Mrs. Taylor leaned forward and looked Josh in the eye. "But it's up to you, Mr. Williams. It's entirely up to you."

Josh said somberly that he would consider Mrs. Taylor's advice. They agreed to keep what had happened strictly confidential until Josh had had a chance to consult with his attorney.

～

Josh's first call after the two women left was to Brad Merriweather, who agreed to take the case and do everything possible to help Josh salvage his business.

Nevertheless, prospects for holding onto the agency looked bleak. The final figures showed that Marge Hanlon had stolen just under $1.3 million from the agency's Workers' Comp clients plus $5,000 from The Pittsfield, leaving the Williams Agency on the hook for a total of $1.2 million after the fidelity bond reimbursement. Equally discouraging, the two insurance companies that issued the Workers' Comp policies that Josh sold dropped the Williams Agency, destroying Josh's fastest growing and most profitable line of business.

Brad managed to work out an arrangement giving Josh five years to repay his creditors, but Josh had borrowed heavily to buy the Duncan Agency, and his business had now suffered a devastating setback. It was a long shot that he'd be able to meet his debt obligations for long and still support his family.

This left selling the business as his only real choice, but if he tried to sell it now, he wouldn't get half of what he'd hoped for. His best option, he decided, was to try to borrow further against the farm and try to scrape up whatever else he could to get through the next six to twelve months. Once the business had recovered a bit, he thought hopefully, he could try to find a buyer.

Fortunately, news of the embezzlement never reached the press, and Josh did his best to carry on as though nothing had happened. At Brad's advice, he agreed to an out-of-court settlement with Marge in which she quietly resigned and promised to reimburse him 25 percent of her future income for as long as it took to pay off his losses. It was clear she could never pay him back in her lifetime, but he had neither the heart to send her to jail nor the desire to see the story splashed across the local papers.

Josh couldn't help but think again and again about Valerie Taylor's comment about Marge losing control of her life. Increasingly, he was afraid, he was losing control of his. Unable to sell the farm, he was now facing the loss of his business.

The embezzlement took a heavy toll on him, triggering an initial period of depression that alarmed Sharon and the children. He had trouble sleeping and was moody, saying little at dinner, sitting alone in the library in the evenings, and avoiding friends. He frequently rose before dawn, pulled on his dark-gray muck boots, and walked the farm, watching the sun come up over the eastern hills and puzzling over how things could have gone so terribly wrong. The family did its best to rally around him, but Sharon became increasingly concerned as the weeks passed. They had each other and they had their health, she reminded him, and in the end that was all that mattered. Somehow, she assured him, they'd get through it.

Josh wasn't at all sure about that, but he slowly began to recover as the spring rains let up and summer came into view. The real breakthrough occurred one Saturday morning in mid-May when Sharon managed to persuade him to leave what he was doing in the horse barn and give her some advice on the perspective for a charcoal sketch she was planning of the bridge over Bixler Brook. He agreed half-heartedly, but once they set up the easel and he began to watch her work, something happened.

Perhaps it was the angle of the sun that hour and the way it filtered through the trees, danced along the brook, and framed her before the easel in her big-brimmed hat. Or perhaps it was the grace of her strokes, the way they caught the curve of the bridge just so and brought the scene to life. Or perhaps it was simply the way she turned and glanced back at him with her irresistible smile. More likely, though, it was a combination of all these things that suddenly touched him, brought tears to his eyes, and made him realize how much he loved this beautiful woman and how incredibly fortunate he was that she was his wife.

The turnaround wasn't instant, but that evening Josh sat in the library taking stock of what he had to do next. It was as though he was getting hammered in one of his tennis matches. Every shot was coming in hard, driving him from corner to corner and pinning him against the baseline. But if you could hit the ball back just one more time, you never knew what might happen next. One shot, one mistake, one piece of luck, and the momentum could change. He'd seen it happen a thousand times. The key was to stay in the game. And for now that meant keeping the farm, taking care of his family, and rebuilding his business as best he could. Sunday was the best day he'd had in two months, and by dinner on Monday the whole family knew he was on his way back.

One result of the embezzlement was that Josh became even more determined to stop the Northerns' casino.

He reviewed every page of the tribe's recognition application, looking for anything the lawyers and researchers might have missed. He peppered Rick Pugliese with questions. And he pressed Gladys Greene to redouble her efforts to come up with additional information on Rachel Amos.

The genealogist continued to harbor strong doubts that Rachel was a Pequot but by the end of May had not been able to find a shred of direct evidence to prove her case. The only documents she had been able to find that mentioned Rachel continued to be two surviving and somewhat sketchy overseer's reports that listed her as living on the reservation in 1800 and dying and being buried there in 1803.

"Interestingly, however," Mrs. Greene told Josh, "the 1798 overseer's report, which is the only surviving report prior to 1800, makes no mention of either Rachel or her daughter, Fanny. This suggests to me that Rachel could simply have been a homeless mother who took refuge on the reservation and had no genealogical ties to the tribe whatsoever. All kinds of down and out people drifted on and off Connecticut's reservations around that time. The only problem is I can't find a single reference to Rachel prior to 1800 to establish who she actually was."

There were very few places left to look, Mrs. Greene cautioned, but she promised to keep trying.

As Gladys Greene pored over old documents, prospects for the casino industry in southeastern Connecticut continued to brighten.

On June 7, 1996, just a little more than three years after the Northerns applied for recognition, the BIA announced it had placed the tribe's petition on active status, which meant the bureau could technically render a preliminary decision one year from that day.

Even Rick Pugliese expressed surprise that the BIA was moving so fast. "The BIA's way behind schedule on just about every other case I know of," Pugliese commented, "so this can only mean that somebody high up is pushing the Northerns' application very hard."

Meanwhile, the Mohegans' new $305 million casino rushed toward completion just ten miles away, finally opening on October 12 as Mohegan Sun.

An estimated 18,000 people jammed their way into the lavish facility in the first hour, overwhelming the 180 gaming tables and 2,672 state-of-the-art slot machines and packing the place so tight that it was questionable anyone even noticed the casino's Northeast Woodland Indians theme. The opening-day crowd was so enormous, the papers reported, that developer Sol Kerzner and his Mohegan partners immediately began planning a major expansion.

Lest anyone worry that Mohegan Sun and Foxwoods might cannibalize each other, analysts predicted that the presence of two of the world's largest casinos within a few miles of one another would in fact vastly expand Connecticut's gaming market by attracting thousands of new players. Indeed, the November 1996 slots revenues reported by the two casinos bore out that prediction, soaring to $64 million from the $47 million made by Foxwoods alone the previous November.

Not only were the total slots numbers incredible, the experts exclaimed, but the daily win, or "hold," per machine was an unbelievable $345 at Mohegan Sun and $284 at Foxwoods, blowing away the $200 per machine in Atlantic City and $100 in Las Vegas.

By year-end, Connecticut's Indians seemed to be winning across the board. The state's fiscal authorities were euphoric about the skyrocketing casino revenues, and the Department of Environmental Protection had moved John Mason's bronze statue from Mystic to the town of Windsor, which he had helped found. The statue's new plaque briefly described Mason's life, but made no reference to the war against the Pequots except to note that the monument had been relocated "to respect a sacred site of the 1637 Pequot War."

25

The Nautilus

March–April 1997

Jim Grimaldi called Bobby in mid-March to say he and Paul Ivy wanted to come up to the reservation to talk about the status of the recognition application and show him preliminary designs for the casino.

Bobby agreed immediately, although he mentioned that Mavis was away on vacation and would be sorry she missed them.

"Anything new on the application?" he asked.

"Not really," Grimaldi said. "Paul says there's been one small glitch, but that everything's still on track. He'll fill you in when we get there."

Ivy coming to the reservation had to mean they were getting close to a favorable decision in Washington, Bobby thought, because Ivy hadn't been in Sheffield since his first visit almost six years ago, and Bobby had only talked to him on the phone a couple of times since. Otherwise, Ivy had remained almost completely in the shadows. As far as Bobby could tell, no one but Ivy's closest associates and a few select officials in Washington were aware of his involvement with the Northerns, and no one in Sheffield knew who was quarterbacking the tribe's drive for recognition and a casino. According to Grimaldi, the tribe had no legal obligation to reveal the names of its financial backers until it actually entered into a casino agreement with them, which meant Ivy should be able to continue to operate behind the scenes until the deal was done.

∽

Ivy and Grimaldi arrived in a stretch limo just before 2:00 on March 20, and Ivy popped out almost before the car stopped.

"Hello, Chief," he boomed, giving Bobby a bear hug as though they were old buddies.

"Welcome back to the rez, Paul," Bobby said, figuring it was okay to use

Ivy's first name if they were such good friends. "And you, too, Jim," he added as Grimaldi joined them. "Can't believe it's been almost six years since you two were here last."

"Neither can I," Grimaldi said. "You've done a lot of work."

"Yeah, looks like you really know how to spend my money," Ivy said with a frown. "Just kidding," he added quickly, laughing at his own joke and draping his arm around Bobby's shoulder to prove it. "I'm glad you spruced the place up. It looked like shit the last time I was here."

Now sixty-seven years old, Ivy still had the smooth shaved head and wrestler's build that Bobby remembered, and he looked tan and fit in a cashmere overcoat, light blue shirt, and solid red tie. According to Grimaldi, Ivy was an avid sailor and diver, still beat men half his age at handball, and was still quite a lover and party animal to boot. He had been married four times, most recently to a Miss Florida whom he'd divorced three years ago, and since then he'd been flying a small entourage of his friends to his casino in Aruba each year for what had to be the most exclusive stag party on the planet. Each guest's cabana came stocked with its own private showgirl, and there were plenty more at dinner each night. The only rule at dinner was that Ivy got the first pick.

Bobby spent a few minutes explaining the improvements to the reservation, then the three men trooped into Bobby's mobile home. Ivy immediately shed his topcoat and suit jacket and, without a word, commandeered the chair at the head of the kitchen table. He motioned for Bobby and Grimaldi to take a seat, then loosened his tie and rolled up his sleeves as he settled in. He was wearing a gold chronometer encrusted with diamonds on his left wrist, and his perfectly manicured nails looked newly polished.

Christ, Bobby thought, the man certainly didn't stand on ceremony. But then, he figured, somebody with that kind of money didn't have to. The guy's watch alone looked like it cost more than the trailer.

Jumping straight to business, Ivy said he'd gotten a little scare two weeks ago when he'd been told that the BIA unit charged with evaluating recognition petitions was raising questions about the Northerns' ability to meet the social and political continuity requirements.

The problem, Ivy explained, was that the unit, known as the Bureau of Acknowledgement and Research, consisted of the most independent and professional people at the BIA, and they were a lot harder to influence than the political appointees at the top.

"Fortunately," Ivy said, "our guy at Interior thinks the BAR people will eventually go along, and he says that even if they balk, the head of the BIA can always overrule 'em. I also checked with the White House and my Senate friend, and they both say not to worry. So I gotta believe we're probably going to be okay.

"The one thing I am concerned about, though," Ivy continued, "is this genealogist, Gladys Greene. If she were ever able to show that Rachel Amos wasn't a Pequot, it'd be a killer.

"Our own genealogist says he's confident he didn't miss anything on Rachel, but the last thing we need at this point is a genealogy problem, and I just wanna be sure you don't know of anything that could possibly trip us up. You don't, do you, Chief?" Ivy asked, fixing Bobby with a piercing stare.

Bobby was taken aback by the question. It was as though Ivy thought Bobby was withholding something.

"Absolutely not," Bobby said, opening his hands and shaking his head for emphasis. "If you're referrin' to the conversation I had with Jim the other day, all I said was I'm uneasy having a former BIA researcher out there tryin' to dig up somethin' negative on Rachel and not knowin' what she might be comin' up with."

"But you're saying there's absolutely nothing you know about Rachel that could hurt us?"

"Absolutely nothin'," Bobby said firmly. As he stared back at Ivy, it struck him that the man's bald head, slightly elongated at the top, was shaped liked an artillery shell—a perfect match for his personality.

"Then why do you suppose this Greene woman doesn't believe Rachel was a Pequot?" Ivy bore in.

"I have no idea," Bobby replied. "But that's why I'm uneasy. We don't know exactly what she's looking for or what, if anythin', she might've found. And if she ever did find anythin', we'd never know until they were ready to spring it on us."

Ivy drummed his fingers on the table as he thought about Bobby's answer. "Okay," he said, "what would you think of bringing in somebody to watch Greene?"

"You mean like a private investigator?"

"Yeah, somebody experienced with this type of thing."

"I think that'd be smart," Bobby said, liking the idea immediately. "It's important to know what she's up to, and maybe this guy could put a little pressure on her, too. Maybe even get her to back off altogether. Know'm sayin'?"

"All right, let us handle it," Ivy said. "You have anybody else who can help keep tabs on her?"

"Not at the moment," Bobby said, "although I'm workin' on the second selectman, Dwayne Fuller. He's part of the Casino Task Force and could help us with a lot of things if we could ever get him past his loyalty to Clark."

"Clark's the first selectman," Grimaldi reminded Ivy.

"That's right," Bobby continued. "Clark and Fuller are Republicans, and they've been runnin' as a team for twenty years. Between the two of 'em, they know everybody in town, and nobody ever even comes close to beatin' 'em."

Ivy thought about that for a moment and then, without leaving his chair, reached over and opened the refrigerator. He grabbed a can of beer from the middle shelf and cracked it open. He took a long pull, then examined the can with a crinkled nose.

"This the only thing you got?" he asked, reading the label out loud.

"Yeah, it's local," Bobby answered. "You don't like it?"

Ivy took another taste, then proceeded to drain the rest of the can in several swallows. He lofted the empty can into an open trash can, where it landed with a clank, and wiped his lips with the back of his hand. "With all the money I pump in here, you oughta be able to do better'n that," he said, and then seamlessly picked up where they'd let off.

"So tell me about this Fuller. You know him well?"

"Yeah, I've known him for years," Bobby replied. "He owns the Gulf station. A bunch of us used to play poker in his back room at night. Fuller usually supports Clark on everything, and he's been backin' him on the casino because Clark feels so strongly about it. But he's told me privately he thinks it's stupid for the town to keep spendin' money to oppose it when it looks more and more like a done deal."

"What would it take to get him to endorse the casino?" Ivy asked.

"One of the problems is gettin' his attention right now," Bobby said. "He's all wrapped up in a fight with the state over cleanin' up some environmental problems at the gas station. He says if he has to do everythin' they're demanding it's gonna cost so much he'll have to close or try to sell the business."

"What if we helped him with the cleanup?" Ivy asked, leaning back and interlacing his fingers behind his neck.

"You mean pay for it?" Bobby asked.

"Yeah. You think that'd bring him over?"

"It might," Bobby said thoughtfully. "He's already on the fence, and the station's his life. But you could be talkin' forty or fifty thousand bucks."

"That's all right," Ivy said, dismissing the price with a wave of his hand. "Why don't you feel him out. If he's interested, we'll send up somebody to talk with him. I like the idea of having two sources on Greene, and it sounds like Fuller could pay dividends in other ways down the pike.

"Okay," Ivy said, turning to a leather architect's case and aluminum easel that the limo driver had brought in from the car. "We've got some plans here I think you're gonna like."

Ivy took out what looked like about a dozen renderings mounted on foam-core boards and set them on the easel. The first board simply had the Northerns' new seal, which showed an eagle alighting on an Indian's outstretched hand and bore the inscription "Northern Pequot Tribal Nation" at the bottom.

"We've designed the casino and hotel to look out over the lake and take advantage of the natural setting, as we all originally agreed," Ivy began, "but we've dropped the Indian theme and the family-oriented touches we originally talked about, and I wanna tell you why before getting into the renderings.

"We all agree," Ivy stated, "that if we were the first ones into this market we could build just about anything and people would flock to the place. But we're not first. We're going to be third, and we're going to be up against the two biggest and most successful casinos in the country. So we're gonna havta put up somethin' that can really draw the crowds."

"We've still got the best location," Bobby reminded Ivy.

"True," Ivy acknowledged. "We're half an hour closer to New York and most of Connecticut's population than Foxwoods and fifteen minutes closer than Mohegan Sun. That's an advantage, but the main thing is we need a place where people want to come."

Bobby didn't argue.

"If you look at what's happening in the industry," Ivy said, "two things are pretty clear.

"The first is that casino gambling's riding a wave right now. It's new and exciting for most people, but the problem is it's starting to turn up everywhere—from riverboats and racetracks to most of the Indian reservations in the country. So I gotta believe people are going to get tired of a lot of what's out there now. And that goes especially for Indian casinos.

"I mean, how many variations can you have on an Indian theme?

"The other thing that's clear if you look at the numbers," Ivy continued, "is that despite all the new interest in gambling, Las Vegas itself has been having some problems. Some of that's because of all the new competition, but basically I have to believe it's because Vegas has lost its way with this family-friendly image it's been pushing lately.

"That's not why people go to Las Vegas," Ivy stated.

"People go to Vegas because it's a little bit of a walk on the wild side. They go there for the glitz and a little bit of sin—to gamble, have a few drinks, see the shows, ogle the showgirls, and hit the strip clubs. They don't go there to ride the roller coaster with their six-year-old.

"And you know who understands that better than anybody?" Ivy asked. "This guy Sol Kerzner from South Africa. The South African government banned gambling, pornography, and interracial sex, but there were no prohibitions in the autonomous black homelands, and Kerzner took advantage of that to build Sun City—or, as everybody called it, Sin City—where whites could go to gamble, watch topless dancers, and get their horn scraped by black princesses.

"Now obviously Vegas has gotta keep it within limits," Ivy said, "but I believe you're gonna see it go back to its roots in the next few years, which is basically to give people a nice, sanitized, comfortable environment where they can cut loose and have a good time in a way they can't back home.

"My point," Ivy continued, "is we gotta stay ahead of the curve. In other words, no roller coasters and no Northeast Woodland Indian scenes, because that stuff's going to be passé by the time we get this thing up and running."

Bobby just nodded. Mavis was going to be upset they were deep-sixing the Indian theme, but she'd get over it. He personally couldn't care less what format they used, as long as it packed people in.

"At the same time," Ivy said, "we havta pay attention to local sensibilities and design something to reflect New England. So what we're proposing is nothing less than the classiest-looking resort casino in America."

He paused to let the idea sink in.

"We've been tossing around some names, and we've tentatively come up with 'The Nautilus,'" Ivy said, taking down the first board and revealing the next one. It had the Nautilus name emblazoned across it next to the silhouette of a graceful sailing ship.

"We've picked the name to play off the region's maritime past," Ivy explained, "and, as you'll see, we've designed the main building to look like an elegant, colonial-style yacht club overlooking the lake.

"Basically," Ivy continued, slowly removing the second board, "we see it looking something like this."

The next rendering showed a sprawling, ten-story structure with white clapboards, paned glass windows, and black shutters. A sweeping green lawn extended down to the lake, and sailboats appeared in the distance.

Bobby's draw dropped. "Ho-lee shit!" he said reverently, his face lighting up in genuine awe of how it had all come together.

Continuing through the next several boards, Ivy explained that the main building would include a two-thousand-room hotel with a thousand suites and the largest ballroom in New England, while a three-story annex would house five separate casinos and private game rooms. The casinos opened off a central square built to resemble a small marina that would showcase modern and antique yachts. "It'll be like a mini-boat show," Ivy said, "where the world's top boatbuilders will compete to show off their sexiest stuff."

His goal, Ivy emphasized, was to create a destination that would draw both midweek and weekend customers and give people some real excitement. "We want New England, but we want it hip, luxurious, entertaining . . . with just the right amount of decadence—something that will bring in the crowds, from locals and tourists to convention-goers and high rollers. That's the goal: just get the people in the door, and we'll keep a percentage of every cent they bring."

Bobby opened his mouth as if to speak, but instead just looked at Grimaldi in admiration of how far they'd come. Grimaldi winked at him and pointed to Ivy. "I told you," Grimaldi said. "He's the man."

Bobby nodded in agreement and gave Ivy an enthusiastic thumbs-up. There was certainly no question he was "the man." He recalled Ivy once stating that aside from his business deals, he never gambled. The only way to win in a casino, he'd said, was to own one. Thanks to Ivy, he was now on track to own one of the most spectacular casinos in the country.

Ivy shrugged off the compliment and continued without missing a beat. In addition to a championship golf course and high-end shops, he said, they were planning, five gourmet restaurants, a couple of edgy nightclubs with go-go dancers, two spas, an authentic Paris cabaret, a theater for burlesque and Vegas-type stage shows, three lounges, including an ultra-lounge with high-priced drinks, and an indoor pool connected to a heated outdoor pool accessed by swimming under a four-story waterfall. Topping it all off, he said as he came to the final rendering, would be a five-thousand-seat concert hall where they could put on high-tech extravaganzas and book the biggest and hottest names in the business.

"Another thing," Ivy added. "We wanna go all out to attract the New York celebrity crowd—you know, the actors, the TV hosts, the models, rappers, and sports stars. We simply want 'em to come and play. We'll send limos for 'em, helicopter 'em in, comp 'em, do whatever we have to do to get 'em here, so people can brag they saw 'so-and-so' up at The Nautilus.

"The whole thing'll be a different kind of New England experience: sin and fun without the guilt. All you repressed Puritans up here should love it."

⌐⌐

The same day Paul Ivy visited Connecticut, Sharon's seventy-six-year-old father suffered a massive coronary at his home in Illinois and died before reaching the emergency room. Sharon immediately flew to Chicago to be with her mother and Josh and the children flew out later the next week for the funeral. The family pleaded with Sharon's mother to come back to Sheffield with them while she recovered, but she declined, insisting she had a legion of friends to watch over her at home. She loved visiting the farm, she said, but she needed to get on with her life.

Then, on April 2, Josh put the Williams Agency on the market. If he could have hung on to the business a little longer he might have gotten a better price, but the debt payments were killing him and he simply had to try to sell. He almost immediately saw that he might have set the price too low, because his broker contacted him within two days with an offer from the Kraft Agency in Hartford. Harold Kraft happened to be looking for an agency in eastern Connecticut and was not only prepared to pay cash but, if there were no problems, to close by the end of the month.

Josh turned over the keys on April 30, roughly thirteen and a half months after discovering the embezzlement. It was both a relief and a heartbreaking loss. The agency had become an albatross, but giving it up was more painful than he'd expected. It wasn't just giving up the business. It was giving up part of himself.

The Kraft Agency offered Josh a job as its sales manager for eastern Connecticut, and he took it for the income, but he had no idea how he would feel going into work every day as an employee rather than the owner. There was no question, however, that he needed the money. The price he received for the agency barely extinguished his remaining business debts, and he still had a hefty mortgage on the farm. In addition, Matt had another year at UConn, and Sarah would be going off to college in the fall. She had also decided to go to UConn, which would at least be cheaper than a private school, but it still meant two kids in college next year, and the income from the farm hardly made a dent in the mortgage.

Sharon insisted on going back to work to help out and found a position as a copywriter for a catalog company in New London. It didn't pay that much, but she'd done similar work back in Chicago, and at that moment anything would help with the bills.

At the same time, Josh began to look for ways to squeeze more income out of the farm. He put off nonessential repairs, decided to add a new field of strawberries, and leased out another ten acres to a neighboring dairy farmer. As part of the belt-tightening, he also sold his and Sharon's horses to the stable that had bought their two Appaloosa colts. It left just Matt's Palomino, Sarah's Morgan, and a second Morgan mare named Jet they'd acquired to replace Jacob's pony.

All in all, it had been a gloomy start to spring.

26

~

Blackjack

May 18–19, 1997

Matt turned twenty-one on Sunday, May 18, 1997, and his mother made his favorite dinner, roast stuffed chicken, along with a chocolate layer cake topped by two giant candles in the shapes of a 2 and a 1. The family sang "Happy Birthday" as Sharon brought in the cake, and afterward Matt opened his cards and gifts, including a sentimental card from his mother and father stuffed with twenty-one $10 bills.

It was more money than the family could afford, but Sharon was determined to make the occasion a special one and had put the money aside during the past month. Matt was surprised by the amount, because he knew how badly his parents were hurting financially, and he went around the table and hugged and thanked everybody. He almost choked up at one point, thinking how lucky he was to be part of such a close-knit family.

Without telling Matt, Kayla had organized a second party for later that evening.

She told Matt she was rearranging her schedule so they could spend a quiet evening together on his birthday, but when she led him into the parlor, she and four of their friends shouted "Surprise!" and burst into "Happy Birthday." The group included Kayla's housemate, Amy, and her boyfriend, Tim Paxton, as well as a Foxwoods dealer named Liam Blackwell and his girlfriend, Allie Carlson.

Before Matt could react, somebody popped the cork on a champagne bottle, the three girls kissed him, the guys clapped him on the back, and Liam stuck a glass of champagne in his hand and offered an Irish toast.

"Happy Birthday, Matt," Liam said. "May you live a hundred years, with one extra year to repent!"

"Hear! Hear!" everyone cried.

"A year may be enough for Matt, but it'll never be enough for you, Liam," Kayla teased.

"That's the whole plan," Liam retorted, and everyone laughed.

"All right, drink up, everybody, we've got to go," Kayla declared.

"Go where?" Matt asked.

"To your party, of course," Kayla said, relishing the surprise. "We're taking you to Mohegan Sun for your birthday!"

Matt and Kayla rode over to the casino with Liam and his girlfriend in Liam's '89 Jaguar.

The newest member of Kayla and Matt's Foxwoods circle, Liam had become one of their favorites. Like Tim, he had Sunday off, and he and Kayla had been the principal conspirators in arranging the surprise party.

Liam was twenty-four and had grown up in Brooklyn with his American mother and Irish father. His father eventually went back to Ireland, and his mother was now living in Texas. After attending St. John's University for a year, he'd dropped out and worked at various jobs in the city. About a year and a half ago he answered an ad and started training to become a dealer at Foxwoods.

Liam was one of the most engaging people Matt had ever met—easygoing and funny, with a million stories, and, thanks to his father, the ability to slip in and out of an Irish brogue in a way that always delighted everyone.

At the same time, Matt noticed that Liam really didn't seem to have any close friends. Even his relationship with Allie seemed superficial. They never seemed to hold hands or show affection for each other. It was as though they were together without having any contact. In fact, aside from Tim, who had introduced Liam into their group, Matt felt he was probably as close to Liam as anyone.

A rabid Big East basketball fan from his year at St. John's, Liam was always interested in talking to Matt about what was happening with UConn. But that was just for starters. Liam, it turned out, was a true sportsaholic. It didn't make any difference what sport came up in the conversation, Liam knew them all, not to mention every player, every horse, every jockey, every record, and every statistic, as well as the latest line on every game or race going. Matt must have told him a hundred times that he should be a sports talk-show host.

Matt was in an exuberant mood as the group entered Mohegan Sun and headed to the Wolf Den lounge. It was incredibly liberating to be twenty-one and able to go anywhere he chose. Everyone in the group—including Kayla, who had turned twenty-one in February—was older than he was. While he had been at parties with all of them, he was always the kid who couldn't go into a bar, order a drink at a restaurant, or go into one of the casinos, where it seemed three-quarters of the people in their crowd now worked.

The Wolf Den was packed when they walked in just before 9:00, and the atmosphere was alive and exciting. A lot of Foxwoods employees came over to Mohegan Sun because they weren't allowed to gamble where they worked, and Tim waved to a couple of people he knew.

They finally got a table and crowded around within inches of one another. What a terrific group, Matt thought as he sipped a martini and they bantered back and forth. He never thought he could get used to martinis, but this one tasted great.

"I just want to say to my young friend here," Liam said, looking at Matt, "that you are one lucky son of a bitch—to be twenty-one, to have a gorgeous woman like Kayla, and to have fabulous friends like us to watch out for you!"

"Damn straight," Tim agreed, pounding the table.

"I just hope we're going to be able to make it home tonight," Kayla said, as Liam signaled the waitress for another round.

"Come on, girl," Liam said. "Drinkin' keeps you loose."

"Which reminds me," Liam added, "did I tell you about Jimmy Flaherty?"

"Probably," Tim laughed, "but tell us again!"

"Well," Liam began, "Jimmy goes into the confessional and says, 'Bless me Father, for I have sinned. I have been with a loose woman.'

"'Is that you, Jimmy Flaherty?' the priest asks.

"'Yes, Father,' he says, 'it is.'

"'And who was the woman you were with?' the priest asks.

"'I can't be telling you, Father,' Jimmy says. 'I don't want to ruin her reputation.'

"'Well, Jimmy,' the priest says, 'I'm sure to find out sooner or later, so you may as well tell me now. Was it Brenda O'Malley?'

"'I cannot say.'

"'Was it Sheelah O'Brien?'

"'I'm sorry, but I cannot name her.'

"'Was it Kathleen Morgan?'

"'I'll never tell.'

"'Was it Patricia Kelly, then?' the priest asks.

"'Please, Father,' Jimmy pleads, 'I can't tell you.'

"'You're a steadfast lad, Jimmy Flaherty,' the priest sighs, 'and I admire that. But you've sinned, and you must atone. You must make a novena by saying the rosary once a day for the next nine days. Be off with you now.'

"So Jimmy walks back to his pew and his friend Sean whispers, 'How'd it go?'

"'Great,' Jimmy whispers back. 'I got four new leads.'"

The girls in particular roared with laughter.

"Tell 'em the one about the pharmacist," Tim urged.

"If you insist," Liam said, clearly loving the attention.

And so it went for the next ten minutes, the table howling at each new story to the point that Matt was sure someone was going to come over and tell them to tone it down.

"All right," Liam finally announced, "it's time to get serious. Now that Matt's come of age, Tim and I are going to take him out on the floor and teach him how to play some of these games. It's our birthday present to him. Everybody go out and have a good time. We'll all meet back here at eleven-fifteen."

Liam, Tim, and Matt headed for the least-crowded craps table and stood watching for a few minutes while Liam and Tim explained the action.

"This is the coolest, classiest game in the casino and has the best odds for a novice," Liam began, "because if you stick to certain bets, the house has less than a one percent edge."

Tim agreed. "You've just got to get used to the table and a few basic rules. It sounds complicated, but it's really not."

"There are four people running the game," Liam pointed out. "The guy sitting behind the middle of the table is called the boxman. He's the boss and watches to make sure nobody cheats and nothing goes wrong. The two dealers on each side of him pay off the winners and rake in the losers' chips, and the stickman there controls the action.

"If the shooter throws a seven or an eleven on his first roll, it's called a natural and it wins. If he rolls a two, three, or twelve, that's called craps and it loses. And if he rolls a four, five, six, eight, nine, or ten, that becomes his point number.

"To win his bet, the shooter has to keep rolling the dice until he rolls his point number again without rolling a seven first. If he rolls a seven before making his point number, he 'sevens out' and loses.

"Seven's the most likely number to come up on any given roll," Liam added, "but don't ever say the word 'seven' at a craps table, because craps players are superstitious as hell and believe just saying the number can make it pop up at the wrong time."

"Okay, here's a new shooter," Tim said, pointing to a fat guy with a mass of blubber for a chin. "He's putting his bet down by placing his chips on the big band there around the outer edge of the table that has the word 'pass' on it. That's called his pass-line bet, and the other players around the table are putting down their bets, which will win or lose depending on what the shooter rolls."

With all bets down, the stickman pushed several sets of dice to the shooter, who picked a pair and rolled them down the table so they bounced off the wall at the end.

"What'd he roll?" Tim asked, craning his neck to get a better look.

"Nine," Matt said.

"So nine's his point number," Tim said, "and he's got to throw another nine before he throws a seven in order to win."

"Oh, shit!" Liam exclaimed as the shooter raised the dice to his mouth.

"What's the matter?" Matt asked.

"Nothing," Tim said with a chuckle. "Liam can't stand it when a shooter blows on the dice. You just don't want to do it. It gets spit all over 'em. It's gross."

"It's fucking disgusting, is what it is," Liam said, without taking his eyes off the table.

"Well, it doesn't seem to be helping the guy," Matt said, watching the shooter roll a ten. The next roll came up a six and a three, however, and the crowd around the table broke out in a cheer.

"See how simple it is?" Tim said. "You've just got to stay away from proposition bets, where you make a specific bet on the next roll. The odds are murder on those bets, and they can clean you out pretty fast."

"All right, let's move on," Liam said.

"How about roulette?" Matt asked, as they passed a line of roulette tables.

"Nah, stay away from roulette," Liam said. "You can play it for fun, but the odds stink, and there really aren't any strategies that'll do you any good. No matter how you bet, the house always has a five percent edge.

"What you want to do is to find a game like craps that narrows the odds. For a beginner like you, the next two best games for doing that are blackjack and this one," Liam said, stopping at a long table with two large, identical semicircles at either end. "Baccarat."

"Yeah," Matt lit up, "this is the one where you see James Bond playing for a hundred thousand dollars a bet, right?"

"Exactly," Tim said. "This is supposed to be an elegant game for rich, sophisticated people. As a matter of fact, I was thinking of putting you in a tux and Kayla in an evening gown and bringing the two of you over to my baccarat table some night just to draw a crowd."

Matt laughed. "I'd have to learn how to play first," he said, actually loving the image.

"Well, that's no problem," Liam said, "because this is about the easiest card game in the casino."

"All you have to do is make two decisions," Tim said. "How much you want to put down and whether you want to bet on the player, the banker, or a tie. After that, it's all luck."

Liam ordered three more drinks from a waitress, and they stood discussing the baccarat action until the drinks arrived. Then they wandered off to find a blackjack table.

Matt was pleased to find something he knew more about. "This is the same as twenty-one, right? You try to get as close to twenty-one as possible, but if you go through it, you bust."

"Right," Tim said. "Blackjack's a nickname for twenty-one."

"Yeah, we used to play it at school Las Vegas Nights," Matt said.

"It's by far the most popular table game in the casino," Liam said, "because a skilled player's got a real chance to win. But there's a huge difference between a typical player and a skilled one.

"The casinos figure an experienced player with a good card-counting system has as much as a two-percent edge over the house, but the casino still makes a hefty profit at the end of the day, because its edge against the typical hunch player runs from six to fifteen percent. But the good news is that if you just take time to learn a basic strategy, with no counting, and you stick to it, you can cut the house edge to under half a percent."

"All right," Tim said, motioning to Matt, "there're some seats opening up at the next table."

"Jeez, I don't know," Matt hesitated. "I don't know if I can afford it."

"Come on," Liam said. "We'll make sure you don't lose much."

Matt felt for his wallet. He had $40 with him from the money his parents had given him for his birthday that evening.

"Come on, before somebody else sits down," Liam pressed. "I'll stake you to your first bet as a birthday present, and I'll lend you a few bucks if you need it. This is a good chance to learn."

The three of them sat down with Matt in the middle, and Tim and Liam bought chips from the dealer.

"Here's fifty dollars in chips," Liam said. "The first ten bucks are on me, and you can owe me for the rest. That's the max you can lose tonight.

"That's actually the most important lesson you can learn," Liam added. "Decide how much you can afford to lose before you start playing, and never go over it. Never. That's the difference between keeping this a game and getting into trouble."

"Shit," Matt was thinking, he couldn't afford to lose anything.

Liam explained to the dealer, a cheerful middle-aged woman, that this was Matt's first time at a casino; anything she could do to help teach him the game would be great. Reluctantly, Matt put down $5, and with all bets down, the woman began to deal, starting at her left and making two passes around the table.

"Remember," Liam said softly, "an ace can count as either one or eleven, and the jack, queen, and king are all valued at ten."

Matt lost his first two hands, going over twenty-one both times and watching the dealer collect his bet and remove his cards from the table immediately. Poof, the money was gone, just like that.

The next hand sent his spirits soaring. His first two cards were an ace and a queen, giving him twenty-one. He won. Or at least he thought he won until he saw the dealer had an ace and a ten, giving her blackjack as well.

"Too bad," Liam said, simultaneously watching Matt and playing his own game. "You know that's a push, right?"

"What's a 'push'?" Matt asked.

"You know, a standoff . . . a tie."

Son of a bitch, Matt thought. If he couldn't win with that hand, what could he win with?

Matt lost the next hand, but then won the next two. Liam and Tim gave him a pointer here and there, and as the table began to thin out, the dealer began to explain how he could double down, split pairs, and take insurance, or how he could surrender by giving up his first two cards and losing only half his original bet. He got so involved that he forgot entirely about the time and was startled when he suddenly felt two hands massaging his shoulders. He looked around to see Kayla standing behind him with the rest of their group.

"I thought we were going to meet back at the lounge at eleven-fifteen," she said.

"What time is it?" Matt asked, looking at his watch.

"It's almost midnight," Amy said. "We finally decided to come looking for you."

"Sorry," Matt said, "I totally lost track of the time."

"Fine chaperones you guys are," Kayla said, addressing Liam and Tim. "I hope you're all at least winning."

"Tim and I are doing okay," Liam said, "and Matt's doing great."

"Not that great," Matt said, looking at his remaining pile of six $5 chips.

"That's not true," Liam said, "he's having fun, and he's staying in the game. He's a quick learner."

"Okay, one more hand," Tim said, "and we'll go back."

Matt was down $20 from the $50 he started with and couldn't make up his mind how much to bet on the last hand.

"I'll tell ya what, Matt," Liam said. "Why don't you bet the whole thirty? If you win, you'll go home with a profit. If you lose, you'll be down the fifty-dollar limit you set, but you'll have had a great night. Either way, you're a winner."

That wasn't what Matt wanted to do, but with Kayla and everybody watching him, he felt he'd look bad if he didn't take the chance.

"All right," he said, as he pushed the small stack of chips forward.

His first card was a nine and the second a seven, giving him a sixteen, the worst possible hand he could get. It was unlikely to win as it was, and it was very likely to bust if he drew to it. Nonetheless, he decided to go for it, and drew his final card as everyone watched.

"A five!" Kayla squealed, and the others cheered.

Now they all watched the dealer, but happily Matt's hand held up as she busted.

Kayla gave Matt a hug and a kiss, while everyone else began pounding him on the back and congratulating him. "Unbelievable," Liam said, shaking Matt's hand and grinning ear to ear. "Just like I said, you are one lucky son of a bitch!"

Liam took everybody back to the lounge for a nightcap, and the four couples left together about 1:00 a.m.

An hour later, Matt and Kayla were lying together naked as a soft breeze fluttered the curtains next to her bed. It was all like a dream he never wanted to wake from. He knew some of it had to be the buzz from the martinis, but all in all, it had been the best day of his life.

~

Matt left Kayla's just before 4:00 a.m. to drive back to Sheffield. He wanted to get home while it was still dark so he could slip into the house without anyone knowing what time he'd come in.

Still feeling the martinis, he was on top of the world as he drove, reliving the evening over and over in his head. Fortunately, Route 36 was practically deserted at that hour, and he encountered only one car once he crossed into Sheffield. He saw its headlights coming toward him just after he turned onto Cedar Road, and he squeezed so far to the right to make sure he avoided the car that he almost hit a tree.

"Whew," he said aloud, sitting up straight and trying to shake the cobwebs from his brain. Having come this far, the last thing he wanted was to have an accident now.

Moments later, he turned left onto Stoddard Mill Road.

Made it, he thought when he saw the farmhouse, and flicked off his lights to reduce the risk of waking anyone.

Then as he turned into the driveway, he noticed a strange glow just beyond the dairy barn. The glow got brighter as he reached the courtyard, and suddenly he felt a surge of panic.

The old English barn was on fire.

Matt threw open the car door and leapt out.

The house and the courtyard were dark except for a single floodlight. There was no sign of life anywhere—just the glow from the barn, which was growing brighter. Even Max, he assumed, had to be asleep upstairs.

Still a bit woozy, he hesitated, not sure whether to wake his parents or run to the barn first to free the horses.

Finally, his mind clearing, he ran to the back door, pushed the fire alarm in the kitchen, then dashed back outside and ran as fast as he could toward the barn. He had to run the length of a football field, and the flames had already begun to break through the roof before he was halfway there. By the time he reached the barn and managed to throw open the two wagon doors, the entire interior was engulfed in fire and the horses were bellowing with terror. A wall of heat rushed at him, driving him back. He stumbled, recovered, and with his arm against his nose and mouth, tried to push his way through the thick smoke into the barn. He called blindly for his horse, General, and the two Morgans, but their cries were increasingly drowned out by the growing roar of the fire. The flames began to singe his hair and he heard the first ominous groans of the old beams beginning to give way.

Giving up, he staggered out of the barn, stopping just outside the entrance, coughing and gasping for air. Suddenly Sarah's horse, Honey, burst past him, her eyes wild, knocking him to the ground and galloping frantically out into the field.

Matt rolled off to the side and waited expectantly for General and Jacob's horse, Jet. They didn't come. He scrambled to his feet and began shouting again, but the intensity of the fire forced him to back farther and farther away from the barn. It was hopeless. He heard a loud, sickening crack, and all he could do was watch in horror as the roof collapsed in front of him.

Matt wasn't even aware the others had arrived until he felt his mother hugging him. Sarah was crying hysterically, and his father was asking urgently if the horses had gotten out.

"Just Honey," Matt responded, shaking his head. "She's off somewhere. But General and Jet didn't make it. I tried, Dad.... I tried with all my might," he said, and then broke down and wept.

When the firefighters arrived, they hooked hoses up to a nearby pond and poured water on the fire until the pond was sucked down to the mud. But there was nothing to save. Only a few thick supporting beams remained, and the fire was still smoldering late that morning.

The wooden barn had stood for more than two hundred fifty years and one of the firefighters guessed it was completely engulfed in less than twenty-five minutes.

They found the charred corpses of General and Jet in their stalls; Josh thought he could see the terror of being trapped on their blackened faces. He brought in a front loader to take the bodies out to the far end of the south pasture, where the family buried them that afternoon. The vet treated Honey for smoke inhalation and Josh helped Sarah prepare a stall for her in the dairy barn.

It was a miracle, the vet said, that Honey had escaped, and he reminded everyone how fortunate they were that they'd sold Sharon's Appaloosa and Josh's quarter horse just a month earlier.

But that did little to lessen the pain.

The family was devastated. Jet, with her beautiful head and high, arched neck, had won Jacob over the first moment he'd seen her, and General, the first horse they had acquired, had helped Matt through his most difficult times. It was, both boys said, as though they had lost their best friends.

With the casino debate becoming nastier, Josh at first couldn't help but wonder if one of his growing number of enemies was responsible for the fire. The scary part was that just a month ago he'd had an anonymous call warning that he was "playing with fire" in trying to block the casino and telling him "to go back to Chicago, where belonged." But he'd dismissed the warning as simply a figure of speech, and the more he thought about it now, the harder it was for him to believe there was any connection. It simply didn't make sense. If a casino supporter was found to have burned down the barn, the majority of people in town would turn even more vehemently against the casino than they were now. And while the investigators were unable to establish the exact cause of the fire, there was no evidence of arson. The most likely cause, they reported, was a faulty electric wire. "I'm afraid," the fire marshal told Josh, "that after all those years the wood was so dry it was just an accident waiting to happen."

Josh had never mentioned the threatening phone call to anyone, and based on the fire marshal's conclusion, he saw no point in bringing it up now. It would be just one more thing for his family to worry about. Furthermore, he decided, there was no need to look for any explanation for the fire other than his continuing skein of bad luck.

27

On a Roll

June 20–30, 1997

The phone was ringing in the tribal office when Bobby returned from lunch on Friday, June 20. It was Paul Ivy's secretary. Mr. Ivy was urgently trying to reach him from the Bahamas.

"Hello, Chief?" Ivy's voice finally came on the line. "Get out the champagne, my friend! I just got off the phone with Washington and they say the BIA's putting out a press release at three p.m. announcing a preliminary decision to grant you federal recognition."

Bobby pumped his fist in the air. "Yeesss!" he shouted, his voice bouncing off the metal walls of the construction trailer. "Fan-tastic! I can hardly believe it. You really came through for us, Paul."

"We're on a roll, buddy," Ivy said, enjoying the moment. "I'm told we should get a final decision within ten months. So get ready, because you're going to have half the reporters in the state all over you this afternoon.

The newspaper headlines blared the story across Connecticut the next morning.

Northerns Win Preliminary Recognition
Take Major Step Toward Third State Casino

Feds Give Preliminary Nod to Northern Pequots
Tiny Tribe Could Rake in Billions

In announcing its preliminary decision—or as the bureaucrats put it, their "proposed finding"—the BIA stated that the Northern Pequots had met all seven criteria for recognition. The finding would be followed by a six-month public comment period, after which the tribe would have sixty days to respond before the BIA rendered its final decision. If that decision were favorable, the press reported, the Northerns would become Connecticut's third federally recognized tribe, behind the Mashantucket Pequots and the Mohegans, and would qualify to negotiate a gaming compact with the state.

Reporters and television crews flocked to the Northerns' reservation to interview the upstart Indian chief who had led the tiny tribe's resurrection and to get pictures of the rustic setting that now seemed destined to be turned into Connecticut's third great resort casino.

Bobby had never been in higher spirits as he welcomed the media and shook hands with more than sixty tribe members and supporters who had heard the news and made a beeline for the reservation to celebrate. Mavis and her daughter passed out plastic tumblers of Dom Pérignon and Bobby mounted the office trailer steps for a brief speech.

"When I think of all our ancestors who persevered generation after generation to make this day possible," he told the crowd, "it almost makes me weep. I can only hope their spirits are celebratin' with us today."

Afterward, Bobby and Mavis took an enterprising TV reporter and her cameraman down to the cemetery, where Bobby pointed out Rachel Amos's tombstone and laid a spray of flowers on her grave. When he explained that virtually all of the tribe's roots went back to Rachel, he became so choked up that Mavis thought for a moment he actually *was* going to cry.

The media found a far different atmosphere when they arrived at the town hall. First Selectman Clark was waiting for them, but there were no refreshments and no celebration. Clark distributed a press release that the town had already faxed to the major news outlets and agreed to take questions. The gist of his message was that the town was dismayed by the BIA's decision. The BIA, he charged, had shown rank favoritism toward the Northerns by repeatedly ignoring or stretching its own rules in order to see social and political continuity where none existed. He promised the town would prepare a detailed rebuttal of the BIA's findings in an effort to persuade the agency to reverse its preliminary decision, and he vowed that if the BIA went ahead and granted the tribe final recognition, the town would appeal the agency's decision all the way up the line, beginning with the Department of the Interior and extending if necessary to the U.S. Supreme Court.

Josh put out a similar press release on behalf of Citizens Against the Casino, and he fielded questions from several reporters who called him at home that night. The toughest question came from his friend, Julie Boyer, from the weekly *Sheffield Advertiser*.

"Do you think it's over?" she asked off the record.

Josh hesitated, not wanting to mislead his friend, but emotionally unable to admit how bad it looked.

"Look, Julie," he said. "This is a big blow. There's no denying it. These bastards are pulling strings in Washington like we never imagined. But the game's not over. If the town will just stick together, we can still win."

"That's actually pretty good," she said. "Can I use it?"

"Which part?"

"'The game's not over, we can still win if we stick together' part."

"Sure, why not?"

It was the lead headline in the following week's *Advertiser*.

✌

Despite the First Selectman's and Josh's brave words, the BIA's preliminary decision had a decidedly dampening effect on the town's will to resist. Even the town's Washington attorney was pessimistic. In a conference call with Clark and Josh, Pugliese reminded them he had warned from the beginning that the BIA had broad discretion in the way it interpreted and applied its guidelines. Clearly, he said, the BIA had seriously bent those guidelines, but there was little anyone could do about it.

"Furthermore," he said, "the hard fact is that the BIA has never reversed a favorable preliminary ruling. So unless we can come up with something new and compelling to rebut their findings, I have to tell you honestly I see very little chance of reversing this one."

"That means," Pugliese cautioned, "that you've got to begin considering how far up the appeals ladder you really want to go. The higher you go, the more it's going to cost, and the way it looks now, I'd say there's little chance of success."

The prospect of a costly and unpromising appeals process presented a major challenge to the town's leaders. More than a few townspeople were already grousing that Sheffield had now spent more than $500,000 for lawyers and researchers, and more and more residents were beginning to ask if it was worth it.

Even Josh's helper, Ben Chapman, expressed doubts.

"You know, Josh," Ben said as they worked around the farm, "I'm not so sure we should keep tryin' t' block the casino if the tribe wins this next round. It might be a lot smarter t' let 'em have the damn thing in return for whatever we can get."

⟿

The only remaining hope of blocking the Northerns' final recognition, Josh now believed, was Gladys Greene. She'd been working on the Northern Pequot project for more than two years, far longer than any of her other current assignments, but she still had not been able to prove her suspicions about Rachel Amos. Yet if she were able to do so, it could single-handedly destroy the tribe's case for federal recognition.

A slight, scholarly-looking woman in her early fifties, Mrs. Greene prided herself on her knowledge of eastern Indian tribes and the federal recognition process. Not only had she been retained by three different eastern tribes over the years, but she had worked for the BIA's Bureau of Acknowledgement and Research for two years in the early 1990s, when her husband had left his job at the Bayer pharmaceutical company near New Haven to join a biotech startup in Maryland. The startup had folded and Gladys and her husband had returned to Connecticut, but she had loved her job at the BIA and still had friends there.

She'd been reluctant to accept the Sheffield assignment because it appeared to her that the Northerns' bid for recognition was another example of a moribund tribe being revived for the sole purpose of opening a casino, and she didn't want to get caught up in what she was sure was going to be a nasty political fight. But she had allowed herself to be talked into the job, and she had been pulled deeper and deeper into the project until uncovering Rachel Amos's genealogy had become almost an obsession.

She continued to suspect that Rachel might not have been a Pequot Indian because of the utter lack of information about her before she had shown up on the reservation overseer's list in 1800. But despite exhaustive research, Gladys had so far been unable to determine who Rachel actually was. Still, every professional instinct told her she was right, and Josh Williams in particular had continued to urge her to keep looking.

Gladys had therefore continued to work on the case along with other assignments, but her work has suffered a serious setback in May when someone broke into her car at the supermarket and stole her laptop computer, which contained some of her most important research on the Northern Pequots. Then when she heard about the BIA's preliminary recognition of the Northerns on June 20, she considered giving up on the project altogether and probably would have if Josh hadn't called and urged her to keep at it. She had reluctantly agreed and spent all of Friday, June 27, trying to come up with new leads on Rachel.

That evening she and her husband went out for an early dinner, and they returned home just as a thunderstorm was about to hit. Gladys went into the house while her husband retrieved a wheelbarrow he had left out and put it in the garage. The first intimation that something was wrong was the draft she felt as she headed toward the back of the house; it didn't make sense because they'd left the air conditioning on and all the windows closed. When she turned on the lights in the bedroom, she saw that the sliding door to the patio was wide open and the drapes were billowing into the room. Her first thought was that she must have opened the door for something and forgotten to close it, but then she looked around and her heart almost leaped out of her chest. Both chests of drawers had been ransacked, and the contents of her jewelry boxes lay scattered across the bed and floor. How stupid to go after her jewelry, she thought, since none of it was of any real value. Then she remembered her new laptop and almost tripped over herself rushing to the study down the hall. The room was in shambles. Desk and file drawers hung open, papers and documents were strewn everywhere, and her new laptop and a portable television were gone.

Gladys's husband came running when he heard her scream and had to hold her in his arms for several moments before she stopped trembling. "The car was one thing," she said between sobs, "but this … this is our home."

The New Haven police suspected crackheads, but Gladys couldn't believe drug addicts would ransack her files. Instead, she was convinced both break-ins were meant to scare her off the Northern Pequot project, and she became so nervous and paranoid that three days later she called Josh and resigned. Josh did his best to get her to reconsider, including offering to go to the state police with her to discuss her suspicions, but it was clear she was too emotionally spent to do either. Josh left it that she was welcome to return to the project any time she chose, but he assumed that he had lost her permanently, and with her the last outside chance of coming up with any new information that could stop the Northerns from gaining final recognition.

28

The Scam

June 1997–January 10, 1998

Matt spent the last few weeks of spring working with Ben Chapman around the farm, then took a road-paving job with the town, which was the best-paying work he could find. Pouring and spreading asphalt made for long, hot days, but he got a huge shot of adrenaline in mid-June, when Kayla finished the last of her college courses and received a promotion at the hotel that freed up her evenings. As a result, he and Kayla began seeing each other more frequently, going out to a movie, driving down the shore for steamers, or occasionally returning to Mohegan Sun for an evening with some of their Foxwoods friends. To Matt, Kayla was more irresistible than ever, and he didn't really care what they did as long as he was with her and they wound up alone together at the end of the night.

Then everything changed.

The first sign of trouble arrived on a Thursday night in mid-August when Liam called Matt at home to offer a couple of tickets to a Norwich Navigators baseball game.

"How's everything with you and Kayla?" Liam asked casually in the course of the call.

It was an innocent enough question, but there was something about the way Liam asked it—really, the fact he asked it at all—that gave Matt pause.

"Fine," Matt began, but sensed something was wrong. "Why?" he asked.

"Just wondering," Liam said, immediately realizing he had made a mistake. "I just haven't seen you guys for a couple of weeks, that's all."

"Yeah, Kayla had some kinda bug last weekend," Matt said, but his mind was already trying to decipher what was going on.

Matt barely slept that night and agonized all day Friday about how he should act when he saw Kayla that evening. Tonight he was simply planning to take her out for a pizza and then go back to her place for a little TV and the usual lovemaking, so they were going to have plenty of time alone together. Should he probe to see if there was a problem, or just wait and see? Better wait, he told himself as he pulled into her driveway and tried to fight off his anxiety. The last thing he wanted to do was create a problem where there wasn't one.

Matt thought Kayla acted a little aloof on the ride to the restaurant, but she seemed fine during dinner, and after a couple of beers he started to relax. He began to think he must have read Liam wrong. He had to be careful—watch the paranoia and jealousy—or he was going to shoot himself in the foot all over again.

When they got back to Kayla's house, she suggested they take a walk. Matt's stomach sank. They never went for walks. "Okay, whatever you like," he replied, feeling the words stick in his throat.

Kayla took his hand as they started out along the tree-lined sidewalk, lights from the houses and street lamps casting pale shadows across the quiet street. She was wearing jeans and had pulled on an old sweatshirt against the evening chill, but whether it was the light or his fear of losing her, she struck him as more beautiful than ever.

They walked along without a word at first, and then Kayla broke the silence.

"There's something I have to talk to you about, Matt," she began, a trace of tension in her voice.

Even though he had been expecting it, the actual words came as a shock. He glanced over at her, but she was looking straight ahead as though concentrating on what she was going to say next.

"We've had some wonderful times together," she said. "You, me, Tim, Amy, Liam, and just the two of us together. I couldn't ask for more...."

Matt sensed her look up at him, but he couldn't make himself look back and kept on walking. He felt he should probably should let go of her hand, but he couldn't do that either.

"But my life's changing, Matt, and so is yours. I'm done with school now, and you'll be graduating next year. It's important we both step back and decide what we want to do with our lives."

Matt stopped and faced her, taking her other hand as well.

"Kayla," he said emotionally, "I know what I want to do with my life. I want to marry you."

Kayla closed her eyes and shook her head. "Matt, we're too young, and no matter how much I care for you, I'm not ready. I told you when we got back together two years ago that I wasn't ready for a serious relationship, and I'm still not ready. This is the time for both of us to step away...before things go any further. You've got to see other girls, and I've got to be able to go wherever I want, take whatever job I want, and see other people, or we're both going to all of a sudden wake up and wonder where our lives went."

"So is that what you want...to see other guys?" Matt asked, releasing her hands and feeling the old jealousy boil up inside him.

"Matt, please," she said, "don't make me say it. I simply want to be free to explore what I want out of life."

Matt took a deep breath, but he couldn't control himself.

"So who is it this time?" he flared, thinking back to Greg Elliot. "A stockbroker, a lawyer...or some high roller you met at the hotel? What's this guy drive, Kayla—a Ferrari?"

"Please, Matt," she pleaded, reaching for his hand. "Don't make it worse."

"Don't make it worse?" Matt retorted, refusing to let her touch him. "The girl I love just dumped me, and you're telling me not to make it worse?"

Kayla closed her eyes and shook her head, as though willing him to stop.

"It can't get any goddamn worse, Kayla. Not for me. I...," he began, but then caught himself. He was doing exactly what he had promised himself he wouldn't do, and there was no point to it. He didn't want her to remember him this way.

"Okay," he sighed, all the fight suddenly draining out of him. "I think I get the picture."

They walked back to her house in silence, Matt too choked up to say anything more. When they got to his car, he turned and kissed her softly on the cheek. "Good-bye, Kayla," he half-whispered, then got in the car and drove away.

Matt was in turmoil as he drove home, his emotions a mix of anger, grief, and utter despair. At one point, he considered swerving into an oncoming semi on Route 36, but his survivor instinct took over at the last second and he hewed to his lane as the big rig flashed by. He caught the trailer's taillights in his rearview mirror and trembled at the thought of how close he'd come to ending his life.

〜

Matt drifted aimlessly for the next two weeks and then returned to UConn, where he started his senior year with zero interest or motivation. The only thing he looked forward to during the fall was seeing some of his Foxwoods friends on weekends, but it was entirely different without Kayla.

Tim Paxton told Matt that Kayla was still living at the house with Amy, but that he rarely saw her, and in late October he mentioned she had a new boyfriend. "The guy's an investment banker from Wall Street and drives a Porsche," Tim said, "but that's honestly all I know about him."

Matt feigned indifference, but the picture of Kayla being squired around New York or riding through the eastern Connecticut countryside in the guy's sports car ate at him like sulfuric acid. His own car was now eleven years old, had 183,000 miles on it, and was ready for the scrap heap. Liam tried to help him get his mind off Kayla by fixing him up with dates a couple of times, but Matt showed little interest.

The one thing Matt did enjoy was playing blackjack at Mohegan Sun. He was actually getting pretty good at the game, and it was something he could now lose himself in for three or four hours at a time and pretty much break even. His biggest worry was that his parents might find out about his gambling, but he went to great lengths to keep it from them, secretly driving back and forth between UConn and Mohegan Sun or pretending to visit friends when he was actually at the casino.

Other than worrying about his family, however, Matt hardly gave going to the casino a second thought anymore. It seemed that half of eastern Connecticut now either worked at or frequented Foxwoods or Mohegan Sun, and that just about everyone else took the existence of the casinos for granted.

⌒

Matt made his first mistake over the Thanksgiving weekend, going over his self-imposed $40 loss limit and losing $100 for the first time in his life.

The need to win back his money preoccupied him the entire next day, and he went back to the casino the next night determined to do that and more. But he must have been having a streak of bad luck, because he lost another $50 before he finally got up and left the table. Even that wouldn't have been a disaster if he hadn't tried to force a change in his luck by playing craps on the way out.

He'd played the game only once after the lesson Liam and Tim had given him back in May, but he figured his luck was bound to turn. It didn't. He lost another $50 before he ran out of cash and had to quit.

Matt couldn't believe it. He'd lost $200 in two nights. He was beginning to realize that gambling under the pressure to win back losses was entirely different from playing the way he had been, cruising along under his loss limit. Instead of backing off, however, he began to press even harder, driving down to Mohegan Sun from school two and three evenings a week, drawing down the last $100 on his credit card, upping his bets, and finally withdrawing all of the $900 he'd told his parents he'd saved to help make his final tuition payment.

The harder he pressed, the more he lost, and within three short weeks he was down more than $1,200.

Now he was totally broke. He had exhausted everything he'd saved, was tapped out on his credit card, and barely had enough money for gas. He was so distraught he found it almost impossible to focus on his semester-end exams, and instead of looking forward to UConn's month-long midyear break, he worried about how he was going to be able to buy simple Christmas gifts, let alone find the $900 to help pay his tuition.

Matt solved his immediate cash problem by begging Mr. Boudreau at the drugstore to put him on full-time during the break and advance him his first week's check, but the problem of the money that was to go toward his tuition consumed him over Christmas. He wrestled with it over and over as he sat in church with his family on Christmas Eve, as they gathered around the tree the next morning, and as they sat down to Christmas dinner that afternoon.

He thought of selling his computer, but he needed it. He considered trying to pawn his watch and electric shaver, but they were worth peanuts. And he even thought of sitting down with his parents and admitting what had happened, but he couldn't face them.

His only realistic option, he decided, was to try to borrow the money, and he knew of only two people in the world who might lend it to him. One was sitting across the table from him—his sister Sarah, now a freshman at UConn. The other was Liam Blackwell.

Matt debated for several days about which to approach. Sarah, he was reasonably confident, would lend him the money, but he worried about her ability to keep it from their parents. Liam, on the other hand, would be a tougher sell, but at least the secret would be safe.

In the end, he chose secrecy.

On New Year's Eve afternoon, Matt took a chance and dropped in on Liam, figuring he was probably scheduled to work that night and would be home before leaving for the casino. Liam lived with two other Foxwoods dealers in a rented cape just off Washington Street in Norwich; the three were watching a bowl game when Matt came in.

"You guys all working tonight?" Matt asked as Liam led him into the living room and the others waved hello.

"Yeah, biggest night of the year," Liam answered. "Just takin' it easy till we have to go. Have a seat. I'll get you a beer."

Instead of sitting down, Matt walked into the kitchen with Liam and asked if he could talk with him in private for a few minutes. Liam looked quizzical but tossed Matt a cold beer and suggested they go up to his bedroom.

Liam closed the door and gestured for Matt to take the only chair while he sat on the half-made bed. "What's up?" he asked.

Matt glanced around uncomfortably, taking in the Knicks, Giants, and Yankees posters plastered on the walls. He'd mapped out exactly what he wanted to say but had grown increasingly nervous about how Liam would react to being asked for a loan. They were friends, but he had to admit he knew surprisingly little about Liam. Despite his hail-fellow manner, Liam was three years older and had a private side that Matt had never really cracked. In fact, Matt increasingly suspected one of the reasons they got along so well was that Liam had something of the loner in him that Matt recognized in himself. As a result, their conversations rarely went beyond the local social scene and sports.

Matt cleared his throat and began explaining his predicament, but by the time it came to asking for the loan, he felt so awkward he simply cut to the chase. "So anyway, Liam," he said, "I'm sorry to come in here on New Year's Eve like this, but I was really hoping you might be able to lend me the money."

Liam studied Matt in silence, as though appraising him and his request.

"So let me get this straight," Liam finally said with an edge that Matt hadn't seen before. "You want me to lend you nine hundred dollars to make up for your gambling losses?"

"Just for a month," Matt said defensively.

"Where you gonna get nine hundred dollars in a month?" Liam asked.

"I'm working full-time at the drugstore for the rest of the break," Matt replied.

"I thought you told me you were only making minimum wage?"

"I am, but I'm gonna keep working there weekends and take a job in the dining hall when I get back to school."

Liam took a deep breath and exhaled slowly.

"I'm sorry, Matt," he said. "I can't do it. I'm a little tight myself right now, and besides, I gotta be honest. I'm really pissed off at you."

"Why, for losing?"

"No, not for losing," Liam replied. "For ignoring every fucking thing I told you.

"The first thing was never to go over your loss limit. Second was never to chase your losses. And the third thing I told you was never to borrow to gamble. Don't you listen to anything, for Chrissakes?" Liam shook his head in frustration.

"Look, Liam, I know I screwed up," Matt pleaded, "but I've got to come up with the money, and there's nobody else I can turn to."

"You know," Liam said coldly, "even if I had the money, I'm not sure I'd give it to you. Not in the condition you're in, because chances are you'd go right back out and lose it all over again."

"No way!" Matt protested. "I swear. . . ."

"And if you think things are bad now, where would you be then?" Liam interrupted.

"Liam, please," Matt tried one more time, "I'm in deep shit. You gotta help me."

Liam didn't answer right away. Instead he got up and walked over to the window and stared out absently, then returned to the bed. Matt watched him intently.

"I tell ya what," Liam finally said, sitting down again, "I'm not going to lend you the money, so forget it. But there may be another way I can help. You around tomorrow, New Year's Day?"

"Yeah, the drugstore's closed," Matt said, seeing the first flicker of hope.

"All right, give me a call around noon. I should be up by then," Liam said. "I may have an idea, and if I do, you can come over tomorrow afternoon and we'll talk about it.

"I'm sorry about your problem, Matt," Liam said, getting up. "I really am. But that's the best I can do."

Liam genuinely liked Matt and felt for him, but he had his own problems, and they were a lot bigger than Matt's.

Liam was not only a sports nut, but he was also an inveterate sports bettor. By the time he'd dropped out of college, he was betting on everything from basketball to luge runs. He had a head for statistics and read the odds on everything, but he had a dangerous weakness for long shots and hunches that rarely paid off.

His sports gambling had gotten him into trouble several times, but he had always managed to extricate himself until two years ago, when he'd built up a $14,000 debt to a New York bookmaker. The debt had felt like a boulder crushing his chest. There was no way he could raise that much money, and he'd decided to skip town to avoid paying it. He had tried to erase every trace of himself, closing his bank and credit card accounts, stopping his subscriptions, and leaving no forwarding address for anyone, including his mother. Then he'd come up to Connecticut to train to be a dealer at Foxwoods.

It was a great choice. He missed New York, but he liked eastern Connecticut and he loved his job. He still gambled, but he was able to save a little money, buy a nice car, and gain a little perspective on the importance of controlling his losses by watching others gamble.

Then everything had changed a little over two months ago when he got a call out of the blue from the New York bookie to whom he owed the $14,000. The bookie said he'd happened to be up at Foxwoods and had been surprised to see a blackjack dealer who looked a lot like Liam. He said he'd checked around and, son of a bitch, it was Liam. So he said he was calling just to say hello and to suggest they get together to talk about the money Liam owed. Liam thought momentarily of bolting again, but there was no way he could disappear at a moment's notice, and he reluctantly agreed to meet the bookie at a Denny's the next afternoon.

The restaurant was almost deserted when Liam walked in and spotted the bookie sitting at a table with a short, balding, muscular man who had to weigh at least two hundred pounds. Neither man got up when Liam approached, but the bookie broke into a broad grin and motioned for him to pull up a chair and sit down.

"Coffee?" the bookie asked. Liam saw their coffee mugs and that the bulky guy was eating a hamburger, but he declined to order anything.

"I gotta say you're lookin' good for a guy who's been on the lam for two years," the bookie allowed, looking Liam over approvingly. "The fresh air up here must be agreein' with you."

Liam raised his eyebrows and gave a little "What can I say?" nod.

"I don't have a lotta time, but I wanted to introduce you to my associate here," the bookie said, gesturing to the man next to him. "Nick's from over in Providence, and among other things does a little collection work. Since you seem to be havin' trouble comin' up with the money you owe me, I thought he might be able to give you a little help."

Liam met Nick's flat, dark eyes for a split second and quickly looked away.

"Perhaps, Nicky," the bookie said, "you could explain to Mr. Blackwell how you work."

"No problem," Nick replied with a thin smile. He had a husky, slightly nasal quality to his voice, as if he had a cold. "We work on a very basic principle," he said, catching and holding Liam's eyes. "Those that pay, walk away. And those that don't pay, don't."

But, he added, he was sure that wasn't going to be a problem for Liam, because he had no doubt Liam intended to pay. He also said he assumed Liam would probably like to see a current statement since so much time had passed. He wrote something on a napkin and slid it across the table.

Liam blanched. The napkin read "$28,000," double the original debt.

"That's with two years' interest," Nick said. "It's our lowest rate."

"How much time do I have to come up with the money?" Liam asked.

"Thirty days," Nick replied matter-of-factly.

"Do I have an alternative?"

"That depends on you," Nick said.

At that point the bookie got up and excused himself, saying he had to get back to New York. "Nice seein' ya again," he said casually, patting Liam on the shoulder and heading for the door.

Liam watched him go and then turned back to Nick. "So, what's the alternative?"

Nick let the question hang for a moment while he took the last bite of his hamburger and wiped ketchup from the corner of his mouth. He then pushed his plate aside and leaned in close enough for Liam to smell the meat and onions on his breath.

It just so happened, Nick said, that he had some friends who liked to play blackjack, and if Liam were to look the other way when they capped a bet from time to time, they'd be willing to give Liam 25 percent of their winnings. Nick estimated it could mean close to $4,000 a week to Liam, and said he'd be willing to see that Liam got a third of it in cash while the rest was deducted from his $28,000 debt. If Liam were to cooperate, Nick said, he was sure the bookie would be willing to wait a couple extra months to be paid out in full.

Liam closed his eyes and massaged his forehead, thinking about the money and the consequences if he were caught. Nick was asking him to take part in an illegal scheme where crooked dealers let certain players secretly add to their winning bets after the bets were placed. There was no question a well-organized capping scheme involving several dealers and players could generate a lot of money for everybody involved, but if a dealer were caught he'd be arrested and could well go to jail. Finally, Liam looked back at Nick and shook his head. "Sorry," he said, "I can't do it. I'd rather see if I can get the money together on my own."

Nick shrugged. "Your call," he said, "but you and I both know you're never gonna find twenty-eight grand in the next thirty days. And don't think you can skip again, because this time we're gonna be watchin'."

When Liam didn't respond, Nick wrote down a phone number on another napkin and handed it to him. "If you change your mind," he said, "gimme a call." He then got up and left, sticking Liam with the bill for two coffees and a hamburger.

⤸

Liam had no illusions about where he stood. He only had two options: play ball or skip town. And they both sucked. If the proposed scam went on long enough, it was almost certain to be uncovered, while skipping had suddenly become a much bigger challenge than the first time around. Not only would Nick be watching him, but this time Liam would have to figure out how to totally disappear. He decided to sleep on the decision for the next several days, but before he could make up his mind, Nick forced the issue by turning up at Liam's blackjack table with two other players. The three of them played a couple of routine hands, and then Nick deliberately caught Liam's eye and capped a bet.

Liam would never forget the moment and the feeling of intimidation when Nick added the chips to his bet. Nick stared at Liam with a small, cold smile, daring him to do something about it.

Liam's immediate instinct was to turn back the bet and, if Nick persisted, to call security. It was a moment of truth, and it just hung there in time as though someone had hit the pause button on a video player. Liam stared back . . . frozen, uncertain. Nick waited. Finally, the video started up again, and Liam paid off the bet.

Nick's two friends continued to show up and play at Liam's table for the next two nights, although Nick stayed away and contented himself with walking by the table occasionally to check on things. Liam assumed Nick was the organizer and enforcer of the scam and that he was probably running a couple other dealers and players as well.

Nick slipped Liam a note the third night saying he wanted to meet him after work in the parking lot of a twenty-four-hour diner south of Foxwoods. When Liam arrived, he saw Nick standing by a gray Lincoln Continental, and when he pulled up next to it, Nick opened Liam's passenger-side door and got in.

"Nice car," Nick commented, looking around the interior of Liam's Jaguar.

"Would you believe it's ten years old?" Liam asked, not wanting Nick to think he'd blown a bundle on the car instead of paying off the bookie.

"You're doin' good," Liam heard Nick say, not certain whether he was referring to the car or his handling of the capped bets. "This is for you," Nick said, handing him an envelope. "Open it."

There was $800 cash inside.

"That's a third of what you've earned so far," Nick said. "The other two-thirds goes against your tab. So you're down to owing us twenty-six thousand four hundred. The way you're goin', you'll be gettin' your full cut in cash in no time."

Liam put the envelope in his jacket pocket.

"I need your work schedule," Nick said, taking out a small notebook.

〜

By the time Matt showed up at his house on December 31, Liam had been participating in the capping scheme for eleven weeks.

The first week, Liam had feared almost every moment that the scam was going to be discovered. With several dealers and players presumably involved, Foxwoods' security people patrolling the floor, and the casino's "eye in the sky" camera surveillance system in constant operation, he couldn't believe that something wouldn't go wrong somewhere.

But the weeks ticked by and nothing happened.

The one scare came when Nick introduced a third player to Liam's table during the second week, and a floor supervisor who happened to be walking by the table noticed the new player capping a bet. Fortunately, the supervisor simply turned back the player's bet and told him sternly not to do it again, after which the player disappeared for a couple of nights.

Liam received his cuts like clockwork, meeting Nick every night after work in the parking lot of the diner. By Christmas he had earned more than $39,000, with $26,200 going toward his $28,000 debt and $13,100 paid to him in cash. Assuming all went well, he figured he should easily be paid up within a week.

Liam had to hand it to Nick. He'd put together a sweet operation. But nobody's luck lasted forever. At first, Liam had intended to use all his earnings from the scam to pay off his debt as quickly as possible and leave town before things unraveled. That way he'd be square with the mob, and he could hopefully avoid the law ever catching up with him. However, with things going so well, he'd gotten greedy and decided he could disappear a lot more easily if he had some serious money. Now that he'd put together a decent bankroll and was about to extinguish his debt, he was ready to vanish.

⤴

Without a word to anyone, Liam gave notice to Foxwoods and set January 1, 1998, as his last night at the casino. He told Nick and a few friends he was planning to fly to Florida for vacation beginning January 2 and would be back in a week, but in fact had a very different itinerary. He intended to collect his final money from Nick after working New Year's night and then drive to Chicago, where he'd sell the Jaguar and hop a train for Los Angeles. From there he was thinking he might go to San Diego or even to Mexico for a while, but wherever he went, he was determined to make it as hard as possible for anyone to find him.

Then, just as Liam was getting ready to make his exit, Matt showed up with his problem.

There was no way he could lend Matt the money. He was going to need every cent he had to successfully disappear, not to mention he wasn't going to be around to get the money back. But he genuinely wanted to help his friend if there were a way to do it.

He had toyed briefly with the idea of having Matt play at his table New

Year's night and either letting him cap his bets or possibly even rigging the cards in Matt's favor, but the last thing he needed was to get caught through some freakish turn of events and have all his carefully laid plans fall apart at the last minute.

An alternative popped into Liam's head as he listened to Matt on December 31, and by the time Matt called on New Year's Day, Liam was convinced his idea was almost foolproof.

⌒

Matt rang Liam's doorbell just after 1:00 p.m. and stood blowing into his hands to keep warm as he waited. He was still smarting from the way Liam had turned him down and could only hope they were still friends and that Liam really did have something for him.

When Liam opened the door, Matt was surprised to see he was in his bathrobe and bare feet, but he was immediately heartened by the way Liam greeted him.

"Hey, Mattie—Happy New Year!" Liam said cheerfully and ushered Matt in. "Looks like a cold morning out there . . . or is it afternoon?"

Matt managed a smile. "Happy New Year to you, too," he said. "Just get up?"

"Yeah, I musta dozed off after you called," Liam answered, leading the way into the kitchen. "Long night, and then I made it longer by going over to the Sun for a few pops. Why don't we sit here," he said, gesturing toward the kitchen table. "The guys are out so I'm the only one home."

Matt sat down while Liam went to the refrigerator and pulled out a carton of orange juice. "Juice, beer?" he asked Matt.

"Maybe some juice," Matt replied.

Liam poured two glasses and came over and sat down opposite Matt. "You do anything last night?" he asked.

Matt forced a laugh. "Like I could afford it," he said.

"Yeah, probably a dumb question," Liam admitted. "I hope you at least watched the ball drop."

"No, actually I didn't even do that," Matt answered honestly.

Liam drained his glass and got up to get a refill.

"Look, Matt," he said as he returned to his seat, "I know you're bummed about yesterday, but I think I got a way to get you your nine hundred dollars and then some."

Matt felt a jolt of electricity go through him.

"But it's gonna take some balls on your part," Liam continued, "and I have to be sure I can trust you never to tell Tim or anybody else that I suggested it to you. Otherwise, you could get me into serious trouble."

"Liam, you're the only friend in the world I can go to right now," Matt said, "and I guarantee you can trust me."

"Okay," Liam said, "let me start real slow. If I could arrange it, what would you think about an opportunity to earn a couple of thousand dollars real quick?"

"You kidding!? What would I have to do?"

"That's the thing." Liam said. "All you'd have to do is to continue to play blackjack the way you do now . . . but with a twist."

"What's the twist?" Matt asked, becoming cautious.

"The twist," Liam replied, "is that after the cards are dealt and you've got a winning hand, you slip more chips onto your bet without anyone seeing in order to increase your win. It's called 'capping your bet.'"

Liam watched Matt carefully for his reaction, and when Matt didn't say anything, he went on.

"It's against the law, but there's a special situation at Foxwoods right now that makes it extremely unlikely you'd be caught, and even if you were, all they'd probably do would be to give you your chips back and tell you not to do it again. And if that happens, you simply walk away and forget the whole thing. I figure you can make two thou in one week and then you stop."

"What's the 'special situation'?" Matt asked.

Liam pursed his lips and looked Matt in the eye. "Matt, you've gotta tell me honestly if you're interested before I get into it any further. You don't have to make up your mind until you hear me out, but you have to at least tell me you're interested, or there's no point continuing."

"I don't know," Matt said after a long pause. "You really think it's safe?"

"Believe me," Liam replied, "if I can arrange this, it's a hundred-to-one you'll come out with your money and nobody'll be the wiser. I wouldn't suggest it otherwise. This is the best bet you'll ever see at a casino in your life."

"Okay," Matt said, "I'm interested, but I gotta hear more."

"That's fine. The minute you want to stop, tell me, and we'll just agree we never had this talk.

"Let me start by giving you a little background," Liam said.

"There are casino scams going on around the country all the time," he began.

"Even at Foxwoods?" Matt asked.

"It happens everywhere," Liam said. "And there are at least a dozen basic kinds of scams.

"One of the simplest is a guy comes in and drops some coins on the floor next to a slot machine, and when the player bends down to pick 'em up, the guy grabs the player's coin bucket. They call the guys bucket thieves, and security people usually catch 'em if the player notices in time.

"Or a guy will use counterfeit coins in the slots or some kind of electronic device to trick the machines into paying off. Another guy will try to steal chips by reaching into the cashier's cage when the cashier's not looking. Somebody else will try to grab a player's chips off a craps table just after he shoots and everybody's watching the dice at the other end. Or an employee in the counting room will try to smuggle money out in his underwear.

"Then there are the scams players try at the various table games, like substituting loaded dice, switching cards, capping bets, or marking cards by cutting the edge with their fingernail, smudging the back with grease, bending the card slightly, or doing anything else that lets them identify the card the next time it's dealt."

"How do you switch cards?" Matt asked.

"That depends, but the best switches usually involve a team of two or three players. One of the players diverts the dealer's attention, and the players then switch cards with each other in order to improve one of the hands.

"For example, the ultimate con in Caribbean stud poker would be for three players to switch cards with each other so the player in the middle winds up with a royal flush.

"But the switches have to be very quick, almost like card tricks. Every move has to be done in less than two seconds. They say the best con is the one nobody can see."

"And what about capping?" Matt asked.

"Capping's easier to hide, because there's no passing cards back and forth and the player can cover his move with his hands, so it's hard even for the surveillance cameras in the ceiling to pick it up unless the security people are focusing on a particular table. But even then, if it's done right, capping can be very hard to detect."

"So to really make this work, you're sayin' you gotta get past both the dealer and the security cameras, right?" Matt asked.

"That's right," Liam said. "You've got to get past both, as well as any floor people who happen to be watching.

"But the biggest problem is the dealers. They can be momentarily distracted, but unlike the people monitoring the surveillance cameras, the dealers are focused on their own tables all the time."

Liam paused. "You still with me?" he asked.

"Yeah, I'm still with you."

"Okay. There are two or three dealers at Foxwoods right now who are in on a scheme where they allow certain players to cap their bets in return for a percentage of the profits. It's been going on now for several months or, for all I know, longer.

"The whole thing's run by a guy out of Providence who recruits the dealers and players and makes sure everybody gets their cut. He's a little rough, but runs a real smooth operation."

"You saying he's Mafia?" Matt asked.

Liam shrugged. "Mafia, mob, syndicate . . . it's all the same."

Matt rubbed his chin. "Jesus, Liam," he said uneasily, "I don't know."

"Come on, Matt," Liam said impatiently. "Who else do you think is gonna organize something like this, the friggin' Boy Scouts?"

"The beauty of this," Liam continued, "is that you'd be in and out in a week. Basically you'd be taking advantage of both the casino and the mob by hitching a ride on something that's already going, then getting out before anything can happen."

"How do you know this Providence guy would even let me in on his deal?"

"I don't, for sure," Liam conceded, "but my sense is he's always on the look-out for new players to keep the thing fresh, and the fact is you'd be perfect."

"Isn't he going to be pissed at you if you introduce me and then I quit a week later?"

"I'm not worried about it," Liam said, "so don't you be. He won't be happy, but what can he do? He's sure as hell not going to do anything that could rock the boat."

"The key," Liam emphasized again, "is for you to get in and out in a week. That way you'll be long gone if the thing ever blows."

Matt sat back and sipped his orange juice.

"So when would you talk to the guy?" he asked.

"It'd have to be tonight," Liam said, "because I'm going to Florida on vacation tomorrow."

"How would I get in touch with him?"

"Assuming he's interested, I'll call you in the morning with a phone number," Liam replied. "The guy's name is Nick."

"And you really think it's a hundred to one I could pull this off?"

"Believe me, Matt, what I'm proposing is almost foolproof. If you've got a better idea for coming up with some serious money, God bless you."

"How would I learn the mechanics? I mean, how do you actually cap a bet without being spotted?"

"I'll show you right now," Liam replied. "It'll take about four minutes."

Nick was all smiles when Liam met him after work on New Year's night. He congratulated Liam for paying off his debt so quickly and joked that they should have a debt retirement party for him when he got back from Florida. From now on, he confirmed, Liam would get his full cut in cash, with nothing taken off the top.

"You still looking for potential players?" Liam asked.

"Sure. You got somebody?"

"Maybe," Liam replied. "He's a college kid. Just started playing last year. Got in over his head and needs the money. Might give you a little variety."

"You say anything to him?"

"Just that I knew somebody who might be able to help him," Liam replied.

"Okay, have him give me a call.

"And Liam," Nick said, as he got out of the car, "have a nice vacation."

Matt agonized over whether to make the call.

He went back and forth over it in his mind for the next twenty-four hours, deciding one way one minute, changing his mind the next. It finally came down to his confidence in Liam. Liam obviously knew more than he was saying, and he seemed so sure. A hundred to one. Where was he ever going to get odds like that? He picked up the pay phone at the drugstore and made the call.

Nick sounded a little gruff when he came on the line, but he was very businesslike and recognized Matt immediately when he identified himself as "the Irishman's friend," as Liam had instructed. Nick said he'd like to meet Matt and asked if he could drive over to Providence Sunday evening.

Matt said he could, and Nick gave him the address of a club called Elaine's.

Elaine's was a popular strip club that drew hundreds of customers nightly from Rhode Island, Massachusetts, and Connecticut. Matt had never been there, but he'd heard about it from some of the guys at UConn and the Foxwoods crowd, although the Foxwoods people he knew preferred another Providence club called the Foxy Lady. They did, at least, until a year or so ago, when the casino's management had put the Foxy Lady off-limits for Foxwoods employees because of allegations that organized crime figures had been working out of the club.

A few of Matt's Foxwoods friends had complained bitterly that Foxwoods had no right to dictate how they spent their private lives, but Matt figured that Foxwoods probably had a pretty good reason for its decision. Despite repeated crackdowns, Providence still hadn't lived down its reputation as the headquarters of the Patriarca crime family and was still considered a center of the New England mob. Now, as he drove toward Providence, he had to wonder how long it would be before Elaine's went on Foxwoods' list as well.

Elaine's was just getting going when Matt walked in at 7:00 p.m. and was escorted by a beefy doorman to the back of the club. A nearly naked blonde was languidly making out with a pole as he came in, and there were several scantily dressed girls congregated by the bar, apparently waiting for their first customers. A waitress in hot pants and high heels smiled at him, and a second waitress, her chest spilling out of her top, disappeared into a large, softly lit lounge where he glimpsed a stage and a couple of girls performing lap dances for some of the early arrivals.

The doorman escorting Matt stopped for a moment to say something to the bartender, and a dark-haired girl dressed in a flimsy negligee sidled up to Matt and asked if he'd like a dance.

"Maybe later," Matt said weakly, feeling her hand run up the inside of his thigh. Her perfume reminded him of Kayla, but otherwise she didn't come close.

"Well, I'm Stacy, and I'll be waiting," she purred, brushing up against him as she passed.

The doorman took Matt down a dingy hall to a door marked "Private" and knocked softly. Nick opened the door and gestured for Matt to have a seat while he finished a phone call. The room had a small desk, a couple of chairs, and a cheap vinyl couch; otherwise it was completely bare, evidently just a place to meet rather than an office. Nick sounded much rougher now than when he'd spoken with Matt on the phone, but once he finished his call he switched to a friendlier mode and came over and shook Matt's hand.

"So you're the college boy," Nick said, squeezing Matt's hand so hard it hurt.

"Yes, sir," Matt replied.

Matt towered over Nick by a good six or seven inches, but he had no illusions about who was in charge. Nick looked like a block of concrete. Probably in his early forties, he had short muscular arms that extended from a short-sleeved shirt, and his neck was nearly the width of his head. Although he was smiling, he was clearly a guy you didn't want to mess with.

"Where you go to school?" Nick asked, sitting down at his desk.

"UConn," Matt replied, taking the chair facing him.

"No shit? You a basketball fan?" Nick asked.

"Just about everybody up there is," Matt said. "I played in high school, but UConn's a different league."

"I always wanted to play myself," Nick said. "But I couldn't dunk."

Matt didn't dare laugh but couldn't help smiling. "Yeah, I shoulda been able to dunk, but I was never that good at it myself," Matt commented.

"So whadaya studyin'?" Nick asked.

"Economics," Matt replied.

"But it sounds like maybe you're not doin' so good in it right now."

Matt wasn't sure how to answer.

"That's okay," Nick said. "Everybody needs a little help once in a while. That's why I'm here. You play blackjack, right?"

"Yeah," Matt said.

"How long you been playin'?" Nick asked.

"Six months."

"Foxwoods?"

"Mostly Mohegan Sun," Matt answered.

"You like the game?" Nick asked.

"Yeah, I like it," Matt said, "but I'd enjoy it a lot more if I did a little better."

"Well, what if I could show you how to do a little better. Win, say, at least a couple grand a week. Would you be interested?"

"Yes," Matt said simply.

"You ever cap a bet?" Nick asked.

"Not in an actual game, no."

"You think you could do it?"

"Yeah, I think I could, with a little practice," Matt replied.

"Well, look, it ain't that hard. All you need is to be quick with your hands, and I gotta believe you got pretty quick hands if you play basketball.

"Here, let's take a look," Nick said, opening the top right-hand drawer of the desk and pulling out a deck of cards and a fistful of chips.

Nick worked with Matt for about fifteen minutes, instructing him on technique, how to work with the dealer, how the overhead cameras worked, and what the floor security people were looking for. If Matt were careful, Nick said, it was a slam dunk.

When they were done, they agreed Matt would give it a try Wednesday night, after which he was to drive to the twenty-four-hour diner to turn over his winnings to Nick and receive his cut. If things went well, they'd decide then when he'd play next.

Nick complimented Matt on the way out. "You're a quick study, kid," he told him. You'll do all right."

⌐⟋

Matt wound up playing blackjack at Foxwoods Wednesday, Friday, and Saturday nights that week. Nick was there to give table assignments and supervise the action, and then met Matt later at the diner to settle up.

Matt was so nervous the first night he played that he had to run to the men's room twice with diarrhea, and he later threw up in the casino parking lot. He began to calm down by the second night, and by Saturday morning, January 10, he was beginning to believe he was not only going to make it through the week but was going to come away with the $2,000 Liam and Nick had predicted.

Matt spent much of Saturday debating how to tell Nick he was quitting when he turned in his money that night. But the more he thought about it, the more he began to think that maybe he should ease his way out instead of quitting so precipitously. It now appeared Nick wanted him only on weekends, anyway, and he had begun thinking about the extra money he could pick up if he could hang in just a little longer. It would take him more than three weeks working full-time at the drugstore to make what he could make in a single night at Foxwoods.

Wanting to at least begin to prepare the groundwork for quitting, Matt told Nick that night he wasn't sure he was up to continuing but that he was willing to give it another try next Friday and Saturday if Nick wanted him. The second he said it, though, Matt realized he sounded like a wuss, and he began to worry Nick might simply drop him.

Nick didn't say anything at first but just sat there in the front seat of Matt's car, his face partially in shadow, scrutinizing Matt.

"Okay," Nick finally said. "We'll give it another shot. Eight–thirty Friday. Don't be late," he said tersely and left.

29

Bixler Brook

January 12–14, 1998

There appeared to be little hope of stopping the Northerns as the New Year began. The town submitted a vigorous rebuttal to the BIA's preliminary recognition of the tribe, but without some startling new discovery it seemed certain the government would grant the Northerns final recognition by summer.

It took Josh a few moments to adjust when Pugliese called from Washington on Monday, January 12, to say he had some potentially good news.

"You sure you're calling the right client?" Josh asked.

"Oh, hell," Pugliese said, pretending as if he'd called the wrong number, "I thought I dialed California."

"Just what I thought," Josh replied.

"God, you're getting cynical."

"Can you blame me?"

"No," Pugliese said, "but maybe this'll cheer you up."

"Let me guess," Josh said. "You've got proof Rachel Amos was an extraterrestrial beamed down from a spaceship, so even Congress can't turn her into an Indian."

"No again," Pugliese said. "Forget about Rachel and stopping the Northerns from getting recognition. It's over. They're in. But I've come up with a technicality that could block them from ever building the casino."

Suddenly Josh was all ears. "Tell me," he said.

When Pugliese finished explaining, Josh had to concede it might just be the most important technicality he had ever heard of in his life. It was so important that he agreed Pugliese should come up to Sheffield and brief the Casino Task Force as soon as possible. He made a flurry of calls and set the meeting up for 4:00 the next afternoon.

Clark held the meeting in his office to assure confidentiality, and the group officially went into executive, or closed, session. The space was cramped, but they all managed to squeeze around the conference table comfortably enough that no one complained. In addition to Clark and Pugliese, the group included the Second and Third Selectmen, Josh, and the Task Force's other two public members, both women.

Pugliese started by telling the group nothing had happened to change his view that the Northerns would almost certainly be granted final recognition. Until yesterday, he said, he believed that would leave the town with two basic options: they could try to make a deal with the tribe in which the town supported the casino in return for as much compensation as it could get, or they could begin the appeals process.

"However," he said, "it now looks like we have a third option." He opened his briefcase and pulled out a large map that Clark helped him tape to the wall behind him. The map was a blowup of the southeast corner of Sheffield showing the reservation and everything around it.

Pugliese produced a pointer and tapped the map.

"The red star here is where they'd presumably put the casino," he said. "This," he continued, pointing to Route 36, "is the state highway that runs past the Standish farm. And this squiggly line is Cedar Road, which runs past the reservation and connects with the highway."

Everyone nodded their familiarity with the area.

"As we know," Pugliese went on, "the casino needs direct access to the state highway and the only way for the tribe to get it without the town's cooperation is to extend the reservation to the highway by annexing the Standish farm. We've consequently assumed all along that the tribe would request that the BIA allow it to take the farm into federal trust the minute it received federal recognition. Equally important, we've assumed the BIA would almost automatically grant the request."

Again, everyone nodded.

"The reason I'm up here today," Pugliese continued, "is that it suddenly looks like the tribe may not have as easy a time taking the farm into trust as we thought, and we now believe there's a real chance to stop or at least seriously delay them from doing so."

"Why, what's changed?" the second selectman, Dwayne Fuller, asked skeptically.

"What's changed is our view of this stream right here," Pugliese replied, pointing to a thin blue line that separated the Standish farm from Deer Run and the reservation. "It's called Bixler Brook."

"Know it well," Fuller said. "It feeds the millpond, then runs through Josh's farm down to the lake."

"Right," Pugliese said. "We've known all along that the brook poses a potential problem for the tribe, because the Indian Gaming Act forbids taking land into trust for gaming purposes unless it's contiguous with an existing reservation. Having an intervening road or other right-of-way like this stream technically means there's no contiguity.

"Until now we never considered the contiguity provision more than a technicality, because we assumed the BIA or ultimately the courts would consider the Standish farm essential to the tribe's ability to exercise its right to build a casino and wouldn't allow a twelve-foot-wide stream to stop them. But according to a piece of intelligence I picked up at Interior on Monday, the BIA's lawyers have become increasingly concerned about the provision, and they're now advising the BIA to attempt to get it changed before approving any annexation requests in which it could be an issue."

Fuller looked troubled. "So why don't they just get it changed?" he asked.

"It's not that easy," Pugliese answered. "The provision was put into the law for a purpose, and with more and more communities up in arms over annexation, they may not be able to get a change through Congress. At the very least, it means uncertainty and delay.

"Consequently," Pugliese said, "we think Sheffield's best shot at stopping the casino at this point is to oppose annexation of the Standish farm rather than to expend any more effort on trying to block the Northerns' recognition. As we've seen over in Ledyard, annexation's something townspeople can really get worked up about, and we think most people in town would be ready to go to the mat on annexation if they thought it could stop the casino."

Clark and the Third Selectman nodded in agreement, but Josh was more cautious.

"That's true at the moment," he said, "but once the tribe sees our strategy, they're certain to come in with an offer to try to get the town to drop its opposition. If that happens, we're going to have to take the offer to a referendum, and if the offer's big enough, I don't think anybody can be sure how the town'll vote."

Nevertheless, Josh acknowledged it looked like the best option available. The only dissenter was the Second Selectman.

"This is asinine!" Fuller protested, throwing up his hands in frustration and directing a withering glare at his old friend, Jim Clark. "Continuing to fight the tribe's the biggest goddamn mistake this town could possibly make. They got the money and they got the political clout, and in the end I can't believe they're gonna let a little stream stop 'em. We could miss out on everything if we don't sit down and negotiate with 'em."

Everyone, and especially Clark, was taken aback by the vehemence of Fuller's objections, but in the end the Task Force voted five to one to adopt Pugliese's recommendation.

The group also agreed to keep their strategy quiet for the time being in order not to tip off the tribe. By that night, however, Fuller was on the phone to Bobby Kingman, giving him a full report on the meeting.

⟿

Paul Ivy could hardly contain his fury when he learned about the contiguity issue on an emergency phone call with Grimaldi and Bobby the next morning. He praised Bobby for enlisting Fuller but curtly instructed both Grimaldi and Bobby to be available for a conference call early that afternoon. In the meantime, he said, he wanted to do some checking of his own.

The moment he hung up, Ivy buzzed his secretary. When she didn't pick up, he opened his door and yelled for her at the top of his lungs. She immediately came running and he gave her the names of two people he wanted to talk to as soon as she could get them on the phone. He went back into his office, slammed the door, picked up a putter, and hurled it across the room. It shattered a table lamp. Four minutes later his secretary buzzed him with his first call.

When Ivy finished the second call, he instructed his secretary to set up a 1:00 p.m. conference call with Grimaldi, Bobby, and the three attorneys working the Northern Pequot deal.

"What if the lawyers can't make it?" the secretary asked.

"Then tell 'em they're fired," Ivy barked, and slammed down the receiver.

⟿

Everyone was on the call at 1:00, each of the attorneys calling in from different locations. Ivy's chief of staff also joined his boss in Ivy's office.

Ivy began by describing what they'd learned from Dwayne Fuller and then lit into his attorneys for not knowing about the contiguity problem.

"What I can't understand is where you three guys have been on this issue. I mean, Driscoll," he said, addressing the lead partner, "how is it I pay your firm half a million dollars a year and I have to find out about this fucking stream this way?"

"I apologize, Mr. Ivy," Driscoll groveled. "We obviously missed it, but we'll check it out right away."

"Check it out?" Ivy scoffed. "I've already checked it out, and the town's lawyer is dead-on. The BIA's changed its position on contiguity just like he says, which means this stream could kill us."

Ivy paused for emphasis.

"Let me make it clear to all three of you one more time," he said. "We've got to be able to annex the Standish farm in order to build the access road to the state highway, or this project is dead. Do you hear me, Driscoll?"

"Loud and clear," Driscoll replied. "We'll have a brief on the contiguity provision on your desk first thing in the morning, including our opinion on whether there's any way to get around it."

"Fine," Ivy said, "but from what I can see, this thing could hold us up indefinitely. You miss something like this again and you're out."

"Yes sir," the senior partner said crisply.

"Okay, we're done," Ivy said, dismissing the lawyers. "Jim, Bobby . . . stay on the line."

There were three separate beeps as the three attorneys dropped off. When they'd gone, Grimaldi asked Ivy if he'd had a chance to talk to "the senator."

"Yeah, I talked him this morning," Ivy replied. "He says he'll see about getting the law changed, but there's no certainty as to if or when he can get it done. In the meantime, he's saying our best course is to get the town to support or at least not oppose our annexation request. That'd let the BIA approve it without having to worry about defending the decision in court."

"How's he expect us to do that?" Bobby asked, seeing the casino begin to slip out of his hands.

"We're simply going to have to strike a deal," Ivy answered.

"Williams will never go for it," Bobby said, recalling his visit to Josh's office almost two years ago. He'd never mentioned the visit to either Grimaldi or Ivy out of fear of they'd criticize him for risking the possibility of Williams going to the press, but talking to Williams that day had made it clear what they were up against in trying to deal with him. "And neither will Clark," Bobby added.

"Forget Williams and Clark," Ivy retorted. "We'll go around 'em. We'll make the town an offer it can't refuse, and we'll force a town-wide referendum to decide it."

Bobby sounded skeptical. "I doubt money'll do it," he said pessimistically. "I think most people'll keep fightin' if they think they can beat us."

"Look," Ivy snapped, "I know what they're saying now—that they want to protect the town's character and values and all the rest of that bullshit. But I've been reading about these people whining about money and taxes for five years now, and I'm willing to bet they're more concerned about their wallets than they are about their precious little town. They may take a little time to come around, but I'll tell you right now—if we play our cards right, a majority will go with us."

30

Cornered

January 16–February 25, 1998

Matt drove over to Foxwoods after dinner on Friday, determined to participate in the blackjack scheme just two more nights. He had earned almost $2,000 the first three nights, and he figured he should be able to make another $1,500 that weekend because he was getting better each time he played. In fact, he thought, it was a shame to have to quit just when he was getting the hang of it. But Liam had been emphatic about getting in and out quickly, and he didn't want to push his luck.

The parking garages and closest parking lots were already jammed when he arrived shortly after 8:00. He finally parked in a far lot and walked briskly through the cold night air past scores of idling buses and long lines of traffic still pouring in. Kayla had once said you had to walk the grounds to appreciate how huge the place had become, and he was beginning to appreciate what she meant. Foxwoods now consisted of more than four million square feet of enclosed space and was spread out over hundreds of acres.

Matt began to feel butterflies in his stomach as soon as he entered the concourse, but it wasn't nearly as bad as that first night. He even stopped for a moment to check out one of the shop windows and managed to smile back at two young honeys as he continued down the long walkway. It was amazing, he thought, what having a few bucks in his pocket did for his self-confidence.

He finally spotted Nick up ahead by the Rainmaker, but he was surprised when Nick started toward him and motioned for Matt to follow him back the way Matt had just come. They finally reached the exit and went outside, where Nick let Matt catch up to him.

"Little change of plans tonight," Nick said matter-of-factly. "I want to introduce you to somebody."

"Okay," Matt said. "Where we headed?"

"Just over to my car," Nick said. "It's in the first lot."

"Who am I meeting?" Matt asked, relieved that Nick had at least parked closer than he had.

"You'll see," is all Nick answered.

When they reached the gray Lincoln, Matt saw there was somebody in the driver's seat. The driver started the engine as soon as Nick opened the back passenger-side door.

"Get in," Nick said, then slid into the back seat next to Matt.

As soon as they were inside, Nick startled Matt by telling him to unzip his jacket and hold out his arms.

"Why, what's goin' on?" Matt asked, totally taken off guard.

"Just a precaution," Nick said. "I gotta make sure you're not wearin' a wire."

"You think I'm wearing a wire?" Matt asked in disbelief but did as he was told.

Nick ignored him and quickly ran his hands up and down Matt's back and sides and chest, into his pants, and then down both legs, from Matt's crotch to his ankles.

"Take off your shoes," Nick ordered, and inspected those also.

"This is ridiculous," Matt protested weakly.

"Okay, he's clean," Nick said, and the driver eased out of the parking space.

"Oh, yeah, I almost forgot to introduce everybody," Nick said a moment later. "Matt, this is Tony. Tony, this is Matt."

"Hello," Matt said uncertainly, while Tony simply glanced back at him in the mirror and nodded.

"We thought we'd go up the road and talk," Nick said, as Tony turned left onto Route 2 and headed toward Norwich.

Five minutes later they pulled into the parking lot of a restaurant Matt had passed dozens of times. Tony drove around to the back where it was darkest and parked under a tree. There was nobody in sight, and Matt could feel the sweat break out along his hairline and his pulse begin to throb in his throat.

"Tony's an associate of mine," Nick said, as the driver shut off the engine and turned in his seat to face Matt.

Matt had no doubt that was true, given their similar plaid sport coats and bull necks. The main difference between them appeared to be that Tony was taller and had all his hair.

"We were wonderin' if you've talked to Liam in the last couple of days?" Nick began.

"No, I haven't," Matt replied nervously. "He was supposed to be back from vacation on Wednesday, but I haven't seen or heard from him."

"You sure?" Nick asked, as if he didn't believe him.

"Yeah, I'm positive," Matt insisted. "Why, is there a problem?"

"The problem," Nick said patiently, "is that Liam is an important part of our little business arrangement, and he seems to have disappeared."

"Disappeared?" Matt asked incredulously.

"Yeah, disappeared," Tony said with a scowl. "Can't you understand fucking English? Your friend has disappeared. He never came back from vacation. We checked, and he's quit his job."

Matt felt disoriented. He couldn't believe this was happening.

"And what we were hopin'," Nick continued, "is that maybe you could help us understand what's goin' on—like, why he called me about you the day before he left."

Matt did his best to regain his composure. "I don't know what to tell you. I swear. The last time I saw Liam was at his house on New Year's Day, and then he called me the next morning with your number. I haven't seen or talked to him since. I assumed he was back from vacation and that I might see him tonight."

"So what's your deal with Liam?" Tony asked.

"Deal? I don't have any deal," Matt said. "Liam's just a friend. He knows I like to play blackjack, and he was just trying to do me a favor, help me out of a jam, that's all."

"How long you known him?" Nick asked.

"I don't know—maybe a year, a little less. I met him through my old girlfriend. I liked him. I thought he was a cool guy. He kinda took me under his wing."

"So, you don't think he'd screw you by blowin' the whistle on our little setup here?" Tony asked.

"No way," Matt shot back. "I told you, we're friends. He was trying to help me."

"All right, look," Nick said, "what we're concerned about is Liam going to the casino or the cops to make a deal for himself, but it doesn't make any sense for him to mix you up in this, unless. . . ."

"Unless what?" Matt asked.

"Unless you're some kinda plant and are workin' with the cops."

"That's crazy," Matt protested. "The last thing I want to do is get involved with the police, for God's sake. All I wanted to do was make a few bucks, and Liam said this was foolproof."

Nick continued to study Matt, trying to decide whether or not to believe him.

"Okay, relax," Nick finally said. "All we know is that Liam's gone, and suddenly you show up. You sure you have no idea where he is?"

"I told you—all he said was he was going on vacation to Florida. Maybe he just stayed another week."

"No, I don't think so," Nick said. "Liam has a history of cuttin' out when he can't handle somethin'. It puts us down a dealer, but I can handle that. What I don't like is that he knows our operation and I have no idea where he is or who he's talkin' to.

"So, you know what I'm thinkin'?" Nick continued, looking at Matt.

"I'm thinkin' maybe it's a good thing you're involved, since as long as you're still in the game, maybe Liam'll be content just to hide out. Because he ain't gonna give up his friend, right?"

"He wouldn't do that," was all Matt could say.

"But to be safe, I want to find Liam," Nick said. "Just to be sure. So what I want you to do is go back to Foxwoods and play tonight like everything was normal. Then tomorrow I want you to go to Liam's house and talk to the guys he lived with to see if you can get a line on where he might be. Understand?"

"Yeah, I understand," Matt replied, not wanting any part of getting Liam into trouble, but not knowing what else to say.

"Then I want you to play again tomorrow night and every weekend for the next few weeks, and we'll see what happens," Nick said.

"One other thing," Nick added. "Tony's in charge tonight. He'll give you your table assignment and be at the diner afterward to make sure everybody gets their cut. You got any questions?"

"No," Matt replied.

"Good," Nick said. He patted the back of the driver's seat. Tony started the car and headed back to Foxwoods.

⤸

Matt went directly to the men's room when they got back to Foxwoods and stood at a sink soaking paper towels with cold water and pressing them to his face. Christ, he thought, he'd never been so scared in his life as when they pulled into the back of that parking lot. Had they really thought he might be working for the police? he wondered. What should he do now? And where the hell was Liam?

Matt's first inclination on the drive back to the casino had been to bolt as soon as Nick and Tony dropped him off. Simply head for his car and drive home. Stay away from the casinos for a couple of months and let the whole thing blow over. After all, what were they going to do? Come after him and try to strong-arm him into continuing. He doubted it.

Yet the more he thought about it, the more he realized he couldn't be sure how they'd react. He was supposed to meet Tony at the Rainmaker in five minutes, and if he didn't show, Tony and Nick were going to be incredibly pissed. What if they did come after him? The last thing he wanted was to see one of those goons walk into the drugstore tomorrow or show up on campus when he went back to UConn next week. Even worse, what if they tried to call him at home? He could just hear his father asking who the tough guy on the phone was.

Maybe it'd be better if he just went ahead and played a little longer, Matt reasoned. Prove he could be trusted and then kind of ease off. There was even an upside to doing it that way. If he went ahead and played tonight and tomorrow night and then stuck it out just two more weekends, he should be able to walk away with at least another $4,500. That was an enormous amount of money at this time in his life. In a sense, he even felt he was getting back in a small way for the money his father's bookkeeper had gambled away.

That was the irony of the whole thing. His father hated the casino and had never gambled there, but he had lost his life's savings and his business to Foxwoods. The goddamned place was going to rake in a billion dollars this year. It sure as hell wasn't going to miss it if Matt took out another $4,500.

Matt finally turned off the faucet and looked at himself in the mirror. He still had another sixty seconds to make up his mind. He thought he still looked a little shaky, but he was encouraged by having faced down the mobsters and so far come out in one piece. He could still quit anytime he chose. He smoothed back his hair and screwed up his courage, then walked out of the men's room to meet Tony. He'd go ahead and play tonight just as they'd asked and then drive over to Liam's on Saturday before work to make them happy. He doubted he was going to learn where Liam had gone, and even if he did, he certainly wasn't going to tell Nick.

Matt arrived at Liam's house just before noon, but neither of the dealers Liam lived with were able to tell him anything about Liam's whereabouts.

Both dealers had hectic schedules, and they said they hadn't even realized Liam hadn't come back until Thursday night. One of them had checked at the casino on Friday to see when he was scheduled to work next and found out only then that he'd quit. They'd then used a credit card to get into his room just a couple of hours ago and had found the room cleaned out. Dealers came and went all the time, they told Matt, but they were absolutely at a loss to explain why he would have picked up and left without even saying good-bye.

Matt also went to see Tim Paxton, then called Liam's girlfriend, Allie Carlson, all to no avail. They were as much in the dark as anyone.

Tim said that he'd seen Liam at the casino on New Year's Eve, and that he had been looking forward to Florida. He just hoped, Tim said, that Liam didn't have some family crisis or serious health problem he didn't want anyone to know about.

Allie was less generous. They had had some good times together, she said, but Liam was a very difficult person to get to know. She doubted he'd ever had a really close friend in his life.

Matt played blackjack at Foxwoods Saturday night and afterward dutifully reported what he had learned to Nick.

"It looks like he left without saying anything to anybody," Matt said, "and nobody has any idea why."

Nobody knew why, Nick thought to himself, because they didn't know Liam's history. The more he analyzed what had happened, the more he was inclined to think that the Irishman had simply gotten cold feet and had decided to take off just as he had before. Besides, it didn't make sense to bring Matt into the picture then turn around and rat everybody out. It was too bad because they had a good thing going at Foxwoods and Liam's departure hurt. He was going to have to recruit a replacement as soon as possible. But unless he was missing something, he probably didn't have to worry about Liam coming back to haunt him.

And this kid Matt looked like he was okay—which was good, because he could find a lot of uses for a clean-cut kid like him.

Despite his intention to stop at the end of January, Matt continued to cap bets into February, and by the time he walked into Foxwoods on Saturday, February 14, he'd earned just over $10,000. This was the night, however, he absolutely intended to quit. He was going to tell Nick he just didn't have the stomach or the need for it anymore.

Matt had been rehearsing his lines all day, and he was totally preoccupied with what he was going to say when he walked past the complex's Al Dente restaurant and spotted Kayla and a tall, good-looking guy talking to the maître d'. Matt stopped in his tracks, then backed up so Kayla wouldn't see him. Then he slowly approached the entrance again and peered inside.

It was Valentine's Day, and a number of couples were standing in the reception area waiting for tables. Kayla was wearing an elegant black silk dress that clung to every curve and set off a silver necklace and earrings Matt had never seen before. She had her hair pulled back so that the soft light caught every angle of her face, and she looked more dazzling than he had ever seen her. It was as though the restaurant had put her there as a centerpiece.

Finally, the maitre d' gestured for Kayla and her escort to follow him, and the two walked hand-in-hand to their table.

Seeing Kayla like this shook Matt to his core, putting him in a deep, dark funk. As a result, he played half-heartedly all night, thinking alternately about Kayla and about how badly he'd screwed up his life. His mood was reflected in his meager winnings, which totaled less than $1,000, from which he'd get to keep less than $250. Nick was going to be doubly pissed, Matt thought as he cashed in his chips and headed for the exit.

Having to face Nick, however, turned out to be the least of his problems. As he stepped off the gaming floor, two Foxwoods security guards and a third man quietly came up from behind and asked him to step over to the side of the concourse, jolting him out of his despondency.

"What's the problem?" Matt asked, but even as he said the words he knew his luck had run out.

The third man identified himself as Detective Lacey—or maybe he said Casey, Matt wasn't focusing—of the Connecticut State Police and held out his badge.

"May I see your identification, please?" the plainclothes officer asked.

Matt had never felt so helpless in his life. "Yes, sir," he said, taking out his wallet and fumbling for his driver's license.

"Mr. Williams," the officer said, "you're under arrest on charges of second-degree larceny and conspiracy to commit second-degree larceny. You have the right to remain silent...."

After reading Matt his rights, the officer patted him down and placed him in handcuffs, and he and the two security guards escorted Matt to a private area where the state police casino unit maintained several rooms that functioned as a small barracks.

Matt was searched, booked, photographed, and fingerprinted, and the $970 he had collected that night was confiscated. He was told he would be transferred to the state police Troop E barracks in Montville, where he would be held on $10,000 bond. The charges against him were Class C felonies and carried penalties of up to ten years in prison and $10,000 in fines.

Stunned, Matt sat staring at the floor.

"You look a little pale, son," the arresting officer said. "You all right?"

"Yes, sir," Matt said softly.

"Do you feel up to answering a few questions about how you got involved in this?" the officer asked in a surprisingly friendly tone.

Matt continued to look at the floor without answering.

"Look, Matt," the detective continued. "You look like a pretty smart guy. I'm sure you realize we wouldn't be filing these charges unless we had some pretty strong evidence against you. We have you on camera. We know what you were doing. We know how you were doing it. And we know who you're involved with. So if I were you, I'd try to cooperate."

Matt felt so cornered that he almost agreed to answer anything the detective wanted to ask, but he simply couldn't bring himself to owning up to what he'd done. The consequences were too overwhelming.

He thought about Liam's assurances and about how stupid he'd been not to quit when he was supposed to. He thought about Kayla and what she would think of him. He thought about his friends and teachers at UConn and from high school. He even thought of Mr. Boudreau at the drugstore and his old tutor, Mr. Conner. But most of all, he thought about his father. He couldn't bear the thought of facing him.

What Matt needed was a lawyer who could help him think things through and get him out on bail in time to at least go home and talk to his parents; that way they wouldn't have to learn about it from the police and see him in jail.

It was now almost 3:00 on Sunday morning. Since breaking up with Kayla, Matt had stayed overnight with friends several times on Saturday nights, but he had said nothing to his parents about not coming home tonight. They'd be concerned when they didn't see his car in the driveway. They'd probably go to church with Jacob and Sarah, who was home that weekend, and then start really worrying about him if he wasn't home when they returned.

The only lawyer Matt knew was Brad Merriweather. The upside was that Merriweather was a family friend and a criminal attorney. Even if he could reach him, however, the question was whether he'd be willing to help without going to Matt's parents first.

But there was little choice.

"I don't think I should say anything until I've talked to a lawyer," Matt finally said to the officer.

"That's up to you," the officer replied. "We're going to transfer you over to Troop E. If you'd like to talk, let 'em know over there."

Matt called Brad Merriweather from the Troop E barracks at 7:00 and got him just as he and Janet were leaving for a day of skiing in the Berkshires. He'd been arrested, Matt said, and he desperately needed Brad's help.

"What's the charge?" Brad asked.

Matt explained as briefly as he could.

"Look, Matt, I'll try to help you," Brad said, "but under two conditions. First, that you level with me as to what this is all about. And second, that if we can get you out of there this morning, you sit down with your parents and tell them everything before they hear it from someone else."

"Yes, sir," Matt said softly.

"I'll tell you right now," Brad said, "I don't like the sound of what I'm hearing."

⤙

Brad arrived at the state police barracks in Montville at 8:20 a.m., and after arranging bail, he drove Matt back to Foxwoods to retrieve his car. By 9:15, they were sitting in Brad's law office in Norwich.

Brad listened to Matt and asked questions for more than an hour, going back in detail over his meetings with Nick, the amount of his illegal winnings, and precisely what he had been told by the police when they booked him. When they finished, Brad reviewed his notes for several minutes and then asked Matt how he was holding up.

"I'm scared, Mr. Merriweather," Matt replied honestly. "I know what I did was wrong. All I wanted to do was get my money back, but everything's gotten out of control, and I don't know where it's going to end."

"Well, you've obviously gotten involved in something a lot more serious than you bargained for, Matt. Normally, this so-called friend of yours, Liam Blackwell, would probably be right. If the casino spotted a kid like you trying to cap a bet, they'd presumably just slap your wrist and tell you not to do it again. But the conspiracy charge says they think they're onto something much bigger than that."

Matt put his face in his hands and shook his head.

"So, the question is," Brad continued, "what do they think they're onto, where are they in their investigation, and where do they think you fit in all of this? And the only way I can find out is to talk to the State's Attorney in New London, which I'm going to do right now if I can reach him.

"What I want you to do, Matt, is go home, sit down with your mother and father, and tell them what happened. Tell them I'm working on it, and then stay near the phone until I call you. Can I rely on you to do that?"

"Yes, sir," Matt said.

Brad and Matt shook hands at the door.

"Thank you, Mr. Merriweather," Matt said. "I'm sorry I'm such a jerk. And I'm sorry to be ruining your Sunday. You have no idea what your help means to me."

"Look, Matt," Brad said, "what you did was illegal and incredibly foolish. But it's not the end of the world. What you've got to decide is if you've learned your lesson. Gambling's a trap for a lot of people, and that's exactly what's it's proving to be for you."

Matt got home just after 11:00 and had to wait twenty minutes before his family returned from church. It was the hardest twenty minutes of his life.

He sat quietly in his bedroom until he heard his father's car pull into the driveway and his parents come up the stairs and go into their room to change. He followed them in and asked if the three of them could go down to the library to talk. Sharon and Josh looked at each other momentarily but accompanied Matt downstairs without asking any questions.

Matt still wasn't sure exactly how he was going to start, but once they'd closed the door and sat down, it all simply tumbled out.

He related how he had begun gambling, had gotten in over his head, had been desperate to recover his losses, and had gotten involved in the scam. He explained how he intended to get in and out but had gotten caught up in the money, stayed too long, and been arrested. He knew what he had done was wrong and against everything he had ever been taught. He was sorry he had broken the law, but above all he was sorry he had so completely broken their trust.

He only hoped, he said, that they could forgive him. He had no idea when he started that gambling could be such a powerful lure. But he understood now. It was like playing with fire, and he swore he'd learned his lesson.

Sharon and Josh listened open-mouthed at first, then simply in numb silence.

"Matt, how could you?" his mother finally said, shaking her head and fighting back tears. She then got hold of herself and went over and sat down next to him on the couch.

"Matt," she said, hugging him, "we love you and we'll do everything we can to help you. But we're so disappointed. I hope you mean it when you say you've learned your lesson."

Josh was harsher. He couldn't believe Matt had done what he had. Where, he asked, was his moral conscience? Equally incredible, where was his common sense? Obviously, he said, he and Sharon wouldn't have been happy if Matt had come to them and confided about his gambling and his losses, but it would have been infinitely better than facing what he was facing now.

Nonetheless, Josh also finally walked over to Matt and embraced him, telling him he loved him and would do everything he could for him.

But Josh was seething inside, and he had no sense at all where this was all likely to wind up. He was furious with Matt, with the casinos, and with the people who had sucked him in. He was angry at the police for not distinguishing between Matt and the others, and with himself for not staying closer to his son. And he was bitter beyond words about the way life seemed to be conspiring against him and his family. Thank God for Brad, he thought. The only smart thing Matt did in this whole pathetic affair was to call him.

⌒

Brad finally called about 2:30 to say he was leaving New London and would be there in about twenty-five minutes. It was important, he said, that they all sit down together as soon as possible.

In the meantime, the house was as quiet as a morgue. It was impossible to keep the situation from Sarah and Jacob, who wanted to know what was going on the moment Matt went upstairs to take a shower, then kept their distance because they didn't know what to say to him.

"Do you think Matt'll have to go to jail, Mom?" Jacob asked.

"I hope not, honey," Sharon replied, almost unable to believe she was being asked such a question. "He's gotten himself into a lot of trouble, but Mr. Merriweather's trying to help him."

"I feel so sorry for him," Sarah said tearfully. "I know he's been upset ever since he broke up with Kayla, but I had no idea he was gambling. We've been driving back and forth to UConn together, and he never said a word about this to me."

When Brad finally arrived, he, Josh, Sharon, and Matt went back into the library, while the two younger children hung around the house to see what would happen next.

"Matt," Brad began once they sat down, "I assume you've told your parents everything, and you have no objection to my talking to you all together. I've just spent an hour with the State's Attorney for New London County, who's going to be prosecuting the case, and I'm afraid there's no time for niceties or sensibilities here."

Everyone looked at Matt.

"Yes, I told them," Matt said softly. "And no, I have no objection. I know I need everyone's help."

"I'm amazed the prosecutor'd talk to you on a Sunday afternoon," Josh said.

"Well, fortunately I've known him a long time," Brad said. "But that's not the important thing. What's important is that there's something he wants from us, too, which we can talk about in a minute. But let me explain first where things stand."

Everyone listened intently as he took them through what he'd learned.

"About two weeks ago," he began, "the casino's surveillance cameras spotted a player who looked like he was capping a bet at a blackjack table. They zoomed in on him, but it was late and they couldn't get a clear shot of him in the act before he left. However, they identified the guy when he cashed his chips that night, and they focused in on him again when they saw him playing with a different dealer the next night.

"This time," Brad said, "they not only got several clear shots of the player capping bets, but they began to suspect the dealer was in on it.

"So they began wondering about the previous dealer as well, and they went to the state police, who arrested the player at a local motel that night and brought him back to the Montville barracks for questioning.

"It turned out," Brad continued, "that the player already had a criminal record, and if they'd reduce the charges against him, he'd agree to tell everything he knew about a blackjack scam that had been going on for more than five months. As a result, he not only identified the dealers and three other players who were involved, but he also identified two Providence mobsters who he says organized and ran the operation."

"At that point," Brad said, "the state police and the casino decided to let the thing run long enough to collect additional evidence, and the Connecticut police also brought in both the Rhode Island state police and the FBI because of the organized-crime angle."

Matt turned increasingly pale as he saw how oblivious he'd been to what had been happening.

"Last night, when they thought they had enough evidence," Brad continued, "they swooped in and made six arrests: the two dealers, three players, including Matt, and a guy they identified as a mob enforcer named Anthony Palo. And this morning, the Rhode Island police arrested a second mob type named Nicholas Carini on a Connecticut warrant.

"They say Carini was the mastermind, and he and Palo are made members of what's left of the Patriarca crime family. They both have records up to here, including armed robbery, assault, racketeering, and loan-sharking."

Sharon winced at the description of the two mobsters, but Josh's face was frozen as he listened.

"Matt said the charges against him were second-degree larceny and conspiracy to commit second-degree larceny," Josh interjected. "What about the charges against the other players?"

"Same charges against the other two players arrested last night, but a lesser charge of fourth-degree larceny against the player who originally cooperated," Brad replied.

"And how about everybody else?" Sharon asked.

"They charged both Carini and Palo with first-degree larceny and conspiracy to commit first-degree larceny," Brad said, "and they charged the two dealers with the same thing. I'm sure, though, that they'd be willing to reduce the charges against the dealers and the other players in return for their cooperation."

"Anything about this Liam Blackwell?" Josh asked.

"Oh, yeah, I almost forgot," Brad said. "They didn't give his name, but Connecticut's planning to issue a warrant for the arrest of a third dealer who resigned from Foxwoods and disappeared around New Year's. So it must be him."

Matt felt a stab in his gut. Liam had got him involved in this whole mess, but Matt was convinced Liam had genuinely tried to help him at considerable risk to himself. If he had just listened to Liam and not gotten greedy, he would've been in and out of the scam in a week and never been caught.

"So where does that leave me, Mr. Merriweather?" Matt asked uncertainly.

"We've got two choices," Brad said. "We can go to trial, and maybe I can get the charge reduced to fourth-degree larceny. But even then it's going to leave you with a record that'll stick with you for the rest of your life."

"What's the second choice?" Matt asked.

"The second choice is to give the State's Attorney what he really wants: full cooperation, including every detail of the scam, from how you got involved to how it operated, and your agreement to testify in court if the prosecution needs you.

"If you're willing to do all that, maybe I can work out a deal to get the charges dropped. Maybe," Brad emphasized.

"You mean tell them everything?" Matt asked. "Including about Liam?"

"Yes," Brad replied.

Matt didn't respond. Instead he just stared at the floor. Josh started to say something, but Brad waved him off.

"Is that going to be a problem for you, Matt?" Brad asked.

"I know this may be hard to understand," Matt said, finally looking up, "but Liam's a friend. He's one of the only real friends I have. He was the only one I could go to, and he tried to help me even though it was risky for him. And if I had done what he told me, we wouldn't be sitting here now. So, yeah, it's a huge problem."

Brad considered Matt's answer and then leaned forward in his chair, his hands folded and his forearms on his knees. "Matt," he said, looking him in the eye, "I understand how you feel, but let me explain in a little more detail what's at stake here."

"For starters, I don't think you owe this guy Liam anything. You may consider him a friend, but he dragged you into a criminal scheme, and the result is that you're under arrest while he's hiding out somewhere.

"Furthermore, he's already been implicated by a witness who capped bets at his table. So there's nothing you can say that's likely to get him in any more trouble than he's already in.

"But the more important thing is that we need the prosecutor's help, and he's not going to help us unless he thinks you're willing to tell him everything.

"The fact is, Matt, you've already been arrested, and I can't undo that. Consequently, the only thing I can do now is to try to make the best possible deal for you, and I'm going to be asking the prosecutor for a lot."

Brad held Matt's eyes.

"I'm going to start by asking that he recommend reducing your bond, but the main thing I'm going to asking for is that he agree to *nolle* the case against you, which means not to prosecute it, and dismiss the charges.

"At the same time I'm going to ask him to ask the court to seal your file, and I'm going to request that he grant you immunity to prosecution on any other charges that might arise out of the case.

"That's a pretty long list of requests," Brad said, "and whether we can get them all will depend on whether the prosecutor wants your help badly enough and whether he believes he's getting your full cooperation.

"It's up to you, Matt. If you're willing to cooperate, you and I need to go and see the State's Attorney this evening and show him we're serious. If we wait and something new develops, he could decide you're not worth the concessions. So you've got to decide now. You want to give my plan a try, or do you want to go through the rest of your life explaining away your record?"

Matt looked away and chewed his knuckles. "I don't know," he said to no one in particular. "I just don't know."

"Matt," Sharon pleaded. "You've got to let Brad help you."

There was a long silence. Matt thought about Liam. He glanced at his parents, then looked back at Brad.

"All right, Mr. Merriweather," he finally said. "I'll do it."

⟜

Brad took Matt to meet with the State's Attorney on Sunday evening and by Monday afternoon reported he had an agreement on all the key points, although as Brad had anticipated, the prosecutor insisted on keeping the case against Matt pending until the cases against the others were disposed of. The prosecutor also wanted to be certain, Brad said, that Matt understood he would have to return all the money he'd made from his illegal winnings to the casino.

The next step in the legal process would take place the following week, when Matt had to appear at State Superior Court in New London for arraignment. Brad expressed satisfaction with the deal, but he warned that Matt and his family should brace themselves for the next couple of days because the state police were about to put out a press release on the arrests, and he was sure the media were going to be all over the story.

It was just the kind of story the press loved, Brad said—the casino being taken for hundreds of thousands of dollars by the mob, its own dealers, and a few of its customers, including a twenty-one-year-old college kid.

Brad's prediction proved to be an understatement. The story broke on television Monday evening and filled the local papers for the next three days. It was splattered across the front page of the first paper Josh picked up Tuesday morning.

Eight Arrested in Foxwoods Scam Probe— Possible Mob Link Seen

Ledyard—Two blackjack dealers, four players, and two reputed Rhode Island mobsters have been arrested in what police claim was a mob-run table-game scam at Foxwoods Resort Casino."

State police said Monday that the alleged scheme, which reportedly cost Foxwoods hundreds of thousands of dollars, began to unravel on January 31, when casino surveillance cameras picked up a blackjack player "capping" a bet in apparent collusion with the dealer. Capping entails a player adding to a winning bet after the final cards have been dealt in order to increase the size of his win.

The blackjack player, Robert Houley of no certain address, was arrested on a charge of fourth-degree larceny and agreed to cooperate with police. Houley reportedly implicated seven other participants, ranging from Nicholas, "Nicky," Carini of Providence, a known organized crime figure and the scheme's alleged mastermind, to Matthew J. Williams, a 21-year-old University of Connecticut student from Sheffield who was allegedly recruited by Carini as one of the players.

"Scam May Have Gone On for Months, Cost Foxwoods Over $1 Million," another headline proclaimed on Wednesday. According to this story, the four players arrested in the scheme were believed to have won close to

$1.1 million in illegal bets over a five-month period, keeping 25 percent of their winnings for themselves and splitting the remainder with the crooked dealers and the mob. "The illicit winnings," the paper stated, "reportedly ranged from more than $400,000 for Robert Houley, who allegedly pocketed over $100,000, to approximately $40,000 for UConn student Matthew Williams, who police said kept just over $10,000."

"Arrest Warrant Issued for Third Foxwoods Dealer in Blackjack Scam," a third headline read on Thursday. The dealer, Liam Blackwell, the article reported, "was allegedly a close friend of UConn student Matthew Williams, one of the four players arrested in the costly bet-capping scheme."

As brutal as the week was for Matt, it was in some ways even more difficult for Josh and Sharon. They dreaded going out for the newspaper each morning, winced at each new revelation, held their breath in the hope that Matt's name wouldn't be mentioned in each new article, and anguished over what their friends and neighbors must be thinking.

Matt stayed in his room on Monday, Tuesday, and Wednesday except to come down briefly to look at the papers and get something to eat, but otherwise Josh insisted family members go about their business as best they could.

Josh went to work but kept a low profile. Sharon went to her job in New London but avoided eye contact with her co-workers. Sarah got a ride back to UConn on Monday and buried herself in the library when she wasn't at class. And Jacob plodded along as though someone had died, saying little and showing none of his usual cheerfulness.

Matt himself finally drove back to campus on Thursday but cut half his classes, then brought Sarah home with him on Friday afternoon.

Sarah's roommate, who was from New London, mentioned how sorry she was to hear about Matt, and at school a couple of kids asked Jacob about his brother, but other than that the only people to say anything were the Congregational minister, who called to ask if he could be of any assistance; Marge Hanlon, who called Josh to express her sympathy; and Janet Merriweather, who called Sharon to lend moral support. It was the fact that no one else said anything that cast the biggest pall. Everyone knew, but they found the situation too awkward to discuss.

Josh and Sharon drove Matt to New London on February 25, meeting Brad at the State Superior Court on Broad Street just after 9:30 a.m.

The courthouse was an old, imposing Romanesque building that Brad explained was primarily used for motor vehicle, small claims, and lesser criminal cases. He said Matt would be arraigned there, but any trials involving the Foxwoods scam defendants would be held at a newer facility around the corner.

Brad escorted Matt and his parents into a large courtroom on the first floor, where they took seats in one of the middle rows of benches facing the judge.

Matt was almost oblivious to the surroundings at first but gradually noticed there were only about twenty-five or thirty people in the room, and many of them appeared to be court officials. The room itself was spartan, with a high ceiling, drab yellowish walls, and poor acoustics that made it somewhat difficult to hear the case already in progress. It was against a big, brawny kid in a muscle shirt. From what Matt could make out, the accused had gotten into a fight and knocked out the windows of a car with a baseball bat.

When Matt's name was called, he and Brad approached the judge together. As Josh watched, all he could think of were other occasions—at school or at a banquet—where he'd watched Matt get up to receive an academic or sports award.

Josh and Sharon strained to hear the prosecutor outline the charges against their son. It was an enormously painful moment. Sharon took Josh's hand, and when he looked over he saw tears in her eyes.

The whole thing was over quickly. Brad entered a plea of "no contest," the judge lowered Matt's bail to $1,000 on the recommendation of the prosecution, and the case was left pending.

"It's not over yet," Brad said when they returned from the judge's bench, "but we're headed in the right direction."

Hopefully that was true, Matt thought as they walked down the driveway toward their cars. But at the moment he stood accused by the state of Connecticut of two felonies, and he faced the prospect of having to testify against five people, including one of his few friends, on charges carrying penalties of up to twenty years in prison.

31

The Stone Wall

March 1998

It was still dark when Josh walked out to get the papers the following Sunday morning, March 8, and he almost didn't notice that a seven-foot stretch of the old stone wall on the west side of the driveway had partially collapsed.

"Damn," he swore under his breath, "just what I need, another project."

A large tie stone that ran through the width of the waist-high wall had caved in, taking several capstones and a pile of other stones and rubble with it. It was going to take him hours to repair it.

Josh couldn't concentrate on the sermon as he sat in church that morning; instead he kept thinking about the collapsed wall. There was something about the wall that bothered him, but he couldn't put his finger on it. Perhaps it was simply the fact that he'd always been fascinated by New England's old stone walls and it always pained him to see one falling apart. Their mystique and beauty were part of the region's charm, and he hated to see them gradually disappear.

The stones they were built with were originally part of the massive mountains that once towered over northern New England. Successive glaciers tore off whole slabs of the mountains, breaking them into billions of pieces that became trapped in the ice as it moved south and that, as the ice melted, were deposited across the land. Once the last glacier receded, a layer of fertile soil developed, burying most of the stones and creating ideal growing conditions in many parts of the region. Then, as farmers cleared and plowed the land, the winter frost burrowed deeper into the ground, causing frost heaves which lifted the stones toward the surface. As a result, most early New England farmers not only had to clear their fields of trees, but constantly had to "pick stones," a euphemism for prying, digging, and pulling out the new crop of stones that nature—or, some swore, the devil himself—produced each year.

The farmers used crowbars, chains, and oxen along with their own brute strength to coax the stones from the soil. They rolled them onto ox-drawn sleds and hauled them to the edges of their fields, where they dumped them in heaps or piled them along existing fences made of brush, stumps, or wood. As they cleared more land and began running out of timber, they increasingly built their fences entirely of stone.

As Josh had learned from his grandfather, the farmers had built basically two types of stone walls. Both were dry walls, built without mortar and totally dependent on gravity to keep them in place. Beyond that, they were very different. The overwhelming majority were what Josh's grandfather called "stacked walls," because they were thrown up quickly by simply stacking one stone on top of another. These were the walls that lined the country roads and marked the boundaries between farms, fields, and pastures. His grandfather had referred to the second type of wall as a "laid wall," because the builder first dug a foundation below the frost line and then carefully built up from there, meticulously laying and filling in around each stone. Laid walls, like the one which ran along his driveway, were normally two rows wide and typically built to grace front yards, gardens, and public places.

Sadly, both kinds of stone walls were steadily disappearing as they either toppled with age or were dismantled by builders, landscapers, and homeowners for their own use. Some were purchased from farmers, but others were simply being pilfered from both working and abandoned farms. Just a few months ago, thieves had driven two trucks up to a working Sheffield farm one night and brazenly carted off one the most scenic stretches of stone wall in town, leaving nothing but muddy tire tracks.

It was ironic, Josh thought, that these once-cursed fieldstones, the bane of the early farmer's existence, should now be so coveted that they were being stolen at night. But whether lost through sale, theft, or simple aging, the result was the same: New England was gradually losing its old stone walls and with them part of its past.

As he drove home from church, Josh finally realized what it was about his own stone wall that was bothering him. It was not simply that a section of another lovely old stone wall had collapsed, but that a section of this particular wall had collapsed. His father had told him that according to the old family diaries, the laid stone wall that ran alongside the driveway had been built in 1678 by Ethan Williams himself, and that keeping it in good repair had apparently been a point of pride for the family for generations. So why, Josh wondered, had a section of the wall collapsed now? He routinely inspected the wall just as his father and grandfather had, and he hadn't recently noticed any problem. Yet some shift had occurred inside the wall to start an avalanche that had brought down an entire section. Josh had no idea when that shift might have begun, but he couldn't help thinking that the collapse of the old wall, which had stood rock-solid for centuries, was reflecting the family's current travails.

～

Despite the cold weather, Josh felt a compulsion to repair the wall as soon as possible, and that afternoon he recruited Matt to give him a hand.

Rebuilding a section of laid wall was far easier than building one from scratch because the foundation and stones were already there, but it was still backbreaking work. Matt provided additional muscle, however, and they made good progress figuring out which stones went where, filling in with smaller stones and rubble, and finally hefting the heavy capstones back where they belonged.

It was also Josh's first opportunity to really spend time alone with Matt since his arrest, and he was grateful for the chance to begin to reconnect with his son.

When they finally stepped back to appraise their work, Josh nodded approvingly and offered Matt a high-five that Matt returned with the first smile Josh had seen from him in two weeks. The ancient, lichen-covered wall, with its shades of gray, blue, green, and brown, truly did look as solid as ever.

"You see this?" Josh asked, taking off a glove and running his fingers over a three-inch gash in one of the capstones. "I'll bet old Ethan Williams did this with a plow more than three hundred twenty-five years ago. Here, feel it. You can almost feel your ancestor's energy embedded in the rock."

Matt pulled off one of his gloves and ran his index finger along and down into the groove. "Probably his frustration," he responded.

Josh nodded and touched the gash again. In his mind's eye he could see Ethan grimace as the plowshare struck and bit into the large, flat stone.

"Finding something like this really makes you think about how long the family's been here, doesn't it," Matt said.

"That's true," Josh replied. "One thing about the farm—the longer you live here, the more you appreciate just how deep the family's roots go in this little town."

That evening, Josh went into the library and pulled down the dusty, leather-bound diaries that his father and grandfather—and who knew how many Williamses before them—had kept on one of the top shelves. Josh had promised himself ever since moving back to the farm to make a project someday of reading them, but at the moment he simply wanted to see if he could find the reference to the stone wall that his father had mentioned.

There were five volumes in all, written in now partially faded ink on discolored paper. The first three had been written by Ethan Williams, the fourth by Ethan's son Samuel, and the last by Ethan's grandson Daniel. It was Daniel whose portrait hung in the upstairs sitting room and who had such a remarkable resemblance to Josh.

The first three volumes were written in a sometimes hard-to-read scrawl that was the main reason Josh hadn't made a more serious effort to read them in the past. Attached to the inside cover of the first volume was an unsigned, typed summary of Ethan's life.

Josh lit a fire in the fireplace and sat down to read. According to the brief biography, Ethan Williams had come to America in 1635 and migrated from Massachusetts to Connecticut in 1636. His first wife, Susan, had been killed in the Pequot attack on Wethersfield in 1637, and Ethan had fought in the Pequot War, participating in the assault on the Pequot fort at Mystic. He had married his second wife, Anne, three years later, and they subsequently moved to Saybrook, where she died childless in 1658.

Ethan then pulled up stakes again, moving into the wilderness northeast of Saybrook and helping to found Sheffield in 1659. He married his third wife, Sarya, in 1660, had two boys in quick succession, then lost Sarya and a third child in 1667. He never remarried and lived at the farm with his youngest son and his son's family for the rest of his years, dying in 1698 at the age of eighty-two.

Josh thumbed through the first two of Ethan's volumes, then picked up the third volume to see if he could find the reference to the building of the stone wall in 1678.

The third volume ran from 1668 to 1698. It began with a deeply personal remembrance of Sarya, who had died exactly one year earlier. Ethan had loved Sarya dearly. She had given him the children he had never had, and he would mourn her all the days of his life. She was, he wrote, "a kind, loving and sensitive soul," as well as "a beautiful woman with striking green eyes and lustrous dark hair that gave her a countenance no man could soon forget."

At least the Puritans knew a good-looking woman when they saw one, Josh thought with a smile. He'd have to give them more credit from now on. And he'd have to see what else the diaries said about Sarya, who intrigued him. He assumed she must be buried near Ethan, but he couldn't really remember. He'd have to stop at the cemetery on Monday and have a look.

At the moment, however, he was looking for a reference to the stone wall, so he jumped ahead to the 1670s. Then he slowed down and began to read certain entries more carefully as particular items caught his eye. Samuel was outgrowing his older brother, Thomas; a heated controversy erupted over the selection of a new minister in the fall of 1672; and gray wolves posed such a threat to livestock in 1673 that the town offered a bounty of twenty shillings for every "howler" killed within five miles of the commons. These entries were followed by increasing references to Indian war scares and then an entire section on King Philip's War. Josh skipped over the war, figuring he'd come back to it when he had time to read it properly, and went directly to the postwar years. Finally he saw the entry he was looking for in a summary Ethan had written of the things he had accomplished during 1678: "Made 7 rods of stone wall along front garden with Thomas and Samuel."

Seven rods, or roughly 115 feet, was just about the length of the old wall that ran along the west side of the driveway. Josh smiled when he found the reference and couldn't help but feel a growing connection with his ancestor. He and Matt, after all, had just finished rebuilding a section of the same wall that Ethan had originally built with his sons, working with the same stones and using the identical muscles to lift and wrestle them into place. Rebuilding the wall, and then finding the gash in the capstone, reminded him of the feelings he had experienced at the Stowe House almost seven years before, when he had imagined he was Ethan waiting for Ebenezer Stowe to come to the front door, and then at the history lecture afterward, when he had imagined helping carry a wounded soldier from a wagon into the meetinghouse during King Philip's War.

Josh had never forgotten the almost out-of-body sense of actually being at the meetinghouse with the wounded soldier, and he flipped back to the section on the war to see if there might be an entry about using the meetinghouse as a hospital. Surprisingly, there it was. A chill shot through him as he read on. According to the entry, the town had cared for five soldiers, including a nineteen-year-old boy who arrived unconscious in the back of a wagon. "The lad's left cheekbone had been shattered by a Narragansett musket ball," Ethan wrote, "and the two men with him were trying to get the boy home before he died. Caleb Foster and I carried him in on a litter, but he passed away the next morning."

Shock turned to confusion as Josh realized that the account of what had happened was just as he had imagined it, and he tried to recall exactly what the town historian, Charlotte Dodson, had said during her lecture. He was positive she had said nothing about the wounded boy and that he had imagined the scene entirely on his own. Yet suddenly here was an incontrovertible record that the scene had occurred in the meetinghouse, precisely as he'd imagined it. What were the odds of imagining something that specific and then reading about it in a diary written more than three hundred years ago? A million to one? Ten million? But it made no difference. Whatever the odds, it had to be a coincidence. Either that, Josh thought, or he had to have in some way—physically or psychically—been at the meetinghouse three centuries ago. Or, he wondered fleetingly, could he have inherited the memory? Of course not, he told himself. All those explanations were ridiculous. He had never believed in reincarnation or anything with even a hint of the paranormal. It had to have been something the town historian had said. Still, the discovery was profoundly disturbing, and he couldn't shake the eerie feeling that it was more than coincidence. At the very least, it added a troubling new strand to the curious bond he seemed to be developing with Ethan.

Josh took a deep breath and tried to clear his head before placing the diaries back on the shelf. He promised himself he'd return to them to read more about Ethan as soon as he had a free evening, and the next day he went over to the church cemetery during the lunch hour to see if he could find Sarya's tombstone.

The temperature had dropped into the low twenties and there was a dusting of snow on the ground as Josh walked up the Congregational Church driveway and entered the lovely old cemetery, with its carefully maintained lawns and trees and shrubs. The oldest headstones began just to the right of the entrance and were arrayed along the slope of a gentle hill. There were row after row of large and small sandstone and slate markers, some so decayed they were largely illegible.

Josh recognized many of the old Sheffield names: Sherman, Neal, Carter, Poole, Sayer, Knowlton, Paine. The more elaborate gravestones, Josh's father had explained, were fascinating combinations of Puritan art and religion. The Puritans' cemeteries, he'd pointed out, were meant to be places of reflection, contemplation, and instruction. If you didn't understand that, Josh thought, some of the gravestones could be pretty macabre, with their hollow-eyed skulls and grim admonitions about the certainty of death.

One of the tombstones he remembered best was a well-preserved red sandstone with a particularly gruesome winged skull. He stopped for a moment to study it.

The winged skull was a commonly used symbol of death and resurrection, and it hovered over the Latin words MEMENTO MORI–FUGIT HORA, carved just above an hourglass. Cherubs rose toward heaven on either side of the epitaph, which described the deceased and then ended with an exhortation.

AS YOU ARE NOW,

SO ONCE WAS I.

AS I AM NOW,

SO YOU MUST BE.

SO PREPARE FOR DEATH

AND FOLLOW ME.

Ethan and Sarya were buried next to each other. Both graves were marked by slate tombstones, although Ethan's was smaller and in better condition. It had a simple border and brief epitaph that read:

IN MEMORY OF

LIEUT ETHAN WILLIAMS

A SOLDIER IN THE PEQUOT WAR

AGED 82 YEARS DECEASED

YE 12 OF NOVEMBER 1698

Josh thought of his own resemblance to Ethan's grandson, Daniel. *Could he look as much like Ethan as he looked like Daniel?* Josh wondered. *Why not? If characteristics could be passed down ten generations, why not twelve?*

At that moment, a frigid gust of wind swept through the cemetery, cutting through Josh's overcoat, and he looked up as though he sensed someone else's presence. Realizing it was just the wind, he pulled up his collar and turned to Sarya's gravestone. It had a large sun at the top, which was another symbol of resurrection, and a lengthy epitaph. Josh put on his glasses and dropped to his haunches to read it. The stone was chipped and badly decayed in places, but the inscription was still legible. He took his time and read it slowly.

HERE LIETH THE BODY OF

MRS SARYA WILLIAMS

LOVING CONSORT OF

LIEUTENANT ETHAN WILLIAMS

WHO DEPARTED THIS LIFE

MAY YE 19 1667

AGED 25 YEARS

AND IN HER ARMS DOTH LYE

YE CORPS OF HER SWEET

BABE BORN 2 DAYS BEFORE

Deeply moved, Josh read the inscription again. Ethan and Sarya had been together for only a little more than seven years. While brief, those years had to have been the fulfillment of everything he'd ever dreamed of. Rising to his feet, Josh looked down at Sarya's grave just as Ethan must have done hundreds of times and wondered how Ethan had ever made it through the rest of his life.

Sarya's epitaph haunted Josh on his walk back to the office, and he found himself still thinking about her and Ethan on his way home that afternoon. Thoughts about his ancestors were immediately pushed aside, however, the moment he walked through the kitchen door.

"Did you hear the announcement?" Sharon asked. "It was just on the five o'clock news. The BIA granted the Northerns final federal recognition. The town has ninety days to appeal."

The announcement was the top story in the local media for the next forty-eight hours, along with endless interviews, analysis, and predictions about what it all meant for Sheffield and the state.

Sheffield's officials blasted the decision, reserving the option to appeal, while the tribe hailed it, urging the town to forgo an expensive and pointless appeal and instead to work with the tribe to ensure that the entire community benefited from the casino.

Each side, however, knew that the town had no intention of appealing, and that once the appeal period was over, the fight was headed toward a referendum on whether to allow the tribe to annex the Standish farm.

Both the town and the tribe immediately began preparing for the expected vote.

Jim Clark leaned increasingly on Josh for advice and support, while Paul Ivy consulted continuously with Bobby Kingman, honing the offer he intended to make to the town and hiring one of the country's top public relations firms to plan and manage what they anticipated would be a no-holds-barred political campaign.

Clark publicly acknowledged in late March that Sheffield had decided not to appeal the tribe's recognition. But, he stated, the town would strongly oppose any effort to annex the Standish farm and would use its planning, zoning, and environmental powers to block the tribe from building either an access road or any part of its proposed casino on the Standish property.

The announcement constituted a formal declaration of war because, as Paul Ivy had admitted in January, failure to annex the Standish farm meant the casino was dead.

32

Fired Up

April 1998

The first few days of April were damp and gray, which pretty much fit Bobby's mood as he worked on plans for the referendum. He'd pulled off a miracle by recreating the Northern Pequot tribe and gaining federal recognition, but he now faced a vote on annexation that he doubted he could win. No matter what they offered the town, he simply couldn't see it supporting the casino in the end.

Discouraged and depressed, Bobby barely spoke as he and his latest girlfriend, a twenty-four-year-old fitness instructor named Adrienne, drove to New London to attend a Saturday night party at the home of one of her friends.

"What'sa matter, sweetie?" Adrienne asked, reaching over and rubbing the back of his neck. "You got something against me tonight?"

"No, no, just got a lot on my mind is all," he answered.

"Personal or business?" she asked.

Bobby managed a wry smile. "Personal, business . . . what's the difference? For me, they're the same thing."

"You want to talk about it?" she pressed.

"Not tonight," he said, and squeezed her thigh. *And especially not to you,* he thought to himself. Not that he didn't like her. She was the best piece of ass he'd ever had, but she was half his age, and he had no idea to whom or how much she talked. Besides, he was nearing a tipping point in his life. If the casino went through, he could have any broad he wanted. And if it didn't, Adrienne would probably dump him. He'd had six girlfriends since he'd become chief, and each one had been a step up. But if the vote went against him, he'd be lucky if he could find a date.

Once they arrived at the party, Bobby began throwing down shots of Jack Daniels like they were Dr. Peppers. He normally would have regretted it in the morning, but not this time. If he hadn't gone to the bar for a fifth refill he wouldn't have heard a nearby group rehashing how the mob and a college kid had taken Foxwoods for more than a million dollars.

"The kid was supposedly an economics major," Bobby heard someone say.

"Yeah, he was probably just trying to earn a little extra credit," someone else remarked, and everyone chuckled.

"Well, I probably shouldn't say anything," a tipsy brunette confided, "but what makes the whole thing even more incredible is that a couple years ago the boy's father got ripped off by a woman who embezzled a million dollars from him and lost it all at Foxwoods. The story's never come out, but the father wound up losing his business."

"I gotta tell ya," another added, "the stories coming out of that place just keep getting wilder. I heard one the other day about this surgeon who...."

Bobby, who'd never heard about the embezzlement, almost spilled his drink. He waited for the group to break up, then approached the woman who had mentioned it. It turned out she had worked for the Williams Agency as a temp following the embezzlement and had learned what had happened. She proved to be even more into her cups than Bobby was, and within ten minutes she had told him everything she knew.

⌒

Bobby had assumed Williams had made a bundle on the sale of his agency and, despite the problem with his son, was at least riding high financially. But now it appeared that Williams may have lost his shirt in an embezzlement. If that were true, it might finally provide a way to get to him. This time, however, Bobby was determined to involve Grimaldi and Ivy rather than try to deal with Williams on his own. The last time he'd done that, Josh had thrown him out of his office, and if he had ever publicly accused Bobby of trying to bribe him, it could've gotten ugly.

Bobby reached Grimaldi at home the next morning, and within two days Ivy's sources confirmed what Bobby had heard. Williams' Norwich office manager had embezzled over a million dollars and Josh had lost all his equity in the insurance agency. Furthermore, Josh and his wife owed more on the farm than it was currently worth, Sharon Williams had maxed out on her two credit cards, and the family had apparently run through all their savings.

Ivy seized on the opportunity immediately.

"Looks like they're barely scrapin' by," he told Bobby over the phone.

"Here's what I want you to do, Chief. Call Williams and offer 'im a million and a half for the farm. Tell him the tribe needs it for housing and needs to close in the next ninety days. If he accepts, it'll look like he's bailing on the anti-casino people because he thinks it's a lost cause. And if he doesn't accept, nothing's lost. If the story gets out, it's an honest, straight-up offer that makes us look confident we're gonna win."

"And what if he accepts, and we lose the referendum?" Bobby asked.

"Don't worry about it," Ivy said. "If the casino goes away, the residential market will come back, and I'll flip it. Give 'im a call this afternoon."

Josh thought twice about taking Bobby's call, but his curiosity got the best of him and he told his secretary to go ahead and put him on the line.

"Hello, Bobby," Josh said coldly. "What can I do for you today? Got another offer for me?"

Bobby ignored the provocation and got right to the point.

"As a matter of fact, the tribe *would* like to make you an offer, Josh. We're lookin' for a piece of land near the reservation, and we're prepared to offer you a million five for your farm."

There were several seconds of silence. Bobby could imagine Josh weighing a response. *Not so arrogant anymore, are we?* Bobby thought.

"You want to run that past me again?" Josh finally replied, his tone noticeably changed.

"Sure," Bobby said, smiling at the sudden transformation. "We're interested in buyin' a tract of land near the reservation where we can build houses for our members, and the tribal council has authorized me to offer you a million and a half dollars for the farm if we can close by the end of June."

"And this is serious?" Josh asked.

"Dead serious," Bobby replied. "We're prepared to give you a written offer tomorrow if you're interested . . . plus a five-hundred-thousand-dollar deposit to show our good faith."

"Look," Josh said, "I'm afraid you've caught me at a bad time. I've got three people waiting for me and another meeting after that. Why don't you call me back in about an hour and a half, and we can discuss this some more."

"Fine," Bobby said. "I'll call you at four-thirty."

The guy's stallin' for time, Bobby thought as he put down the phone. *But I definitely got a hook in 'im. Now I've gotta play 'im.*

⌐⌐

Josh removed his reading glasses and sat at his desk massaging his eyes. There were no meetings. He simply needed time to think. The tribe had obviously learned about his financial predicament, and they were making one last effort to get him out of the way before the vote. The problem was, it was so tempting. It would solve so much. A million and a half dollars would get him out of his mortgage and leave him with a couple hundred thousand to start over somewhere. He and Sharon could walk away from the entire incredible mess. But it was basically just another bribe, and to accept it would be the ultimate act of betrayal—of the town, of his friends, and of everything that made him who he was.

Josh stared absently at the wall, gradually realizing he was looking at an ancient map of the town he had found at the farmhouse and framed for his office. His gaze then fell to his desk and a photo of Sharon and the kids. He felt light-headed, almost disembodied, as though he were literally being pulled between the present and the past.

He shook off the feeling, forced himself to get up, and paced the floor, going over the offer again and again until he finally went back to his desk and stood by the phone. There was no point agonizing over it any longer. There was no way he could accept the offer. Not now, when it looked more and more like he might be able to stop the casino. He didn't care how much they offered him.

Josh picked up the phone and dialed Bobby's number, upset with himself for letting Bobby think for even a minute that he might sell.

Bobby answered on the second ring.

"Josh!" Bobby said, surprised to hear his voice. "I was gonna call you at four-thirty."

"I know," Josh said, "but I got through early and wanted to save you the trouble. The answer is no," he said firmly and hung up.

Bobby listened to the line go dead, then slammed the phone down in frustration.

⌐⌐

Infuriated by Bobby's second attempt to bribe him, Josh went to Jim Clark's office the next morning and asked if Clark were still interested in having him manage the campaign against the casino in the referendum. Clark had been urging him to take the position for almost a month now but had given up because Josh was already so stretched between his job, the farm, the Casino Task Force, and CAC.

Clark consequently lit up like a Christmas tree when Josh asked the question. "Absolutely," he said. "Just tell me what you need and you got it."

Josh smiled at the older man. "How can you say that? You don't know what I'm going to ask for."

"Try me," Clark said confidently.

"Okay. What I need is for you to let me resign from the task force and let me use CAC to run the campaign."

Clark raised one bushy white eyebrow. "I understand why you want to use CAC, but why do you have to resign from the task force?

"See," Josh said. "I warned you not to commit before you knew what you were committing to."

"Look," Clark said, "I'm not objectin', I'm just askin' why you think you have to resign. Is it because of Fuller?"

"To some extent," Josh replied, "but why don't I take you through the whole thing?"

"Good idea," Clark said, leaning back in his chair.

"You and I both know the tribe is going to come at us with everything it's got," Josh began. "They're going to make the town some kind of unprecedented offer—could be as much as five or six million dollars a year—to try to get people to go along with the casino. Then for the next six or seven weeks they're going to mount an all-out campaign to win fifty point one percent of the vote. I can't even guess what they'll spend, but I guarantee it'll be at least a hundred times what anybody's ever spent per vote in the history of Connecticut."

"You know what I spent to get reelected last year?" Clark interjected. "Six hundred twelve dollars."

"Yeah, but you don't even campaign anymore," Josh said with a little chuckle. "The tribe'll probably pay their top PR guy that much an hour."

"If we're going to compete against that kind of money," Josh continued, "I'm going to need two things: the ability to move fast without having to clear everything with a bunch of other people and confidence that our plans aren't being leaked to the other side. CAC gives me both those things, but the task force is a problem on both scores. It's a public committee I can't control and one of its members is probably already leaking everything we say to the tribe."

Clark grimaced. "You really think Fuller's gone that far?"

It was a delicate subject, because Clark and Fuller had been politically inseparable ever since they started running together, and Josh knew Clark had taken it hard when Fuller split with him on the casino back in January. Fuller hadn't publicly come out for the casino yet, but Josh was certain it was just a matter of time.

"I can't prove it" Josh replied, "but he's done such a sharp U-turn recently that it's obvious something's happened. I know he's your friend, but at the very least we'd be foolish to trust him with any information that could hurt us."

Clark thought about it for a moment, then let out a deep breath. "Okay," he said, "I can't argue with that."

"What about CAC?" Clark asked, shifting away from Fuller. "You see any negatives in my turnin' the campaign over to you guys?"

"I'm sure you'll get a complaint of two," Josh said, "but other than that, I think it's all pluses. CAC's a volunteer group open to anybody, but I've got an executive committee I can trust to keep the sensitive stuff quiet. I've got to do a little reorganizing for the campaign, but even as it is CAC's the best weapon the town's got."

Clark nodded. "Okay, so far I'm on board. You got any other requirements?"

"Just one," Josh said.

Clark waited.

"You've got to promise you'll work side by side with me on this. I don't care if we have to talk ten times a day. There's nothing I want to do more than bury the casino, but I can't run the campaign alone."

Clark smiled and pushed himself up out of his chair. "Deal," he said, reaching out to shake Josh's hand. He'd always liked Josh. But he especially liked seeing him this fired up.

⌇

Josh resigned from the Casino Task Force the next day and immediately began revamping CAC in an effort to transform it from a loose group of volunteers into a streamlined campaign organization. He and CAC's vice president, Carol Zajak, began by going over every name on their membership list, then assigning individuals to specific groups responsible for developing strategy, preparing literature, writing letters to the editor, scheduling speakers, and recruiting door-to-door campaign teams. By mid-April, they had selected captains for each group, and Josh had become cautiously optimistic they should be able to win the referendum almost no matter what offer the tribe made.

Then Rick Pugliese came up with a new piece of intelligence that, if used right, promised to further bolster the town's chances.

Pugliese passed the information on in a three-way conference call with Josh and Jim Clark on April 21.

"You ever heard of a guy named Paul Ivy?" he asked.

"No," Clark and Josh both replied.

"Who is he?" Josh asked.

"He's a billionaire real estate developer from Miami," Pugliese said. "Really big-time. Sixty-third-richest man in America, according to *Forbes*. He's got shopping malls and office parks up and down the East Coast, plus a half-dozen casinos in the Caribbean and two more he's building with Indian tribes in California.

"He's also one of the biggest political contributors in the country," Pugliese continued. "He's supposedly very circumspect but is on a first-name basis with half the committee chairmen on the Hill and was one of the first guests Clinton invited to sleep in the Lincoln Bedroom."

"And?" Clark asked, impatient for the punch line.

"And according to what I just learned from a friend over at Interior this morning, he's the main investor behind the Northern Pequots."

"Since when?" Josh asked incredulously.

"Apparently since the beginning," Pugliese replied, "so it looks like he's gone out of his way to hide it."

"Why?" Clark asked.

"That's the question," Pugliese said. "Ivy evidently shuns publicity like the plague, so that may be the only reason. But it also appears he's very controversial with people who've dealt with him, and that the environmentalists in particular hate his guts.

"So what I'm assuming is he's also stayed in the shadows because he's afraid his reputation could further stir up the town against the casino."

"Either way, he's got to be the reason the tribe's been getting such favorable treatment in Washington," Josh said.

"No question," Pugliese agreed.

"I can't believe we never knew about him," Josh said. "The only investor's name I ever heard was Grimaldi's. Isn't there any requirement that tribes divulge their investors' names?"

"Not until a tribe's officially recognized and the investor has a casino deal with the tribe," Pugliese said. "I'm assuming Ivy's had a deal with the tribe for years or he never would have invested the kind of money he has—which means once the tribe's officially recognized, they have no choice but to acknowledge his involvement. I'm also assuming he never expected to have to reveal his role until the casino was a done deal or he would have disclosed his involvement the same time Grimaldi disclosed his. Now Ivy's stuck with having to go public just before the referendum, when it can hurt the casino the most."

"This actually cuts both ways," Josh said thoughtfully. "On one hand, it means the tribe's got a lot more money behind it than we ever imagined. But on the other, you're right. If Ivy's reputation is bad enough and we can make the case that the tribe's been hiding him, it could give us a huge boost going into the referendum."

"Exactly," Pugliese replied.

"So how do you think we should handle it?" Josh asked.

"Well, first I want to fax you an article we've dug up on him," Pugliese said. "It's a little dated, but it goes into a project in Georgia that he took a lot of flak on, and I was hoping, Josh, that you might be able to call one or two of the people quoted in the story to get a little better read on what actually happened there.

"I could do it," Pugliese said, "but they might be a little more open with you than with a Washington lawyer. We'll continue to look into the guy on our end, and then we can compare notes. The goal is to control the way the town learns about Ivy and to let people know there's a reason he's tried to stay invisible."

꩜

According to the article, Ivy was a former Miami home builder who had originally hit it big buying and developing large tracts of land bordering the Florida Everglades.

Admirers called Ivy a "ferocious competitor" who didn't hesitate to take on opponents seeking to block his projects, but critics saw it differently, describing him as "predatory" and charging him with "callous disregard" for the impact of his projects on the communities where he built. The classic example was Ivy's attempt to build a 1.5-million-square-foot mall on a site near Kennesaw Mountain, Georgia, where Confederate and Union forces had clashed during Sherman's march on Atlanta. Confederate troops had held the ground for two days against overwhelming odds, and it was believed there were unmarked Confederate and Union graves nearby.

In 1986 Ivy's firm, Diversified Construction, won approval to build a golf course, homes, and a community shopping center on the site. The original plans called for blending the project with the environment and protecting key areas of the battlefield, but three months later Diversified announced it had decided to alter the plans by including a massive regional shopping mall.

Area residents immediately cried foul, but Ivy's company insisted that the original approval, which gave permission for mixed-use development, gave it leeway to alter the project, and the company threatened to sue the county if it didn't let the revised project proceed. County officials began to buckle, and it appeared for several months that the expanded project would go forward. Before it could, a seventy-eight-year-old former army sergeant named Millard Malloy put together a coalition of environmentalists, preservationists, Civil War buffs, and ordinary citizens to fight it, and once their campaign began to draw national attention, Ivy backed off. It was apparently the only time in Ivy's career, the article said, that he had been stopped from developing land he'd acquired.

Malloy might have died in the meantime, so Josh was heartened when he found the now ninety-year-old veteran in a Marietta, Georgia, retirement home. The moment Malloy heard Ivy's name, Josh couldn't have stopped the old sergeant if he'd tried.

Malloy took Josh through the entire story—battle by battle as Sherman advanced on Atlanta, and maneuver after maneuver once Ivy came into the picture. Ivy had tried to remain out of the public eye the entire time, using his lawyers, PR people, and company executives as shields, but the coalition had dragged him into the spotlight, characterizing him as a greedy predator who cared nothing about the battlefield or the men who'd died there.

"Even then," Malloy said, "the man pulled so many political strings he almost got away with it. But in the end, we figure he simply couldn't take the continuing hit to his reputation and risk scaring off his political friends."

Malloy promised to send Josh copies of key newspaper clippings about the fight against Ivy and even volunteered to come up to Sheffield at his own expense and address a town meeting about what Sheffield was in for if Ivy were involved.

"I'll tell you right now, son," the old man said, "you can't believe a thing that lying son of a bitch says. If he thinks he can make a buck, he'll pave over your entire town."

⤶

Josh spent the better part of two evenings going through the newspaper articles Malloy expressed up to Sheffield. It appeared the old man had copied every story ever published on the Kennesaw Mountain project, and Josh carefully read every one, trying to glean everything he possibly could about Ivy and the way he operated. He then sat down in the quiet of his library to take stock of the billionaire and the town's chances of stopping him.

Josh was confident Ivy's record in Georgia and the secrecy surrounding his role with the Northerns would hurt the tribe in the coming referendum, but he was also extremely wary of the man. Ivy was clearly an extremely shrewd opponent with enough money to surprise the town with a much more seductive offer than anyone anticipated.

Josh had no idea how much Ivy had invested in the Northern Pequots to date, but it had to be millions, and in the meantime Connecticut's gambling market and the financial opportunity it represented had done nothing but grow.

Americans, it was forecast, would wager more than $630 billion on legalized gambling in 1998, including slot machines, table games, lotteries, bingo, and video poker, compared with $17 billion in 1974. And nowhere, it seemed, was gambling on a bigger roll than in Connecticut.

Moreover, Josh was now convinced that Ivy, supported by his lawyers, political friends, and lobbyists, had the federal government in his pocket. If he hadn't been convinced before that government officials were being bought off, the developing scandal involving the Chippewa Indians proved it.

According to press reports, the White House was being accused of using its political influence to block the construction of a casino by three poor Chippewa tribes in Wisconsin in order to protect the gaming operations of several wealthy tribes in the area. The wealthy Indians had contributed heavily to the Democratic National Committee to help reelect President Clinton in 1996, and many newspapers had called for an investigation into whether Secretary of the Interior Bruce Babbitt had improperly intervened on their behalf and then lied about the White House's involvement. The issue had mushroomed to the point where Attorney General Janet Reno had asked for an independent prosecutor to investigate the affair.

With so much Indian gambling money sloshing around Washington, Josh was certain the Chippewa situation was just the tip of the iceberg. It would be a miracle, he thought, if Sheffield could beat back all the financial and political interests now arrayed against it.

33

The Proposal

June 8–18, 1998

With no appeals forthcoming, the BIA's recognition of the Northern Pequots became official on Monday, June 8, 1998, and the tribe immediately announced it would hold a public meeting the following Friday evening to unveil its casino plans. Rick Pugliese predicted the tribe would also use the occasion to introduce Ivy, because now that the tribe was formally recognized and about to negotiate a casino compact with the state of Connecticut, its biggest investor would have no choice but to come out of the closet. Once again, the Washington attorney was right on the money.

The tribe's public relations team rented the regional high school's gym to accommodate the expected crowd, bringing in hundreds of folding chairs and setting up a sophisticated image-magnification system that projected the speaker and his presentation onto a giant screen.

More than six hundred mostly hostile townspeople had filled the place by the time Bobby mounted the makeshift podium and his oversize likeness flashed on the screen. Josh sat between Sharon and Carol Zajak about six rows back, while Pugliese, who'd flown up that afternoon, sat nearby with First Selectman Clark.

Bobby began by introducing himself and the eight individuals who sat in a row facing the audience: the five-member tribal council, the project's chief architect, Mr. Richard Sayo, and the tribe's two financial partners, Mr. James Grimaldi of New York City and Mr. Paul Ivy of Miami. Each of the eight stood as he or she was introduced, with Ivy standing and acknowledging the crowd last.

So here at last was the infamous Paul Ivy, Josh thought, studying the broad-shouldered man with the bullet-shaped head. Ivy was tastefully dressed in a blazer and tie, and Josh was surprised at how young and agile he looked for his age. When Ivy sat down, he crossed his legs and looked back at the audience with a warm, friendly smile, as though he were Mr. Clean come to help with the housework. *You phony son of a bitch*, Josh thought, *you may beat me, but everybody in this room is at least going to know who you really are.*

Bobby finished the introductions, looked into the camera, and then raised both arms high in the air and declared enthusiastically: "Bo zho nikanek!" which, he explained proudly, meant "Hello, my friends!" in the Algonquin language. "This is the language my ancestors used here in southeastern Connecticut hundreds of years ago," he said, "and I am truly honored to greet you with their words tonight."

There was a scattering of polite applause, and then Bobby launched into his presentation, acknowledging that there was some understandable skepticism about building a casino in Sheffield, but expressing the hope that the town would give the proposed project a fair hearing and that the town's residents would ultimately become as enthusiastic about it as he was.

"As you've probably read," he said, looking out over the sea of faces, "our tribe began negotiatin' a gaming pact with the state on Tuesday, but the fact is we've been plannin' the casino for more than two years now. We've gone to great lengths to design a facility the town can be proud of, and we're delighted to finally be able to show it to you."

The architect joined Bobby. Wielding laser pointers, they took the audience through the plans for The Nautilus, beginning with a slide of the reservation as it was today, then drawing an audible gasp with a color rendering of the proposed white resort set against the deep blue waters of Jepson Lake.

The architect introduced the crowd to the two-thousand-room hotel, Bobby covered the ballroom, and they used a mix of models, sketches, and computer-aided walk-throughs to show the five casinos, the indoor marina, and the clubs, spas, restaurants, and lounges. In a brief video interview the project's chief environmentalist spoke of the great pains being taken to preserve the natural beauty of the area, and the presentation then turned to the five-thousand-seat concert hall, including video footage of some of the famous entertainers who could be expected to play there.

The audience appeared overwhelmed. Even Josh was unprepared for the size and scope of the project.

"Can you believe this?" Sharon whispered in Josh's ear. All he could do was shake his head.

"We estimate," Bobby stated, bringing up a new slide containing three bold bullet points, "that The Nautilus will cost one point three billion dollars, will create ten thousand permanent jobs, and will provide the state treasury with more than a hundred million dollars in slots revenue in its first full year of operation.

"The only obstacle to movin' forward," Bobby continued, "is the fact that other than Cedar Road, there is currently no way to get from the state highway to the reservation. But this problem is easily solved."

With another press of a button, Bobby brought up a multicolored map showing the reservation, Cedar Road, and the Standish farm, which the tribe now owned.

"Now that the tribe's been officially recognized," he continued, "we've applied to the Bureau of Indian Affairs to take the Standish farm into federal trust. As you can see from the map, that will allow us to extend the reservation to the highway. We have no doubt the application will be approved, but at the same time we recognize that the town could conceivably delay its approval and thereby delay the project.

"We don't want to risk delay," Bobby said firmly, "because as the old adage goes, 'Time is money.'

"We're therefore prepared to invite the town to share in our good fortune if it will support our land-into-trust application."

Sheffield's budget for the upcoming year, Bobby pointed out, projecting another slide onto the screen, totaled $12.4 million and was expected to increase to $13.5 million in the year 2000.

"Except for about a million dollars in state aid," he explained, "almost all of that money will have to come from local property taxes, meanin' that Sheffield can expect a property tax bill of approximately twelve and a half million dollars for fiscal year 2000. But if you'll work with us on the Standish farm, we're prepared to offer you enough new revenue to eliminate the town's property taxes completely."

A total hush fell over the audience. Connecticut's property taxes were the third highest in the nation.

"Let me be specific," Bobby continued, relishing the feeling of having the people who had once dismissed him so lightly now hanging on his every word.

"If we can come to an agreement, the tribe will pay every cent of the town's property taxes the first year the casino is in business. Right now, we project that to be between thirteen and fourteen million dollars. We'll then figure what percentage that represents of the casino's first-year slots revenues, and we'll pay the town the same percentage every year for as long as we're in business.

"That would mean that Sheffield and the tribe would become true partners, since Sheffield's revenue would rise, or fall, with the success of the casino's slots operations.

"Assumin' the casino is successful," Bobby declared, flashing a final slide on the screen, "the town could look forward to at least a hundred fifty million dollars from the casino over the first ten years alone, and probably a lot more.

"As a result," Bobby concluded with a flourish, "Sheffield would become the only town in the state with no property taxes—which would not only save most of you thousands of dollars every year but should significantly raise your property values as well."

The hall erupted in a Babel of competing conversations, as people reacted to the astonishing offer. Bobby waited patiently, then pleaded for order. He and the architect, he announced, would now be happy to take questions.

Hands immediately shot up all around the gym, and tribe members took mobile microphones to each questioner.

"Why is it necessary to build a project that chews up and paves over so much land?" an attractive, fortyish woman wanted to know.

The yacht club theme, the architect explained, required a relatively low structure. The last thing the tribe wanted to do, he added, was to build a tall tower that would mar the rural landscape.

"What about traffic, crime, and social problems?" a frail older woman asked.

The tribe believed the complex's location on the edge of town and the fact that most traffic would come up from I-95 would keep traffic problems to a minimum, Bobby replied. The Nautilus would have a state-of-the-art security program designed to keep undesirables away. And the Northerns would be leaders in contributing to the Council on Problem Gambling and other social programs.

"What about the unlucky homeowners at Deer Run?" a man demanded angrily. He was an executive at Pfizer and had one of the most expensive homes in the subdivision.

The tribe was prepared to buy their homes at fair market value, Bobby answered, and would welcome the opportunity to do so, since the land they were living on was part of the reservation until it was illegally taken from the tribe in the 1800s.

Josh rose, and one of the Northerns came over with a microphone. "This is the first we've heard about Mr. Ivy," Josh stated. "Can you tell us when he became an investor and what his background is?"

Bobby had been waiting for the question, and he listened carefully to exactly how Josh phrased it. Grimaldi had told Bobby about Ivy's Kennesaw Mountain fiasco after the three of them had begun working together, but none of them had ever expected to have to reveal Ivy's involvement with the Northerns until after the casino was in the bag.

"I'd be happy to answer your question, Mr. Williams," Bobby said, acknowledging the casino's most outspoken foe by name. "As you know, Jim Grimaldi was the tribe's first investor when we announced our intention to seek federal recognition back in 1993. We . . . that is, Jim and I . . . then asked Mr. Ivy to come in as a second investor when it became clear the project we were planning had the potential to become larger than we first envisioned. Mr. Ivy is a major international real estate developer whose portfolio includes casinos in California and the Caribbean, and we believe he and Mr. Grimaldi give us a truly outstanding development team. We have resumes of both men up here for anyone who'd like them after the meeting."

It was a slick reply that didn't specifically answer how long Ivy'd been behind the tribe, but that was okay with Josh. Bobby's unwillingness to give a date and repeated references to Grimaldi confirmed just how eager he was to keep the spotlight off Ivy. To press Bobby further on Ivy risked suggesting that CAC already knew who Ivy was, and that was the last thing Josh wanted. It was better to let Bobby think he'd dodged a bullet for the moment.

"How soon could you start construction if you got the town's cooperation?" a heavyset man who owned a plumbing business asked.

"If the town approves the casino," Bobby replied, "our goal is to begin site work in September and open the casino by January 2001."

To facilitate the town's reaching a decision, Bobby continued, the tribe was asking that Sheffield hold a special referendum the week of July 20. That would provide a six-week period for a thorough discussion of the proposal and give every voter in town an opportunity to help decide the matter.

A tall, crusty old dairy farmer who was a fixture at Sheffield town meetings asked the next question. He was dressed in a T-shirt and coveralls, and stood as erect as a Marine. "What if we don't accept your offer?" he asked in a clipped Yankee twang.

"We hope that won't happen," Bobby replied, "but if it does, we'll be forced to withdraw the offer and proceed on our own. It could mean a delay in getting started, but in the end we believe the biggest effect would be to cost Sheffield hundreds of millions of dollars."

There was a break in the questions as the audience considered that sobering thought, and Bobby used it to bring the session to a close. He announced that the tribe would be mailing details of the proposal to every home and business in Sheffield, and he invited anyone with questions to call him personally at the reservation. His phone number, he said, would be on the mailer.

Josh and Carol Zajak stayed afterward to mix with the crowd and try to get a better feel for its reaction. It didn't take long. Josh had to overhear only a few conversations to know the tribe had achieved everything it could have hoped for in terms of getting people to begin thinking of the casino in a new light.

"What's your gut feel?" Carol asked as they left the building.

"My gut feel?" Josh said. "My gut feel is that we're in for a war, and they just won the opening battle."

⌒

The tribe's spectacular offer was the lead news story in the state on Saturday morning, and when Sheffield's residents checked their mailbox later that day they found a glossy, four-color brochure describing The Nautilus and detailing the once-in-a-lifetime proposal.

Based on the news accounts, moreover, it appeared that Josh's assessment of the proposal's impact was dead-on. One newspaper did a random poll of people filing into the meeting Friday night, and found that 80 percent were opposed to the casino, 13 percent were in favor, and 7 percent were undecided. In a second random poll done as people left, only 52 percent said they were opposed to the proposal they had just heard, 16 percent said they were in favor, and a whopping 32 percent said they were undecided and needed more time to think about it.

Jim Clark announced first thing Saturday morning that he would call a special meeting of the Board of Selectmen for Monday, where he'd propose a town referendum for Tuesday, July 21, to vote on the tribe's offer. That would give both sides exactly six weeks to campaign.

Then Josh called several reporters to tip them off about Ivy's background and raise the question of why the tribe had kept his involvement in the casino secret. He said it appeared the tribe had kept Ivy under wraps for more than five years, and if they dug into in the aborted Kennesaw Mountain project in Georgia, they'd understand why. Afterward he worked with Carol Zajak to put the finishing touches on a statement CAC planned to release that afternoon and to distribute door-to-door on Sunday.

The statement hit back hard at the tribe's proposal and urged its defeat.

The Nautilus, CAC declared, would change Sheffield forever, beginning by attracting thousands of cars and buses each day, overwhelming its schools and other services, and destroying its rural New England character.

As it did so, the statement warned, it would:

- prey on the most vulnerable people in our community, including pathological and problem gamblers, the poor, and the retired

- entice our youth to gamble

- contribute to divorces, broken families, and child neglect

- spread debt and bankruptcy

- increase suicides

- add to the number of drunk drivers

- attract criminals and shady operators to a town that doesn't even have its own police force

"Here are just a few statistics to think about when deciding whether to invite The Nautilus into Sheffield," the statement continued.

- The casino business is based on constantly encouraging people to gamble and keeping up to ten percent of what they bet.

- Casinos lead to eventual social costs of two-to-six dollars for each dollar of direct benefits.

- Seventy percent of casino profits come from increasingly addictive slot machines.

- Suicide rates in Reno, Las Vegas, and Atlantic City are up to four times higher than in cities of the same size where casinos are illegal.

- Pathological and problem gambling doubles within fifty miles of a casino.

- Calls to Connecticut's Problem Gambling Hotline are soaring, having risen by seventy-six percent last year alone.

"When," CAC asked, "are we going to stop the spread of gambling across southeastern Connecticut?

"Who is going to say no to predators like Paul Ivy, who hid his involvement in the casino as long as he could; who is reviled by the nation's environmentalists and preservationists; and who once tried to turn a hallowed Civil War battleground into a giant shopping mall?

"How is this so-called 'businessman' really any different from the drug lords who ship their products into our communities and then sit back to collect their profits while those communities wrestle with the consequences?

"Sheffield," the statement read, "is one of the oldest and most pristine towns in America. How could anyone who cared for this beautiful little town propose to deposit this monstrosity in our midst?

"The answer is obvious. Mr. Ivy couldn't care less about what happens to Sheffield. And he thinks so little of us that he believes he can buy us by offering to pay our property taxes.

"We urge you to tell Mr. Ivy that he's wrong. We urge you to tell him that Sheffield is not for sale."

⌐

The newspapers gave CAC's statement a good ride Sunday morning, and for the next several days the media jumped all over the Ivy story.

They had a field day with the real estate and casino mogul, noting he was one of the richest men in America, was a friend of the President and powerful Congressmen, and had slept in the Lincoln Bedroom despite the fact that he had tried to rip up the graves of Union and Confederate soldiers in order to build a shopping mall. "No wonder the billionaire tried to hide," one of the state's largest papers editorialized.

One reporter even flew to Georgia to interview Millard Malloy and other participants in the battlefield saga.

"Ivy is the most deceitful son of a ##### you'll ever meet," the old veteran told the reporter. "If he'd had his way, a piece of the South's and America's history would be gone forever. That's why we called him 'Poison Ivy.'

"If Connecticut's smart," Malloy concluded, "it'll throw him out on his ear just like we did down here in Georgia."

CAC was gleeful over the stories, and casino opponents began referring to Ivy by his Georgia nickname.

The tribe's PR team initially ignored the attacks on Ivy out of fear any response would only fuel the fire, and instead concentrated their guns on what they termed CAC's "knee-jerk rejection" of the tribe's offer.

"It is obvious," the tribe said in a statement released for Tuesday morning's papers, "that CAC is so biased against the tribe that it had already made up its mind about the proposal without even considering it."

The tribe was confident, the release stated, that townspeople would make their own decision based on the facts, and it was greatly encouraged by the random newspaper polls taken at the meeting on Friday showing that many people formerly opposed to the casino were now willing to consider it.

In addition, the release said, the tribe was pleased to report the results of a scientific poll of Sheffield voters conducted over the weekend. According to the poll, which was carried out by a leading Washington research firm, 18 percent of respondents supported the tribe's proposal, while 33 percent were now undecided. That meant, the release pointed out, that 51 percent of the town's residents either favored or were willing to consider the offer, while only 49 percent were opposed.

"The tribe is certain," the statement concluded, "that more and more of the undecideds will become supporters as they come to recognize the enormous benefits of partnering with the tribe in this exciting venture."

By Wednesday, however, Bobby and the PR people were so concerned about the continuing negative publicity about Ivy that they felt there was no choice but for the tribe to issue a new press release addressing the issue.

"We are saddened," the release stated, "by CAC's attempts to characterize our proposal as some kind of nefarious scheme concocted by out-of-towners.

"We have made the proposal together with our partners in good faith. It is part of our desire to share our good fortune with our neighbors if they will only help us realize it.

"Moreover, we especially regret CAC's personal attacks on Mr. Ivy. He is an honorable man, a leading developer, and a successful investor, and we believe the town will come to respect his ability and integrity as it gets to work with him, just as we have."

Josh smiled when he read the tribe's statement on Thursday morning. It was obvious the Ivy revelations were drawing blood. He wanted to call Pugliese and read him the article, but he was going to have to wait until the afternoon. This was the day Matt was scheduled to testify in the Nick Carini casino scam trial, and he and Sharon had set aside the morning to accompany Matt to court.

34

Ultimatum

June 18, 1998

Josh and Sharon had become increasingly concerned about Matt over the past two months.

He had given some early signs of bouncing back from his arrest but had withdrawn again that spring and never really come out of it. He struggled through his last semester at UConn with barely passing grades and came home each weekend, spending most of the time working around the farm by himself and rarely seeing friends. When graduation time arrived, he chose to receive his diploma by mail rather than accept it in person. He finally went back to his old summer job with the town's road crew, but other than that, he showed little interest in anything.

The one thing Matt didn't want to do was to testify in the scam case, and he became visibly upset when Brad Merriweather called unexpectedly on Monday, June 15, to say the State's Attorney had decided he needed him to testify against Nick Carini that coming Thursday. With the exception of Liam Blackwell, who was still unaccounted for, all the dealers and players involved in the scam had now pleaded no contest to their charges, but both Carini and his sidekick, Anthony Palo, had pleaded innocent, and the prosecution was going all out to convict them.

Brad went over Matt's testimony with him for more than an hour Wednesday morning and tried to calm him down, but by that evening Matt was an emotional wreck. Josh and Sharon could hardly get him to speak when they drove him to the courthouse the next morning, and at one point Josh had to pull over on I-95 because Matt thought he was going to be sick. Sharon straightened his tie and brushed back his hair on the courthouse steps, and Josh gave him some last words of encouragement before they went inside to meet Brad.

When Matt was finally called to the stand, the prosecutor had him take the jury through his part in the scam in excruciating detail, including his initial conversations with Liam, his visit to Carini in Providence, how much money he won, his interrogation by Carini and Palo in the restaurant parking lot, and where he met Carini to split up the take. The prosecutor even produced a deck of cards and some chips, and asked Matt to demonstrate how he capped a bet.

Then Matt had to endure an intense cross-examination by Carini's lawyer. Nick stared at Matt the entire time, and when Matt and his parents left the courtroom they ran into Tony Palo, who gave Matt a murderous look as they walked past him. Sharon saw Matt start to look back at Palo, but she took his arm and pushed him forward.

Outside, Josh and Sharon and Brad praised Matt for the way he'd handled himself, but Matt appeared shaken and humiliated by the experience and sat silently in the back seat staring out the window all the way home. When they got back to the farm, he went directly to his room, and he didn't come down for dinner.

Josh had to go out that evening for a strategy meeting with CAC, and when he got home he went to the library to finish up some insurance work before going to bed. He'd just sat down at his desk when Sharon came in and closed the door behind her.

It was obvious she'd been crying, but when Josh approached her, she avoided him and sat down on the couch instead. He sat down next to her.

He started to put his arm around her, but she pulled away and turned to look at him, her beautiful green eyes now bloodshot and tense.

"Josh," she began, "do you remember what you said to me that last night in the Keys...that you'd never let sentiment or the past keep us in Sheffield if it came time to go?"

"Yes," Josh said. "And I meant it."

"I hope so," she said. "Because after this morning, it's time to go."

"Look, I know how much the trial....," he started to say, but she cut him off before he could continue. He'd never seen her so intense.

"This casino situation is destroying us, Josh. First your business, then killing ourselves to hang on to the farm—and now, Matt. My God, did you see how that Nick stared at him the whole time, and the look on that other gangster's face when we passed him? How do we know what they might do to Matt for testifying against them?"

She wrung her hands and shook her head. "We've already waited too long to go, and you know it," she said accusingly.

"You're right," Josh acknowledged, trying to placate her. "I beat myself up every day for dragging you and the kids into this and not getting out when we could. But you know leaving's not that simple anymore. Every cent we've got is tied up in the farm, and nobody's going to buy it until the casino situation's resolved."

As he said it, however, Josh realized immediately that that wasn't true. Bobby Kingman had offered to buy the farm two months ago.

But that was different, he told himself. The tribe had tried to buy the farm in order to get him out of the way and increase its chances of winning the referendum. He had pushed the offer entirely out of his mind and never mentioned it to anybody, including Sharon. Now he was getting caught up in a lie.

"And besides," he said, "we can't simply pick up and leave like a bunch of gypsies. We've got to think it through. Where would we go if we left today?"

"I don't know, Josh. Anywhere where there are no casinos. I simply want to go and I want to go now. The farther away the better. We've got to get Matt and the rest of the family out of this place."

"What would we do for money?" Josh asked. "Even if I'm lucky, it could take me months to find a decent job."

"We'll simply start over," she said, as though it were the most obvious thing in the world. "We're not too old. We'll both find something. Matt can support himself. Sarah can take a year off from college. We can rent an apartment. What difference does it make? Whatever we do will be better than staying here and waiting for the next disaster to strike."

"Sweetheart, please, listen to me," Josh said, pleading with both hands. "We'll go. I promise. Just give it another month to see what happens. If we can just win this vote, the whole situation may change. The market may open up again and we'll be able to sell the farm. And even if we lose, who knows, the tribe may buy the farm."

"Josh, you're not listening to me. Whether we win or lose the vote, selling the farm could take another year, two years, five years, who knows? By then Jacob could be in college."

Sharon let out a sigh of frustration.

"I want to go now, Josh," she said, "not in another month or two months or a year. Now!" she repeated, her eyes suddenly flashing with anger. "And frankly, it doesn't make a damn bit of difference to me anymore whether the tribe builds their casino or not. We've already got the two biggest casinos in the world practically next door, and you can see what they've done to us!"

"Sharon, please be practical," Josh pleaded, stunned by her vehemence and filled with guilt over not having discussed Kingman's offer with her. "All I'm asking for is a little more time. We can't just walk away after all these years and turn everything over to them without a fight."

"You see," Sharon screamed, "you're not even thinking about the family. It is about the past. For you, the whole goddamned thing is about the past!"

Josh stared at her, speechless.

Sharon looked away, then finally looked back and nodded, her lips pursed tight. "All right," she said coldly. "I'm willing to stay through the vote, but then I'm leaving. I pray to God you'll come with me, Josh, but if you don't, I'm going by myself, and I'm taking the kids."

⟜

Josh tried his best to make up with Sharon following her ultimatum, but she remained aloof.

She slept in the spare bedroom that night and barely returned his embrace when he went up to her and tried to take her in his arms the next morning. He told her he loved her more than anything in the world and assured her again that they'd leave after the vote no matter what the outcome.

"I love you, too, Josh," she said, "and I want to believe you about leaving. But you're going to have to prove to me you're serious."

Following breakfast, she informed him that she'd be writing letters that morning resigning from the board of education and the Democratic town committee. She showed zero interest at dinner when the conversation turned to the casino and the referendum. And she was already asleep when he got into to bed that night.

Josh closed his eyes and listened to her breathing. Clearly, it was going to be a very difficult next four weeks.

35

~

Spin

June 19–20, 1998

Events were now rushing ahead. Despite the tribe's efforts at damage control, it was clear by Friday, June 19, that the Ivy story wasn't going away, and the PR experts recommended that he come to Sheffield himself for a press conference on Saturday. It was a risk, they acknowledged, but they said it was essential to give people the other side of the story in order to defuse it.

Ivy hesitated. He had always fought hard for whatever he wanted, but for the past thirty years he'd made it a firm rule to stay in the background and let others fight the company's public battles. He was tough, maybe even a bit coarse, as his detractors contended, but he was no fool. Rich real estate developers rarely won much sympathy in a public debate. Moreover, his success relied importantly on his stable of political friends, and they wouldn't remain his friends for long if he became embroiled in public controversies that reflected negatively on them.

Nevertheless, it was clear that the biggest single deal he had ever attempted was on the line, that he was already taking a pounding, and that he was going to have to step in himself if he was going to counter the personal attacks. Reluctantly, he agreed to meet with the press.

~

The tribe had set up a double-wide office trailer as a command post for the six-week campaign, and Bobby and the three full-time PR consultants were waiting when Ivy arrived at the reservation Saturday morning. Ivy was cordial but tense, and he immediately set to work prepping for the 2:00 press conference. For the next two hours, he fielded every question the group could throw at him, then went next door to Bobby's mobile home to be alone and rest.

More than a dozen reporters and TV cameramen crammed the office trailer by 2:00. Bobby sensed they all felt they were attending a billionaire roast and couldn't wait to skewer Ivy in person. *Bastards!* he thought. Ivy could have bought the whole motley crew a thousand times over, but right now he needed them.

Finally Bobby stepped to the makeshift lectern, where he welcomed everyone and introduced Ivy.

"I'm very pleased Mr. Ivy has been able to come up from Miami today to address some of the environmental issues that have been raised in connection with the casino project," Bobby said, as though the afternoon were meant as simply a routine briefing. "Afterward, he's agreed to stay as long as you like to answer questions.

"Mr. Ivy, welcome back to Sheffield," Bobby said, extending his hand. For a moment, the two men stood opposite each other shaking hands—the pony-tailed, formerly broke tribal chief in his trademark buckskin jacket and the bald billionaire in his $4,000 Italian-tailored suit.

Ivy began somewhat formally by thanking the media for its efforts to present both sides of the Nautilus issue.

"I know that protecting the environment is one of the top concerns people have about this project," he continued, "and that's as it should be. Fact is, it's also one of my top concerns, just as it has been in every project I've ever done. Only here, my company and I have to be even more mindful of the environment, because our partner is an Indian tribe. And like all Native Americans, they are particularly sensitive to living in harmony with nature."

Ivy looked over at Bobby to punctuate how seriously he took his obligation to the tribe.

Bobby nodded back his appreciation, but as he did, he noticed two reporters in the rear look at each other and snicker. So far they obviously weren't buying what Ivy was selling.

"Today, therefore," Ivy went on, "I'd like to discuss some of the extraordinary steps we're planning not only to preserve the environment, but to enhance people's ability to enjoy it."

With that, Ivy took his audience through a prepared presentation, pointing out the way in which the planners had made use of the reservation's rugged terrain, how they'd captured spectacular views of the lake, and the efforts they'd made to preserve as much of the woods as possible, including the main stands of cedar. The tribe, he explained, was even planning to create a rhododendron sanctuary accessed by a boardwalk that would enable casino patrons to admire the magnificent wild flowers the area was known for.

Several reporters yawned and others doodled in their notebooks during the presentation, but as soon as Ivy invited questions, hands shot up all over the room.

It was a critical moment for everyone connected with the casino, and for no one more than Bobby Kingman.

Ivy had been the tribe's secret weapon. Bobby estimated he had by now invested more than $13 million in the tribe. He had paid Bobby's and the tribal staff's salaries, underwritten the improvements to the reservation, and funded the tribe's operating expenses. He had paid for the genealogists, the anthropologists, the historians, and the lawyers who had put together the recognition application. He had paid for the architects, designers, engineers, and innumerable other experts who had planned The Nautilus. And who knew what he had spent on the lobbyists, PR specialists, and politicians he was counting on to help push the casino through?

But Bobby had no idea whether Ivy could survive the media, and he held his breath as Ivy took the first question.

Was it true, an aggressive female reporter asked, that Ivy had double-crossed people in Georgia by trying to turn a Civil War battlefield into a shopping mall?

Bobby could see Ivy tense at the words "double-crossed," but Ivy caught himself, managed to smile, and gave a polite, carefully considered answer.

The Kennesaw Mountain project, Ivy said, was probably one of the most misunderstood projects in the history of American real estate.

"The truth of the matter is that that entire corridor between Chattanooga and Atlanta was the scene of battle after battle and skirmish after skirmish during the Civil War," he stated. "I'm a Civil War buff myself, and I know the history. The Confederates tried to block Sherman at every turn and managed to hold 'im up for four months before he finally took Atlanta.

"As a result," Ivy continued, "you can hardly find a piece of land down there that doesn't have some historical interest. Before we bought the site in question, we consequently checked it out thoroughly and found that while there had been a brief skirmish there, it was relatively unimportant historically. Furthermore, it was clear somebody was going to develop the site sooner or later, and I figured they'd be a lot less careful with it than I would be. We therefore went ahead and drew up several options for the site, including one consisting of a residential community and a regional mall. We ultimately picked that one because it enabled us to extract the most value from the land and still protect most of what was left of the old battlefield.

"It was a good plan," Ivy said, "and most of the local officials supported it because we took such pains and it meant jobs and taxes for the county.

"But as so often happens nowadays, a small group of people who didn't appreciate the balance we were trying to strike got together and opposed the project on the grounds it was going to ruin one of greatest historical sites in America. It was ridiculous! I mean, it was as if we were trying to pave over Monticello or the Peach Orchard at Gettysburg. Many of the opponents had never even been to Georgia and had no idea what they were opposing. But the opposition got going and gradually kicked up such a fuss, we decided to abandon the project altogether."

Ivy paused and scanned the room, looking directly into the cameras. "And that's the truth!" he said firmly. "To even suggest I tried to mislead anybody or bend the law is totally inaccurate. Everything I did there was completely legal and ethical. I can give you the names of some of the former county officials who will verify it."

Bobby looked at Ivy almost in awe. Ivy's account barely resembled the one Bobby had heard from Grimaldi or the ones in the papers over the last week. Yet there was just enough truth in it to sound plausible. The man was an absolute spinmaster. And he just kept getting better with each question.

If the situation in Georgia was really what he claimed, why had he hidden his involvement with the Northerns for so long?

He had never tried to hide his involvement from the town, he said, shaking his head as though the very idea was insulting. Why would he? Nothing untoward had happened in Georgia, and what did happen there was a matter of public record. If he had been worried that anything in his background could hurt the Northern Pequots, he would have gotten it out on the table long ago and certainly not waited until just before a referendum. But the fact was, he was only a passive investor in the tribe, and his partner, Jim Grimaldi, had handled almost all the partnership's business with the Northerns until a short time ago. What's more, there was no requirement for an investor to publicize his investment in a tribe until it was federally recognized and the investor had signed a casino agreement with that tribe. "I don't think I've ever made a passive investment public," Ivy said, "but as soon as the Northerns were recognized and the tribe began negotiations with the state, I came to

Sheffield to meet the townspeople and help present the project we're proposing."

Did he think it was unreasonable for Sheffield residents to be suspicious of him after what had happened in Georgia?

Ivy spread his hands. Look, he said, he could certainly understand that some of them might be suspicious after the distorted picture his opponents had painted, but their concern would disappear quickly once they learned the facts and had an opportunity to work with him.

Did he feel any of the animosity toward his old critics that they obviously still felt toward him?

No, he said, he didn't bear grudges. His critics may have gotten a little carried away, but you had to have pretty thick skin to be a developer these days, and fortunately he did.

Did it bother his conscience at all to come in and build one of the biggest casinos in the world in this little, picturesque New England town?

"Sheffield *is* a beautiful town," he said with great empathy, "and I'm committed to do everything possible to preserve its uniqueness. But I want to emphasize I wasn't the one who decided to open up Connecticut to casinos. The courts and the politicians were. My job is to help build the best, most attractive, and most environmentally friendly facility I possibly can for both the tribe and the town."

Did he think that he'd become a liability to the tribe, and that he should possibly withdraw from the project to improve the tribe's chances of winning the referendum?

Ivy thought about that for a moment. "I think," he said, turning toward Bobby, "I should really let the Chief answer that one."

Bobby was so relieved and fired up by Ivy's performance that he wanted to stand up and cheer. Instead he simply rose from his chair and walked slowly back to the lectern, aware that every eye in the place was on him. "All right," he said, looking around the room with a poker face, "are there any other questions about the rhododendrons?"

Everybody laughed, and the tension was broken.

"Look, I understand your interest in this Georgia thing," Bobby said seriously. "It's natural, because it makes for a good story. But I want to say emphatically that we have complete confidence in Paul Ivy.

"He's not only a consummate professional, he's a standup guy. You asked him some pretty brutal questions just now, and he never flinched under fire. That's exactly the kind of guy I'd always hoped to find as a partner.

"Thanks for comin', everybody," Bobby concluded with a cheerful smile. "I hope you'll all stay and have some refreshments."

After the last reporter left, Ivy asked Bobby to take a walk with him, and the two men headed down toward the lake. A breeze blew Ivy's tie over his shoulder and ruffled the fringes on Bobby's jacket as the two men made their way across the meadow.

"I gotta tell ya . . . you were terrific, Paul. All those cocky reporters jammed into that trailer just waiting to nail you, and you stopped 'em cold."

"We'll see," Ivy said. "That ugly broad who asked the first question especially pissed me off. For a minute I wanted to reach out and grab her by her scrawny little neck."

Bobby chuckled. "Yeah, but you know, she really did you a favor. Because it was that first answer that really began to turn things around. By the time you got through, they didn't know what to think."

Ivy shrugged skeptically. Bobby could see he was still seething from the rough questioning, and he sensed Ivy wanted to talk to him about something in private.

"You know, Chief," Ivy said, "I'm concerned about the opposition being better organized than we thought. They've obviously known about me for a while and were just waiting to hit me with this Georgia business at the right moment. And the other thing is that it's clear Clark and Williams don't trust Fuller anymore, because they never breathed a word to him about what they were planning."

"Yeah, I've been thinkin' the same thing about Fuller," Bobby said. "Whadaya think we should do with him?"

"Well, he's no use as a source anymore," Ivy said, "so we might as well have him come out and back the casino publicly. His endorsement could give us a boost right now and could also help take some of the attention off me."

"The only problem with that," Bobby replied, "is that we were hopin' to save him until right before the vote when he'd have the biggest impact."

"I know," Ivy said, "but I've been thinking about how to deal with that, too. What we need is another big name to come out for us a couple of weeks after Fuller—somebody equally or even more influential who hasn't taken a position on the casino yet or maybe's even been against it . . . maybe a doctor everybody loves and respects or the local bank president. It'd be a hell of a one-two punch and give us some real momentum going into the vote.

"You know anybody like that we might talk to?" Ivy asked.

Bobby pondered the question. "No doctors or bankers," he said, "but there is one guy who'd be perfect if we could ever get him. Problem is, he's out of the question."

"Who's that?" Ivy asked, brushing off a wayward leaf that had blown onto his lapel.

"Our state rep, Reid Dowlin'," Bobby said. "Next to Clark, he's probably got the biggest followin' in town and he certainly fits the bill of bein' against the casino. The son of a bitch's been against it from day one."

"You ever approach him on it?"

"Nah," Bobby said, dismissing the idea with a shake of his head. "It'd be pointless. He voted for the Mashantucket casino back in 1991 and took so much heat he's gone overboard to oppose ours in order to make up for it. There's no way he could reverse course now."

"You get along with him otherwise?" Ivy pressed.

"Not especially. Guy's a total hypocrite on the casino, and he's hit me pretty good in the press a couple of times."

"Why'd he back Foxwoods?" Ivy asked.

"He owns a travel agency, and I always assumed he did it because it'd be good for his business. He's a real political junkie, so I can't imagine him riskin' his seat for any other reason."

"But you don't think he'd risk it a second time?"

Bobby stopped and the two men faced each other.

"Jesus, Paul, I know what you're thinkin'. And you're right—if Dowlin' came out for us it'd shake the town to its core. But I can't imagine flippin' the guy."

Ivy held up his hand. "You're probably right," he said, "but why don't you write down everything you know about the man, and then I'll see if I can have one of my people talk to him. This may be exactly what we're looking for."

36

~

The Leather-Bound Book

June 20–23, 1998

It had now been over a year since Gladys Greene resigned as Sheffield's genealogist and she was heavily engaged in other assignments. But the Northern Pequot project was the most frustrating she had ever worked on, and she
couldn't escape the nagging feeling she had missed something about Rachel
Amos that could have resolved the question of whether she possessed Pequot
blood.

The problem was, she simply had run out of places to look.

She had spent endless hours at the History and Genealogy Unit of the
Connecticut State Library in Hartford as well as whole days at the Sheffield
Town Hall, the Sheffield Library, the Sheffield Historical Society, and their
counterparts in adjacent towns. She had examined the Barbour Collection of
Connecticut Vital Records, the Bible and Family Records Index, the Hale
Collection of Connecticut Cemetery Inscriptions, and the Connecticut Pro-
bate Estate Papers Index, all of which went back to the 1600s. She'd gone
through the Connecticut Census Index, old newspaper marriage and death
notices, even passenger lists of ships arriving from Europe. And she'd scoured
the Connecticut Church Records Index, which also extended back to the
1600s, and all the relevant church records in the State Archives that hadn't
been indexed. Yet she hadn't been able to find any reference whatsoever to
Rachel before she showed up on the Northern Pequot Reservation.

It occurred to Gladys several months after leaving the Sheffield project that
the only other thing she might have done was go to the Sheffield Congregational Church and physically examine every document the church had from
the period. She hadn't done that because, like most Congregational churches
in Connecticut, the Sheffield church had sent its early records to the state library for copying and safekeeping, and she had thoroughly examined them
there.

The Sheffield church had a complex history, but it wasn't that different than other Congregational churches Gladys was familiar with. It had been organized in 1659; the first permanent meetinghouse was constructed two years later. The current meetinghouse had been built in 1755 and had served as both a house of worship and the assembly hall for town meetings until 1830. In 1790 thirty-five members withdrew from the church to organize a Congregational church of their own in the Sayerville section of town. The Sayerville church functioned until 1928, when, because of declining membership, it disbanded and reunited with the Sheffield church.

Gladys had been careful to confirm that the Sheffield church had included the Sayerville church's records in the documents it sent to the state library in 1939, and she had been satisfied the library had the originals of all the early documents currently held at the Sheffield church. Indeed, the library's collection appeared especially complete, containing not only membership, meeting, and baptismal records prior to 1900, but even many marriage records, which were often hard to come by because ministers often took them with them from one church assignment to the next.

The only thing that appeared to be missing were the Sayerville church's meeting minutes prior to 1810, but she had assumed that since everything else was intact, those minutes must simply have been lost or inadvertently destroyed along the way.

Nonetheless, she couldn't help wondering in retrospect if she might have missed something by not actually going to the Sheffield church to do an on-site examination. At one point, despite the fact she was no longer employed by the town, she had even considered going back to Sheffield to check out the church on her own. But in the end she decided the last thing she wanted was to re-engage with a project that had ended so traumatically. Besides, she rationalized, the chances of finding the missing minutes and then finding any reference to Rachel in them were so remote as to be practically nonexistent.

Then the Ivy story broke, rekindling all her worst memories of the way the Sheffield project had ended. She followed every twist and turn of the story, and by the time she saw Ivy on TV at his June 20 press conference, she was convinced he had not only bought off the government but had paid the people who'd broken into her car and home.

Gladys was not normally a vindictive woman, but she was consumed the entire weekend with the thought of somehow getting back at Ivy. Unfortunately the only thing she could think of was something she had previously dismissed as the longest of long shots—going back to Sheffield and searching in the one last place where she might conceivably find additional information on Rachel Amos.

On Monday morning, June 22, Gladys called the Sheffield Congregational Church to arrange to go through its records the next day.

Mrs. Greene arrived at the church at 10:00, wearing a long cotton dress and floppy summer hat. She went straight to the church office, where she showed her identification and the church secretary escorted her to a 8-by-6-foot closet that contained all of the church's records back to 1659.

The closet was overflowing with cartons piled on top of one another. The secretary said she was afraid the Sayerville ones were mixed in with the others, so that Mrs. Green was going to have to hunt for what she was looking for. It was amazing, Gladys thought as she began going through the closet, how careless a lot of churches were with their old records, and she cringed at the thought of how many documents may have disappeared from the Sheffield church before the state library began collecting them back in the late 1930s.

She brushed away the cobwebs and dust, and finally found three Sayerville cartons in all. She picked out the one marked 1790–1830 and carried it to a table, prepared to examine every document it contained with a fine-tooth comb.

The Congregational churches had typically kept their most important records in leather-bound volumes, which were eventually delivered to the state library archives along with loose pages and even small slips of paper. The documents were photostated then bound into buckram cotton notebooks. It was standard procedure for the state library to keep the originals and return the buckram notebook copies to the churches.

Gladys opened the carton and noticed a single old leather-bound volume among all the newer buckram notebooks. She could barely believe her eyes. Apparently the old leather volume had never been sent to the library for copying. For all she knew, it might have been misplaced before the rest of the records were sent to the state, then found years later and put back among the photostats. But whatever the reason, there in front of her was a worn leather volume entitled "Church Meetings and Transactions, 1790–1810."

Gladys felt the rush of excitement she always did when her detective work paid off, but she recognized that it was still a million to one against there being anything in the minutes about a poor soul named Rachel Amos.

This time, however, she wasn't to be denied. After more than two years of futility, it took her only fifteen minutes to find what she was looking for. It was contained in a two-page entry midway through the volume. She quickly made several copies of the entry on the office copier, then placed the volume back in the box and returned the boxes to their original locations in the closet. The volume would be safer there, she decided, than if she called attention to it by asking the secretary to store it somewhere more secure. She left the church and half ran to Josh's office, hoping desperately that what she had found could still be of some use.

⁓

Josh hadn't seen Gladys since she resigned from the Sheffield project, and he was surprised when his secretary buzzed him to say Gladys was in the reception area and would like to see him as soon as possible. He recalled how upset she'd been about the break-ins, but if anything, she seemed even more rattled now. She was slightly out of breath when he ushered her into his office, and he noticed that her hand trembled when she sat down and opened her tote bag.

"This is probably too late to do the town any good," she said, taking out a manila file folder, "but I had to let you know immediately. I've finally discovered who Rachel Amos was."

"You're kidding!" Josh said with a look of disbelief.

"I almost wish I were," Gladys said somberly, "because I feel like a fool for not coming up with her identity a long time ago. The information has been sitting right under our noses the whole time."

Gladys explained quickly how she'd gone to the Sheffield Congregational Church that morning and found the information in an old volume of church minutes that had inexplicably never been sent to the state library.

"These are the minutes that concern Rachel," she said, opening the folder and handing Josh one of the copies she'd made. "They're from a meeting at the Sayerville church on June 6, 1799. As you'll see, they lay it all out about as clearly as anyone could ask."

Josh took the copy, put on his glasses, and began to read.

"At a Church meeting held after the Thursday evening lecture," the minutes began, "the subject of Rachel Amos and her sixteen-year-old daughter, Fanny, was discussed."

Rachel Amos, according to the minutes, was the companion of an itinerant tradesman named Luc Fournier who had come down from Canada with

Rachel and her daughter that spring. Fournier had been helping to build a house for a church member named Ezra Sage and had fallen off the roof and died. Sage had asked that the congregation take up a collection for Rachel and her daughter, who were suddenly destitute, and endeavor to place her on the Northern Pequot Reservation as a temporary shelter. The congregation, the minutes reported, agreed to help the poor woman and to seek the assistance of the Northern Pequot chief, who, it was noted, the church had assisted in the past.

Josh's jaw dropped as he read. "So, in other words," he said, looking up at Gladys, "neither Rachel Amos nor any of her descendants were Northern Pequot Indians."

"That's right," Gladys replied. "Neither Bobby Kingman nor any of his relatives have a drop of Pequot blood. The last Pequot descendant to live on the reservation was Louis Jobert, who was killed in the trailer explosion back in 1991.

"And now that Jobert's sister has died," she added, "there's no one in the entire tribe who descended from the original Pequots. These people are no more Pequot than you are."

"God, if we'd only had this earlier," Josh exclaimed.

"I'll never forgive myself, Josh," Gladys said. "I simply missed it. And you're right. It would have changed everything."

"Do you think there's any chance Kingman and Ivy have seen these minutes?" Josh asked.

"No," Gladys replied. "They obviously missed them, too, or they'd have made sure they disappeared."

"Where's the minutes book now?"

"I put it back in the church closet," Gladys said.

"All right, look, I'm going to call the minister to get his permission for us to go over and get it and put it in a safe-deposit box. Then I'm going to call Jim Clark and ask him to come over here so you can go over the whole thing with him, just as you did with me. We may have discovered who Rachel was too late to stop the Northerns from being recognized, but we've sure as hell found out in time to affect some votes!"

37

The New Poll

June 23–July 1, 1998

The consensus among the tribe's PR people was that the Ivy press conference was a home run in terms of rebutting his critics. Not only did it get heavy media coverage, but the tribe followed up the next day with a town-wide mailing containing the full text of Ivy's remarks on the environmental aspects of the project together with a complete set of the maps, renderings, and aerial photographs he used in his presentation.

Two days later, moreover, Sheffield residents woke up to the news that Dwayne Fuller had broken with the rest of the town's leaders to back the casino.

"Major Crack in Casino Opposition," one headline read.

> **Sheffield**–Popular Sheffield Second Selectman Dwayne Fuller stunned residents of this embattled town Wednesday by becoming the first elected official to support the proposed Northern Pequot casino and to call for approval of the tribe's financial offer in the upcoming July 21 referendum.
>
> Fuller's announcement came as a shock because he is a longtime political ally of First Selectman Jim Clark, who, along with CAC president Josh Williams, is leading the opposition to the casino.
>
> Fuller particularly criticized Clark for spending taxpayers' money to oppose the tribe when a growing number of townspeople are for it.

Fuller underscored his break with Clark by formally resigning from the Casino Task Force and then continued his assault on casino opponents in a front-page interview in the *Sheffield Advertiser*.

"I've lived in Sheffield for sixty-four years," Fuller told the paper, "and I've seen the town change so much you can't recognize it anymore.

"I can remember back to right after the war when we had just over a thousand people. Now we got forty-six hundred, and the pace of new people coming in has doubled in the last five years.

"And taxes keep going up, because every time another family moves in it puts new demands on our schools and services.

"As a result, it seems all we do around here now is argue about money. We just finished another battle over the budget, and look at what we've already got on our plate for next year: a new teachers' contract, a new Little League field, and a new emergency communications center, not to mention getting started on the sewers everybody suddenly says we need.

"Where do people think all that money's coming from?

"So once we get by this fantasy about keeping the town the way it was, what I want to know is what's so terrible about the tribe's proposal? It would make us a partner with one of the richest men in America in one of the most profitable businesses in the country.

"Think about it! They're offering to pay us more than enough to wipe out our property taxes and take care of any costs associated with the casino.

"Jim Clark says he's confident the town can block the casino. But what if it can't? The worst thing that could happen is for Sheffield to refuse to work with the tribe and then have the tribe find a way to go ahead without us."

⌒

The Northerns commissioned a second telephone poll on Monday, June 29, which marked the end of the second full week of the campaign. Based on the results, which they kept private, it appeared that they had been able to overcome the Ivy flap, and that the casino proposal had even managed to gain a little ground. Whereas the numbers from two weeks ago had showed 49 percent opposed to 18 percent in favor, with 33 percent undecided, the new poll showed the proposal down 43 percent to 21 percent with an even higher 36 percent undecided.

Bobby was encouraged that they were at least headed in the right direction, but Ivy called from Miami just before midnight on July 1 to express his unhappiness that they hadn't made any progress moving the undecideds into the yes column.

"Why do I get the impression our people are all sitting around on their asses up there?" Ivy barked into the phone. "There's less than four weeks left. We gotta move, Chief!"

"Everybody's workin' eighteen hours a day," Bobby assured him. "Fuller's out beatin' the bushes, and we've got another mailin' goin' out tomorrow. We also heard from the brother of one of the CAC people a couple days ago, and he says CAC's disappointed that the campaign against you has petered out."

"Well, at least that's positive," Ivy said, "but what we need now is some offense!"

"You had any luck settin' up a meeting with the guy we talked about?" Bobby asked, referring to Reid Dowling.

"Yeah," Ivy said. "Someone's meeting with him up in Connecticut tomorrow."

38

~

Bombshell

June 23–July 5, 1998

Jim Clark's first reaction to learning Rachel Amos's identity was that the town should immediately demand the BIA revoke the Northerns' recognition. But when he and Josh phoned Rick Pugliese to tell him about Rachel, Pugliese said the chances of getting the BIA to do that were almost nil.

"No question the Rachel discovery is huge," Pugliese said, "and, yes, it would have presumably blocked the Northerns from being recognized if it were made earlier. But given the way the BIA pushed the tribe's application through, they're not going to reopen this case now short of some enormous uproar in Congress over what happened."

"Why?" Clark asked. "If there's hard evidence that nobody in the tribe is related to the original Northern Pequots, why wouldn't they reopen it?"

"Because they're going to argue that they spent years trying to come up with significant genealogical information on the Northerns prior to 1800, and that when they couldn't, they had no choice but to define the 'historic' Northern tribe as those individuals recorded as living on the reservation in 1800. Based on that logic Bobby Kingman and everybody else descended from those residents qualify as Northern Pequot Indians."

"Yeah," Clark shot back, "except that Rachel Amos was never listed as an Indian in any document and we now know that neither she, her husband, her daughter, nor any of their line had an ounce of Indian blood."

"True," Pugliese said. "But all the BIA knew was that Rachel lived on the reservation, was buried there, and had a daughter who married an Indian and was subsequently identified as an Indian herself in a reservation overseer's report. So the BIA can claim it did the best it could based on the information available, and you can go pound sand."

"Hold on, Rick," Josh interjected, "I understand what you're saying, but even if the BIA refuses to reverse itself, the fact is we've got a bombshell here—proof the government's about to give an Indian casino to non-Indians.

That's a dynamite story that can hopefully turn even some of the casino's supporters against Kingman and Ivy and this whole stinking scam. So I'd argue our strategy should be to play the Rachel story to the hilt—which means demanding the BIA rescind the Northerns' recognition and doing anything else we can to put the story on the front page and keep it there as long as possible."

"Look, don't get me wrong," Pugliese responded. "I agree with the strategy, including demanding a reversal. I just don't want you and Jim getting your hopes up that the BIA's going to cooperate. Although," he added after a momentary pause, "who knows? If we can stir up enough of a storm in Washington, it's not inconceivable Congress could step in."

Josh and Clark spent the next week considering how best to break the Rachel Amos story. They finally decided to drop the bomb on Thursday, July 2, which would give the news a chance to sink in over the Fourth of July weekend. They held a final meeting Wednesday evening in Clark's office, then headed over to the Sheffield Tavern for a drink.

The main dining room was almost empty when they arrived, but the downstairs taproom, with its antique cherry bar and potbellied stove, was still going strong. The taproom offered live music every night, and tonight a banjo player was singing sea chanteys as Clark and Josh headed for a corner table.

"I've always loved this room," Clark said as their drinks arrived. "People always talk about the meetinhouse, but I s'pect more of the town's business got done here in the old days than anywhere else. I don't know if you ever heard of 'im, but we had one first selectman, name of Ward, who apparently held almost all of his monthly selectmen's meetins over here while he was in office."

"You have proof of that, do you?" Josh asked, not sure whether Clark was putting him on.

"You think I'm kiddin'?" Clark said, and motioned Josh to follow him over to a wall where there was a framed page from the tavern's 1765 account book. It read: "Expense for selectmen and Licker, pound 3. 4s."

"They got about twenty of these bills in an old ledger upstairs," Clark said, "and the guy was only in office for two years, so he musta held most of his meetins here. Been tempted to move the meetins here myself, but then I keep thinkin' that's probably why Ward wasn't reelected."

They both laughed and touched glasses, wishing themselves luck the next day.

"The town's been lucky to have you all these years," Josh said, and meant it.

Although doubtful at first that Clark was up to leading the battle against the casino, Josh had gradually become genuinely fond of the older man and had come to regard him as a close friend.

"So tell me, honestly, how do you see the vote going?" Josh asked.

"I don't know, Red," Clark sighed. "I was pretty confident a few weeks ago, but I'm not so sure now."

"I wish we could get a look at the latest polling the tribe's been doing," Josh said.

"Yeah, that'd help," Clark agreed, "but even without a poll, I can tell that things're tightenin' up. You can tell just by the stress level in town. I can't walk down the street without gettin' into an argument with somebody about the casino, and you got whole families split on whether to keep fightin' or throw in with the tribe.

"It's unbelievable," Clark went on. "My wife told me she saw two women get into a shoutin' match over the casino at the A&P the other day. Said it was so bad she thought they were gonna start smackin' each other right there by the pork chops."

"I can believe it," Josh said, imagining the scene.

"The big worry, though," Clark said, "is obviously all these undecideds. I s'pect there's even more of 'em now than when the tribe did its first poll, and the more I talk to people, the more uncertain I am as to how they're gonna break."

"How do you think people are going to react to the Rachel Amos news?" Josh asked.

Clark shrugged. "You'd think they'd feel so duped they'd come out and vote against the casino in droves. But who knows? The problem is that a lot of the people you'd think'd be mannin' the barricades against the casino are mesmerized by the money."

At that point, two construction workers who had been drinking at the bar sauntered over to the table.

"You're Jim Clark, the first selectman, right?" the bigger and apparently drunker of the two asked Clark.

"Right," Clark said, and stood up to shake hands.

"Well, let me tell ya somethin', Clark," the man said. "I'm sick and tired of you usin' my money to block the casino."

"That goes for both of us," the second man chimed in. "When's the town gonna get smart and go with the Indians?" he demanded, leaning into Clark's face.

"Hey, watch yourself, fella!" Josh said, springing up and trying to get between them.

"Nobody's talkin' to you, asshole?" the man said, and tried to push Josh back into his chair.

Josh almost lost his balance but caught himself and shoved back so hard the man fell back against his companion, and both drunks crashed into an empty table and onto the floor.

The bigger man scrambled to his feet first and grabbed a captain's chair that he hurled at Josh. It missed his head by an inch and shattered against the wall. Before the man could pick up another chair, the bartender and two customers came running over to break up the fight, and the bartender, a beefy six-footer dressed in a colonial-era shirt and knickers, grabbed the two drunks by the back of the neck and hustled them out of the tavern.

The whole thing was like a scene from a Western, Josh thought as he smoothed out his shirt and watched them go. He hadn't been in a barroom brawl since he got his nose broken in Saigon more than twenty-five years ago, but even there nobody'd thrown a chair.

"Just a coupla boys who drank too much," Clark said, seemingly unfazed. "Kinda underscores what I was sayin' about people bein' stressed out. The sooner this whole thing's over, the better, as far as I'm concerned."

Ed Goggins, the manager, came bustling over and apologized profusely, insisting they each have a drink with him on the house.

"Thanks, but one'll do it tonight, Ed," Clark said as they got ready to go. "Got a big day tomorrow and gotta stay sharp."

$$\backsim$$

Jim Clark notified the media first thing Thursday morning, July 2, that he'd be holding a press conference that afternoon at 3:00 to discuss a major new development in the casino battle that he was certain would be of national interest. It was short notice, but the casino continued to be the hottest news story in the state, and by 2:55 it felt as though the entire Connecticut press corps had gathered in the town hall's first floor auditorium.

Clark sat at a folding table bantering with reporters before getting started. The four remaining members of the Casino Task Force sat to Clark's left, while Gladys Greene and Rick Pugliese, who had come up from Washington, sat to his right. News that something big was up had gotten around town, and about two dozen spectators, including Bobby Kingman and the tribe's three PR consultants, were standing behind the seated reporters.

Clark gave it an extra minute, then began in his usual folksy style.

"I guess everybody in Connecticut knows by now," he said, "that the government has a law that says federal Indian tribes can open casinos even when it's illegal for everybody else.

"Now I don't think that's a particularly good law, but the federal government's full of a lot of smart people, and I figure who am I to argue.

"But even the government says the law should only apply to people who can prove they descend from real Indians. And that's particularly important here in Connecticut, because when we give people the right to open casinos, we're givin' 'em the right to open billion-dollar businesses.

"So I thought everybody'd want to see a new document that proves the federal government's made a colossal mistake in givin' that right to Bobby Kingman and his relatives, who it now turns out are no more related to the original Northern Pequots than they are to George Washington."

Josh watched Bobby turn angrily to the PR consultants, but whatever he was saying was drowned out by a burst of questions directed to Clark.

Clark raised both hands and pleaded for people hold their questions, because, he said, he wanted to turn the floor over to Gladys Greene, the town's genealogist.

"Just in case you don't know or don't remember," Clark added, "Mrs. Greene is a former BIA researcher and one of the best in the business. She's made up press kits for all of you and is gonna take you through this whole thing step by step."

⤳

Clark was absolutely right about the story's national appeal.

The first wire service report set the tone:

GOVERNMENT BLUNDER COULD GIVE INDIAN CASINO TO NON-INDIANS—U.S. APPARENTLY MISSED KEY DOCUMENT IN RESEARCHING CT TRIBE

Sheffield, CT—The U.S. Department of the Interior, already under attack for alleged political corruption connected to Indian casinos, came under new fire today for authorizing a group with no Indian genealogical ties to open an Indian casino in Connecticut.

In June the group, which calls itself the Northern Pequot Tribal Nation, won federal recognition from the Bureau of Indian Affairs, but a document recently unearthed from a local church appears to prove the group has no Indian ancestry. The BIA is a unit of the Interior Department.

Experts say the mistake could hand the Northerns and their key investor, controversial billionaire real estate developer Paul Ivy, a multi-billion dollar windfall in the form of Connecticut's third Indian casino. The state's two current casinos are already the largest in the world.

The report noted that Sheffield First Selectman Jim Clark stated the town would demand the BIA revoke the Northerns' recognition and that he urged residents to vote overwhelmingly against the group's proposed casino in a July 21 referendum.

Radio talk shows picked up the story as an example of the latest government screw-up, two television networks used the story on the evening news, and late-night TV comics lampooned government bureaucrats for turning con men into Indians. Jay Leno cracked that he was so inspired by the Northerns that he intended to form his own tribe and take back Manhattan.

Local newspapers led with the story Friday morning, and papers from Maine to Hawaii carried wire-service accounts on the front page or under national news.

Josh and Clark were jubilant about the coverage, and Rick Pugliese called from Washington late Friday morning to say it looked as though the BIA was in crisis mode over the damaging publicity. There was such confusion, Pugliese reported, that he was sure the BIA wouldn't be able to respond before Monday, enabling CAC to have the story all to itself over the weekend.

But BIA officials proved far more resilient than expected and held a hastily called news conference Friday afternoon to respond to the growing ridicule.

They regretted the rush to judgment, they declared, because the Northern Pequot situation had been unfairly represented and badly understood by the media.

The BIA, their spokesman stated, had conducted a lengthy review of the Northern Pequots' acknowledgment petition and had concluded the tribe met each and every requirement for recognition based on the information presented by all parties, including the tribe's opponents. Furthermore, he contended, even assuming the church document was genuine, it did not negate the BIA's recognition decision.

"The BIA faces a special challenge in attempting to verify the lineage of eastern Indian tribes," the spokesman stated, "because those tribes came into contact with Europeans long before western tribes and in many cases were decimated and dispersed prior to 1800, making it difficult and sometimes impossible to obtain genealogical or other records from before that time.

"Our only interest," the spokesman continued, "is to verify that a petitioning tribe has genealogical ties with the historic tribe. In the case of the Northerns we were forced to rely on tribal membership lists from the early 1800s to establish the membership of the historic Northern Pequot Tribe, and those documents indicated that Rachel Amos was a member of the tribe at the time of her death in 1803."

One of the ranking Republicans on the Senate Indian Affairs Subcommittee issued a press release immediately following the BIA press conference, expressing confidence in the bureau and noting the Northerns had gone through a grueling, five-year recognition process in which opponents had never succeeded in casting doubt on the tribe's genealogy.

"The sudden appearance of this previously unknown church document," the senator stated, "is little more than a tempest in a teapot. It is regrettable that the tribe's opponents have tried to use it in this last-ditch effort to block the Northerns from exercising their legitimate rights."

Jim Clark fired back that the BIA's defense of its decision was nothing but sophistry, and that it threw out the genealogical criteria that had always been the most important part of recognition decisions. No matter how the BIA tried to explain it, Clark declared, it was now clear that the current Northern Pequot Tribe didn't have a drop of Pequot blood. The whole affair, he charged, simply highlighted the extent to which gambling money was now driving the federal recognition process.

The national media continued to cover the story through Sunday morning, but then dropped it as too complicated and arcane for the general public. It was enormously disappointing to Josh and Jim Clark that the story didn't have more national staying power, but they took comfort in the fact that they had at least turned the tribe's legitimacy into a major campaign issue as they headed toward the finish line.

39

The Deal

July 2–10, 1998

The one thing Bobby had taken as gospel when he first began angling for a casino was that he was a descendant of a genuine Pequot Indian, and he couldn't help but feel a sense of loss at discovering he wasn't.

Sure, maybe his Pequot connection had always been a bit hazy and he'd never had the slightest interest in it before this whole casino thing. But, goddamnit, he'd simply put too much into trying to become an Indian over the last eight years to suddenly be told he had no Indian blood.

Hell, he had even come to think and feel like an Indian, or at least the way he thought an Indian thought and felt. He had become an Indian chief, had lived in a goddamned trailer on the reservation, had even done his best to dress and look like an Indian. Not only that, but he had held all those pow-wows, bought his girlfriends all that turquoise jewelry, and learned all those Indian words that peppered his talks to school kids and civic groups.

He'd become so persuasive in responding to questions about his ethnicity that few people bothered to challenge him anymore. The only exception might be the occasional little kid at an elementary school, but he had long since learned to turn those instances to his advantage, just as he had when talking to a bunch of first-graders a couple weeks ago.

A cute little girl had popped up out of nowhere and exclaimed: "But you don't *look* like an Indian."

As always, Bobby had explained that his Indian ancestor, Rachel Amos, had married a man who wasn't an Indian, and then he'd added his favorite line: "But you know, sweetheart, it's not how you look that counts, but how you feel in your heart. And in my heart, I'm an Indian."

"Me too," the little girl had said with a big smile, and Bobby had figured he'd made another friend. In fact, Bobby thought that if they could confine the referendum to first-graders, the tribe would win in a walk.

As upset as Bobby was when he learned the truth about Rachel, he could only imagine how much harder it was going to be for his poor Aunt Mavis, who was enormously proud of her Indian heritage, had increasingly come to dress like an Indian, and was truly the heart and soul of the tribe. And then there was his fifteen-year-old son, Eddie; Bobby had bought him a ton of Indian books and made him take Indian dancing lessons. God, he thought, he was really going to have to think about what to say to Eddie.

Bobby kept reminding himself, though, that the only thing that really mattered was winning the referendum, and his impression was that while the Rachel Amos document had been a major blow, it hadn't been fatal. When you cut through all the clutter, the referendum seemed to be boiling down to simply one question: Did the money make tolerating the casino worthwhile? At the moment the jury was still out.

Then on Wednesday, July 8, six days after the Rachel Amos revelation, the tribe caught a break when one of the local papers ran a feature story highlighting the enormous difference between the amount of money being offered to Sheffield by the Northern Pequots and the paltry amounts the Mashantuckets and Mohegans were providing their host towns. The article quoted a Wall Street gaming analyst who said any way you sliced it, the Northerns were making Sheffield "a phenomenal offer."

The tribe made five thousand copies of the article, handed it out at the shopping center and along Main Street, and mailed it to every household and business in town.

Ivy couldn't stop raving about the article when he talked to Bobby on the phone that evening, and he said he had another good piece of news.

"I talked to 'our mutual friend' this afternoon," Ivy said, "and I think we're close to a deal. I'm flying up Friday morning to meet with him personally. I'd like you to pick me up at the Groton airport at ten."

Bobby was elated. Their "mutual friend" was Reid Dowling.

⌒

Bobby stood at one of the windows of the small airport terminal waiting for Ivy's private jet to arrive. He caught sight of the sleek, ten-passenger Dassault Falcon as it came in over the Sound, then watched it land like a graceful bird and taxi toward him. Grimaldi had told him it was the best corporate jet in the air, and Bobby thought longingly that it was exactly what he'd like to get for himself if they ever managed to push the casino through.

Ivy got off the plane with nothing but a briefcase and strode confidently into the terminal. "Hello, Chief," he said breezily and shook Bobby's hand with his usual iron grip.

"Good flight?" Bobby asked, appreciating the fact that Ivy was still calling him "Chief." He hadn't been sure how Ivy would address him after learning Bobby wasn't actually an Indian. At the same time, though, Bobby had the impression Ivy had been acting a little warmer toward him since Ivy's press conference. Grimaldi had mentioned that Ivy had been very appreciative of the ringing endorsement Bobby had given him, and that he was impressed with the way Bobby was holding up under the pressure of the campaign.

"Not bad," Ivy replied. "Did a little work and actually managed to get in a few winks."

Bobby led Ivy to the car, a new top of the line BMW sedan he'd borrowed from a dealer to take Ivy to Old Saybrook, roughly half an hour away. Ivy had booked a hotel room there for an 11:30 meeting with Dowling, after which he planned to return to Miami.

"I was surprised when you said you were comin' up," Bobby said as he eased the car out of its parking space.

"Yeah, I hadn't been planning to, because I thought we had things worked out with Dowling last week. But then that fucking Rachel Amos document came along, and he backed off. Now that things are settling down, he's interested again, and I want to nail this down myself before something else happens."

Bobby just nodded. He found it hard to believe Ivy was willing to risk talking with Dowling personally rather than through a third party. What if Dowling turned on him in order to solidify his anti-casino credentials? The fallout could kill the casino for good and destroy Ivy personally. The only explanation was that Ivy was so driven to win the referendum that he was willing to take the risk.

"How *you* doin', Bobby?" Ivy asked, looking over at him. 'That Rachel Amos stuff had to be pretty rough on you and Mavis, huh?

"Yeah, it was tough," Bobby acknowledged. "Especially on her."

"Well, just so you don't worry about it, Grimaldi and I couldn't care less whether you're an Indian or a Bulgarian. Truth is, Jim told me the first day you walked into his office he suspected you weren't any more Indian than he was. But he liked the situation and the way you handled yourself, so here we are ... homing in on the biggest score in my career. The important thing is that you had the balls to do what you did. Fact you're not an Indian makes it even more spectacular. The key now is to put everything behind you and just keep pushin' until you're over the goal line. Don't let anybody stop ya or you'll regret it the rest of your life."

Bobby hadn't been sure where the conversation was going when Ivy started in about Rachel Amos, but he suddenly felt enormously appreciative toward Ivy for turning the revelation about her into a positive. It was the first personal pep talk anybody'd ever given him in his life.

"I got a close friend who's Estonian," Ivy went on. "He was a nineteen-year-old kid when the Russians took over Estonia just before World War Two. The Ruskies drafted him and forced him to fight for them against the Germans in forty-one. Then the Germans captured him, and he turned around and fought with them against the Russians. One morning they ran into a squad of Siberians that'd been wiped out by a German dive bomber, but there was this one Siberian who was still alive, lying on the ground and moaning for water. Despite the fact he hated the Commies, my friend knelt down and handed the guy his canteen. The Siberian suddenly grabbed my friend's wrist and bit into his hand like he was trying to bite it off. My friend screamed and tried to pull his hand away, but the Siberian wouldn't let go. Then there was a gun shot, and a bullet opened a huge hole in the Siberian's forehead. When my friend looked up, there was this German lieutenant with a Luger. 'Be careful. They're animals,' was all he said, and walked away.

"The moral of the story," Ivy said, "is finish what you start. And that's exactly what you and I both gotta do here."

Bobby drove in silence for the next few moments, thinking about the German lieutenant with the Luger.

"You confident we can trust Dowlin'?" he finally asked, changing the subject back to the man Ivy had come to meet.

"Yeah, I think so," Ivy replied. "It's gonna cost more than I thought, but that's all right. He's putting his political career on the line, and I think his support could make the difference. Fortunately, he's the kinda guy you can do business with."

"What's he willin' to do?"

"He's offered to send a letter to every voter in Sheffield urging them to vote for the casino," Ivy replied. "He's already written the letter, and assuming I can close the deal, our PR people can pick up enough of his stationery and envelopes to get a mailing out to the entire town this afternoon. That way, everybody'll get the letter by tomorrow and Dowling can spend the final week campaigning for us."

"Have you seen the letter?" Bobby asked.

"No, but he read it to me last week. He obviously wasn't going to give me a copy until we finalized things."

"And it's good?"

"It's better than good," Ivy said. "It's a political masterpiece. He says he's been reevaluating the situation, and he's convinced the tribe will eventually be able to annex the Standish farm and build the casino no matter how the town votes, and therefore it'd be 'a mistake of historic proportions' to reject the tribe's offer and get nothing."

"Good line," Bobby said.

"And you'll appreciate the last part," Ivy continued. "He says because of his concern for doing everything possible to maintain the town's rural character, he's gotten the Northerns to agree to acquire five hundred acres of open space and donate it to the town if it votes in favor of the casino."

"Jesus, who's going to pay for that?" Bobby asked.

"Relax," Ivy said. "I will. It can be wetlands for all anybody cares. I think it's brilliant. I told you, the guy's smart. He's got a real feel for the town, and he says he needs the open space thing for his image."

"That's for his political image," Bobby said. "What's he want for himself?"

"That's what we're still talking about," Ivy answered.

⌒

Bobby let Ivy off at the Saybrook Point Inn, which sat on a point that jutted out into the mouth of the Connecticut River and afforded sweeping views of Old Lyme and Long Island Sound. The inn was part of a large marina complex teeming with tourists admiring the yachts and watching the seagulls float on the heavy summer air.

Ivy said he should be finished by 12:30, and Bobby decided to drive across the street to Fort Saybrook Monument Park to kill time. The small park was the site of the historic English fort that commanded the entrance to the river in the 1600s. Bobby had passed it many times over the years without stopping, but this was a good time to take a few minutes to look around.

The old fort was long gone, but the park had an imposing statue of Lieutenant Lion Gardiner, the fort's builder and its commander during the Pequot War, along with numerous plaques telling the story of the fort and the war between the Indians and the English. Bobby found himself fascinated by Gardiner, who had one hand poised on his sword and a spyglass in the other. Bobby tried to imagine what it must have been like some three hundred sixty years ago as the Pequots tried to starve and pick off the fort's garrison. Eight days ago, it occurred to him, he would have identified with the Indians, but now that he knew the truth about Rachel, he had to admit he really didn't give a shit.

Bobby spent about half an hour browsing through the park and then drove back to the inn to watch for Ivy, who came out just before 12:15. A light fog had begun to roll in off the Sound, and Bobby could hear a foghorn in the distance as Ivy opened the car door.

"Done," Ivy said, settling into his seat.

"You got the letter?"

"Signed on his official legislative stationery. If we hustle, we should be able to get it out this afternoon."

"No problems?"

"Not in the end."

"What'd you finally have to give him?"

"No disrespect, Chief," Ivy answered, "but why don't we just leave it that I agreed to the five hundred acres for Sheffield. That way, you never heard of him personally getting anything."

40

A Tragic Mix

July 11–17, 1998

Representative Reid Dowling's letter to Sheffield's 3,076 voters arrived in their mailboxes on Saturday morning, July 11.

The letter took the town completely by surprise and was the big topic of conversation all weekend. Casino opponents saw it as the ultimate act of betrayal and swore retribution, while supporters were energized and predicted victory. But whatever side one was on, it was clear the town's official opposition to the casino now lay in shambles.

Nevertheless, it was hard to tell from conversations around town exactly what impact the letter was having on its main target audience, the undecideds. Voters in this group seemed more interested in hearing what others thought of the letter and Dowling's about-face than in volunteering their own thoughts.

More telling, a new private poll conducted by the tribe's pollsters on Monday, July 13, showed that with a week to go, the undecideds were beginning to break in favor of the casino. The poll's director reported the results in a late Monday night conference call with Ivy, Grimaldi, Bobby, and the tribe's PR people, describing the developing momentum as "extremely encouraging."

Whereas the poll two weeks ago had shown 21 percent for, 43 percent against, and 36 percent undecided, the new poll showed 29 percent for, 45 percent against, and 26 percent undecided, which, if the poll was right, meant the undecideds were breaking 4 to 1 for the casino.

"So what are you sayin'?" Bobby interjected, unable to contain his budding excitement. You think we got a shot at winnin' this thing or not?"

"It all depends on whether you can keep up the momentum," the pollster replied. "It's hard to believe the numbers will keep breaking like they are, but if they do there's no question you may be able to pull it out."

Sharon Williams normally would have been home when the pollsters called just after 5:15 that afternoon, but she had to work late on Monday to wrap up a catalog scheduled to go to the printer on Tuesday. She called home at 4:30, leaving a message that she should be home at about 9:00.

Her boss, Harley FitzGibbons, brought in pizzas for the small staff, as he always did when they worked late, and they finally put the catalog to bed shortly before 9:00. Sharon spent a few minutes straightening up, then walked out to the parking lot, where she used the remote to unlock her 1995 Honda Accord. She could see how filthy the car was, even in the twilight, and she made a mental note to have one of the boys wash it after dinner on Tuesday. She certainly wasn't going to spend $6 at the car wash.

Sharon took her usual route through the now largely deserted streets of downtown New London toward I-95, turned onto the entrance ramp to the highway, and cautiously merged into the westbound flow of traffic. Then she set her speed control, turned on her favorite FM music station, and settled back for the twelve-minute ride to the Sheffield exit.

The occasional late night was the one thing Sharon didn't like about her job, but she felt lucky to have found something in the marketing and advertising field that was close to home. Although she'd known relatively little about catalog retailing, she'd picked it up quickly, and Harley had not only made her his chief copywriter but was involving her more and more in layout and design.

It was consequently going to be hard to leave the job, but she had no doubts about what she had to do. She glanced at her reflection in the rearview mirror and shook her head at the lines around her mouth and eyes. Another six months like the last, she thought, and she'd begin looking old.

After some initial misgivings, she'd come to see Sheffield as an almost idyllic dream, a place where her husband was more alive and content than she had ever seen him, the perfect place to raise their children, and a community to call her own. But the dream had become a nightmare, and she was convinced she was the only one who could extricate them from it. Josh's emotional roots in the town and the farm simply went too deep. If the casino lost, he'd look for every possible excuse to delay leaving Sheffield. And if it won, he'd want to stay as long as possible to try to sell the farm. She could feel it, and it was the reason she had had to give him the ultimatum.

Sharon had always believed she and Josh had the perfect marriage. She had loved him almost from the first week they'd met. They complemented each other in almost every way, and she couldn't remember another time they'd disagreed on an important decision.

Now she knew she had stung him badly with her demand. It had to be the final affront to his ego after everything else that had turned against him. But she was determined to hold his feet to the fire. Their relationship had been badly strained for more than three weeks now, but if that was the price for getting them out of Sheffield, then so be it. If he wouldn't leave following the referendum, she'd take the kids and go. Josh could come when he was ready.

Sharon was so deep in thought she didn't notice the gray Taurus swing out from behind her and begin to pass. Suddenly the Taurus cut back into her lane, sideswiping her front left fender and forcing her to swerve sharply to the right. She tried desperately to right her car, but it glanced off the metal guardrail and headed back into the travel lane, where it was hit with enormous force by an SUV coming from behind.

The front left side of Sharon's Honda was demolished, and the car was sent hurtling back toward the side of the road, where it finally smashed into a guard post and burst into flames. The SUV veered off to the right, ran up on the grass where there was a gap in the guardrail, and slammed into a tree, while the Taurus began fishtailing and finally hit the center divider, spun completely around, and came to a stop in the center median, facing the oncoming traffic.

Several vehicles drove right through the crash scene. Then others began to stop and drivers rushed out to try to help. Traffic began to build up, sirens sounded in the distance, and the first police cruisers, fire engines, and other emergency vehicles arrived, their lights flashing in a kaleidoscope of reds, yellows, and blues.

The firefighters had to use hydraulic cutters to get to Sharon, who was pinned in tight. As the first ambulance made its way in, men shouted instructions and two-way radios squawked and crackled everywhere. Finally rescue workers cleared enough space for a Life Star helicopter to land on the highway, its rotor blades whipping up a cloud of dust as it came in. Two stretchers were quickly loaded onto the helicopter, and it lifted off and headed toward Yale–New Haven Hospital to the west.

Josh made supper for the kids, then went out campaigning door-to-door with one of his campaign teams until just before 9:00. When he got home, he went to the library and worked on insurance business for a while before realizing Sharon hadn't come home yet. He finally called her office at 10:00 but got her voice mail. He called again at 10:10 but once again no one picked up. He finally called Harley FitzGibbons at home at 10:15.

Harley was immediately alarmed because he and Sharon had left at about the same time. Had Josh checked with the state police just to make sure there were no major tie-ups or accidents? No, Josh said. He would.

The duty officer at the state police barracks in Montville informed Josh there'd been a three-car accident around 9:15 on the New Haven–bound lane of I-95, just west of exit 74 in East Lyme. There had been several injuries, but there was no information yet on the identities of the victims. At least two of the injured had been flown by helicopter to Yale–New Haven. The interstate had been closed in both directions and was just beginning to be re-opened. If Josh's wife had been caught between exits, she could still be in the tie-up.

"I take it your wife doesn't have a car phone," the duty officer said.

"No, she doesn't," Josh answered.

"Well, she's probably just stuck, then," the officer replied. The state police would contact him if there were any word on his wife.

Josh felt a rush of panic the moment the officer mentioned the accident, but he'd been caught in a closure of I-95 himself, and he assured himself that was all it was. Still, it was frightening. The timing was bad. Sharon would have been near exit 74 right around the time of the accident.

He decided to call Yale–New Haven, just in case. When he reached the hospital no one could give him any information on the accident or whether any of its victims had arrived at the hospital. They would call him if his wife were admitted.

He turned on the television. Nothing. He went to a front window and looked out toward the street. Nothing. Fear began to edge back into his brain. He sat. He paced. He went back to the window, and he began to pray.

Josh thought of waking Matt and Sarah but decided against it. They both had to be up early to get to their summer jobs, and it was pointless to wake them when there was nothing anyone could do. Instead he went back to the library to sit by the phone.

Just before 11:00 he got up and went to the front window again. Just as he got there, two headlights turned into the driveway. He felt an enormous surge of relief. Thank God, she was home.

He started back toward the kitchen door to meet her when she came in from the garage. But the car didn't continue into the courtyard. It must have stopped in the driveway. He turned back in confusion. He saw the car through a side window. It had stopped and turned off its lights. He could see a figure headed for the front door. No one ever came to the front door.

Josh got to the door first and opened it. Two uniformed state troopers approached, looking grim and uncomfortable.

"Mr. Williams?" they asked.

"Yes?" Josh answered, his entire being filling with dread.

The senior officer identified himself and his partner, and asked if they could come in. Josh stepped back from the door to let them through, then stood facing them in the narrow hallway.

The older trooper cleared his throat and said he regretted to have to report that there had been an accident. Sharon Williams had been killed when her car was hit by two other vehicles and crashed that evening on I-95.

"We're deeply sorry for you and your family, Mr. Williams," the trooper continued, but Josh was no longer listening.

"Are you sure?" he blurted. "Are you sure it was her? She was in a white Honda...."

The officer closed his eyes and nodded.

Josh felt disoriented. He reached for the wall to brace himself, then felt strong hands help him to the parlor, where he slumped down, dazed, on the sofa. He wasn't sure how much time passed, but he became aware of the children's voices in the hall. He rose from his seat and they rushed toward him, weeping and hugging him in anguish and disbelief.

⤻

Because of the lateness of the accident, Tuesday morning's papers carried only brief reports of Sharon's death, but the impact on Sheffield was devastating. The news brought an outpouring of sorrow from friends, acquaintances, and strangers, and the town's mood became even more somber on Wednesday with the first full accounts of the accident and grisly photos of the charred and tangled wreckage.

Sharon, it was now reported, had apparently tried to escape from her wrecked Honda but had succumbed to the fire.

The driver of the SUV was in critical condition, but the driver of the Taurus that sideswiped Sharon had been released from the hospital and charged with driving while intoxicated after testing for almost five times the legal alcohol limit. A firefighter on the scene was quoted as saying the Taurus's driver had acknowledged spending the afternoon and evening at the two casinos, where he had been drinking steadily. The source said it was hard to believe the man had made it as far as he had, given the condition he was in.

Interstate 95 in Connecticut, it was noted, was one of the most congested and dangerous highways in the country, and accidents had been mounting on the thirty-two-mile stretch between the Connecticut River and Rhode Island since the opening of the casinos.

The news that Sharon had been killed by a drunk casino patron ignited a firestorm of outrage and a paroxysm of soul searching about the impact of the casinos on eastern Connecticut. A spate of newspaper articles reported that drunk-driving arrests were escalating near the casinos, that the local state police troop made twice the number of DWI arrests made by other troops in the state, and that the two casinos had been fined more than $300,000 for violating liquor laws since they had opened.

The casinos' entire business, critics charged, was based to one degree or another on handing out free drinks to customers in order to help make them happy, loosen their inhibitions, and keep them gambling. The two casinos together employed almost five hundred waitresses to do nothing but serve drinks, and every one of those waitresses had a stake in serving as many drinks as possible in order to earn tips.

In fact, alcohol was so central to the casinos' business, critics noted, that the casinos had a special arrangement whereby the state merely fined the casinos for liquor violations rather than also suspending their liquor licenses, as they did with other establishments. The whole situation was absurd, a state police officer commented. Mere fines could never be expected to deter casinos that were pulling in hundreds of millions of dollars a year.

The casinos countered that free alcohol was a tradition in the gaming industry and an important part of the overall customer experience patrons were seeking. Moreover, they contended, they trained their staffs to monitor the amount of alcohol customers consumed, and the reason the casinos weren't closed down for liquor violations was that the casinos permitted the state to place liquor control agents on their premises.

None of it satisfied the critics, who responded that the casinos were like arsonists who poured gasoline on a roaring fire and then came running with a garden hose. The whole idea of the casinos contributing to gambling-treatment programs and allowing a few liquor-control agents in their gambling halls was, they contended, simply part of the industry's massive hypocrisy.

‿

Josh and the children went about the numbing task of arranging the funeral with the help of their pastor and the Merriweathers. Sharon's mother flew east to be with the family, and Josh's sister and her husband came down from West Hartford to help. Flowers arrived throughout the week, a hundred cards came in the mail on Wednesday alone, and friends and neighbors dropped off food and did their best to comfort the family.

All overt campaigning for or against the casino stopped for the week, and an estimated five hundred people overflowed the church for the Friday morning memorial service. The minister spoke poignantly of Sharon's love for her family and the community, and Josh and the children brought the congregation to tears as they took turns speaking of their love for her. The choir sang "Rock of Ages," and a soloist concluded the service with "Amazing Grace," his magnificent tenor voice filling the church and transfixing everyone with the hymn's soulful music and reassuring words. "Amazing Grace, how sweet the sound . . . I once was lost but now am found."

Afterward, the family went out to the old cemetery, where the minister conducted a private graveside service commending Sharon's soul to the Lord. Josh and the children stood side by side, pressed together, each lost in their own grief over losing the one person in the world they loved the most. When it was over, they remained briefly to say their personal farewells, and Josh placed a single yellow-rayed sunflower atop the casket.

‿

Most of the mourners made their way back to the Williams farm, where the neighbors had helped set up tables of food in the old farmhouse.

Those paying their respects came from every neighborhood, every church, every social stratum, and every political leaning in town. Sharon's terrible, untimely death seemed to have penetrated the town's collective psyche, stopped people in their tracks, and caused them to reflect on their own families and mortality. The divisions that seemed ready to tear the town apart were temporarily set aside, passions cooled, and people who in many cases had been battling each other a few days earlier now shook hands and embraced.

The main exception was Josh's treatment of Dowling.

The Northern Pequot tribe sent a huge floral wreath to the funeral, and Bobby Kingman attended the church service. Josh would have politely acknowledged both gestures if he had been aware of them, but he was unable to control himself when he saw Reid Dowling toward the end of the reception. Dowling approached him in the living room with his hand extended, but Josh refused to take it.

"Do you remember the last time you were in this house?" Josh asked.

"I think . . . ," Dowling began to say, slowly dropping his hand and trying to make the best out of the situation.

"It was seven years ago," Josh interrupted. "Sharon and I asked for your help on the casino vote in Hartford. But you stabbed the town in the back then, and now you've done it again."

"I'm sorry you feel that way, Josh," Dowling managed to say. "And I am truly sorry about Sharon. She was a remarkable woman, and I'll always remember her."

"And I'll always remember how she died," Josh said bitterly. "At the hands of a drunk gambler you helped let into her life."

Josh turned and walked away, leaving Dowling speechless.

~

41

Ethan's Diaries

July 17–21, 1998

The town went into the final weekend before the referendum in an uneasy and inscrutable mood, making it impossible to predict how it would vote. Bobby feared that Sharon's death at the hands of a drunk gambler had put a final stake in the casino's heart, while Jim Clark feared the outpouring for Sharon might be the town's way of atoning for the pro-casino vote it was about to cast.

Both sides did a final mailing that arrived on Monday, July 20, but otherwise it was a strangely quiet end to the wildest, most fractious, and most divisive electoral campaign anyone could remember. Sheffield seemed glum, nervous, and exhausted, and one had the sense that hundreds of townspeople were still wrestling with how to vote.

Following the funeral, Josh remained too shattered to think about anything other than Sharon, their life together, and the enormity of the family's loss. The pain and guilt ate at him constantly—he could hear her voice pleading with him to leave Sheffield, but he had been too consumed with the casino and saving his heritage to listen. Friday night was the worst. He loaded up on sleeping pills but even then woke up and reached for her, only to find that she was gone. He buried his head in her pillow and wept, letting his tears mix with her lingering scent.

~

Josh forced himself to get up and go to the office for a few hours Monday morning, then rounded up the kids after lunch to help him cart bales of hay from the fields to the barn for storage. It was a hot, humid day, and loading and unloading the heavy bales onto and off the pickup truck was hard, sweaty work. But it proved to be good therapy, and by the time they all got cleaned up and sat down at dinner with Sharon's mother that evening, Josh felt the family was showing at least the first tentative signs of coming back to life. Matt and Sarah both thought it would be best if they returned to their summer jobs the next day, and they agreed to go over to the town hall together afterward to vote.

Josh went into the library after dinner to begin tackling the cards and letters and bills that now covered the coffee table, but by 9:30 he was so tired he went up to bed. Yet as exhausted as he was there were too many thoughts racing through his mind to sleep. If only he hadn't walked away from his job in Chicago. If only he hadn't brought the family back to Sheffield. If only they'd left before the embezzlement. If only he'd accepted the tribe's million-and-a-half-dollar offer. If only Sharon hadn't worked late that night. The if-onlys were driving him mad. He finally got up and went back down to the library, looking for something to occupy him until he could relax.

Remembering the diaries he'd been meaning to get back to, he reached up and pulled the first of the five volumes off the top shelf.

He thumbed through the diary, which ran from 1635 to 1647, then sat down and started reading from the beginning. As before, he struggled at first with the handwriting, but he soon became absorbed in Ethan's account of the Atlantic crossing, his long trek to Connecticut, his marriage to Susan, and her grisly death a week later at the hands of Pequots.

As Josh continued to read, he was fascinated by Ethan's description of the colonists' preparations for war against the Pequots, then horrified by his account of the torching of the fort and the massacre of the people inside. He could picture the soldiers and their Indian allies ringing the hopeless fortress. He could see the flames, feel the heat, hear the screams, and smell the growing stench of burning flesh that filled the early-morning air. He looked on as a soldier plunged his pike into a boy who'd jumped from the top of the palisade, and he watched as thirty to forty Pequots broke out of the main entrance in a desperate effort to escape.

Ethan told in graphic detail how he had chased one Pequot down, knocking him to the ground with the butt of his musket. The man had rolled and recovered and was crouched like a coiled spring, grasping his hatchet in his right hand, ready to bury the weapon in Ethan's skull. The Pequot's left arm was badly burned and he was bleeding from the temple, but the warrior, a "lusty" man about twice Ethan's age, was defiant and showed absolutely no fear.

It was at that point that Ethan noticed the Indian's wampum necklace and the purple shell pendant that hung from it. "For a brief instant," he continued, "the brilliant flames from the fort reflected in the pendant, as though the man's very soul were aflame, and at that moment it struck me that he surely must be a sachem."

Before Ethan could think further, the Indian rebuked him and issued a stunning curse in English: "'You slay too many. *Matchit.* 'Tis evil. May the gods drive you from our land!'

"'Damn your gods!' I screamed," Ethan wrote, "certain now the Indian was no mere warrior. I raised my sword to dispatch him, but he flew at me like a dragon, slicing my coat with his hatchet and coming within an inch of my heart. I stepped back and then swung my sword and severed his head. Looking down, I saw the blow had also cut the necklace, which had dropped to the ground and which I took as a remembrance of the war."

Josh mulled the words Ethan had penned more than three hundred fifty years ago, then remembered something that made his heart race. He got up and walked quickly down the hall to the parlor. He turned on the lights and went over to a maple secretary desk where he and Sharon had stored a number of small antiques and keepsakes they'd collected from around the house when they first moved in. He began rummaging through the drawers and found what he was looking for—a painted wooden box, maybe an inch and a half deep and seven or eight inches square. There was a wampum necklace with a deep-purple shell pendant inside.

Josh took the box back to the library and returned to his chair, where he sat under the reading light examining the necklace. He didn't want to take it out of the box for fear of damaging it, but he touched the small purple-and-white shell beads with his finger, feeling their hard, smooth finish, and used his handkerchief to polish the pendant, which reflected back his image. The beads were tubular in shape, perhaps a quarter of an inch in length and somewhat smaller in diameter, with tiny bores; they had been threaded with a thin strip of leather and knotted in place. In case there was any question about the necklace's provenance, it had been cut in one place and the two severed ends were stained with what Josh could only assume was the sachem's blood.

But Josh needed no further evidence that it was the necklace from the diary. He knew in his bones they were one and the same.

Putting down the necklace and picking up the diary again, Josh began to read about Ethan's return to Wethersfield, but his mind kept going back to the necklace until fatigue gradually overcame him and he felt himself slipping into sleep. He imagined he was being pulled through a long, dimly lit tunnel, passing generation after generation of his ancestors, half-real and half-ethereal in their period dress, until he emerged on hard ground outside the burning Pequot fort. He dreamed it was he who fired into the fleeing band of Pequots, he who chased down the sachem, knocking him to the ground with the musket that now hung over the kitchen fireplace, and he who cut off the sachem's head.

He then dreamed the sachem was in the front seat of Sharon's Honda as she drove home on I-95. Sharon was wearing the wampum necklace, and the sachem was distracting her so she didn't see the Taurus coming up on her left. Josh felt the Taurus sideswipe Sharon's car, then watched in horror as the Honda was hit a second time and sent hurtling into the guard post. He had one last glimpse of her slumped against her air bag as the fire spread. As he looked on, the sachem reached over and cut the necklace from her neck. Then the Indian and the necklace disappeared ghost-like through the flames.

Josh jerked awake and glanced around uncertainly, as though expecting to see the sachem's ghost carrying off the necklace. But there was no ghost, and the necklace was on the reading table exactly where Josh had left it. It had simply been a nightmare. He shook his head and looked at his watch. It was 7:22. He'd slept for maybe three hours. He was sweating, his head ached, and his neck hurt. He picked up the diary, which had fallen on the floor, and stared at it. God, he thought, he was letting this ancient history consume him.

Josh got up and took the necklace and the diary over to his desk and put them in a drawer. He would come back and read more that afternoon, he decided; right now he desperately needed a shower and some aspirin, and he needed to get going. He planned to vote before going over to the office and wanted to get back to the farm by noon to finish bringing in the hay.

Josh headed upstairs and came down again twenty minutes later, just in time to say good-bye to Matt and Sarah, who were leaving for work. He had a quick cup of coffee with Sharon's mother and left the house just before 8:00.

⌒

It was 4:00 p.m. by the time Josh was able to sit down with the diary again.

He picked up the story just after Ethan returned to Wethersfield from the attack on the Pequots, and followed him through the next ten years as he remarried, added on to his cabin, and planted and harvested his crops. Ethan hired out as a carpenter during the winter, took an active role in the town's militia, and became embroiled in a controversy over who should be chosen as Wethersfield's first full-time minister.

In 1641 the General Court in Hartford authorized a survey of Pequot country for the purpose of "settling inhabitants in those parts," and over the next two years the court moved to open up southeastern Connecticut by providing land grants to Captain Mason and the soldiers who served with him, as well as giving thousands of additional acres to other settlers. Ethan grew restless and was tempted to strike out for the new lands, but his wife, Anne, preferred a more civilized existence, and in 1647 they agreed to move to Saybrook, which was beginning to grow and prosper.

The second volume of the diaries began with Ethan and Anne's arrival in Saybrook, which they took to immediately because of its slightly milder weather and lovely views of the lower river and the Sound. Ethan wrote fondly of their first nine years there, then with growing despair as Anne fell ill with consumption and literally wasted away before him. Her death in 1658, after eighteen years of marriage, left him childless and a widower at age forty-two.

Josh felt a closer and closer bond with Ethan as he read. He imagined himself back in seventeenth-century Connecticut, listening to Ethan argue an ecclesiastical point in Wethersfield or hunting with him in Saybrook's salt marshes. By the time he finished the last entry about Anne, he had completely lost track of the hour and was startled when Jacob knocked on the library door at 6:15 to call him for dinner.

‿〜

When Josh got to the kitchen, Matt and Sarah were telling their grandmother about the mob scene they'd just witnessed at the town hall, where the voting line stretched all the way to the street. They had had to wait more than half an hour to vote and people were saying it was by far the heaviest turnout the town had ever seen.

"Any indication which way it's going?" Josh asked.

"No, not really," Matt said, "although there was one interesting thing we noticed."

"What's that?" his father asked.

"Well, it's a pretty simple ballot," Matt said. "'Yes,' you support the tribe's proposal, or 'no,' you don't.

"All you have to do is go into the booth, close the curtain, flick the pointer to yes or no, open the curtain, and leave. I mean, what can it take, ten seconds?

"But we must have noticed at least a dozen people who took forever in the booth. So we had to assume a lot of people were coming in at the end of the day still not having made up their mind about how to vote."

"You're probably right," Josh said, impressed with their perceptiveness.

⌣

After dinner, Josh helped with the dishes, then about 7:30 went out for a walk. The polls were supposed to close at 8:00, but if the line were long enough, he supposed it could be sometime after 8:30 before the last ballot was cast.

Carol Zajak had called on Monday to say that CAC's key workers would be gathering at her house to wait for the returns and that everyone would love to have him join them, but Josh couldn't bring himself to go. Sharon's death was simply too fresh, and he felt it would be awkward for everyone if he went. If they won, his presence would put a damper on the celebration, and if they lost it would just add to the depression. Carol had promised, however, that she'd call him directly from the town hall as soon as the polls closed to give him the results.

It was a pleasant evening, and he walked almost all the way up Stoddard Mill Road to Route 141 and back, passing the mill pond and broad fields of corn that were almost ready for picking. Walking back, he looked out toward the reservation and wondered what the Indians who had once lived there would think of the people who claimed it now.

He finally got back to the house just after 8:20 and went to the library to wait for Carol's call.

⌣

Carol called at 8:40 on her cell phone. She said the last minute crush of voters was so great that they had just closed the polls, but that they should have the results in a few minutes.

"The turnout's been phenomenal," she added. "They're saying it's over ninety-eight percent."

"You think that's good or bad for us?" Josh asked.

"I don't know, but we're going to find out in a minute. Wait a second— Jim Clark's here and wants to say something to you."

Clark came on the line and said he'd been thinking about Josh and Sharon all day, and he wanted Josh to know how much he appreciated everything he'd done to help bring things this far.

"No matter what happens, Josh, the town will always be indebted to you and your family," Clark said.

"Oh, oh, gotta go," he added hurriedly. "Talk to you later. Here's Carol."

Carol came back on the line and said they were about to open the first of the three voting machines.

"But, first, here're the absentees," she said. "Twenty-four yes, thirty no. I can't believe it's so close, but at least we're ahead!"

There was a pause and Josh waited, not quite able to make out what was being said in the background.

"All right, here's the first machine," Carol continued. "Five hundred three yes, five hundred four no. God, it's close, Josh," she said nervously. "What the hell's the matter with these people?"

There was another pause.

"Second machine," he heard her say. "Four ninety-eight yes, four ninety-four no. We're only up three!"

Josh waited with his eyes closed, trying to will the outcome.

"Third machine," Carol reported, her throat catching this time. "Four ninety-five yes, four ninety no. . . . I'm sorry, Josh. I'm so sorry."

✍

Josh thanked Carol for all her hard work and put down the phone. He stood for a moment absorbing the news, then walked over to the east window, where he looked out toward the barn and the darkening fields beyond. He was bitterly disappointed, but not surprised.

Every indication had been that the town was overwhelmingly opposed to the casino just seven weeks ago. But the tribe's offer had changed everything. The town had looked into its soul and decided it wanted the money. Or at least didn't want to risk losing it. And even then, he couldn't fault the entire town. Half the townspeople had held out to the very end.

Josh shared the news with the children and Sharon's mother, all of whom expressed disbelief that the anti-casino side hadn't been able to eke out a few more votes and commiserated with him over the loss. Josh acknowledged that it was a bitter defeat, but said it was important that the family move on. He said his first step would be to put the farm up for sale, as the family had long planned to do if the Northerns ever got to build their casino, and then to begin thinking seriously of where to go after Sheffield. It would be sad to leave the farm, he added, but the Williamses had had a long run in Sheffield, and time had a way of changing everything. The others listened quietly and simply nodded when he finished. At the moment, there was nothing else to say.

Wanting to be alone, Josh returned to the library and escaped back into Ethan's diaries.

⤳

Anne's death in 1658 prompted Ethan to reevaluate his life, and in the spring of 1659 he left Saybrook with a small group of his neighbors to found Sheffield. The land here was more rugged than in either Wethersfield or Saybrook, but he welcomed the opportunity to start over in a new place, and by late summer he and his fellow-settlers had raised a dozen barns, begun work on the town commons, and erected a temporary meetinghouse where they enacted the first town ordinances and attended services. Wanting to be off by himself, Ethan chose a piece of land three and a half miles from the commons for his farm, and threw himself into the task of clearing it, planting his first crops, and building a cabin.

By November 1659 and the onset of colder weather, the tone of the entries began to change. Ethan remained upbeat, but an element of loneliness began to seep into his writing, and for the first time he mentioned the possibly of seeking a "helpmeet," which Josh assumed meant a wife. What Ethan found, however, he could not possibly have bargained for.

He first saw Sarya on a trip back to Saybrook in December 1659. She was a beautiful, eighteen-year-old, raven-haired girl who was working as a servant for a merchant who had recently moved down from Hartford.

Ethan confided to his diary that he was "instantly smitten" by the girl and "gripped by feelings I didn't realize I still had." He thought of her constantly over the next several weeks, then in January returned to Saybrook through the snow to talk to the merchant about the young woman.

The merchant explained that Sarya had been born out of wedlock to an unknown white father and a Pequot woman who had been given to the merchant's family following the death of her parents in the Pequot War. If Ethan wished to wed Sarya, and if the girl and her mother were agreeable, the merchant said, he would be happy to accommodate him for a small consideration.

The arrangements were made and Ethan took Sarya for his wife and brought her with him to the wilds of Sheffield.

Josh was stunned for the second time in less than twenty-four hours.

Sarya was half Pequot, which meant the entire Williams line was descended from the very people Ethan had helped massacre. It was mind-boggling. No one in his family had ever told him this. He went back and read the passages again to be sure. Then he got up and headed for the front stairs, which he took two at a time.

He flicked on the lights in the sitting room next to the master bedroom and went over to the 1720 portrait of Daniel, Ethan and Sarya's grandson and the ancestor everyone said Josh resembled so strongly.

There was no question that certain of their features were remarkably similar, including the reddish hair, the expressive brown eyes, and the strong jawline, although Daniel's nose was slightly larger and his ears smaller, and the skin tones in the portrait seemed a bit darker. But what did Josh expect? He and Daniel were born two hundred sixty years apart. Ten generations set up innumerable possibilities for differences between them.

What Josh was really interested in was whether he could see any Indian features in his ancestor. He thought he detected them in Daniel's coloring and possibly his cheekbones, but he couldn't really tell. Again, that only made sense, since Daniel would have been only one-eighth Indian if Sarya were half Pequot.

It was now almost 11:00 p.m. and Josh was going on no more than three hours sleep, but he was wide awake. He went into the kitchen to fix a cup of decaf, then went back to the library and the diary.

◦⁀◦

Ethan took Sarya to Sheffield in February 1660, and it became clear that the following years were the best ones of his life.

Josh was mesmerized by Ethan's account of his and Sarya's first years together, moved by Ethan's tenderness and devotion to her, and captivated as she blossomed from a shy servant girl to a vivacious and loving wife. Thomas was born in January 1661 and Samuel twenty months later. Both boys were healthy. The farm was prosperous. And Ethan reveled in his new family, which he considered nothing less than a miracle at this stage in his life.

Ethan taught Sarya to read and write. He took her into Saybrook to see her mother several times a year, and her mother came to the farm to help with the harvest each August. Sarya's maternal grandfather, Ethan learned, had been a Pequot sachem named Chachanen, and Ethan told Sarya he wasn't surprised because he considered her his princess.

The only problem seemed to be that Sarya had difficulty conceiving after Samuel. She finally became pregnant again in 1666, and the family was excited by the prospect of a new child. Then one Tuesday in May 1667, three weeks before Sarya's due date, Ethan came back from the fields earlier than expected, having pulled a muscle picking stones. The boys were outside, and Sarya was alone when Ethan entered the house. He knew immediately something was wrong.

Sarya was sitting at the kitchen table with her head down, and when she looked up, her anguished expression filled him with dread. He thought at first it was something to do with the baby; then he noticed Volume I of his diary on the table next to her, and she suddenly bolted from her chair and rushed past him, collapsing on their bed, weeping and inconsolable.

Ethan wrote that when he went back to pick up the diary, he saw that it was open to his description of the burning of the Pequot fort at Mystic. He assumed that she had been secretly reading the diary for several days and that she had come to the part about the massacre that afternoon.

Sarya was despondent that evening and the next morning, and when Ethan returned from the fields at noon, the boys told him she had gone out to pick flowers near the big bolder and still hadn't returned. Ethan immediately went out looking for her and found her lying half-conscious at the bottom of a ravine. The left side of her head was caked with blood and she appeared to have broken her neck. He brought her back to the house in a wagon and laid her on their bed, where she whispered incoherently in the Pequot language about her mother and referred several times to her grandfather Chachanen by name.

Ethan and Thomas tended to Sarya constantly for the next eight hours, during which she gave birth to a baby daughter she and Ethan planned to name Mary. The baby died that evening and Sarya, who lapsed into a coma, passed away two days later. Ethan went for Sarya's mother, who had been preparing to come to Sheffield to assist at the birth, and she, Ethan, and the two boys buried Sarya in the cemetery by the meetinghouse.

Josh stared at the faded handwriting and once again could hardly believe what he had just read. Ethan hadn't spelled it out in so many words, but Josh could visualize clearly what had happened: Ethan walking in and finding

Sarya distraught over his role in slaughtering her people, including very likely her own grandfather; Sarya waiting for him to leave the next morning and telling the boys she was going to pick flowers; and Ethan finding her in the ravine, knowing she had jumped in an effort to take her own life.

It was all overwhelming. The massacre, Ethan's beheading of the sachem, the blood-stained necklace, Sarya's lineage, and ultimately her suicide. Josh now understood why the diaries had been tucked away on the top shelf over the generations.

Josh sat motionless, contemplating Ethan's turbulent life, the turmoil of his own life since returning to Sheffield, and the increasing sense, heightened by Sarya's and Sharon's tragic deaths, that he and Ethan were linked in ways he could never fully comprehend. It was as though the ancient sachem's curse, originally directed at Ethan, had somehow reached out across the ages to ensnare Josh and finally drive the Williamses from the land.

42

~

Aftermath

July 22, 1998–May 26, 2003

Josh's initial efforts to sell the farm failed to attract a single offer, and he gradually adjusted to the realization that, given his finances, he had no choice but to remain in Sheffield for the time being and wait out the market. While the farm had no residential value because of its proximity to the casino, commercial values on Route 36 soared once the casino was approved, and he had to believe that sooner or later someone would be attracted the farm for its commercial potential.

In the meantime, the Northern Pequots moved quickly to begin constructing The Nautilus, bringing in an army of construction crews that worked around the clock for more than two years to have the world's newest resort casino ready by the beginning of 2001. Neighbors complained bitterly about the constant noise, congestion, and disruption, but the selectmen said there was nothing they could do about the construction schedule because they had no control over the reservation.

As The Nautilus sped to completion, Foxwoods and Mohegan Sun continued to grow, as did the problems associated with them.

The first homicide at a Connecticut casino occurred when a man was shot and killed and another critically wounded at Mohegan Sun; two men committed suicide at Foxwoods, one by shooting himself in the head and the other by ingesting drugs and cutting his wrists; another man, distraught by his gambling losses, was rescued as he stood with a knife to his throat at Mohegan Sun.

Reports of embezzlements and white-collar crime became commonplace, including the stories of the Norwich woman who took more than $100,000 from a Norwich Chevrolet dealer to gamble at Foxwoods; the Ledyard tax collector who embezzled $302,000 from taxpayers to play the slots there; and the Hartford theater employee who was charged with stealing $91,000 in cash receipts from "Phantom of the Opera" and other shows to support her gambling habit. Embezzlements in Connecticut were increasing so rapidly, in fact, that one expert estimated they could soon reach ten times the national average.

In other news, a judge was arrested for falsifying personal bankruptcy papers after losing hundreds of thousands of dollars at Foxwoods; a money-counter at Mohegan Sun was arrested for stealing more than $800,000 by stuffing $100 bills into his jumpsuit; and police warned that Chinese organized-crime groups were increasingly preying on the Chinese and other Asian gamblers who each week flocked by the thousands to Connecticut from New York and Boston to indulge their cultural bent for gambling. Chinese loan sharks were reportedly charging 5 percent interest, compounded daily, which meant that if someone borrowed $100, he owed $105 after the first day and $411.33 at the end of thirty days. In one instance, a local Chinese restaurant owner was said to have gotten so deep into the syndicates that they threatened to blow up his restaurant if he didn't pay.

The Nautilus stayed on schedule through it all, opening its doors on January 20, 2001, as the third-largest casino in the Western Hemisphere, behind Foxwoods and Mohegan Sun. The reviews were fabulous, calling The Nautilus as good as anything in Las Vegas, and the opening-day crowds nearly doubled those that had poured into Mohegan Sun four years earlier.

The huge, ten-story complex dwarfed the surrounding countryside, its lights permanently illuminating the night sky like some kind of enormous spaceship that had touched down in the Connecticut woods. The state turned Route 141 into a four-lane expressway from I-95 to Sheffield, and the state highway that ran past the reservation was widened from two lanes to six. Most of the gamblers coming down from Hartford still came through the center of town, however, and they soon discovered Stoddard Mill Road as the quickest shortcut to the casino, racing by the Williams farm late at night and hopelessly clogging the little country road each weekend.

Given the tight job market, one of The Nautilus's biggest challenges proved to be recruiting enough workers. The Nautilus held job fairs in all of Connecticut's major cities as well as New York and Boston, bused in workers from strategic points around the state, recruited hundreds of trained dealers from Puerto Rico, and even went as far away as Poland to bring in experienced dealers from that country's casino industry. The new casino also targeted Ecuadorians, Peruvians, and other Latin Americans for a host of less glamorous jobs, from kitchen helpers to cashiers, offering bounties and attracting hundreds of illegal aliens whose presence prompted angry demonstrations and increasing calls by locals for a crackdown on illegal immigration.

Sheffield and the surrounding towns expressed alarm about the need to provide housing and social services to the newcomers, and Hispanic community leaders said they were being overwhelmed by the inflow of new people.

The biggest challenge came from the influx of Chinese and other Asian workers, a large number of whom spoke little or no English. Thousands of Chinese now worked at the three casinos, and the region's Asian community seemed to be growing each day.

Chinese investors snapped up a number of the large old houses along the Sheffield town green, turning them into "hot bed" operations, where as many as thirty people lived in a single house, sharing beds with others who worked different shifts. The tenants rode blue Nautilus vans back and forth to the casino with each shift change, spread their laundry on the front lawns and shrubbery to dry, and socialized on the green late into the evening.

Totally dependent on the casinos and their landlords, most of the Asians kept to themselves, much as the French Canadians had when they first came to Connecticut to work in the mills, but at least one man summoned the courage to go outside the community to seek help for their living conditions. In a note he delivered to the town hall, he wrote that he and nineteen others were living in a house that had had no heat or running water for almost three weeks. "Please help us," he pleaded. "The owner knows, but does nothing."

Sheffield held emergency meetings on the housing problem and tried to crack down on the overcrowding, but there was no immediate solution other than throwing innocent people out on the street. The zoning board finally responded by easing restrictions on multifamily housing, and the tribe announced plans for building low-income apartments, but as the new residents kept coming, more homes were turned into de facto boardinghouses, and more and more for-sale signs went up across town.

Traffic exploded overnight as The Nautilus attracted more than 12 million visitors the first year. Sheffield established its own police force, the town tried desperately to recruit more volunteer firefighters and EMS personnel, and the public works department tripled its work crews. Teachers and parents despaired over the decline in standards and discipline in the schools; many of Josh's friends, including the Merriweathers, moved out, and there were growing complaints about the strong sexual orientation of the shows and clubs at The Nautilus, which, it was reported, had put stripper poles in its hotel suites and set up a new promotional unit to attract overnight bachelor parties from across the Northeast.

"My pitch is very simple," the unit's new director, Paul Ivy, Jr., told *New York* magazine. "Beef, booze, and boobs—and right now we're first on each count."

The Nautilus dramatically accelerated southeastern Connecticut's transformation and triggered a surge in overall casino marketing. Television and radio spots constantly invited people to "come play," "be a winner," and revel in "the wonder of it all." Newspaper ads touted the casinos' respective advantages. And a billboard war broke out along the major highways. Bobby Kingman even floated a trial balloon suggesting that Connecticut lower the legal gambling age from twenty-one to eighteen for slots in order beat back growing competition from other states. "Both the state treasury and the casinos would benefit," he told lawmakers.

Perhaps the biggest marketing coup of all belonged to Mohegan Sun. In January 2003, the Mohegans announced they had purchased the Orlando franchise of the Women's National Basketball Association and would be moving the franchise to Connecticut, which, along with Tennessee, was an epicenter of women's college basketball. The team, rechristened the Connecticut Sun, would play in Mohegan Sun's new ten-thousand-seat arena.

The purchase marked the first time a gambling enterprise would own and operate a U.S. professional sports franchise. In the past, the idea of gambling interests owning a professional sports team had been one of the great taboos in American society, and teams had done everything in their power to protect their image by avoiding any link with gamblers. In 1955, baseball commissioner Ford Frick had gone so far as banning major leaguers from overnighting in Las Vegas. Now the Mohegans had ended that taboo, their announcement marking a major milestone for casino gambling in America.

The Mohegans sought to deflect criticism by arguing that they were a family entertainment venue and pointing out that if patrons chose, they could get to the arena without ever passing through any of Mohegan Sun's gambling halls. However, as the *Hartford Courant* observed, the addition of a basketball team was "opening new doors and bringing in customers who might never have dreamed of setting foot on casino property."

Never was that clearer than on opening day. The sellout crowd included large numbers of mothers and daughters, girls' basketball teams, and Girl Scouts and Brownies wearing their uniforms, sashes, and badges. As the fans milled about in front of the arena, the chaotic din of slot machines could be heard no more than thirty feet away.

～

Meanwhile, the spectacular growth of casino gambling in the state began to breed increasing concern about what was happening beneath all the glitz. A young lawyer named Jeff Benedict published a painstakingly-researched book that questioned the Mashantucket Pequot Tribe's legitimacy, becoming the state's leading critic of the federal recognition process and the gambling industry. Economists began to bemoan the growth of low-wage casino jobs at the expense of higher-paying and more productive jobs. The Connecticut Center for Economic Analysis concluded that the state's first two casinos had done little or nothing to spur new business in the surrounding towns, while complaints mounted that the casinos had in fact diverted spending away from local businesses like restaurants, theaters, and sports facilities. And there was growing concern that the likelihood of competing casinos being built in Massachusetts, Rhode Island, and New York meant that Connecticut's casinos would become increasingly dependent on attracting locals to their slot machines and table games.

As these concerns grew, Connecticut residents also began to focus on the likelihood that three more tribes—the Eastern Pequots in the east and the Schaghticokes and Golden Hill Paugussetts in the west—might soon receive federal recognition and open their own casinos. For the first time, significant numbers of people in western Connecticut began to join the growing number of vocal critics and opponents of casino gambling, and as a result a statewide coalition of towns, churches, businesses, and individuals formed to try to block any new casinos in the state.

Under intense pressure from the coalition and Connecticut's congressional delegation, the BIA ultimately denied the three tribes' applications and, in January 2003, the state legislature repealed the Las Vegas Nights statute, thereby creating a formidable barrier to any new Indian casinos in the state.

～

Although pleased to see the legislature finally vote to repeal the Las Vegas Nights law, Josh saw little reason to celebrate. Repeal promised to do nothing to slow the growth of the existing casinos, and in the meantime government support for gambling seemed likely to turn every gas station, convenience store, computer, and cell phone into a place to bet.

Moreover, it was hard for Josh to be too upbeat about the vote when he remained pinned down on the farm by his massive new neighbor to the east. Unable to sell the farm, he had survived the past four and a half years primarily by focusing on his job, his few remaining crops, and, most of all, his children.

Matt had never really recovered from his mother's death, from his experience with Kayla, or from his traumatic brush with gambling and the law. Josh had finally persuaded him to join the army to try to get a fresh start. He was currently finishing up a tour of duty in Korea and was debating whether to reenlist or come home and look for a job.

Sarah had turned out to be emotionally tougher than either of the boys and had seemed to recover from her mother's loss better than either of them. A graceful young woman with beautiful green eyes and auburn hair, she had graduated from UConn with honors in chemistry, had worked at Pfizer as an associate scientist, and was now in medical school in Boston.

And then there was Jacob, whose presence at home had done more than anything to keep Josh going for the past several years. Bright and outgoing, he had inherited his mother's personality and artistic bent and was determined to be an architect. Unlike Matt, he had opted for a small New England college and had received a scholarship from Bates in Maine, where he was now a freshman.

An opportunity to sell the farm finally arrived in April 2003 when the tribe approached Josh with an offer to purchase it for approximately the amount of his remaining mortgage. The rumor was that they were also interested in purchasing the Sadrozinski farm and intended to use the combined properties for parking and employee dormitories. Josh accepted the offer immediately. Within a month, he took a job with an insurance agency in Portsmouth, New Hampshire, within relatively easy driving distance of Jacob and Sarah, and he found a refurbished Victorian on five acres just outside of town. If things worked out right, he thought he might even be able to persuade Matt to join him in the insurance business there once his son was ready to settle down.

Josh closed on the farm on Monday morning, May 26. Afterward, he went over to the cemetery, where he knelt at Sharon's grave, telling her softly how much he loved her and asking again for her forgiveness. Then he said good-bye to his parents and grandparents and drove back to the house for a final walk around the property before leaving for New Hampshire.

It was a pleasant morning, and despite the constant traffic on Stoddard Mill Road, the farm and the immediately surrounding land had changed little from when Josh was a kid. He started out walking along the stone wall that separated the orchard from the south pasture, stopped for a few moments to replace a stone that had fallen to the ground, and thought about the wonderful fall Sundays the family had spent picking apples and then enjoying supper together. He paused at the site of the English barn, thinking of the terrible fire that had trapped the horses, but also of the magical time when the Appaloosa had had her first foal and the entire family had walked back from the barn together in the moonlight. He then continued on to Bixler Brook, following it west toward Stoddard's Mill and recalling spot after spot where Sharon had set up her easel to sketch the pastoral scenes she'd loved so much.

Heading back, Josh climbed a gentle rise that overlooked the southern half of the farm. He watched a red-tailed hawk circle in the distance, then whispered a final farewell to the beautiful land that had sustained his family for nearly three and a half centuries.

No, Josh corrected himself, it had actually been far longer than that. His blood, after all, was as much Sarya's as it was Ethan's, and his roots in the land reached back into the very mists of time.

~

Timeline

1637   English colonists attack and burn the Pequots' fortified village at Mystic *(fact)*

1659   Ethan Williams helps found Sheffield, Connecticut *(fiction)*

1660   Ethan marries Sarya *(fiction)*

1675–76   King Philip's War destroys or damages more than a third of English settlements in New England and decimates the region's Native American population *(fact)*

1686   Connecticut establishes Northern Pequot Reservation *(fiction)*

1803   Rachel Amos is buried on the Northern Pequot Reservation *(fiction)*

1983   Mashantucket Pequots receive federal recognition as an Indian tribe *(fact)*

1987   Josh Williams and his family move to the Williams farm in Sheffield, Connecticut *(fiction)*

1988   Congress passes the Indian Gaming Regulatory Act, giving federally-recognized tribes the right to open casinos in states that permit casino-type gambling *(fact)*

1991   Connecticut legislature defeats effort to repeal the state's charity Las Vegas Nights law *(fact)*

1992   Mashantucket Pequots Open Foxwoods Casino *(fact)*

1993   Northern Pequots announce bid for federal recognition as an Indian tribe *(fiction)*

   Massive public opposition erupts to Mashantucket Pequot proposal to buy and annex up to 7,000 acres of North Stonington, Ledyard, and Preston *(fact)*

1994   Mohegans granted federal recognition as an Indian tribe *(fact)*

1996   Mohegans open Mohegan Sun *(fact)*

1998   Northern Pequots granted federal recognition as an Indian tribe *(fiction)*

Sheffield Referendum on proposed Northern Pequot Casino *(fiction)*

2001   Northern Pequots open The Nautilus *(fiction)*

2003   Connecticut legislature repeals the state's Las Vegas Nights law *(fact)*

~

Acknowledgments

Having grown up in Wethersfield, Connecticut, the site of the attack that directly precipitated the Pequot War, and then having lived on the edge of the Mashantucket Reservation in Ledyard from 1977 to 1998, I couldn't help but be fascinated by the remarkable story of Foxwoods, troubled by the explosive growth of casino gambling and intrigued by the age-old theme of the past impinging on the present.

Predictably, trying to incorporate all of these elements into a novel quickly became a far bigger project than I ever anticipated. The one certainty is that I never would have completed or published it without the invaluable help and encouragement of my wife, Betsy, and numerous others along the way. They include:

Kim Llewellyn, a brilliant physical and ebook designer and production maestro who immersed herself in the story well beyond the call of duty.

Glen Hartley of Writers' Representatives, LLC, who introduced me to Kim and advised me on the rapidly changing contours of the publishing industry.

Pat Fogarty, my tireless and keen-eyed copy editor.

Paul Steele, Peter Marathas, Mark Sullivan, and Maura Casey, who read the manuscript and provided their critiques, suggestions, and advice.

Kelly Sandefer of Beehive Mapping, who prepared the maps in the front of the book.

And the many individuals who took the time to meet with me and/or answer questions at the Connecticut State Library, the Mashantucket Pequot Museum and Research Center, the Connecticut Council on Problem Gambling, the Bettor Choice Compulsive Gambling Treatment Program in Norwich, the Ledyard, Groton, and Deep River Town Halls, the Montville Barracks of the Connecticut State Police, the State's Attorney's office in New London, the Connecticut Forest and Park Association, the First Congregational Church in Essex, and the Hartford office of the United Church of Christ.

To all of them, I express my sincere appreciation.

Bibliography

In addition to the sources mentioned in the Acknowledgments, I was informed by a wide range of books, articles, and documents, including but not limited to:

Adams, Sherman W., and Henry Reed Stiles. *The History of Ancient Wethersfield, Volume I.* Somersworth, N.H.: New Hampshire Pub. Co. in collaboration with the Wethersfield Historical Society, 1974.

Allport, Susan. *Sermons in Stone: The Stone Walls of New England and New York.* New York: W.W. Norton, 1990.

Anquoe, Bunty. "Clinton, once on middle ground, now backs gaming on Indian reservations." *Indian Country Today* as reprinted in *The Day* (New London, Conn. August 20, 1993).

Avery, John. *History of the Town of Ledyard, 1650–1900.* Norwich, Conn.: Franklin Press, 1972.

Baldelli, Ann. "Rainmaker to be focus of an 'awesome' show." *The Day* (New London, Conn., September 3, 1993).

Benedict, Jeff. *Without Reservation: The Making of America's Most Powerful Indian Tribe and the World's Largest Casino.* New York: HarperCollins, 2000.

Blechman, Andrew D. "Christened with class." *Norwich Bulletin* (Norwich, Conn., November 18, 1993).

Bradford, William, and Samuel Eliot Morison. *Of Plymouth Plantation: 1620–1647.* New York: Knopf, 1976.

Casey, Maura. "A Special Report on Problem Gambling." *The Day* (New London, Conn., March 17, 2002).

Caulkins, Francis Manwaring. *History of New London, Connecticut: From the First Survey of the Coast in 1612 to 1852.* New London: the author, 1860.

Cave, Alfred A. *The Pequot War.* Amherst: University of Massachusetts Press, 1996.

Church, Thomas. *The History of Philip's War, Commonly Called the Great Indian War of 1675 and 1676.* Exeter, N.H.: J. & B. Williams, 1842.

Collins, David. "Tribe presses its winnings into plans for huge resort." *The Day* (New London, Conn., July 16, 1992).

Ibid. "Foxwoods' earnings go beyond 'incredible.'" *The Day* (New London, Conn., July 16, 1993).

Ibid. "Sinatra's red carpet ready to roll." *The Day* (New London, Conn., November 17, 1993).

Ibid. "Foxwoods, fans welcome Sinatra." *The Day* (New London, Conn., November 18, 1993).

Ibid. "Tribal fortunes rise in Washington." *The Day* (New London, Conn., April 30, 1994).

Ibid. "State expects $210 million from casinos." *The Day* (New London, Conn., June 23, 1996).

Collins, David, and Virginia Groark. "Mohegan Sun wins $25.9 million in first month of slots operation." *The Day* (New London, Conn., December 5, 1996).

Connecticut General Assembly, Senate and House Proceedings, 1991, Vol. 34.

Day, The. "Broke gambler encamped at Dew Drop Inn forced to move." *The Day* (New London, Conn., October 14, 1993).

DeCoster, Stan. "State Must Negotiate on Casino Plan." *The Day* (New London, Conn., May 19, 1990).

Ibid. "Casino Plan Threatened by Weicker." *The Day* (New London, Conn., May 1, 1991).

Ibid. "Weicker raises stakes against Indian casino." *The Day* (New London, Conn., May 15, 1991).

De Forest, John W. *History of the Indians of Connecticut, from the Earliest Known Period to 1850*. Hartford: W. J. Hamersley, 1851.

Delaney, Edmund. *The Connecticut River: New England's Historic Waterway*. Chester, Conn.: Globe Pequot Press, 1983.

Demaris, Ovid. *The Boardwalk Jungle*. New York: Bantam, 1986.

Eisler, Kim Isaac. *Revenge of the Pequots: How a Small Native American Tribe Created the World's Most Profitable Casino*. New York: Simon & Schuster, 2001.

Fischer, David Hackett. *Albion's Seed: Four British Folkways in America*. New York: Oxford University Press, 1989.

Fromson, Brett D. *Hitting the Jackpot: The Inside Story of the Richest Indian Tribe in History*. New York: Atlantic Monthly Press, 2003.

Goodman, Robert. *The Luck Business: The Devastating Consequences and Broken Promises of America's Gambling Explosion*. New York: Free Press, 1995.

Grant, Ellsworth S., and Oliver Ormerod Jensen. *The Miracle of Connecticut*. Hartford, Conn: Published by the Connecticut Historical Society and Fenwick Productions, 1992.

Green, Rick. "Sun Shining On Mohegans." *Hartford Courant* (Hartford, Conn., January 29, 2003).

Grinols, Earl L., "Gambling Economics: A Primer." *Faith & Economics* 28, Fall 1996. Wenham, Mass.: Association of Christian Economists, Gordon College, 1996.

Haigh, Susan. "Senate kills Bridgeport casino." *Norwich Bulletin* (Norwich, Conn., November 18, 1995).

Hamilton, Robert A. "State must negotiate on casino plan." *The Day* (New London, Conn., May 19, 1990).

Harding, James Ely. *Lyme, As It Was and Is.* Lyme, Conn.: Harding, 1975.

Hauptman, Lawrence M., and James Wherry, eds. *The Pequots in Southern New England: The Fall and Rise of an American Indian Nation.* Norman: University of Oklahoma Press, 1993.

Hileman, Maria. "Wampum Trade Created Wealth and Conflicts." *The Day* (New London, Conn., December 12, 1993).

Hosley, Darienne J. "Mohegans savor dream." *Norwich Bulletin* (Norwich, Conn., October 13, 1996).

Hubbell, William, and Roger Eddy. *Connecticut.* Portland, Or.: Graphic Arts Center Pub. Co., 1989.

Johnson, Edward, and J. Franklin Jameson. *Johnson's Wonder-Working Providence, 1628–1651.* New York: C. Scribner's Sons, 1910.

Johnson, Kirk. "Indians in Connecticut Get Casino Gambling." *New York Times* (New York, October 26, 1990).

Ibid. "Casino Owner Offers Lure: $140 Million in New Taxes." *New York Times* (New York, February 12, 1993).

Jones, Mary Jeanne Anderson. *Congregational Commonwealth: Connecticut, 1636–1662.* Middletown, Conn.: Wesleyan University Press, 1968.

Kaplan, Karen. "Foxwoods says strip club off-limits." *The Day* (New London, Conn., May 2, 1996).

Kimball, Carol W. *The Groton Story.* Stonington, Conn.: Pequot Press, 1965.

Lepore, Jill. *The Name of War: King Philip's War and The Origins of American Identity.* New York: Knopf, 1998.

Lincoln, Charles Henry, John Easton, N. S., Richard Hutchinson, Mary White Rowlandson, and Cotton Mather. *Narratives of the Indian Wars, 1675–1699.* New York: C. Scribner's Sons, 1913.

Mashantucket Pequot Nation of Connecticut. *Pequot Times.* (Mashantucket [Ledyard], Conn., 1992–2003).

Mason, Louis B. *The Life and Times of Major Mason of Connecticut: 1600–1672.* New York: Putnam, 1935.

National Gambling Impact and Policy Commission (U.S.). *The National Gambling Impact Study Commission: Final Report.* Washington, D.C.: The Commission, 1999.

Oberg, Michael Leroy. *Uncas: First of the Mohegans.* Ithaca, N.Y.: Cornell University Press, 2003.

O'Brien, Timothy L. *Bad Bet: The Inside Story of the Glamour, Glitz, and Danger of America's Gambling Industry.* New York: Times Business, 1998.

Orr, Charles, ed. *History of the Pequot War: The Contemporary Accounts of Mason, Underhill, Vincent and Gardener* (Cleveland: The Helman-Taylor company, 1897).

Overton, Penelope. "BIA forum brings 600 to Ledyard." *The Day* (New London, Conn., September 19, 1993).

Ibid. "Cruisin' the Casino." *The Day* (New London, Conn., May 22, 1994).

Peterson, Harold L. *Arms and Armor in Colonial America, 1526–1783.* Harrisburg, Pa.: Stackpole Co., 1956.

Philbrick, Nathaniel. *Mayflower: A Story of Courage, Community, and War.* New York: Viking, 2006.

Rabinovitz, Jonathan. "A Battlefield Topped With Felt." *New York Times* (New York, August 5, 1996).

Ibid. "Can the Man Who Made Sun City Make It in Atlantic City?" *New York Times* (New York, September 21, 1997).

Residents Against Annexation Newsletters, 1993–1996. Ledyard, Conn.

Riley, Laurie. "Connecticut Sun Rises in Casino Arena." *Hartfort Courant* (Hartford, Conn, May 25, 2003).

Shanahan, Marie K. "John Mason Statue Has A Homecoming." *Hartfort Courant* (Hartford, Conn., June 17, 1996).

Slater, James A. *The Colonial Burying Grounds of Eastern Connecticut and the Men Who Made Them.* Hamden, Conn.: Archon Books, 1987.

Tashjian, Dickran and Ann Tashjian. *Memorials for Children of Change: The Art of Early New England Stonecarving.* Middletown, Conn.: Wesleyan University Press, 1974.

Thorndike, Bill. "Night in the life of a dealer." *Norwich Bulletin* (Norwich, Conn., February 12, 1995).

Thorson, Robert M. *Stone by Stone: The Magnificent History in New England's Stone Walls.* New York: Walker & Co., 2002.

Van Dusen, Albert E. *Connecticut.* New York: Random House, 1961.

Viafora, Susann. "Court clears way for Ledyard casino." *Norwich Bulletin* (Norwich, Conn., September 6, 1990).

Ward, Gerald W. R., and William N. Hosley, Jr., eds. *The Great River: Art & Society of the Connecticut Valley, 1635–1820.* Hartford, Conn.: Wadsworth Atheneum, 1985.

Wieder, Lois M. *The Wethersfield Story.* Stonington, Conn.: Pequot Press, 1966.

Willing, Richard. "Special counsel named to investigate Babbitt." *USA Today.* (Arlington, Va.: Gannett Co., March 20, 1998).

Winthrop, John, and James Kendall Hosmer. *Winthrop's Journal "History of New England" 1630–1649.* New York: Scribner, 1908.